DEATH CASTS A
SHADOW

John V Mercurio

ISBN 978-1-63961-432-5 (paperback)
ISBN 978-1-63961-433-2 (digital)

Christian Faith Publishing
832 Park Avenue
Meadville, PA 16335
www.christianfaithpublishing.com

Printed in the United States of America

DEDICATION

This book is dedicated to Jennifer Lynn Fisher Mercurio, my wife, life partner and best friend for her seemingly inexhaustible patience with me in this process. Her encouragement cannot be overstated.

Also a word of recognition for Manuel Guzman, professional artist, illustrator and friend for transforming an idea into original design for the cover of *Death Casts a Shadow*.

Finally, I offer a word of praise to God, the true author behind the ideas and words of this novel.

PROLOGUE

A bead of sweat trickled down Mercurius's temple as he faced a formal Roman military inquest. Someone had to answer for the assassination of eleven Roman dignitaries that happened on his watch. Steadying himself, he cautiously answered questions from the investigating committee.

Speaking in a detached tone, one of the adjudicators asked a question to which he already knew the answer. "Were all eleven members of Ambassador Aurelius' entourage lost?"

Mercurius' answer was curt, his eyes straight ahead. "Yes, all eleven lost, sir."

"Who is responsible for this carnage?"

"We believe it to be the same group that had perpetrated other recent attacks."

"You're referring to the Judean insurgents?" asked another official.

The post commander nodded in affirmation. "That's correct, sir."

"Let me get this straight," barked the most vocal official. "You say you know who did this, yet you haven't made any arrests. Is that accurate, Commander?"

"Yes, sir."

The official looked visibly disgusted. "Ambassador Aurelius is still missing, and you have no clue where these Zealots have taken him?"

Mercurius' response seemed delayed, "Sir, this situation doesn't exactly match the—"

"In fact," the committee member broke in, "you have no idea whether Aurelius is alive or dead, do you, Commander?"

Mercurius offered no reply.

"Where is the examining physician's report?"

Breaking from military protocol, Mercurius made eye contact with the official. "Sir, the doctor was visibly shaken by the level of carnage in this case."

"Did you think it appropriate to use a neophyte in a situation such as this?"

Mercurius felt the heat of anger rising up at the back of his neck. "Sir, this is a field physician with a seven-year track record. I can only say that the ferocity of this attack was something neither he nor I had ever witnessed before."

With a degree of trepidation, another committee member spoke up, "Commander, would you clarify that last statement for us?"

Mercurius' eyes became steely as he annunciated his words with painstaking clarity, "Their bodies were ravaged, brutally butchered, torn apart with what had to be unnatural strength." The floodgates were now open for Mercurius. "Limbs were missing that could not be accounted for. They hadn't been cut off. They'd been torn off! One staffer's face was partially gone. The doctor's best guess was that it had been gnawed off."

Members of the inquest had heard enough. With a look of disbelief, the leader held up an outstretched palm. "That will be all, Commander."

*****

Several hundred years before this incident, a young Hebrew prophet named Jeremiah shared his thoughts regarding the depravity of the human heart. He openly wondered if anyone could even imagine to what depths it might descend. What might happen if the dark side took complete control?

CHAPTER 1
Phantom

At the fortress city of Sebaste, a cricket's serenade amplified the stillness of the night. Seven hundred years earlier, Sebaste had a different identity; it had been known as Samaria. The ancient city had been the capital of Israel's northern kingdom, but in the years that followed, it would be crushed by foreign invaders. The Assyrians were the first, descending like locusts destroying everything in their path. The Babylonians followed them, who in turn were subjugated by Persians. Samaria was reduced to rubble, except for one section that escaped detection. Hidden deep beneath the city, a series of underground mazes remained untouched and intact.

Thirty-seven years before the Roman Empire moved in, Samaria was rebuilt and expanded by Herod the Great, who renamed it Sebaste in honor of Emperor Augustus.

Within Sebaste's city walls, a young Roman sentry sat on the cool stone floor of the watchtower, admiring the night sky. The cricket's song had a tranquilizing affect, but for some reason, the soldier felt restless. He was troubled by an uneasy sensation, the kind of feeling a person got when they knew they were being watched. Glancing at the wall torch, he attempted to assure himself.

"It's nothing," he muttered, but the strange sensation persisted. Leaning forward, he scanned the compound below yet saw no movement. Getting to his feet, he moved around, trying to shake the eerie feeling. "Gives me the creeps," he grumbled. Less than a second later, the torch went out, and the crickets abruptly ended their song.

The hair on the back of his neck stood up straight. Reaching for his sword, his head pivoted right, then left.

The intense silence was interrupted by a high-pitched scream. The youthful soldier scarcely maintained his footing as he watched his fallen helmet bound down the stone staircase.

"What in the name of... What was that?" bellowed a voice below him.

"It came from the ambassador's quarters!" he shouted back. Heart racing, he rushed down the stairs, joining the other legionnaire already on his way to the ambassador's chamber. Together, they pounded on the heavy doors. "Ambassador!" they shouted. "Are you all right?"

No reply.

"Ambassador Aurelius, please open the door!" Panic began to set in as they tugged on the brass rings of the massive portals that would not budge. Sounds of panic erupted throughout the courtyard.

"This can't be happening!" said the first soldier.

"They're barred from the inside!" shouted the other.

"Sound the alarm! We need help!"

Tonight, the garrison was comprised of *immunes*, a rookie police force. The trumpet alarm did its job awakening the sleeping troops. Their quick response followed protocol. Minutes later, all exits are sealed off. As troopers scurried about the compound, Orel, a member of the Judean guard, assisted soldiers outside the ambassador's door.

Not long ago, this compound had been a family mansion, the home of a wealthy Levitical priest named Lamech. Many Judeans were shocked when he offered to share a portion of his estate with the Roman military. Well-educated, intelligent and wealthy, Lamech had always picked up on the shifting winds of change, cleverly manipulating politics, religion and the military for his personal agenda. The Roman military happily accepted his offer, turning a portion of his ancestral home into a fortified fortress in return for certain promises. Lamech's mansion had become the living embodiment of the ancient proverb, "Keep your friends close and your enemies closer." A small contingency of Judean guardsmen remained in the compound to serve as Lamech's personal bodyguard.

A full moon cast a shadowy light on the ambassador's entry door. Orel raised his voice above the chaotic chatter, "How can I help?"

"Axes, we need axes! Got to get through this door!"

Nodding, Orel rushed away, returning within minutes with the requested implements. Wood chips flew like missiles as blow after blow struck the heavy cedar doors. But the sturdy portals held fast, refusing to yield ground. The process was impeded further as the arrival of additional immunes created congestion. Mercurius, the Post Decanus, arrived, issuing a singular order.

"Break it down—*now!*"

Axes were tossed aside as twenty soldiers planted their shoulders against those doors. Grunting, they pushed mightily, but the unrelenting doors stood resolute.

"Next twenty!" Mercurius shouted as the next twenty replaced the last perspiration-soaked crew. Moments later, a thunderous *crack* reverberated through the courtyard as the interior crossbar splintered. Swords drawn, the legionnaires rushed in, struggling to see through the darkness. There was no sound or movement in the dark chamber.

"Ambassador!" The cry echoed through the blackness. Except for the sound of soldiers panting, the room was eerily silent. "We need light! Get torches in here!" Mercurius shouted. The blazing pitch revealed the grizzly remains of the ambassador's envoy, with throats slashed to the bone. The extent of savagery stunned immunes and guardsmen alike. Several rookie recruits gagged reflexively; others turned away, hands over mouths.

"What…happened here?" asked one trembling voice. No one dared to ask the more perplexing question of how this happened. Eleven people were massacred with such ferocity and stealth, and only one managed to scream before being silenced by a knife?

Orel scanned the ravaged remains for Aurelius. "Post Commander, the ambassador isn't here!"

Mercurius, a man as nervous as he was ambitious, stepped forward to do what ranking officers did best: bully the next man down the chain of command.

"Markus! I want an immediate report from all posted sentries! These men didn't kill themselves. I want the ambassador and these assassins found. Stop standing around, they may still be within the compound!"

While Markus dispatched immunes, Lamech's personal body-guard sent word to his compatriots to check on the safety of the priest, instructing them to stay posted outside the old man's door. That being done, he couldn't resist another look at the mystifying scene. Reaching for a torch, he popped his head inside the chamber. Mercurius was still poking around.

"Did something occur to you?" asked Mercurius.

Arms at his sides, Orel offered no comment.

Mercurius' temper flared. "I know you understand me. Without your help, we wouldn't have gotten in here. What do you know about all this?"

Orel replied in perfect Latin, "Why should I help Romans?"

"I knew it!" cried Mercurius. He had always regarded Judean soldiers as inferior to Roman but realized he was desperate for help. Smiling, he took a step closer to Orel. "I've been asking myself that same question, and yet here you are. You're obviously a capable sol-dier, so why are you still here?"

"Perhaps I have a personal interest."

"All right, then let's take a closer look together."

Orel nodded in agreement. Torch in hands, they surveyed the dimly lit room. What they hoped to find was a starting point, but instead, they were left with nothing—no clue to how the killers got in or out.

Markus returned with a report, prompting Mercurius to roll his eyes: "No sign of the assassins or missing emissary." While Mercurius reprimanded Markus, something caught Orel's eye, something that was definitely out of place. Squatting down next to one corpse, he found a small mark, a tattoo, possibly in Hebrew. The body was too blood-smeared to make it out clearly. Using his thumb and spit, he cleared away the blood covering the mark. Behind the dead man's ear was something only a Jew would recognize: the symbol צלמות. The seldom-used word had two parts: *tsal* meaning "shadow," and *mavet* meaning "death," together forming "shadow of death."

Orel decided to keep this discovery to himself, at least until he could make some sense of it. "Why," he mused, "would a staff member of a Roman emissary have a Hebrew word tattooed in a place that would likely go unnoticed?"

"It took several men to subdue so large a group as this!" said a blustery Mercurius. "It has to be the Zealots!" He looked to Orel for a confirming nod but received no such support. His focus returned to Markus, his second-in-command. "This suite has several connecting rooms equipped with oil lamps. Light all of them, and then clear out your men. They're trampling on everything!"

Assuming the order included him, Orel joined the exiting legionnaires.

"Not you, Orel! Please stay. You've been extremely helpful. Your continued assistance would be much appreciated." He turned again to Markus. "Send for the garrison physician. I want these bodies examined."

After another pass through mangled bodies and adjoining rooms, a frustrated Mercurius reached his boiling point. With his hand against the back of his neck, he cursed. "How the hell did they get in and out of here unseen? This chamber has only one entrance and one exit. The sentry posted at the back reports that no one has passed in or out of that door and that both entrances were barred from the inside!" The name of the Zealot leader leaped into Mercurius's head, but he kept it to himself. "Are we dealing with the dark arts here? Is there some kind of demon able to pass through walls and vanish into thin air?" He was thankful Orel didn't respond to such an outrageous postulation. But Orel was still preoccupied with the hidden tattoo.

Additional reports continued to stream in from tower and gate sentries, but all yielded the same useless information: no sightings, no clues. Somehow, the intruders passed in and out unnoticed. Inexplicably, all sentries reported all clear until the moment of that ghastly scream.

"Search the outer walls," ordered Mercurius. "I want patrols outside the compound. Instruct them to look for anything out of the ordinary." Once more, Mercurius turned to Orel. "Can I depend on the assistance of your guardsmen to canvas the village?"

Orel smirked, refusing to disguise his distaste for the way he and his men had been treated by these same Romans who were now asking for help.

"You know the haunts of this place. How did those bloody goat herders get in here?"

"Someone knows," Orel cautiously replied. "Someone either inside or outside these walls. They had help. I suggest you offer a reward to the people of the community for any information that leads to the capture of these butchers."

"Excellent! Markus, take charge of this, and remember, my head is not the only one on the block for this. That insurrectionist dog, Barabbas, is surely behind this," he grumbled. "It's got all the earmarks." Looking like a man possessed, Mercurius grabbed Markus's forearm. "The ambassador may yet be alive. I need answers! Get me some!" With a sharp salute, Markus moved quickly.

The immunes mulling around outside the compound were edgy. Soon, the whispers began to spread.

"Flesh and blood can't pass through locked doors or stone walls," whispered one soldier to another, muffling his words with his hand.

"What kind of man could have done this?" said another.

"What if," the other said and swallowed, "it's not a man? What if the stories are true?"

With his mouth hanging open, the first man warily asked, "St… stories? Wh-what stories?"

"The stories of"—he gulped, forcing his reluctant tongue to speak the word aloud—"the Phantom."

Taking leave from Mercurius, Orel headed across the compound to check on the well-being of Lamech. He thought of the oath he'd sworn to protect the priest. That, of course, was before he knew the old priest the way he did now. For Orel, this was no longer just a job; he respected and cared for the old man. The aged priest and the young guardian shared a mutual admiration. With Lamech's home in view, Orel spied fellow guardsmen, Judah and Seth, posted at the door just as he had instructed.

"Is everything all right?" asked an approaching Orel.

"He's suffered no incident. Everything is secure," answered Seth, the younger of the two. "That's all we know. He's unwilling to talk to anyone but you."

This surprised Orel. "Me, why?" He kept his voice down as he moved closer to the guardians.

Judah, the elder of the two, shrugged his shoulders. "You know why. The priest doesn't see us the same way he sees you."

Orel didn't try to deny it to spare their feelings; he knew it was true. They'd formed a special bond the others didn't have. Stepping up to the door, he raised his fist but then hesitated for a second before knocking. The hour was late, and he wondered if he should risk waking the old man. Raising his fist again, he studied the door holder that housed a miniature replica of the Commandments, then knocked firmly, loud enough to be heard without sounding demanding. As he expected, there was no answer on his first attempt. Lamech was eighty years of age.

"Sir," he called, this time pounding on the door, "it's Orel. May I come in?"

Several minutes passed before there was a sound of rustling inside followed by a sluggish advance. The door opened slowly. Lamech stood silently at the threshold, his eldest servant, Ezra, standing beside him, scowling at Orel.

"He would not let me answer the door," said Ezra, shaking his head. "He insists on answering the door himself, claiming it is he, not I, with whom you wish to speak."

Lamech's smile verified the accuracy of Ezra's summation.

"He's a stubborn old man who refuses to give an inch either to me or his age."

As exhausted as the old priest looked, he couldn't help but break into a chuckle, causing him to almost lose his balance.

"Sir, I'm sorry to disturb you at so late an hour. I'll come back in the morning. I just wanted to make sure you were all right. You need to rest."

Lamech made no reply. He looked at Seth and Judah, then back to Orel. Feeling a bit perplexed, Orel started to repeat himself, but

Lamech's raised palm stopped him. Placing his index finger to his lips, Lamech motioned for him to enter and close the door behind him. With the priest leading the way, they walked to a sitting room. The old man gingerly settled into a chair, motioning for Orel to join him. The two sat for several minutes before the priest finally spoke, "Many things are in motion this night, are they not?" Lamech stated fact over question. The priest's eyes looked heavy. Orel was concerned that the strain of the night might have been too much for him.

"Sir, why don't I come back in the morning? You need your rest. I can—" was all he could get out before Lamech's eyes tightened his tongue.

"As to the details, you may enlighten me tomorrow as I, in turn, will do for you when the hour is decent and our heads are clear. But for now, sit with me a few moments, for there is something you must be made aware of."

Though exhausted, the priest was calm, placid. Each word he spoke carried weight. "The events of this night have produced many questions but few answers. Neither you nor the Roman *Decanus* can make sense of them. However, this isn't your first time to witness this kind of scenario, is it?" Again, the priest's question was more rhetorical than inquisitive.

Orel inhaled and exhaled quickly. Lamech seemed to know more about what just happened than he showed, even though he was safely tucked away in his bedchamber.

"No, it's not," he replied hesitantly. "Not the first time." A shiver ran through him, a warning that he was not going to like what came next. "How do you know about that?"

Ignoring his question, Lamech continued, "You needn't fear for my safety, my young friend." Pausing to take a breath, he raised his weary eyes to meet Orel's. "Of this, I am reasonably confident, though I admit there yet remains a small place in my heart that seeks to convince me otherwise." Lamech's demeanor had captured Orel's attention and silence. "The Romans, however, are in grave danger. Aurelius should not have come here. No amount of planning or secrecy could have guaranteed his safety. He will eventually be recovered, but I am certain he is already dead." Lamech looked intensely at Orel. "This was not a kidnapping as you and Mercurius have presumed."

Sitting motionless, a bead of perspiration trickled down the Judean guard's temple. He swallowed involuntarily but could not bring himself to ask the priest what was running through his mind. How could he possibly accuse so great a man of conspiracy?

A silent chuckle highlighted the age lines of Lamech's tired face. "This isn't a conspiracy, Orel. It's a curse, an ancient evil which has not visited the enemies of Elohim for centuries. Not since…" Lamech's voice trailed off, his eyes moving about the room as though he sensed something unseen. "Come back tomorrow afternoon. We have much to discuss."

CHAPTER 2
Vitus—the Beginning

Is the pathway of life predetermined? Or do we make our own destiny? Does a tragic event, such as the loss of a parent, create an obstacle so great it can't be overcome? Or does it serve as a catalyst for greatness? Are life's stepping-stones purely a matter of chance or part of a grand mystical blueprint laid out before we take our first breath?

Vitus grew up in the Tuscan province of Rome, the only child of parents who loved him as well as each other. His father, Decimus, was a gifted Roman officer who served in the remote region of Judea where Vitus was born. His Judean mother was breathtakingly beautiful and soft-spoken. She gave him the name Vitus for its meaning of new life. He inherited his father's bronze skin, green eyes, six-foot frame, and chiseled features and his mother's kindness.

Vitus was brilliant, a child prodigy waiting to happen until life took a drastic turn. His mother's life was snuffed out by Judean Zealots seeking retribution against his father. Fearing his son might be next, Decimus sent Vitus back to Tuscany, their ancestral home. There he would be raised by Claude, his father's elder brother.

Claude was a political reactionary who longed for the earlier days of the empire. A student of ancient Sparta, he despised excess in everything except discipline. A Spartan's badge of honor was self-denial and arduous development. This was the code Claude employed in rearing his exceptional nephew. His reasoning: hard work would distract the boy from dwelling on his mother's death. Claude never imagined that Decimus would fall victim to the same insurrectionists that killed Vitus's mother.

As he did during many meals, eight-year-old Vitus grilled Claude for details about his parents. "Please, Uncle, tell me about my father."

Claude shook his head. "Again? You've heard the story many times."

Vitus nodded enthusiastically.

"All right," he replied, squaring his shoulders with pride. "Your father was a good man but an even greater soldier. He was commissioned to lead a special task force in a far country called Judea."

"The place where I was born," Vitus interjected.

"Yes." Claude smiled. "Your father was very intelligent. He seemed to know what the rebels were planning before they did, making them furious! He was the only officer who understood the Semitic mind."

Excited to hear the story again, Vitus scooted closer, not wanting to miss a word or gesture.

"Those evil Zealots knew Decimus would eventually destroy them. They schemed and plotted, trying to find a way to outsmart him, but they couldn't. He was far too clever."

Claude paused, wishing there was a way to change the outcome of the story. "The Zealots," he continued, "realized the only way to defeat him was through his family. They slipped into your mother's village and kidnapped her. She was never heard from again."

"They killed my mother."

"Yes, and that proved to be the death of your father as well. He asked for military leave to get you out of Judea. His request was denied. His leadership was too critical for him to be away, even for a short time."

Reaching up, Vitus wrapped his arm around Claude's neck, wanting to comfort his uncle.

Fighting back a catch in his throat, Claude continued, "Decimus remained in Judea while you were escorted to Tuscany. Knowing you were here with me was a comfort to him, but his concern for your mother caused him to lose his edge. This helped the Zealots to trap and kill him."

Anger ripped through Vitus. "Did they make him suffer?"

Claude's jaw tightened. "Yes. If you remember nothing else, remember the name of the Zealots. Perhaps, one day, you'll repay them for the evil they've brought upon this family!"

Eight-year-old Vitus replied, "I will never forget, Uncle."

Claude was determined to raise Vitus in the ways of ancient Sparta. Even in his formative years, the child was extraordinary, showing superior intelligence, analytical ability, and instinctive reactions. Simply put, Vitus possessed skills that couldn't be taught. Limitless potential linked to the finest military academy seemed providential, but his desire to avenge his parents became an obsession, an inner darkness that slowly engulfed him.

*****

On his seventeenth birthday, Vitus joined the Roman Legion, delighting his Uncle Claude. Possessing an extraordinary memory, he quickly became fluent in Aramaic and Latin, giving him yet another advantage. He was soon selected for a Special Forces training unit under the direction of Dmitri, a Greek general cut from the cloth of Sparta's legendary 300. Dmitri liked to mix old-world methods with new-world thinking. The final exam was a rescue mission. The assignment, for what Dmitri termed *the Ten*, was to go behind actual enemy lines, rescue, and return with Roman legionnaires who had been slated for execution. Employing stealth, the Ten passed behind enemy borders undetected. They invaded the compound making fast work of a larger hostile force and rescued five legionnaires while sustaining no casualties. Vitus had distinguished himself as the leader of this remarkable group. This successful mission turned an already tight-knit unit into a band of brothers.

Destiny took a hand when news of a Roman ambassador's kidnapping reached Dmitri. He knew the employment of the Ten would be too tempting to resist any longer. Sure enough, with the rescue mission just days old, Vitus and his nine compatriots were briefed for a secret mission to Judea. They were to locate, isolate, and execute Judea's terrorist leader, a man the Zealots called the Phantom.

Vitus struggled to contain his excitement upon hearing these orders. In little more than a day, the Ten were introduced to their new commander, a former Centurion with legendary battlefield credentials known as Atticus. His failure to control his violent temper resulted in the derailing of a remarkable military career. He had no patience for self-serving officers who lacked real combat experience.

"Those people," Atticus would say, "don't know the end of a sword from the crack in their behind." His failure to follow orders of pseudo-military bureaucrats hadn't gone well. He was busted in rank and shelved. But when the situation in the outlying region of Judea became intolerable, the military turned to the soldier who had distinguished himself against insurgent uprisings. To those who regarded him with derision, putting him in charge of such a mission was an act of desperation. But with his rank restored, the Centurion intended to make the most of this unexpected second chance. Atticus was promoted and briefed on the mission.

News of the attack on the ambassador drew the immediate attention of Rome's military hierarchy. It was this secretive group of Roman leaders that decided that the moment they'd been waiting for had arrived. Without delay, they deployed the special ops unit but provided only basic intel to the newly reappointed centurion. Atticus was told only that these men had received counterterrorism training and that their speedy arrival to Caesarea was critical.

The senatorial committee which commissioned Dmitri to train the Ten sent the Centurion the following orders: "Do not inform your regulars as to the nature of this mission or the specialized training of the Ten."

Atticus was not dissuaded by the lack of information given to him. He'd find out what he needed to know, as always, in the field of action. As instructed, he kept his unit of regulars in the dark regarding the special Ten.

The Centurion's speech to his slightly enlarged troop was brief. "It's critical we arrive in Caesarea as soon as possible, and that, ladies, is what we're going to do!" He gave them twenty minutes to eat and ready themselves before moving them out. After thirty minutes of double time, he barked at a member of the Ten he'd been closely watching.

"Vitus!" shouted Atticus.

"Commander?"

"Fall back, soldier, take up the rear, and keep these dog-eared dust buckets from slowing us down!"

"Yes, sir!" barked Vitus. Wasting no time, he broke formation, moving from the front to the back of the line. Atticus's voice had an unmistakable raw bite to it with vocal assaulting orders. He was nasty, not the kind of man soldiers challenged unless they were crazy or had a death wish. Driving the troop at a relentless pace, they traversed the countryside in tight formation. An average days' travel for a troop, carrying full gear was ten to fifteen miles. Atticus planned to cover twice that distance.

"Pick up your feet, men! We have no time to waste!"

Eighty pounds of legionary gear, plus a twenty-mile jog, equaled exhaustion. The regulars were nearing collapse, while Vitus and the rest of his unit barely looked winded.

Atticus finally barked out an order, "Company, halt! Take five, ladies." The entire unit collapsed into a gasping heap, all except the newcomers, who quickly dropped to the ground, trying to blend in.

CHAPTER 3
No Time to Waste

Atticus was focused on one exhausted soldier. "Keep up or we'll leave you out here for the buzzards!" Except for an early morning break, the Centurion had driven them relentlessly. The gasping sound of spent lungs grew louder by the moment. Unfazed, Atticus showed no sign of letting up. There was a method to this madness as well as a fine line between discipline and brutality. He knew he'd pushed these men to the edge.

Several legionnaires began to stumble from fatigue. Atticus had recognized the signs of dehydration miles ago. Vitus's long-range conditioning allowed him to continue on, but he was sure the collapse of the regulars was imminent.

The Centurion was a master at getting past the facade to discover the underlying motive. It was clear that his sudden promotion in rank was directly tied to these ten new commandoes. The fifty regulars under his command had little to do with the Judean mission other than provide cover for the Ten.

As a young man, Atticus advanced rapidly in rank by demonstrating decisiveness in moments of crisis. On more than one occasion while facing a crucial moment of battle, he forged ahead while his superiors debated. He trusted his instincts, refusing to second-guess himself. He took risks that higher-ranking officers wouldn't take. During the Varus Wars, at only nineteen years of age, he made himself indispensable. His cunning bold leadership could not be ignored.

Now suddenly, as if by sleight of hand, he was reclaimed from the scrap heap and restored to his former rank. It happened so fast that he wasn't even awarded the customary hundred soldiers a Centurion commands; only the Ten had been added. He'd been told they were exceptional but nothing more. Atticus was once again the alpha of an elite fighting team, but he intended to find out just how elite they really were. Would they crack under his baptism by fire? He would use this cross-country passage to find out, even if it meant gambling with the lives of his regulars. "They're only camouflage anyway," he reasoned. "Collateral damage."

A week had passed since the massacre in Judea, an assault so brutal it caused seasoned veterans to shudder. The attack was so carefully planned and executed it left no witnesses to unravel the mystery. Outgoing reports were so outrageous they reached even the most remote outposts. Each time the account was retold, its impact multiplied. According to one account, the attack occurred inside a military compound, the former home of a retired priest. Though heavily guarded by Roman immunes and Judean temple guards, massive carnage still ensued.

"Pick up the pace, boys, we're losing daylight!" Atticus's raspy voice quivered rhythmically with each pounding step. His merciless order seemed to suck the oxygen and stamina from the hearts and lungs of his fifty regulars. "Flavius!" he shouted. "You're falling behind again, causing us to lose time!"

Staggering from exhaustion, the legionnaire stumbled forward, unable to regain his balance. This lapse created a sequential collapse, bringing down a dozen exhausted soldiers with helmets and weapons flying in all directions. Finally, the Centurion gave the order he should have given an hour ago. "Company, halt!" he shouted. The troop collapsed, creating a small tornado of dust. Coughing and panting, the regulars lay face down, breathing in dust and dirt, too weary to reach for the waterskins in their packs. Vitus and the rest of the Ten were winded but still on their feet, awaiting instruction from their commander. Atticus's eyes moved from man to man; he was impressed but didn't show it.

"Knock off, men," his hoarse-sounding voice relented. "We'll rest here a few minutes."

Legionnaires made up Rome's heavy infantry, the military backbone of its war machine. Rome's military had been successful because it had learned to adapt. They applied training techniques of the Etruscans, used Greek-styled weaponry and strategy, and beat the Celtic warriors at their own game by implementing rapid-strike initiatives. It took almost a century, but they defeated the seemingly invincible hill-fighting Samnites through guerilla warfare, literally fighting fire with fire.

A legionary's training was grueling and arduous, intent on building the mind and body. Atticus understood this kind of training better than most, making him marvel at the condition of his new additions. They were extraordinary, like nothing he'd ever seen.

The Centurion could be vindictive, even heartless when it came to the plight or pain of others, but never malicious. He'd been handed something special; the only question was, how special? So far, they'd taken his best punch and stayed upright. The grueling march had shown Vitus to be the most exceptional of these ops.

Once they arrive in Judea, the Ten would operate covertly. Roman intelligence had concluded that the Zealots' precision strikes were successful because they had the support of Judean nationals. The ten special ops would infiltrate the local populace in a way regular legionary units could not.

Still on his feet, Atticus stared at Vitus, searching for signs of weakness. Nearly twenty years older, the Centurion was physically spent from the grueling pace but refused to show it. His raspy voice rose above the still heavily wheezing soldiers.

"Attention!" shouted Atticus. The regulars struggled to get to their feet.

One man, still attempting to gather himself, foolishly spoke out of turn, "Sir, would it be all right if we rested for just a—"

"Get to your feet, soldier, before I kick you to death!"

The rumpled crew did its best to stand straight at attention. Atticus continued, "I received word last night about Special Ambassador Maritus Aurelius, the Legatus who was sent on a peace envoy to Judea. He was there to provide Judea's discontented leaders a forum to voice their complaints. Some of you have heard that the

23

ambassador was kidnapped from inside the compound." Pausing for a moment, he took a drink from his waterskin, allowing some to run down his neck. "His entire delegation is dead, slaughtered as they slept behind locked doors." Shifting his gaze from man to man, he looked directly into the eyes of several. "The ambassador is missing. There's hope he may still be alive. Members of the delegation's throats were slashed so deeply they were nearly decapitated. One man's tongue was pulled backward down the throat and out a slit in the front of the neck. It's a Sicilian calling card. These terrorists were sending a message: they know us better than we know them. They mock us with the ancient lesson of a treacherous tongue."

A grimace of disgust covered his face. "Who can understand these worshippers of one God and their strange customs?" Dropping his muscled arms to his sides, he exhaled deeply, then squared his broad shoulders. "This isn't my first visit to Judea. I've served here before, hunted and dragged them from the holes they hide in. We're going to catch these dogs." His tenor turned to a snarl. "When I'm finished with them, these goat droppings will be running to change their soiled garments. Their days of rebellion are numbered."

None doubted his resolve.

"I don't want to spend one more minute in this hellhole of a country than I have to! Do you understand me?"

Intimidated by his bravado, none responded, fearful of provoking a wrong response.

Finally, Vitus stood and responded, "We do, sir," causing every head to pivot in his direction. If Vitus was frightened, he hid it well, his eyes showing only admiration for his commander.

Atticus, a bit surprised, tried to hide the smile in his eyes, nodding his head in recognition of the kid's courage. "Officially," Atticus continued, "the blame for this mess has been pinned on Barabbas, leader of the Zealots. These rebels have been actively plotting against Roman occupation for years. They play on the hatred local citizens have for us to shield their underground activities. Our mission is to assist, reinforce, and help our forces stationed in Samaria. Our time of arrival is critical. Now see to your basics. We move out in five."

Vitus was the first member of the Ten to peek behind the Centurion's frightening façade, while Atticus saw in Vitus a younger version of himself. When they resumed the march, the Centurion's cadence was markedly slower.

CHAPTER 4
Ancient Evil

Vaulting to an upright position, Orel shouted aloud, "No!" His cry interrupted the morning calm. The lingering effect of his nightmare caused a shudder. Last night's ghastly massacre wrestled sleep from everyone. "Oh G—" he blurts out before catching himself. Judaism forbade speaking aloud the name of Elohim, except in critical situations. The dream was connected to the nightmarish events of the previous night. "At least the old man is all right," he mumbled.

His thoughts of the priest brought him back to the eerie discussion Lamech spoke of before retiring for the night. Spinning around in his bunk, he lowered his legs until both feet touched the cold stone floor.

It took little effort to recall Lamech's haunting words: "This is not a conspiracy. It's a curse, an ancient evil." With his quarters adjacent to Seth and Judah's, he was not surprised by their conversation outside his door.

"Orel!" Judah called. "Come out and see these crazy Romans! Hurry up! They look like ants running all over the compound!" Judah propped his back against the door, waiting for a response. But Orel was in no mood for Judah's flippancy. "Come on, man, you gotta check this out! You won't believe it!"

Orel could also make out Seth's voice laughing at the young legionnaires.

Once the banter between the two of them quieted, Judah tried again. His rapid exhale gave evidence of his impatience. "Orel! You coming out here or what?" Judah tried a different tactic. "The post commander has been asking for you. So has Lamech."

Orel's door flew open. "Why didn't you say so in the first place instead of running your mouth as usual?"

Judah's eyebrows furrowed. "Why didn't I say what?

"That Lamech is calling for me!"

"Mercurius and Lamech have been asking for you is what I said," he insisted.

"What did he say? Does he need something?"

"Who?"

Orel's eyes rolled in disbelief. "Forget it, I'll find out for myself."

Seth jumped into the conversation, "Hey, I'm the one who spoke to Lamech, not him!" pointing to Judah. "I'm also the one who spent the night posted outside his door."

Orel's eyes slid over to Judah who looked down and away. The instructions had been for both of them to stand guard outside the priest's entrance for the remainder of the night.

With arms folded, Orel cast a glaring look toward Judah who refused to make eye contact. Orel knew that Seth had a tendency to state the obvious but disconnected when it mattered most.

His attention turned back to Seth. "So the priest talked to you?"

Seth nodded and smiled.

"What was the message?" asked an exasperated Orel.

Seth gave a sideways glance toward Judah before answering, "He said he wants to see you." He paused to gather his thoughts. "His exact words were...oh yeah, 'Get Orel, and don't come back without him!'" Seth grinned, pleased with himself for remembering the message verbatim. "Yeah, that was it, all right."

Orel's unspoken assessment was dumber than dirt. "Let me get this straight," he said. "After all that went on last night, you boneheads left the priest alone and unprotected?"

Facial expressions took a sudden turn as Orel's words sank in. Seth shifted his weight uncomfortably. "Do you think these Romans are running all over the compound to get exercise?" With a deep exhale, he asked, "So tell me, do you think you can keep Mercurius busy for a few minutes while I talk to Lamech?"

Seth shrugged. "What are we supposed to say to—" was all he could blurt out before Judah jerked him backward.

"We'll see to it," Judah assured Orel.

Taking his leave of them, Orel dodged dozens of scrambling immunes as he headed for Lamech's residence. Standing at the portal entry, he suspended a fist in midair for several seconds before reluctantly rapping on the hard wood frame. The priest's house was a beautifully aged mansion. Roman occupation had forced all Jews to make concessions, even wealthy upper-class Sadducees like Lamech. The current arrangement between Roman occupation and Judean religious hierarchy provided a degree of decorum, but it came with a hefty price tag for people like Lamech. The Sadducees, having the most to lose, seemed most willing to accommodate their Roman overlords. The Pharisees, chief antagonists of the Sadducees, saw things differently. They were openly critical of their religious counterparts but were still highly motivated to keep the Romans out of their personal affairs.

The heavy outer doors slowly opened, revealing Ezra, Lamech's main servant. "Come in." He motioned. "He waits for you."

Stepping over the threshold, Orel was apprehensive. "It's daylight," he reminded himself, trying to ignore the negative vibes from last night. "It was late. I was exhausted," he mused while cautiously keeping his thoughts to himself. "My mind was playing tricks on me. There's nothing otherworldly going on here." He tried to reassure himself.

"Follow me," said Ezra. The walls of the corridor leading to the priest's study were covered with mosaic designs. Extending his hand behind him, he halted Orel's advance. "Sir."

Ezra's voice was distinct, drawing the aged priest's eyes toward his servant. Lamech's failing eyesight didn't prevent him from recognizing his personal bodyguard's troubled aura. "Come in, my friend." He motioned. "Yes, come in and sit for a while." Lamech reclined in a fleece-covered chair, the ilk of which only the rich could afford. "Sit, sit," he repeated, gesturing with both hands for emphasis. "Don't worry, you needn't fear anything from me." Detaching his short sword, Orel slowly lowered himself into an identical chair, taking great care not to damage it. His concern brought a chuckle of appreciation from the old man.

"Sir, you sent for me?"

"Yes." He nodded, his speech labored. "We didn't finish our conversation last night." Lamech's pupils were glazed white from cataracts. "I imagine the Romans are busy scampering about this morning."

"*Scampering* is the perfect word, sir. Yes, scampering over the entire complex."

"Have they requested assistance?"

Orel's eyes narrowed at this question, wondering where the old priest was headed. He shifted his position in the fleeced chair, unaccustomed to such extravagance. "I offered some advice to the post commander yesterday evening," he replied cautiously.

Lamech was silent, offering no immediate remark. Leaning back into his chair, his hand moved slowly to his mouth, pondering the wisdom of his guardian's decision to offer assistance.

Unsettled by the silence, Orel offered an explanation, "I was one of the first to hear the scream." He tried to justify his actions. "I helped them break through the ambassador's heavily barred doors. It was ghastly, like the inside of a slaughterhouse." He stood to his feet, reliving the tension. "The assassins entered and exited unseen. No one has a clue as to how!" Shoulders turned down, he nervously paced the floor. "If it hadn't been for that scream," he continued, "the deed might have gone undetected until morning!" Orel straightened himself, locking eyes with Lamech. "Do you know anything about this, Your Excellency?"

"Is there anything else? Something you haven't mentioned?"

Orel's jaw tightened at the question. More than any other person, he revered Lamech. Orel hadn't told anyone about the mark behind the slain staff member's ear, unsure of whom he could trust. To his knowledge, no one else in that compound knew about it. It seemed improbable if not impossible that Lamech might know of it, yet his probing question suggested otherwise. Now the one man he thought he could trust drew his suspicion. *Am I being paranoid?* he wondered. He decided to play dumb and see where the conversation took them. "No," he answered, trying his best to hide his apprehension, "there's nothing else." Lamech sat quietly, his fingers interwoven. He was the kind of man who said a lot without speaking a word.

"Sadducees refuted the notion of spirits, angels, or resurrection," Lamech said softly, breaking the awkward silence. He slowly shook his head. "But I've lived long enough to see things that neither I nor my contemporaries can competently explain." Dragging two fingers across his lips, the priest's face turned expressionless. "What do you know about the events that led to our people's exodus from Egyptian slavery?"

Again, Orel's eyes narrowed, wondering if Lamech's advanced age was causing confusion. "As a child, I learned how the great *I Am* sent Moses to deliver his message, '*Let my people go,*' to Pharaoh. When Pharaoh refused, several plagues softened his resolve. It was the final plague of pestilence that broke his will."

"Very good, my young friend, and what was that final plague?"

Orel was hesitant, trying to decide if he should redirect the conversation. "The messenger, death angel, demon, whatever it was"—he paused again—"killed the firstborn in every Egyptian household, both child and beast."

Expending considerable effort, Lamech pushed himself up from his chair. Orel reached for his arm, trying to steady him. Secure on his feet, Lamech spoke with conviction, "It is clear to me that the curse is once again at work."

"The curse?"

"The ancient evil, the messenger of death recorded in the scroll of the Exodus. When Pharaoh refused to obey the Lord and let our people go, ten plagues came upon them, each one worse than the previous, until *it* came and slaughtered them. Pharaoh's house was the first to taste the slayer's wrath, his own son killed as he slept. His most skilled sentries were powerless to stop it. The pestilence *passed over* every Hebrew home as well, but they were spared by the lamb's blood painted over each door's entrance." The old priest's legs, weak from age and atrophy, couldn't support him for long. Gingerly, he slid back into his seat, weary from the previous night. Grasping the hand of his bodyguard, Lamech pulled Orel's ear down to his lips, close enough for Orel to feel the warmth of the old man's breath. "*It has returned*," he whispered. "But this time, it comes for the Romans. This time, it will not be our people who leave but our enemies! You have already seen for yourself what you cannot explain. There is no protection from *its* icy fingers of death!"

Orel swallowed involuntarily; a chill ran through his body.

Lamech asked again, "Are you sure there isn't something you want to tell me?"

Sticking to his story, Orel pushed out the words, "I'm sure."

CHAPTER 5
Arrival

Oppius was a career soldier. Infantry grunts called him a lifer, tough as nails, and Atticus's closest friend. Oppius was the kind of friend a man searched for his whole life. When charges of insubordination carried humiliation and demotion, Oppius stood by Atticus, even though it cost him a reduction in rank and pay. Before the age of twenty, Atticus was labeled the Prodigy by Roman military elite. It was no surprise to Oppius that Atticus arrived in Sebaste, brandishing the rank of Centurion. There was no demonstration of physical contact between them, but their smiles displayed a shared admiration.

"What took you so long?" bellowed Oppius. "Guess the years have caught up with you, old man. Five years ago, you'd have made it in half the time."

"One quarter of the time except for your sorry carcass always slowing us down!" Atticus grumbled, causing Oppius to quake with laughter. Atticus, having too much fun to let the exchange end, continued, "Fast? You wouldn't know fast if it crawled up your leg and bit you in the butt! You've had two speeds your whole life: slow and lifeless." Both men shook with laughter. Oppius, hands on his knees, worked to regain his composure for the sake of the men.

Closely watching these two officers, Vitus's smile quickly graduated to laughter. It was the first time he'd laughed in a very long time. Most of the regulars were stunned and silent, none having ever seen the Centurion crack a smile.

Vitus knew his commander had to be bone tired. While the exhausted troop of regulars struggled to stay on their feet, Atticus displayed no signs of fatigue. Taking a relaxed breath, Vitus sensed a kinship with the Centurion.

Atticus had a purpose behind every decision, every action. His cross-country endurance test, for example, provided valuable information about the newly acquired Ten. "Whoever trained this group," he concluded, "did one hell of a job." Their stamina and conditioning were miles above his regulars, no easy task to accomplish. Every Roman legionnaire was given rigorous training, instructors pushing the limits intent on readying them for battle. But when the desert dust had settled, it didn't take a genius to see the difference.

"At ease!" Atticus barked, his back to the toasted troops. "Take a load off." The raspy-sounding order was followed by a total troop collapse, all except the special ops who looked like healthy men in a disease-ridden camp. Vitus stood out, even among the Ten; he possessed an inner force that was different from the others.

Atticus had liked the kid from the first. This strikingly handsome Special Operative had the heart of a warrior, the head of an officer, and a muscular six-foot frame. Using superior speed and balance on the Ten's training mission, he single-handedly overpowered a dozen enemy soldiers, using only his short sword.

Dmitri, Vitus's training instructor, was quick to dismiss any man from his program that lacked superior potential. The Greek training instructor selected only twelve out of one hundred of Rome's most promising soldiers. Two of the twelve perished during his grueling training methods. He turned the remaining Ten into an elite fighting force. It was Vitus's powers of observation that first caught Dmitri's attention.

Vitus had noticed that the Centurion's muscular right arm was more scarred than his left, indicating a warrior who was right-handed in combat. At the same time, he concluded the likelihood that Oppius was ambidextrous since both arms were evenly toned and scarred.

"It's been a long journey, old friend," remarked Oppius, his double-sided meaning intentional. "My men"—tipping his head toward the soldiers behind him—"will take your legionnaires to their barracks while you and I catch up."

"They need water more than rest," remarked Atticus. "They've inhaled buckets of dust the past few days." Raising his voice so the men could clearly hear him, he continued, "They've earned the best meal this base can offer." The tanned leathery lines in Atticus's face were accentuated by his grin.

Oppius signaled to one of his men, "Reus, escort these men to the well and let them drink their fill. The rest of you"—pointing to his regulars—"see that all gear is waiting for them at their stations."

Being back with his old friend uplifted Atticus's spirit. "On your feet!" His gravelly voice bounced off of his haggard-looking legionnaires already tasting the cool water. "Come on, come on, we don't have all day." Dehydrated and fatigued, they began to stumble over each other. "Vitus, take charge. Report back when all is squared away."

Vitus took every order seriously but was careful not to over-step the authority of Reus, Oppius's second-in-command. Vitus's character made it easy for others to trust him. However, the special attention Vitus was receiving from the Centurion didn't sit well with Flavius, the son of a dignitary. He should have been the one getting Atticus's praise, not this late-arriving nobody. Flavius's family's standing was supposed to be his ticket to rapid promotion. Jealous and vindictive, he began hatching ways to derail Vitus, but he was going to need help.

Turning to Aquila, another of his soldiers, Oppius instructed, "Report to the officer of the day. Alert him of the Centurion's arrival. Take the same message to the *sala de mesa* with instructions to pre-pare enough food for an additional sixty men. Wrapping an arm around Atticus's shoulder, he chuckled. "Now, let's get that wineskin I've been saving."

"Sounds good," whispered Atticus, "along with a place to sit before I fall down."

"Both are in my quarters."

Moments later, when the two were alone, Atticus confided in his old friend, "Do you know why I'm here?"

"I imagine it's connected to recent developments here in Judea. You know me well enough, my old friend. Paying attention has kept me alive. The Zealots have stepped up their attacks on our outposts in Sebaste." Intelligence claims Barabbas is the architect behind these attacks. The legionnaires have taken to calling him, or should I say whispering his nickname, the Phantom."

"Is Barabbas responsible for the massacre and kidnapping of the ambassador?"

Oppius nodded. "Guess that's why they dug up an old relic like you for the job." He laughed.

Atticus grinned. "Anything else?"

The lines on Oppius's face smoothed as his expression changed. "Rome labels the Zealots as terrorist thugs, but they view themselves as patriots, freedom fighters, true believers. The Roman Senate doesn't want another full-blown uprising on their hands. They seek only to maintain the status quo. They'd rather let that political pimp, Antipas, do the dirty work. The emperor prefers a carving knife to a battering ram. But if things continue on the present course, the rebels will force the senate's hand. If we fail to contain this most recent insurrection, it will be *alea iactaest*. Palestine will be cleansed militarily, the Varus wars all over again."

Oppius's mood took a sudden turn from somber to light.

"What? What is it?" asked Atticus.

"It's me." He smiled. "I'm turning into an old woman carrying on like this. I'm glad you're here. Glad for the chance to work together again and pleased for this opportunity that has been presented to you. Few soldiers get a second chance, but they've put you in a difficult situation."

"Let me worry about that. What I need is information. I wasn't properly briefed. The consults pressured me to get this troop to Sebaste ASAP, promising additional intel upon arrival." Atticus got serious for a moment. "I have no intention of keeping a lid on things. They expect me to derail this uprising, and that's what I intend to do."

"Pretty tall order," said Oppius as Atticus collapsed into his sleeping cot.

With eyes shut, Atticus asked, "Did you notice anything about my men today?"

"Now that you mention it, a few of them didn't look as beat as the rest."

Smiling, Atticus wiped his stubbled face with his forearm. "Anything else?"

"Yeah, that kid, what's his name, never relaxed. Always watching, listening, hanging on every word. What's up with that?"

"You haven't lost your edge. Just your looks."

"So says the man with the ugliest eye I've ever seen, and don't get too comfortable in that bunk. The base commander has been awaiting your arrival. Or did you think it was coincidence that I was out there when you arrived? I was supposed to bring you to his quarters the moment you got here."

Atticus took another long swig from the wineskin. "Will this be the briefing I was promised?"

"Word is they knew you were coming and were planning an ambush."

"They?"

"The Underground, the Phantom—whoever *they* are. They must have underestimated your arrival time. Lucky break!"

The muscles in Atticus's jaw pulse with anger, a look Oppius knew all too well.

"Maybe *they* were the lucky ones," said Atticus. "These guys are no ordinary soldiers!"

CHAPTER 6
A New Wrinkle

Military barracks

Roman barrack cots were rigid and uncomfortable; the Sebaste outpost was no exception. "Vitus, wake up, man! You gonna get us in hot water our first morning here!" said Scipio, shaking his slumbering friend.

"Leave me alone," grumped Vitus. "Quit shaking me!"

"Roll call was minutes ago! What's up with you today?"

Vitus grudgingly rose, readying himself for inspection. He'd been dreaming of the rebels who'd killed his father. Revenge was almost in reach when Scipio started shaking him. Since joining Special Forces, the same dream haunted him nightly, but last night's version had a new twist.

*****

The nightmare always began in a desolate Judean town. Vitus was alone, standing in full combat gear with his back to the setting sun.

In the distance, a faint voice called to him, "Vitus, help me!" He was eight years old when he last heard his father's voice. "Hurry, Vitus!" the voice pleaded.

The dream was unswervingly repetitious. A rapidly setting sun turned to darkness and dense fog. Vitus peered into the gloom, trying to determine the direction from which the voice traveled. His hands extended in front of him, he moved blindly through the darkness before bumping into the rough surface of a stone wall.

"Vitus, where are you?" the voice cried. "Help me, son!"

The wall was too high to scale and too long to get around. "I'm coming, Father!" The voice was definitely coming from the far side of the wall. Running his hands along the wall's rough edges, he searched for any kind of a crevice to gain a foothold.

"They're killing me, son! Help me!"

In the darkness, he stumbled over a grappling hook and rope. Taking hold of them, he swung the three-pronged hook in a circular fashion, letting it fly over the wall on the upswing. As soon as the hook grabbed, he was over the barrier. Decimus was several hundred yards away, surrounded by twenty Zealots cloaked in black. Leaping from the twenty-foot precipice, Vitus dropped and rolled, drawing his sword in a seamless motion, and was instantly in a full sprint. Decimus's tormentors arrested their torture to ready themselves for Vitus's attack.

The words of Dmitri, his training instructor, echoed in his brain. *Stay in control, keep your wits!* Heart racing, Vitus struggled to comply. For a frozen moment, he was suspended between the past and the present. His battle cry shattered the stillness. The shrouded horde of antagonists were ready for the engagement with weapons drawn. Spinning and leaping, he burst into the center of them, leaving a wake of death in his path. No match for his unchained rage, each fell, leaving him standing alone, covered in their blood. Turning, he saw Decimus nailed to a makeshift cross with a solitary figure pressing a knife against his father's throat.

The dream had followed its usual path, except for the translucent looking specter standing behind Decimus. The ghostly enemy was eerily different, hovering just above the ground.

"You're too late!" it shrieked, sinking the blade up to the tang. Decimus's head slumped forward, lifeless.

"*No!*"

"You're too late to save your father," jeered the specter, "but your mother is still—"

*****

The dream collapsed into a swirling vortex as Scipio attempted to wake him.

Thirteen summers had passed since Vitus witnessed a Judean sunrise. Now at last, the long hard years of discipline and rigorous training were about to pay off. Vitus couldn't remember a time when he was free of this obsession for revenge. Though he didn't know it, he desperately needed closure. The recurring dream never varied until last night. A new element had been added with the specter referencing Vitus's mother in the present tense. What could this new twist mean?

Rays of early morning sunlight streamed into the barracks. "The troop is already out there!" said a puzzled Scipio, pulling his still dazed friend to his feet. This behavior was way out of the norm for Vitus. "Do I have to carry you on my back?" he exclaimed.

"No," Vitus replied, teetering between sarcasm and sincerity. Finally, the two men sprinted to the already assembled troop awaiting inspection. The Centurion was not amused.

Vitus could still feel the grit from yesterday's arduous march on his teeth. None of the regulars would dare complain about their blistered lips or sandpapered skin, not to a man like Atticus. Legionnaires were expected to march until they dropped, if necessary. A Roman soldier never asked for a break, not even to relieve himself. When he could no longer fight the pressure to urinate or defecate, he prayed his next rest stop was near a source of water so he could restore his dignity.

The Centurion's rank had been restored from *Tesserarius,* a field sergeant. He had no delusions about the reason for his promotion. If the rebels hadn't brought Palestine to the brink of disaster, he'd still be shaking scorpions out of his bedroll in the Syrian Desert. In a strange twist of fate, it was the Zealots more than the special ops that were responsible for this second chance. His caustic voice lashed the troop the way a chariot driver cracked his whip.

"Attention, mudslingers! Time for a little perspective! You're here to restore order to the region." Atticus's movements were slow and measured as the veins in his massive arms bulged. "You're not here to be emissaries or politicians. Not here to make friends!" His arms and legs were a mosaic of scars, a warrior's badge of honor.

After several moments standing at attention, a soldier's neck and back grew weary trying to remain motionless. Vitus's height put him head and shoulders above most of the regulars, affording him excellent peripheral vision. Careful to avoid eye contact, he watched this mountain of a man abscond the notion of personal space, getting up in the face of several legionnaires. Clearly, his intent was intimidation. A stream of spit inadvertently landed on Vitus's cheek, but he didn't flinch, allowing the spittle to slide down his neck.

The Centurion's left eye appeared to be misshapen; the wounded orb was partially covered by a shredded eyelid. Vitus wondered, *Was it damaged in combat or ripped away by a wild animal?* Atticus's massive hands were another source of rumor. The first night the Ten arrived, Flavius entertained the troop with a corresponding story.

"Have you ever seen hands on a man like that?" queried Flavius. "And that temper. Whatever you do, don't get between him and what he's after." Enjoying the spotlight, Flavius continued, "That explosive temper got the best of him several years ago. The Centurion lost it completely right in the middle of a campaign. Those mammoth mitts ended up around the throat of a pompous general, nearly choking the life out of him. That lapse in judgment caused him to suffer *gradus deiectio.* He was stripped of rank and a promising career, or so it seemed at the time."

Vitus's daydreaming was disrupted by Atticus's continuing rant, "Remember why you're here!" his volume increasing. "The damned insurgents must be stopped! So says the senate, and what they demand we will perform!" His fiery eyes bore into his attentive troop. "Did you hear me, boys?"

"Sir, yes, sir!" the unison response returned.

Legionary Rufus's hastily devoured breakfast was still embedded in his stubbled face. It seemed his morning shave was less than perfect. Legionnaires were required to be clean-shaven, even in remote outposts. But the concept of personal hygiene seemed lost on Rufus. His slovenly appearance matched his slow nonaggressive movements. The dried-out stubble-embedded porridge looked like an early frost had settled on his chin and cheek. Atticus hadn't yet noticed it.

"You're here to serve the emperor. That means shutting down Zealots in whatever form or shape they present themselves. This ghostly Phantom is more fable than fact!" His cadence and tone become distinct, methodical. "He's flesh and blood, nothing more." Satisfied that he'd made his point, a smile cracked his resolute grimace until he noticed Rufus's stubble-adorned face. Rufus stood directly behind Vitus who had already interpreted his commander's body language. He instinctively shifted his weight to one leg, ready to clear the path between himself and Rufus. Flinging soldiers aside like paperweights, Atticus parted the seas until he was toe-to-toe with a wide-eyed legionnaire hovering menacingly over the gangly young soldier.

"You seem to be having a little trouble shaving your face, soldier." His tone was laced with sarcasm. "Let me assist you."

Roman soldiers kept their weapons sharp at all times, especially their *pugio* or dagger. This versatile weapon doubled as a razor for shaving. Atticus glared at Rufus while slowly pulling his pugio from its casing. Pressing the knife hard against the trembling man's cheek, he slowly and deliberately shaved away the stubble-encrusted porridge. Beads of blood rushed to replace the vacated beard. Rufus's eyes were wide with horror as the blade slid from his jaw to his throat, coming to rest just above his Adam's apple. Operating with surgical skill, Atticus cut deep enough for blood to trickle down his chest, but not so deep to penetrate the artery. The visibly shaken soldier looked straight ahead, perspiration pouring out of him. He uttered not a sound. Placing the bloody knife against Rufus's cheek, Atticus leaned in close enough for the trembling soldier to feel his hot breath. "You need to get a little closer when you shave, soldier. Either you will or I will!"

Still holding the bloody knife, the Centurion took a step back to address the entire company, "As I said, you're here to serve Rome and the emperor, so serve well!" He glanced back at a visibly shaken Rufus before continuing, "Take care of the little things, and the bigger things will fall into place. Unless their women are assaulted or taxes raised, these Judeans barely know they're alive. We want to keep it that way. Let them go on sleepwalking through their miserable existence. Hands off their women. Don't try to make nice with the natives. Don't think kindness will provide an invitation to a bedroom. Don't give them a reason to hate us more than they already do. Take the rest of the morning to rest and recover. This afternoon, you'll be assigned to patrols."

He turned to the bloody nearly whimpering legionnaire one last time. "And you...clean yourself up!" The unwitting Rufus had provided the perfect vehicle to reinforce Atticus's dark side to the troop, reminding them he was not a man to take lightly. "Troops dismissed."

As the men broke ranks, Flavius blocked Vitus's path with three of his buddies providing backup.

Doing his best impersonation of the Centurion, Flavius deepened his voice. "Better watch your step around here." He motioned toward the departing commander. "He's not the only one you should be afraid of." His toadies encircled Vitus. Flavius, unaware of Vitus's training, imagined he could set the pecking order in his favor. He poked his index finger into Vitus's chest. "You understand me? Or do you need a little demonstration?"

Vitus stood silently.

Watching as all this developed, a steaming Scipio stepped beside his friend, ready to take on all four of these fools. "Are we having a problem?" asked Scipio, his eyes sliding horizontally from man to man while patting his friend's shoulder. Scipio's gaze was locked on Flavius, who still thought he had the advantage in numbers. He got so close to Vitus that they were barely a breath apart. Vitus, who was not intimidated, simply smiled at so foolish an action. Fear flashed through Flavius, now regretting his miscalculation. Trying to maintain the pretense of bravado, he slowly backed away, but his mouth was still running.

"Just remember what I said, hotshot. You're nobody around here until I say otherwise!" Flavius had no idea what might have happened had he pushed his charade any further. The four instigators turned and walked away.

"Their moment will come," said Scipio.

"Think you're right," Vitus sighed. "Let's get something to eat. I'm starved." But his thoughts quickly returned to the dream. Could this *Phantom* be the same man that took his parents' life so many years ago?

CHAPTER 7
Rebecca

The village of Emmaus

Several days later, four members of the Ten stood dressed in local garb, brandishing week-old beards. Emmaus held no more intrigue than the next town, but it was a convenient place to rest before moving on to their next destination. Their throats were dry from dusty Judean roads, so their first stop was the village well. There they could quench their thirst while taking discrete inventory. The well's ancient shaft reached down to an underground spring. This was the perfect meeting place for travelers, merchants, and citizens.

It'd been several weeks since the team enjoyed sour wine, a Roman legionary staple. After guzzling several long drinks of water, Scipio, Julius, and Leonidas were ready for something a little stronger.

Turning to Vitus who possessed the best grasp of Judean geography, Leonidas asks, "Where does a man get a drink around here?"

"You'll find an inn down this next street," said Vitus, pointing them in the right direction.

"You're not coming?" asked Scipio.

"No, gonna hang out here a while longer."

Scipio's eyebrows furrowed. "You sure, Vite?"

"I'm sure. Just don't spend the rest of the afternoon there."

After a shrug, Scipio ran to catch up with the others, taking a last glance over his shoulder to check on his friend.

Vitus had been discreetly watching a woman in her late twenties transfer water she'd drawn from the well into a colorful ceramic jug. With deceptive ease, she hoisted the heavy container to her shoulder. An almost imperceptible smile enhanced the corners of her mouth. She was flattered by this handsome stranger's interest, even though she feigned indifference. Relying on youthful recollections, he summoned up a vision of his twenty-five-year-old mother.

*****

Vitus pictured his mother balancing water jugs suspended from a pole that she supported atop her shoulders. She was about to depart from their home for the village well. Young Vitus opened the door for her. Her voice was gentle. "Thank you, my son, and now please shut the door behind me."

"Why can't I go with you? I can help draw the water so you don't have to work so hard!"

"You do help me, but you know what your father said about you going with me."

"When I return, you can help me to—" She stopped abruptly upon noticing a dark circle under his left eye. Putting down the container, she took a closer look, assessing the damage. "What happened here?"

Vitus didn't answer.

Sitting her son down, she dipped a strip of cloth into water, dabbing then kissing the bruised area. "This isn't the first time." She sighed, unable to hide the hurt in her voice. "They've been after you again, haven't they?"

Vitus nodded twice. "Why do those boys hate me, Emma?"

She took hold of both his shoulders. "They don't hate you. They're afraid of you."

His face scrunched up, trying to make sense of her logic. "They say bad things about you."

"It's all right." She sighed, holding him close. "Nothing they say can hurt me."

45

Vitus straightened his shoulders. "I'm not going to let them say those things about you!"

*****

The bleating of a thirsty lamb ushered Vitus back into the present. Realizing he'd been sitting too long by the well, he rose and walked over to a merchant hawking his wares. *Better this than nothing*, he thought. Pretending to be interested in the chattering banter, he spied another woman heading for the well. Like the woman before, she was carrying several large pots for her family's needs for the day. She was younger than the first woman, not yet in her twenties, and breathtakingly beautiful.

Vitus wasn't the only one who'd noticed her. Several legionnaires, also on patrol, had been following her along the same road his friends had used to get to the tavern. Their drunk and offensive behavior had her frightened. She quickened her pace to avoid them, but they blocked her way, encircling her.

"Don't be so unfriendly," said an inebriated Flavius. "We just want to talk." He and his companions had no intention of letting her get to the well. She didn't understand their Latin tongue, but she didn't need to; it was clear what they were after. One grabbed her wrist, jerking her up against him, sending her ceramic pots tumbling. Her struggle to free herself only heightened their aggressive behavior, laughing and hooting at her predicament. Flavius was so drunk he groped her with no concern to the public surroundings. Her eyes flashed with terror as she struggled to get away. Two of the men began dragging her away from the well, searching for a more private place to finish what they'd begun. Flavius covered her mouth firmly, preventing her cry for help.

"No, we can't have that now, can we?" His speech was slurred. But as he looked up, his path was blocked by a villager whose face was partially covered. The veins in Vitus's arms bulged with tension and disgust. The four regulars assumed he was a local Judean.

"That's enough," he said in Latin. "You've had your fun. Now let her go!"

Three of them instinctively reached for their short swords while Flavius maintained his grasp of the struggling maiden.

When Vitus uncovered his face, the thugs reflexively stepped back. Only Flavius, whose brain was slushier than the others, maintained his position.

The two men locked eyes. "Is there something wrong with your hearing?" Vitus asked rhetorically. "Walk away now while you still can!"

The girl's lungs heaved in and out from her panicked state. Vitus's stare was fierce, his intentions clear.

For most of his life, Flavius had enjoyed the silver spoon treatment of the rich. He wore an air of superiority like a person wore a garment. His liquored mind assumed this situation to be no different, and he stubbornly refused to yield.

"You walk away, sheep dip!" His words were slurred, but he maintained his grip on the struggling female. "There are four of us and one of you. If we find you still here when we're finished, we'll do to you what we're going to do to her."

When Vitus stepped toward them, Flavius pulled her even tighter to his chest, restraining her with one arm, muffling her mouth with the other.

"What are you waiting for?" Flavius shouted to the other three. "Teach him some manners!"

Vitus's aura of confidence was unsettling to the three regulars. The men hesitated for an instant before rushing him, committing to an action they were about to regret.

Having already calculated their attack, Vitus countered with a foot-first horizontal lunge. The sound of ribs cracking filled the open square. Bones splintered from a direct strike to the solar plexus. Two of them hit the ground, sliding backward, writhing in pain. Pugio in hand, the third lunged but found only empty air. Rolling and spinning, Vitus flanked his would-be attacker, latching on to the hand holding the weapon, twisting it in a direction that nature never intended it to go. Undaunted by the dropped weapon, he continued until the regular was immobilized and gasping for air. With a look of controlled fury, his focus returned to Flavius, who looked as frightened as the young woman he was holding.

"I'll say this slowly so even you can understand. If you wish to leave here in one piece, *let...her...go!*"

Dropping his hand from the girl's mouth, he shoved her toward Vitus, grasping for his weapon. Catching her, Vitus shook his head in disbelief. "Wrong decision!"

When Flavius regained consciousness, his nose and jaw were out of place along with three fingers on his right hand. Vitus yanked him up on his feet.

Meanwhile, the young woman sat speechless. She momentarily lost track of her fear, distracted by the speed and ferocity of the stranger who saved her. Propping up a nauseous Flavius, Vitus kicked at the sides of the fallen trio.

"Get up and take his sorry carcass with you back to the command post!" The three regulars struggled to collect themselves, staggering to maintain their footing before starting their painful trek back to the post. "Just a minute, you're not going anywhere until you've made your apologies." The badly damaged three looked at him, then each other, wondering, *Is he serious?*

He was. Each man apologized repeatedly until Vitus was convinced of their sincerity. Dropping down to their knees, they bowed and begged for the young woman's forgiveness.

"All right, that's enough! Get up! Now listen carefully. You're going to leave this place and never return again. If I ever see any of you in this village again... Now beat it."

As the four men staggered away, Vitus knelt beside the still traumatized young woman. Trying to gather her composure, she reached for her water jar. Despite what had just happened, she couldn't return home without the family's water for the day. Vitus was amazed at her resolve and courage. He spoke softly to her in Aramaic, her native tongue, the language of his youth.

"Are you all right?"

Surprised by the words coming out of his mouth, she wiped away her tears to study his face. He sat down cross-legged by her, being careful not to crowd her. She was even younger than he originally estimated. Even with all she'd been through, she was stunning in appearance—olive skin, large hazel eyes, and delicate features.

"I'm sorry," he whispered. "I promise this will never happen to you again."

He didn't realize he was holding her hand until she pulled her knees up under her to get eye level with him. Her face was calm, her fear beginning to dissipate. She saw through his disguise. "How is it that a Roman can speak my language?"

"I was born here. My mother was Judean."

A look of surprise covered her beautiful face. Vitus felt a little funny. It was a sensation he'd never experienced before. He couldn't look away from those hazel eyes. She didn't object when he continued to caress her small hand in his. Helping her to her feet, he quickly retrieved her water jar. Refusing her objection, he filled to the brim. Shyly looking down, she accepted the heavy jug, attaching it to her carrying pole.

"May I ask your name?"

"Rebecca." Her voice was soft and gentle.

"Rebecca," he repeated, pronouncing her name as if it were royalty, "will you allow me to accompany you to your home?"

She dropped her head, looking only at the ground. "You can't. My family would not permit it. You're a—"

"Hated Roman," he finished her dangling phrase for her. Still looking down, she nodded and then began to walk away, steadying the jar.

Vitus couldn't let her go, not like this. "Do you come to this well each day?"

Without turning toward him, she paused and nodded yes.

"This time each day?"

This time, turning toward him, she nodded affirmatively, a slight smile pursing her lips. "Thank you." Her voice was barely above a whisper.

"Vitus," he added.

"Thank you, *Vii-tuss*, for saving me."

His eyes followed her until she disappeared from sight. A spark of hope stirred in both of them.

CHAPTER 8
Antipas

Historians have recorded the good, bad, even forgettable exploits of leaders. Herod Antipas had worked diligently trying to avoid that last label. However, the tetrarch of Galilee in reality was the puppet governor of Emperor Tiberius. His leadership was always under the watchful eye of intrusive Roman occupiers, but Antipas refused to see himself as a pawn. He was a cunning manipulator, always vying to improve his political grip. From his vantage point, the Romans were a means to an end, and scruples were sentiments for the weak. He would not hesitate to use horrific measures if they worked to his advantage. Power was simply a matter of timing and perception; if he made the right decisions at the right time, the Romans may one day be dancing at the end of his strings.

Herod Antipas was the son of Herod the Great, a shameless politician who used public works to charm the Judeans. His popularity with Judean natives soared when he made good on his promise to rebuild their temple. Herod I was an Idumite, not a Jew by birth, a detail that made all the difference to Judeans who never accepted him as their legitimate king. After substantial repairs on the Temple were completed, he wanted to be called *Messiah*. The move backfired. He was not only disliked; he was despised by most of the Jewish populace.

His detached brutality wasn't limited to competitors. Marimae, his first wife along with three sons, would suffer terrible fates. This was the same man who entertained the three Magi from the Far East. When the star they had followed mysteriously disappeared outside of

Jerusalem, they sought an audience with Herod, looking for help to complete their quest.

"Where is the *promised one*, the newborn king of the Jews?" inquired the Magi. The ancient scroll of the prophet Micah pinpointed Bethlehem as the place.

Feigning benevolence, Herod made one request of the wise man. "When you find him, please return and bring word to me so that I may worship him also" (Matt. 2:8 paraphrase my own). His true intention was the swift end to another threat to his kingdom.

Being warned in a dream, the Magi never returned to Herod. The enraged king sent soldiers to slaughter, every male child born in Bethlehem three years of age and younger. This was Antipas's role model.

Herod the Great's death was gruesome. His swollen, disease-ridden, insides burst and gushed out just as he collapsed. The man literally dropped dead, leaving Judea in a vacuum of political instability. Palestine was only a remote eastern outpost in Rome's Mediterranean empire, but when rioting in Jerusalem turned into open rebellion, Governor Varus of Syria crushed it with two Roman legions. His troops pursued the rebel forces, publicly crucifying two thousand of them. The rest of the demoralized force of ten thousand surrendered without a battle.

Antipas used his considerable political skills to ensure this kind of thing would not reoccur during his reign, even if it meant crucifying his own people. It's worth noting that one Centurion in the Varus' invasion of Judea was a young promising field general named Atticus.

To sustain Judean peace and protect his sphere of power, Antipas pacified Emperor Tiberius. It was his good fortune the brutal Tiberius showed more liberality toward Judea than any other conquered territory of the empire. Antipas persuaded Judean citizens to suppress their complaints by publicly flogging any dissidents. His clever mix of politics and religion gained him the support of the Pharisees, a nationalistic religious order. He also gained the support of the aristocratic Herodians by disgracefully marrying his half-brother Philip's wife, Herodias.

In the twenty-seventh year of his reign, Judea was thrown into an uproar. A young prophet, who had been living like a hermit in the desert, set up shop along the Jordan River. This powerful preacher was irresistible. Thousands came to the Jordan, awestruck by his rugged individualism.

John the Baptizer's words had a way of stripping away all pretenses. The crowds embraced what John was offering: a new life through peace with God.

"*Repent!*" John shouted. "Clear away the clutter in your life! Make room for the Messiah who will soon show himself!" (paraphrase my own)

Weeping, they came reverently to John, asking forgiveness, wading into the waters of the Jordan to be baptized to seal their commitment to Yahweh.

It didn't take long for the news of John's activities to reach Antipas's doorstep.

After John's death, Antipas would relive the steps leading up to John's execution. His fateful command, "Off with his head!" would echo relentlessly in his brain. One night, his restless sleep was interrupted by a palace guard with urgent news.

"Your Majesty"—he bowed—"you've received a message from Governor Pilate."

Staggering from lack of sleep, he read the communiqué: "Sebaste Command Post attacked yesterday evening, eleven visiting dignitaries dead, Ambassador Aurelius missing."

A shudder ran through him. "It's John's ghost!" murmured the superstitious tetrarch. "He's returned to take his revenge on me!"

CHAPTER 9
One Step Ahead

The sleeping cot made a high-pitched *creak* of relief as the Centurion rolled out of his borrowed bunk. His brief nap was hardly sufficient.

"No rest for the weary," he muttered.

"Haven't you rested enough for the past eighteen months?" snapped Oppius, referring to Atticus's derailed career. "Maybe you would rather be wasting your life away back in the desert."

"Guess I'm getting old." He stretched and cracked his neck. "Something went down with several of my men yesterday," noted Atticus.

"They haven't been here long enough to get into trouble," Oppius sighed.

"It takes less time for some than others. Just before dusk, four regulars dragged themselves past my quarters. Flavius, the biggest mouth of the unit, looked the worst. Two of them were keeping Flavius upright. But all four had taken a pretty good beating."

"Great! It's not enough to fight the enemy. They have to beat on each other too?"

Atticus rubbed the partially denuded eyelid, smiling at his friend. "What makes you think they were fighting with each other? How do you know it wasn't the underground getting a pound of flesh?"

Oppius rolled his eyes. "If it had been, they wouldn't be limping back. We'd be collecting their carcasses."

"You're getting good at this, old friend. You're right. This was an internal matter, which is why I refused to get involved last night.

That smart-mouthed punk had it coming. Sometimes the best thing to do in situations like this is let them play out. As far as the party responsible, I'm pretty sure I know the answer to that too. My ten new legionnaires are special. One is exceptional and unlikely to take any nonsense, especially from the likes of that pompous yak."

"This is all very interesting, but Quintus Fabius is waiting to see you. It wouldn't be wise to put him off now that he knows you're here."

"Quintus Fabius—the *Tribunus Cohortis* commander of the special ops auxiliary unit in Venetia? Here in Judea?"

"That's the one."

Atticus rubbed his always irritated eye. "It begins to make sense."

"Does it? I'm still in the dark as to why a special forces tribune stationed a world away would be here in Judea now."

Atticus strapped on his leather-cased armor, cradling his helmet under one arm. "Ready?" he asked Oppius.

Oppius offered a sideways glance. "Let's go."

Walking stride for stride, they were escorted by two foot soldiers into the room where Post Decanus Mercurius and Tribune Quintus Fabius were seated. The escorts, positioned on the outside of each man, snapped off a salute, eyes straight ahead. Atticus and Oppius's salutes were slightly less enthusiastic. Both officers remain seated.

"We've been expecting you, Centurion," said Mercurius, "but not this soon."

"I was told time was critical," Atticus interjected. "My men sacrificed comfort for speed."

Quintus signaled to the foot soldiers to exit.

"Sit down," said Quintus, sounding more like an invitation than an order. "You must be physically spent." As they complied, the tribune chuckled, "Did all your men survive the trip?" Quintus liked this no-nonsense centurion who wasn't concerned with making a good first impression on a ranking officer. Rising to his feet, Quintus maintained eye contact. "You must be wondering what this is all about."

"Not really, sir." Atticus's self-assurance was impressive. "You're about to enlighten me regarding my ten legionnaires' unique training and mission."

Mercurius's back straightened; this was information Atticus wasn't supposed to know. Meanwhile, an inwardly smiling Oppius wondered how his friend could still take a man's legs out from under him after all these years.

"As I said, you don't disappoint, Commander!"

"It was clear from the start. The Ten weren't regulars. Their conditioning sets them apart. It wouldn't surprise me if they prove themselves more capable than any soldier who has served under me. The Ten, my sudden promotion and the succession of events—it doesn't take a soothsayer. Your intention was for the regulars to provide cover for the Ten as we crossed the countryside. Combine this with the blatant attack and kidnapping of an ambassador, nothing but a quick response would suffice. What I don't know is what happens to me now that I've delivered the package."

Mercurius glanced at Quintus Fabius, who was openly enjoying the Centurion's deductive skills.

A grinning Quintus, not caring about proper military behavior, stood up, shaking his head in approval. Oppius and Atticus quickly joined him, getting to their feet.

"We picked the right man for this mission and these men." He beamed. "Your estimations are correct, remarkably so. You impress me, Commander, and that's not easy to do. The recent developments you mentioned forced us to move sooner than originally planned. That's why information was withheld from you until you arrived here in Samaria. You're also correct about the task force which you've deemed the *Ten*, but you need details." Pausing, Quintus glanced at Oppius, then back to Atticus.

"There's no man I trust more than this one." Atticus nodded toward his friend.

Once again, the Centurion's unapologetic nature caused the Tribunus Cohortis to laugh. But his mood darkened as he turned to Mercurius. "This is the man those geniuses put on the shelf, wasting this kind of talent while the Judean underground rips us apart!"

Again facing Atticus, he continued, "The Ten are as unique as the Greek who trained them, a true son of Ancient Sparta. I was the overseer for what we called the Venetia Project. The Ten are mostly native-born Romans. Several speak more than one language, all are superior athletes and warriors, but one has distinguished himself above the other nine. He's called—"

"Vitus," Atticus completed his sentence. "Unquestionably Vitus."

Quintus smiled. "Yes, he's extraordinary, and though it seems impossible, head and shoulders above the rest. Their commencement exercise was a rescue mission, not simulated, the real thing. This young man risked his life to rescue a trapped soldier. Under normal conditions, he would have received the *Corona Civica*, the highest honor a legionnaire can be awarded, but his courage and ability must remain unseen for now. To do otherwise would risk the purpose for which he and the remaining nine have been so meticulously prepared." He stared into Atticus's good eye. "These ten men are ghosts. They don't exist, except to the man who trained them and a few select others. As their commander, you will answer to me through Mercurius. Everyone else is on a need-to-know basis only."

Quintus's demeanor became deadly serious. "I'm confident you're a man who isn't easily intimidated. Take great pains to prevent leaks, careless banter or action that might compromise this clandestine mission. The terrorists have their ears to our walls. Don't underestimate them. They're clever, resourceful, knowing more about us than we do about them. But now for the first time, we have an edge. If we use it correctly, we just might beat them at their own game. Are we clear?"

Atticus came to attention. "Yes, sir!"

Mercurius extended the missive in his right hand. Atticus motioned for Oppius to retrieve it. "It contains the names and personal information of the Ten and particulars you'll need to optimize the mission."

Atticus scanned and read aloud, "Vitus, Scipio, Anthony, Decima, Julius, Caius, Didius, Virius, Leonidas, Cyrus."

"Each man is a killing machine, able to engage and defeat ten or more men in single combat. Vitus is special. Teach him, learn from him, but use his talents wisely and cautiously. Your mission is to infiltrate, expose, and destroy the insurgent underground cell groups.

"Vitus is a Roman citizen but also a native-born Judean. He knows their language, customs, and beliefs. This young stallion has a fire within that drives him but also holds the potential to destroy him if not properly channeled. The leader of the Zealots has capitalized on our fears. He portrays himself as an avenging spirit. It's time we turn that around. Remember what I said about keeping the fire within Vitus under control. If you fail, it might come back to burn all of us! Find out what happened at the compound here in Sebaste, locate and rescue Aurelius—if he's still alive—and find that damned Phantom! I want his carcass openly displayed on a Roman cross as soon as possible."

A beam of light from an upper window finding the exact angle gleamed off Atticus's damaged left eye.

He raised an arm to shield it. "What about the other one?"

"The other one?"

"The Nazarene rabbi. He seems to have a greater following than the Phantom."

"I'll leave that matter to your capable judgment."

"I will report and answer only to the post commander in your stead."

Quintus nodded affirmatively. "Yes, he was present the night of the attack and will bring you up to speed." Leaning forward, Quintus Fabius's fingers grasped the edges of the desk. "One last thing, Commander. The Ten are a fraternity, a band of brothers willing to do whatever it takes to save one other. I know you'll capitalize on such loyalty. It's one of the things you do best."

Atticus and Oppius saluted respectfully, making their exit. Once outside, Atticus spoke first. "Tomorrow morning, I want all regular legionnaires assembled and ready with full packs. You will lead the regulars southeast to a town called Antipatris. That will keep them busy and out of my way for now. Besides, scuttlebutt says outlying villages of Samaria are hotbeds for insurgent activity."

"And what of the Ten?"

"We'll travel southwest toward the village of Sychar. Most Jews avoid that region like the plague, taking the long way around, even though it costs them time and money. That village might even hold a personal attraction for me."

Oppius smiled broadly. "Samaritan women are beautiful and lonely, perfect for the likes of us."

"I'll take the direct route to Sychar and communicate by courier, if necessary. Mercurius has provided several excellent runners."

"And what are your plans for the Ten when you get them there?"

"To take them on a ghost hunt."

CHAPTER 10
The Tetrarch's Tirade

The king's palace appeared still as if bathed in a serenity of silence. This was the dwelling place of Herod Antipas. The lower palace halls were empty, its servants settled down for the night. The only visible signs of life were the palace guards standing their evening posts. Any passerby would assume all was well within, but in the king's bedchamber, a tempest stirred.

"Must you continue with this pacing?" His wife's remark was more of a rebuke than a question. "I cannot sleep with this incessant demonstration of futility."

However, Antipas's concern was not the loss of sleep but power. "Can't you understand what this means, woman? This time, he's gone too far! A Roman envoy is massacred the night after they arrive. Ambassador Aurelius has been kidnapped and is probably dead, and you expect me to calm down, relax, and come to bed?" His emotional tirade acted as a catalyst to further agitate the king who resumed his pacing more erratically than before.

Herodias lay back on her bed, resting on one arm. She made no comment, realizing that even if she knew the right thing to say, it would bring her husband no solace.

"This incompetence is going to cost me my throne...my authority!" he steamed. "The man can't even be trusted to protect a special envoy!" Herod mimicked what he imagined Pilate's condemning words about him would be. "How can we expect Antipas to control the province of Galilee?" he asked aloud in a mocking tone. Looking like a caged animal stalking the limits of its confinement, he moved to and fro frantically, then abruptly stops. "He even has our soldiers believing it!"

Herodias's scorn had turned to concern. She wondered, *Has he lost his mind?* "Believing what?" she asked in a confused but stern tone.

"That he's more than a man!" His discussion now moved in a different direction. "That he has supernatural powers, able to move through solid-barred doors that even temple guards with axes can't get through! That he might be"—he paused with a dazed look and an involuntary swallow—"*the One*," his voice trailing off.

"Who? Who might be the One?" Herodias, frustrated with a train of thought that she couldn't follow, shouted back at Antipas. "You're raving! Who might be what?"

He paused, glancing over at her now standing beside the bed. A sneer of contempt curled his upper lip, stunned at her ignorance, or worse, her stupidity. "Barabbas, Barabbas, don't you pay attention to anything other than your stupid jewels and ways to make yourself beautiful? They're calling him Phantom among other things, and the scary thing is they're beginning to believe it. Can't you understand the reasoning? No ordinary man could do such a thing, only the promised one—the Messiah!" Wringing his hands in the manner of a fanatical fool, he suddenly pointed a finger directly at Herodias. "This is entirely your fault!"

Anger quickly replaced worry, her head shaking in disbelief. "My fault? My fault?" she shouted. "Now I know you're crazy!"

"Crazy, am I? Oh, that's so like you, but I'm not nearly as crazy as you are cunning! You set this up so carefully, planning your strategy, spinning your webs, even using your own daughter to get exactly what you wanted from me!"

"If you're referring to the execution of the Baptist at my daughter's request, remember, it was you, not I, who boasted to grant such a promise in front of so many prominent guests." Gesturing with both hands for emphasis, she spat the fateful speech back in his face. "'Ask whatever you wish, and I will grant it, up to half my kingdom!' Those were your words, not mine! But what does any of this have to do with Barabbas or this talk of a Messiah?"

Her question resulted in the king slumping down, collapsing into a pile on the cold stone floor. "It's a judgment against me," he said mournfully, "a judgment from God for executing his messenger."

She stared at this heap of a man she married sprawled across the floor of their bedchamber. A wave of contempt engulfed her as she considered this commoner, this poor excuse for a king that she called husband. Gritting her teeth, she enunciated her words for emphasis, speaking slowly, succinctly, each syllable exuding revulsion, "Get off that floor, you miserable excuse for a man! You're not some whimpering child who needs his mother. You're the king! The light of Israel!"

Her tone immediately snapped Antipas out of his malaise. Standing to his feet, he gathered his composure, listening intently but saying nothing. It was as if they had switched positions; she had usurped his authority during his dearth of courage.

"In the morning," she continued, "you will send an urgent messenger to Prefect Pilate requesting an immediate audience regarding the insurgents that trouble the peace of this region. You will offer your royal palace as a meeting place but state your willingness to meet on his grounds. You will affirm your allegiance, not your subordination to Rome, and you will carry yourself as a king, not a pawn in his presence. You'll do what you do best as a politician. Use that mouth of yours to cover up your lack of insight and leadership."

The king, in a state of semiconsciousness, sat down backward on the bed, his wife towering over him, his face bearing the look of someone in shock. Bowing his head, he slowly nodded a silent yes.

CHAPTER 11
The Woman at the Well

The warming rays of the sun tempered the chilly morning air. Oppius, eyes closed, drank in its warmth, waiting for the troop to assemble. His repose was shortened by the arrival of the physically imposing Centurion.

"Attention!" bellowed Oppius to the assembled troop. "We have a matter that needs addressing!"

Four of the regulars looked woozy and were having considerable trouble standing up straight. Just before morning inspection, Atticus stopped at the base infirmary to speak with an orderly regarding the severity of their injuries. The list was long: cracked ribs, a broken nose or two, several dislocated fingers, and several deep contusions. The attacker exerted just enough force to create temporary, not permanent injuries—a skill all to itself. As Atticus expected, Flavius took the worst of it, but none of them slept last night.

Glaring at the four regulars, the Centurion exhibited a combination of disgust and disbelief.

"It seems we had some trouble within our ranks yesterday."

Vitus's eyes remain straight ahead, displaying no emotion or remorse. For the first time in his life, he was having trouble staying focused, his thoughts continually drifting back to Rebecca.

The change didn't go unnoticed by the Centurion. "Something on your mind, soldier?"

"No, sir," he quickly replied, quickly snapping back to attention.

The Centurion lowered his gaze to the ground, his words directed toward Flavius and company but penetrating the entire troop. "I expect every man to be battle-ready every day, no excuses, no exceptions." Looking up, he brought the battered four into his direct line of sight. "I repeat, every day, able-bodied, battle-ready. The only acceptable excuse is death! Should you fail to satisfy these simple rules, you will answer to me, and that, gentlemen, is something you'd better pray you never have to do!" His words were slow and deliberate. Pausing, he took a step back. "Sergeant Oppius, forego inspection this morning. If we look any closer, someone is going find themselves in worse condition than they already are. Give the orders for the day and move them out within the hour."

Oppius saluted to his retreating commander as did the regulars, which Atticus refused to acknowledge.

"You heard him, full pack in one hour. Troop dismissed!"

*****

Moving at double-time pace, the unit of Ten and their commander arrived at the village well of Sychar late in the day. The Samaritans credited their ancestor, Jacob, for digging the well there. Like most wells, it had an attached rope and vessel for drawing water but no drinking vessel. The women of Sychar carried their vessels to the well daily. The Centurion planned to capitalize on this cultural nuance.

"Fan out," he barked to the Ten. "Find something we can use to drink from, and be quick about it."

The order seemed odd as each man was carrying his own supply of water, and they could easily be filled from the well.

"Vitus, you and Scipio remain here with me." Atticus rested his back against the base of the stone well. "These Zealots are a clever bunch. They fight by their rules to their advantage. They attack under the cover of darkness and never on a field of battle." Removing his helmet, Atticus rubbed the top of his close-cropped head. "They hide in plain sight in places just like this village. Who knows? Maybe we'll get lucky today, but it won't be with the help of these villagers. Our presence here reminds them that the empire is a daily disruption to their worthless lives."

Vitus and Scipio returned no comment.

Atticus smiled. "The prefect thinks we were sent here to keep a lid on things, to keep these cavemen clad in camel hair in line! I suppose Governor Pilate also tolerates Herod Antipas, the Judean ruler of Galilee, because the emperor demands it. But Pontius Pilate doesn't know which way the wind is blowing regarding our mission here." He swiped at the air with his hand. "Oh, man, what is that stench? We must be downwind of sheep dip." Atticus stood and moved farther away from the well. "Regarding the insurgents, we need intelligence, gentlemen, and you're going to get it for me. What I want to smell is the stench of insurgent carcasses impaled on crosses, starting with Barabbas!"

In the distance, Atticus spied a woman supporting two water jugs on her lovely shoulders. With each approaching step, the Centurion's mood improved. She was probably in her late thirties, and Atticus was expecting her. He knew her reputation, a lonely outcast shunned by the other women of her village. He had calculated his time of arrival to correspond with her visit to the well. Scipio and Vitus studied him as she approached. Speaking in his best broken Aramaic, Atticus fumbled his way through introductions. "Woman, permit me to help you fill your jug." The two soldiers shot each other a look, quickly surmising this *chance* encounter was nothing of the sort. She was attractive but feisty.

"I'm in no need of your help," she snapped. "I collect water every day without your assistance, thank you!"

Atticus burst into laughter, loving a woman with a sharp tongue.

"I insist." His raspy voice sounded uncharacteristically soft. Tossing the well's bucket in, he waited for the sound of a *splash*. "Scipio," Atticus pointed to one of the heavy ceramic containers—"fill it to the brim." Turning back to the woman, he made his play. "I need to question both you and your husband about insurgent activity here."

"I have no husband," she said, adding a touch of seduction to her reply.

A broad smile embraced the Centurion's face. They clearly understood each other.

"Take me to your house. I need a good meal and bath. I'll pay you well."

She stared at him for several seconds, then answered in a soft but deliberate tone, "I'll provide what you desire but not because I'm afraid of you." Her spirited indifference delighted him.

"Vitus, pull out that flask of oil in my pack and bring it over here. Scipio, draw enough water to fill her other container. When the rest of the men return, have them make camp at the outskirts of the village for tonight. Keep them out of trouble. I'll be back at daybreak." Atticus offered the woman the costly flask of olive oil which she willingly accepted. Hoisting the water-laden staff atop his shoulder, they walked off together, leaving Scipio and Vitus wide-eyed.

*****

In the distance, a rooster's braggadocios crow awakened Vitus. Squinting through the dusky morning light, he saw the unmistakable silhouette of the Centurion poised to rouse the unit. Within minutes, the Ten were on the move.

"We're headed back to Sebaste," his voice shook from the lively pace at which they were moving. "Let's pick up the pace, men! Convince me your speed in crossing the Palestinian countryside wasn't a fluke!" While Oppius's troop of regulars slumbered soundly in Antipatris, Atticus's Ten were a quarter of the way back to Sebaste. Atticus, his thoughts drifting back to last night, was already planning a second visit to Sychar.

CHAPTER 12
Back to Sebaste

The Centurion possessed an innate sense of a man's physical and psychological breaking point, wielding the knowledge like a weapon. But his seemingly gruff indifference didn't drive soldiers to rebellion. On the contrary, it engendered their loyalty. He had pushed the limits of the Ten while returning to Sebaste's military compound but followed it up with a long night's rest and especially hearty breakfast.

Instead of the usual field assembly, they met for a conference inside his quarters.

"Today," Atticus began, "we find out if the time and effort Dmitri invested in this unit was worth it. We'll see if you're as extraordinary as the senate thinks you are!" "They're counting on you to prevent another full-scale military purge and extend the Pax Romana here in Judea. For the rest of this week, my regulars will patrol the surrounding countryside and villages of southern Samaria, affording you the liberty to sweep every inch of this garrison. I want answers regarding this massacre." Atticus's eyes narrowed with intensity, making the damaged left orb appear even more abnormal than usual.

"This morning, Vitus and Scipio will assist me in a Q&A session with PC Mercurius. The rest of you will comb the inside and outside of these grounds. Gather every bit of information you can from immunes, house servants, and physical surroundings. Anthony, you will catalog all findings and report them to me at the end of the day. All information is to be reported only to me! Are we clear on that?"

"Clear, sir," the Ten responded.

"All right, then, let's see if you can find what others have missed. We need something that will lead us to the ambassador." Atticus paused. "Do I think the man is still alive? No, but the recovered body will render a great deal of information. My gut tells me that whatever is left of him isn't far away. Reach beyond your training, trust your instincts. They're what make you special. All right, let's move out!"

Without delay, the ops plunged into their assignment. Until now, Atticus's most difficult challenge had been making the Ten look like regular legionnaires. Now with the regulars out of the way, he could focus on the real assignment: to infiltrate the insurgents and capture or kill their leader.

With an unspoken admiration, Vitus and Scipio escorted the Centurion to the PC's post. Atticus was counting on Vitus's keen powers of observation to provide him with a second set of eyes equal to his own. Scipio had already proven himself to be a shaker and a mover, a man who got things done. Atticus would lean on both of them for superior detection results.

After obligatory salutes, the trio listened attentively to Mercurius's recounting of that fateful night. A name that continued to surface was a Judean soldier called Orel.

"Who is this Orel?" Vitus interrupted, momentarily forgetting his place. Atticus had intentionally held back, putting Vitus to the test. Vitus sheepishly glanced at his commander; diplomacy was an area Dmitri had addressed.

The crusty Centurion, finding no fault in his protégé, emphasized the point, "Yes, Post Commander, tell us about this Orel."

Mercurius's eyes shifted between Atticus and Vitus. "Orel is not under my command. He's not an immune or even Roman. He's a former Temple guardian. The principal bodyguard of Lamech, a distinguished retired Hebrew priest, who has shared these grounds with us the past three years."

Scipio broke in, "Why is a Jewish priest living in a Roman compound?"

"This place was his home long before it was a Roman garrison," Mercurius answered. "Judean religion and politics are practically married. Historically, the Sadducees have been much more cooperative with the empire than the other religious groups. Being wealthy, they have more to lose than most if the status quo with the empire is disturbed. For this reason and others, Lamech willingly opened the doors of this massive estate, allowing us to convert part of it into a military installation."

"I've heard of the wealthy temple vaults," interjected Vitus.

Atticus grunted sarcastically. "It's about money kid, it's always about the money."

"I'm not sure that holds true when it comes to the Zealots," countered Mercurius. "It's not money they're after. They see themselves as liberators, selfless heroes who will sacrifice everything for *the cause*."

"What is the cause?" asked Scipio.

"Zionism is what they're calling it now, the return to independence and Hebrew tradition. Their intent is to make things so uncomfortable for us that we finally decide it's not worth the trouble and pull out." Mercurius paused, considering his next words. "The extremist's fringe is led by Barabbas who believes he's paving the way for something or someone greater, a coming leader who will rally all of the Jews to rise up and push the empire out of Palestine."

"Call it whatever you like," said Atticus. "Riches, freedom, *the cause*—it all boils down to power."

"Do you think it possible that Barabbas believes he is the messenger of El Shaddai?" asked Vitus.

Mercurius was taken aback—not by the question but who was asking it. He was surprised by this young soldier's awareness of a culture so foreign to him. Sitting back with his arms folded, he shook his head and smiled in appreciation. "I can see why you want this young legionnaire at your side," he said to Atticus. Redirecting his response to Vitus, he said, "Yes, I think Barabbas does suffer from a Messiah complex."

"And you believe he's the one who perpetrated the catastrophe on this garrison?"

"I do. Barabbas is the name directly linked to insurgent activity in Judea. His legend has spread like a disease, even among our own soldiers. They've taken to speaking his name in hushed tones as if he were lurking in the shadows, waiting to strike. He plays on the ignorance and superstitions of our men, using their own fears against them."

With a sense of urgency, Vitus turned to his commander. "Sir, shouldn't we speak with Orel?"

Atticus turned to Mercurius. "Can you arrange a meeting with him?"

"I have no authority over him. He's Judean, but he's been of great assistance at the time of the attack and since." Mercurius's next comment struck a nerve with Vitus. "He's quite intelligent for a Jew."

"Intelligent for a Jew?" Vitus's repetitive response was laced with shards of cynicism.

For the second time, Mercurius was taken aback by Vitus. Completely unaware of this young man's mixed Jewish/Roman heritage, Mercurius was perplexed by his response.

Rising to his feet, Atticus broke the awkward silence. Vitus and Scipio followed his lead. "I'll need access to the chamber where the killings took place," said the Centurion in his gravelly voice.

"You'll have it," remarked Mercurius, still glancing at Vitus from the corner of his eye. "I'll give the order as soon as we're done here. Full access to the ambassador's chamber along with anything else you need."

"It's critical we speak to Orel as soon as possible," insisted Atticus.

"Assuming his cooperation, I'll arrange the meeting."

"If there's anything else you need, just send word. Keep me in the loop. I expect regular updates on your progress."

As they made their way across the grounds of the garrison, Atticus turned toward Vitus, unable to wait any longer. "What the hell just happened back there?" his raspy-sounding voice barked.

"It's personal," snapped Vitus, his eyes downward as they walk.

"Yeah, I know, kid. It always is. Fill me in as soon as you can."

CHAPTER 13
Investigation

Atticus was still thinking about Vitus's uncharacteristic reaction, as they walked to Aurelius's chamber. Two immunes blocked their way at the entrance. Revised orders from the post commander hadn't yet reached them. Atticus, never one for patience, issued an order of his own, "Step aside." Wide-eyed and blinking, the two glanced at each other, unsure of their next move. The Centurion moved closer to the guard on the right. "Soldier, I don't repeat myself for anyone, but I'm going to assume you're confused. Now for the second and last time, I'm ordering you: *stand down!*"

This second command causes one of the young immunes to shake involuntarily. Caught in the middle, he was afraid to disobey previous orders but was petrified of the towering brute.

"Stand down!" cried an approaching runner. "The PC's new orders instruct you to give these men entry!"

But the news had arrived a moment too late. The hapless sentry had already been tossed aside by Atticus. Vitus's attention, however, was trained on the second man accompanying the messenger. He was not Roman military.

"You're Orel," remarked Vitus in Aramaic, the native tongue of the region. Scipio shot a look Vitus's way, having no idea his friend spoke their language.

"That's right," Orel answered in Latin, Rome's native tongue.

Vitus greeted him with a nod of approval and a smile.

Atticus wasted no time. "We've heard a lot about you from Mercurius."

Standing several feet away, Orel shifted his weight to one leg.

"We're anxious to hear your take on events of that night. Maybe you can provide a different perspective than what we've already been told."

Orel was just shy of six feet with a muscular symmetrical frame that supported his 190 pounds.

Atticus dismissed the messenger and guardians with a wave of his arm. Redirecting his gaze away from the dark chamber, he snapped at the three soldiers, "Are you coming in or not?" Atticus directed his next words to Orel, "There're good at what they do, so share whatever conclusions you hold with them."

Sporting a wry smile, Orel remembered Lamech's sobering words: *The ancient curse, messenger of death.* They'd surely think him deranged if he were to mention any of this.

"It was the scream that first alerted me, a shriek so startling the entire compound must have heard it."

Listening intently, Vitus was anxious to begin questioning Orel. "A single scream?" he broke in. "Are you certain? So many men viciously mangled and only one manages to cry out?"

"Absolutely certain. One…solitary…terrifying scream," he answered succinctly.

"There is only one way in and out of this suite," interjected Scipio, peering through the dark chamber.

"That's correct. Why don't we all take a closer look?" Orel reached for one of the torches holstered on the wall. Scipio grabbed the other. Torches in hand, they entered the windowless chamber that bore no natural light.

"This place gives me the creeps," Scipio remarked, shrugging off a shiver. "Feels like a mausoleum." Running his fingers along the walls, he walked to the far end of the shadowy chamber. "Only two doorways," he cried, confirming the obvious. "Were guards posted at both of these?"

"Immunes are always at their posts," added Orel. "But the doors to the chamber were locked from the inside. This combined with the young soldier's inexperience, didn't serve well." Pausing for a moment, he wondered if he could trust these men. He had to tell someone about the slain man's tattoo. Vitus might be a kindred spirit, but he couldn't yet bring himself to share his secret.

Waving his arms from the other end of the chamber, Scipio proclaimed, "This door is clean. No blood marks!"

"The doors were locked from the inside," said a pensive Vitus. "The assailants never used them."

"They sure as hell got out," bellowed Atticus who had silently been taking it all in, "since they're not here now!"

"It makes no sense! I'm beginning to understand why he's called the Phantom!" said Scipio. "Eleven men savagely butchered, a missing dignitary, only one scream heard, and no witnesses to any of it? It doesn't figure. Someone is messing with us, and we're not getting it. These butchers didn't vanish into thin air!"

"Your people haven't been able to get anywhere," said Orel. "No matter how many times they go over it, they end up with lots of questions and few answers." Orel delayed for a moment before posing the question, "Could there be something else going on here?"

Atticus's eyes narrowed, accentuating his deformed eyelid. "Keep those thoughts to yourself, mister, we're here to expose this charlatan, not fuel his myth."

"How is it you got yourself involved in this?" Vitus cautiously asked. "You're the bodyguard of the priest. Why weren't you at his quarters?"

The question delighted Atticus.

Orel laughed, releasing tension that seemed days old. "I've been asking myself that question. All I had to do was mind my own business. But instead, here I am in the middle of it."

"So do you agree with Mercurius that this is the work of Barabbas?" asked Scipio, still mulling Orel's leading question.

Orel smiled broadly. "Barabbas? Barabbas is a convenient faceless villain your military uses to suggest the Judean insurrection is under control. But the real problem is far bigger than one man. My people are proud and stubborn. Our continued defiance should convince you of that. Who do *I* think is responsible?" he said, shrugging his shoulders. "I suppose Barabbas is as good a choice as any."

With each passing moment, Vitus's admiration for Orel grew. Orel was not afraid to speak his mind but maintained a guarded approach to life. Mercurius's backhanded compliment of Orel was accurate; he was intelligent and slow to pass judgment, even on Romans. His track record the night of the massacre was nothing short of exceptional. His obligation was to protect Lamech, but he ignored convention to assist Mercurius, and now he was doing it again.

"I'm heading back to my station, but I want a progress report as soon as possible," said Atticus, but his words were lost on the three men's concentration. They continued their examination of floors and walls as if he'd never spoken. "Did you hear me, Vitus? I get that report by the end of the day!"

Vitus acknowledged Atticus with a nod and a quick salute. "You'll get everything we discover, sir. Do you still want it funneled through Anthony?"

Squaring his shoulders, Atticus exhaled, "Bring it directly to me." Rumbling out the door of the chamber, he muttered to himself, "This trio needs no additional motivation from me."

The trio now regarded this mystery as an enemy to defeat.

"There had to be a lot of blood," insisted Scipio. "Why isn't it splattered all over the place? With that kind of butchery, there should be more blood visible."

"I agree. Throats were cut so deeply that heads were nearly decapitated," said Orel, making a slashing motion along the base of his throat.

"You were here. Did they clean the place up?" asks Vitus.

"I can't say for certain. That night was bedlam. I wasn't looking at walls or the floor when we broke through the doors. I was expecting a battle! If Mercurius is anything, he is cautious. Why would he give instructions to scrub the place down?" Orel paused. "I do remember the bedding. It was blood-soaked."

"Maybe they were attacked as they slept," said Scipio, moving around the room, trying to visualize it. "That could explain the singular scream."

Vitus walked over to the cots. "They look out of place, and the bedding has been tossed around. Were things jostled when they removed the bodies?"

"I have no idea. I was only involved in the initial break-in and then later discussion with Mercurius."

"If these beds were close enough to each other, one or two assassins could have killed them as they slept without a struggle or a scream," said Vitus, moving from bunk to bunk, replicating the action. "If their throats were cut as you had said, it would be impossible to cry out, even if they regained consciousness. One or two silent stalkers might have been enough."

"However it happened, one woke up," Orel reminded. "His bloodcurdling shriek carried into the courtyard!"

"It had to have been the last man or there'd be more evidence of a struggle," said Scipio.

"The only heavy blood splatter is over here." Vitus pointed to a section of the stone wall.

"It's all very interesting, but it doesn't explain what happened to the ambassador," said Scipio, rubbing the top of his head.

"According to Mercurius and Orel, the doors were barred from the inside." Vitus points to the battered remains. Orel nodded. "If the plan was to kidnap the ambassador, it may have been his scream you heard. That could mean he's still alive."

"No," Orel butted in, "I don't think so. Only a person being skewered lets out a cry like the one I heard. As a temple guardian, I watched priests prepare a lamb for a burnt offering. The lamb's bleating became a high-pitched yelp as the knife slashed its throat. I've heard that death scream hundreds of times. I still hear it in my sleep, a sound you never forget."

Vitus's eyes scanned the chamber walls. "There's another way out of this place. There has to be. A secret portal, a hidden passageway somewhere in the floor or walls. It's here, I'm sure of it!" Vitus turned around in the dimly lit room. "This compound is not a standard Roman outpost, is it?"

Orel nodded. "It wasn't a military installation at all. These buildings and grounds were the exclusive estate of Lamech, the priest who still lives here."

"What prompted the new arrangement? Was it commandeered by Roman military?"

"Not commandeered, volunteered by Lamech. He brokered the deal with the governor. He was willing to share part of his estate as a gesture of goodwill, but not out of the goodness of his heart. That's not who the man is."

"They knew a way to get in and out without being seen or heard," remarked Scipio. "They knew a way to get in and out without being seen or heard. Except for that scream, it was perfect. Only someone with precise knowledge of this place could have accomplished it." The priest could be in league with the Zealots. The old man's family mansion a Roman military post—who better to know the secrets of this place than Lamech?

Orel thought of the man with the imprinted tattoo, צלמות. What if he was one of the attackers posing as a Roman? In either case, something went very wrong. There had to be an inside man helping the Zealots, but for now, Orel refused to accept Lamech as that person.

"Scipio!" Vitus barked. "Get back to Atticus. Tell him we need water, bucketloads of it."

Scipio's eyebrows creased, puzzling over Vitus's request.

"Just do it and hurry!"

CHAPTER 14
The Shadow of Death

Twelve men moved through shadowy light, speaking in hushed tones, anxious to begin their secretive meeting. The last man to enter barred the door behind him. The main body of the Shadow of Death was ready to commence. Shimron, who was an exceptionally savvy scribe, opened the discussion.

"Our concerns regarding the Baptist's rising popularity are no longer an issue."

"Yes," interrupted Tola, another influential member of this powerful group. "We have Antipas, the mighty tetrarch of Galilee, to thank for that."

"I think you mean Herodias," chuckled Shimron. "'Bring me his head on a silver tray!'" he mocked. "That woman gets her man one way or another." He laughed outwardly but inwardly shuddered at the thought.

Iri, another member of the Shadow, spoke up, "There's a second issue we dare not sleep on. The Nazarene, the one called Jeshua, has the potential to upset the status quo with Rome."

"Our people retrieve information daily from his meetings. We intend to discredit and embarrass him publicly," replied Shimron.

"Really? And how is that going?" asked Tola. "To my knowledge, our most skilled debaters have failed to put a dent in his armor. He manages to counter the most carefully designed questions to trap him, twisting them into pitfalls for our agents. He's a hero to these ignorant masses who have no idea what's good for them. How much longer before they start calling him Messiah? We must come down hard!"

Iri stood up beside Tola, hosting a calm facial expression. "Perhaps it is time to involve the Phantom." The undercurrent mumblings abruptly stopped, the room becoming deadly silent. "I was contacted by one of his messengers yesterday. When the Romans finally discover their missing ambassador, his mutilated corpse will incite the kind of rage the Phantom has been after."

"He goes too far with these fanatical acts of brutality!" cried Tola. "What will happen when news of this debauchery gets back to Emperor Tiberius? Will his liberality toward us continue? Or will the full weight of the imperial army come crashing down on us?"

Pockets of murmured discussions broke out in response to Tola's sobering remarks.

"Your mistake is in your assumptions, Tola."

All heads turned to engage the words of Korah, a lone figure standing at the far end of the circle. Korah was something of a double agent in this assembly of Sadducees and scribes. Publicly, he posed as a member of the Herodians, but behind closed doors, he supplied this group with invaluable insider information.

Unnerved by Korah's remark, Tola demanded an explanation. "Just what is that supposed to mean?"

"You give Barabbas too much credit and not enough blame."

Tola was perplexed by Korah's cryptic comment. "Speak plainly!" he demanded.

"The attack on Aurelius didn't go quite the way it was planned. Is that clear enough for you? He didn't intend to kill the ambassador." sighed Korah.

"The potential for things to go awry is something we all recognize. I don't hold Barabbas responsible for killing Aurelius as you obviously do! Barabbas didn't kill the ambassador, nor did any of the daggermen."

A stunned Tola sat down. All eyes in the room fastened on Korah. "Do you finally understand? Aurelius will shortly be discovered by legionnaires nailed to a cross in a remote area south of

Samaria. But he didn't die from crucifixion. The plan is misdirection, to lead our enemy away from the truth."

"What did happen?" asked Shimron.

"The ambassador's wounds are far worse than any of the others. But Aurelius's wounds were inflicted postmortem to disguise what actually killed him."

Shimron, losing patience, cried out, "What is the reason for this subterfuge? Who killed Aurelius if it wasn't Barabbas?"

"The creature…" Korah's voice trailed off. "The beast that still roams the lower chambers of Lamech's estate."

"Impossible," cried Iri. "The creature hasn't been seen or heard from in years!"

"It was seen the night of the massacre! It came up from the depths, surprising the team of assassins, instantly killing one of them, and wrestling Aurelius away from Barabbas, tossing the Phantom aside like a sack of wheat. It was devouring the ambassador alive, biting off chunks of his torso until Barabbas thrust a burning torch to the back of its head, setting its hair on fire, sending it back into the tunnels. Its horrific scream is what alerted the Roman sentries that night. Seeing no recourse, he killed the ambassador and took his mutilated body with them. Our inside man was collateral damage. His neck had been snapped like a twig by the beast. The Zealots cut his throat like the rest to disguise the truth. The rest you already know."

Korah paused, leaving the group stunned and silent, then continued, "We have many things to consider tonight. The Nazarene is certainly one of them. I haven't told you all this to dissuade you from infiltrating his inner circle. On the contrary, I hope I've done the opposite. I applaud Barabbas's quick reaction to an impossible situation. It was the creature, not the Phantom, that put us into so precarious a situation."

"But what does any of this have to do with the Nazarene?" demanded Shimron.

Korah drove his point home, "When Aurelius's body is discovered, Pilate will pressure Mercurius to take countermeasures. What if we can deflect the Roman military anger toward the Nazarene? If we can connect him to Barabbas, it gives the Romans an easy target to strike."

"Interesting," remarked Shimron, "but how do we accomplish such a thing? This young rabbi is no fool."

"There's always a way, Shimron. We've worked together long enough for you to know that. Barabbas will plant evidence that points to Jeshua. The scam will require a man to infiltrate the Nazarene's ranks. He has thousands of followers but a small inner circle. Barabbas believes he has the perfect man for the job."

*****

Lead by Oppius, Atticus's regulars had searched the outlying regions of Samaria for insurgent activity with no luck. Oppius had hoped to capitalize on the generational hatred between Jews and Samaritans. Divide and conquer; a simple but time-tested strategy was doomed to fail. It seemed the only thing Jews and Samaritans hated more than each other was Roman occupation. Samaritans had provided hiding places for Zealots to thwart Romans and doom Oppius's plan.

In the past, Roman military had relied on brute force and over-whelming numbers, not stealth. The Zealots were not yet aware there were special ops in Judea targeting them for extinction.

While Oppius's soldiers spun their wheels; Zealot militants staged a faux crucifixion using Aurelius's battered remains. They were intent on leaving an easy trail for the legionnaires to follow. Enemy archers would ambush and kill all but a few of the unsuspecting legionnaires, intentionally allowing a remnant to escape and report their discovery.

CHAPTER 15
Aurelius

The winded courier refused to surrender his communiqué to the sentry who blocked his way. In turn, the sentry wagged his head, refusing to grant him passage. It was a classic case of irresistible force meeting immovable object. The exhausted runner struggled to catch his breath. "I'm Athos," he declared, "sent by Sergeant Oppius with a message of critical importance for Centurion Atticus!"

"That's interesting," said the sentry in an official sounding voice. "Give it to me and I'll see he receives it."

His breakfast interrupted, Atticus joined the ongoing fracas, raising his own voice above the shouting match. "Is that for me, soldier?"

The courier was taken aback by the size of the Centurion. "Are you Commander Atticus?" he stuttered.

"I am indeed! Let him pass, Tertullian." After coming to attention, the overzealous sentry stepped aside. Clutching his waxy correspondence, the young courier stepped past Tertullian, giving him a sideways glance. The Centurion motioned for the runner to follow him as he walked back to his now cold breakfast. "Sit down, son, you must be hungry."

Athos, still grasping the communiqué, suddenly noticed the Centurion's left eye. The young courier's open mouth prompted a chuckle from Atticus. This battle-scarred veteran had seen that look hundreds of times. He considered the injury a mark of distinction. Athos swallowed involuntarily, trying to act like he hadn't noticed it.

Coaxing his semiparalyzed tongue to cooperate, he finally pushed out the words, "Sir, I—"

But Atticus's raised hand left his sentence dangling in the air. "You just arrived with an important message for me."

Looking a bit unnerved, he tried again, "Yes, sir, it—"

The Centurion's open palm stopped him again. "It's of an urgent nature?" Atticus said with a smirk.

The courier nodded.

"Then why is it still in your hand instead of mine?"

Trying to hold back another swallow, Athos sheepishly handed the missive to the Centurion. "Should I wait for your response, sir?"

A curt "Yes" was followed by a finger pointing to the door. "Out there, soldier."

Athos started for the door but then stopped. He knew he shouldn't ask, but he couldn't help himself, "Sir, I—"

Atticus's raspy voice blistered him. "*Outside!*"

With color draining from his face, Athos tripped trying to get out the door.

Forcing down a spoon of cold oats, Atticus read Oppius's communiqué:

> *Troop attacked by archers—several dead.*
> *Ambassador's stripped body discovered*
> *on hillside cross—throat slashed.*
> *Awaiting orders.*

Atticus's fist came down hard, sending bits of porridge flying in several directions. "Damned Zealots!" he seethed. "They set this up, wanting us to find the body! Athos," he bellowed, "get in here!"

The nervous courier reentered. "Sir," he replied.

"You will carry a message back to Sergeant Oppius with all speed."

The young wide-eyed runner was fully focused.

"Commit these words to memory: 'With all dignity possible, return the ambassador's body to Sebaste, escorted by a company of five legionnaires. The remainder of the troop will remain in the region.' Have you got that?"

Coming to attention, Athos tried to avoid looking at the Centurion's distorted eye.

"Repeat that message back to me!"

Making no eye contact, the runner complied.

"Good, now get some food and drink at the mess hall. I want you en route within the hour."

*****

Just about dusk the following day, Flavius and four additional regulars arrived in Sebaste, dragging a litter behind them. One entry guard sprinted off to inform the Centurion of their arrival, but the odor of a badly decaying corpse had already alerted him. Inside the infirmary, the five legionnaires stood silently at attention. Atticus peeled back the covering, exposing the grisly remains. The pungent stench was so overwhelming the regulars covered their mouths trying to keep from gagging.

The Centurion shook his head; the grotesquely swollen body barely looked human. "Crucifixion is an excruciating way to die, sometimes lasting for days. But this man didn't die from crucifixion." Pointing to the throat, he continued, "These gashes tell a different story. His artery was severed. He would have bled out in minutes.

Flavius was pale and silent, perhaps realizing for the first time what he'd gotten himself into. There were no rules of engagement, no lines that couldn't be crossed in this web of terror, and no easy way out of this assignment.

"What's wrong, soldier, cat got your tongue?" The grossly disfigured body had been gashed in several places, chunks of the lower region missing completely.

"Was he alive when they did this to him?" asked a shaken Flavius.

Pulling the canvas back over what was left of the ambassador, Atticus answered, "Let's hope not. Go to the post commander. Tell him to come and see for himself what's become of Aurelius. That is, if he has the stomach for it."

Atticus looked up to see Scipio jogging toward them, yelling something about water. "Sir," his voice getting clearer as he got closer, "Vitus asks you send water, a lot of it!" he shouted.

"Water?" he snarled with the tone of a man who had an especially bad day. "He wants water?" he repeated. "Did he say why?"

"No," Scipio shrugged, "just that he'd explain later."

"That's when he'll get his water—later. Go back and tell him I need him to meet me here at the infirmary. I want him to examine the ambassador's corpse."

Scipio saluted and bolted.

Disgusted, Atticus dismissed the five legionnaires with a sideways wave instead of a salute. "I'm going to get that SOB," he seethed. "I'm going to find him and disembowel him slowly in front of his people. He's going to wish he'd never been born!"

CHAPTER 16
Discovery

His patience growing thin, Vitus paced the floor in the ambassador's empty chamber. Orel followed him with his eyes. This was a side of Vitus he hadn't seen.

"What's taking Scipio so long? He should have been back by now!"

Of course, neither man had any way of knowing Aurelius's remains had just been delivered to the Centurion. Obsessed with the killer's baffling entry and departure through barred doors, Vitus was impatient to test his theory.

"What in the blazes is he doing?" Vitus's attitude seemed out of character to Orel, who gave him a sideways glance.

"Something unexpected has delayed him. He wouldn't intentionally leave you hanging."

Vitus blew out a breath of acknowledgment. He knew Orel was right, but his patience was spent.

"You and you," Vitus ordered the young immunes, "round up as many men as you can find. I want a line of ready hands stretching from that well to this door, at least thirty men. Have you got that?"

The two immunes were the same age as Vitus, but they regarded his words as those of a seasoned leader.

"If anyone questions you, tell them you're following Mercurius's orders."

They quickly saluted before rushing off to carry out his instructions.

Orel exhaled, "I sure hope you know what you're doing."

"So do I."

Within minutes, a line of immunes stood shoulder to shoulder stretching from the well to the chamber entrance. The two soldiers who had gathered them stood smiling, an assortment of buckets under each arm.

Shaking his head, a smiling Orel looked back at Vitus. "Pretty impressive, Post Commander," he laughed.

Vitus's praise of the bucket-hauling immunes caused the two men to straighten with pride. He then addressed the entire company, "Your objective is to keep water moving man to man, without breaking rhythm. The man at the end of the line will run the empty container back to the well, each man following his lead. All right, then, let's get this brigade started."

Soon, sloshing pail after sloshing pail of water took on a kind of symmetry and speed. The last man sprinted back to the beginning, not wanting to slow down the process. Scipio, returning empty-handed from his meeting with Atticus, found Operation Water Flow in full swing.

Vitus caught sight of him. "Keep it going, men, this is going to work!" he shouted, while shooting Scipio a perturbed scowl.

"Vite, I—"

"Not now, Scipio, already lost too much time."

"But Vitus, I've got to tell you—"

"Not now, Scip! Get in here and help us! Follow our lead."

Scipio watched Vitus and Orel send buckets of water splashing against the wall, forming a pool at its base. "Take notice of the run-off!" he shouted. "If it doesn't puddle on the floor, sing out!" Turning back to the line of firemen, he shouted, "Keep that water coming!"

The thirty soldiers had no idea why they were doing this, but it doesn't matter. They'd bought into Vitus's charismatic leadership. Orel had picked up on Vitus's plan, but Scipio was still bewildered.

"Vite, what is all this?"

"Look for a hidden entrance!" he yelled back, continuing the assault of water against the stone walls. "It might not be in the walls," he shouted. "Watch the dispersion of water on the floor." "Keep it coming, men!" "We'll soak this entire room, if necessary. I know it's here."

"Over here!" Orel shouted. "It's over here!" Vitus and Scipio rushed to the place. "See how strangely the water behaves." Scipio splashed more water where Orel stood.

"That's it!" cried Vitus, signaling for the fire brigade to stop. Water seeping into the stone floor brought a smile to Vitus's face. "This is what we've been looking for," he whispered, examining the area. "Pour another one here and here," pointing to the outer edges of both sides.

Orel, relieving a gawking immune of his bucket, watched the formation of a watery outline. The faint pattern quickly faded as the water ran through the stones.

"We need tools!" Vitus declared, grabbing one immune by his helmet's chin strap. "Find shovels, picks, anything to pry up these stones."

Soldiers tripped over each other, trying to get to the door. "Orel, we need more water. Got to define these edges."

Scipio, thinking he had an opening, tried to deliver the Centurion's message to Vitus. "Vite, the Centurion has ordered—"

"Not yet, Scip, hand me your pugio."

Scipio hesitated briefly before pulling his dagger from its sheath. The eyes of both men locked for an instant, causing Vitus to smile. "Really, Scip?" he said, extending his outstretched palm. Flipping his knife in the air, Scipio caught it blade first before handing it to Vitus. Still smiling, Vitus poked and probed the quickly fading edges. Orel carefully poured another bucket, revealing a rectangular-shaped outline in the floor.

"There has to be a lever release somewhere in this room," said Scipio, now just as excited as Vitus.

"It might not be in the floor," said Orel.

"Spread out! Run your hands along the walls. Feel for irregularities," shouted Vitus.

Scanning with their eyes, their hands ran along the rough stone surface.

"We need more light in here!"

Orel's mind returned to his last conversation with Lamech. He heard the priest's warning: "Ancient curse." Caring deeply for the old man, he tried to rationally consider the possibilities. This chamber—the entire compound, for that matter—had been the home of an extremely powerful priest. If anyone would have known about the existence of a secret passage, it would be Lamech. This would not go well for him with the Romans. Hoping against logic, he wondered, *Could the old man have lived there all those years and not know about this?*

"Over here," yelled an energized Vitus. "I've got something!" Nudging a stone from side to side, he dislodged it. Reaching inside, he remarked, "There's definitely something in here!"

Scipio and Orel flanked him, anticipation building. Feeling inside, Vitus carefully wraps his hand around a lever, first pushing then pulling it toward him.

"I don't believe it." Orel's voice was barely above a whisper as he watched the stone floor slide downward. A staircase appeared in the darkness below. Scipio, ready to jump down, was stopped by Vitus's hand against his chest.

"Not yet, Scip. I want you to gather up the rest of the Ten and get word to the Centurion."

"What are you going to do?"

"Orel and I—" He paused, not wanting to assume anything, but quickly received a nod of approval. "Orel and I are going to take a look down there. Follow us down as soon as you return."

"You sure about this, Vite? Maybe I should go with you."

"Remember our training. Gather the others, get word to Atticus, and this time, get back as quickly as you can." Vitus's quick smile told Scipio that everything was okay between them. "Ask the immunes to stay ready outside, and hand me my sword before you go."

Orel, a torch in hand, descended into the dank-smelling blackness with Vitus right behind him. As if lodging a complaint, each tread creaked under Orel's weight. Before taking the final step, the tattoo, צלמות, flashed in Orel's mind. He wondered if he would suffer the same fate as the man who bore the words "Shadow of death." As his foot touched the last step, it triggered a secondary lever, sending both of them sprawling forward. The torch was quickly quenched in a puddle of water. Behind them, the retractable stairs reset to an upright position, leaving them in total darkness.

CHAPTER 17
A New Element

Barabbas, a militant extremist, was the leader of the Zealots. For most of his life, he had believed extreme action was the only realistic way to push the Romans out of his country. Lately, however, he had been mulling over an alliance with the *peaceful* young rabbi from Nazareth. Such a plan would be in direct conflict with the secret society that had supported his underground rebellion. This same order had begun pressuring him to infiltrate Jeshua's inner circle of disciples. He had serious reservations about their motives, but if he failed to comply with their wishes, their financial backing would abruptly end. But if he could somehow arrange a face-to-face meeting with Jeshua, Barabbas was convinced he could win him over to his side. He could then bypass the power-grasping religious faction.

His military leadership and Jeshua's charismatic influence could usher in a new era of freedom, the very stuff that dreams were made of. But how did a man like Barabbas approach a man like Jeshua? One of his soldiers, Simon the Zealot, could be the answer. No one had a quicker wit or smoother tongue than Simon. If anyone could successfully penetrate the Nazarene's inner ring, it would be Simon.

A curse escaped his lips as he thought of the hours of planning that went into attacking the ambassador. They were supposed to kidnap Aurelius, not kill him.

"Barabb, it's time to go!" said Issachar, one of his closest associates. Peeking out the doorway, Issachar looked up and down the dark street, checking for any movement in the quickly fading daylight. Looking back, he signaled all clear but found a glassy eyed Barabbas, deep into another one of his episodes. These spells had been increasing in frequency and becoming worrisome to Issachar.

Barabbas had no greater friend than Isa. They grew up together on the streets of Damascus. Both experienced the icy finger of death at a tender age. Studying Barabbas' faraway stare, Isa found himself back in time on the streets of Gazara, reliving a moment neither of them have ever forgotten.

*****

"Have mercy!" came a pitiful cry, but it fell on deaf ears. These legionnaires were not concerned with civility; Rome's, iron fisted, military crushed all resistance with appalling violence. Orders were issued to extinguish all resistance. Rumors of insurgent activity in the region of Gazara resulted in the legion's youngest centurion being sent there.

"Have no concern for troop behavior in this maneuver." These were the orders of General Varus from the famous Varus Wars. In the heat of combat, it was easy for soldiers to lose a sense of morality, but in this particular mission, reprehensible behavior was actually encouraged. "Leave an impression they will not forget!" was an order some legionnaires enthusiastically carried out.

The merchant citizens of Gazara were attacked unmercifully. They were killed in the streets as a public spectacle. Some managed to escape, but Barabbas's family wasn't so fortunate. His father was first beaten then herded into a group of men to be used as slave laborers. Women who had not been killed would be used to satisfy the sexual appetite of legionnaires. Houses were turned into makeshift barracks, the former inhabitants' personal possessions became military property. Young Isa watched a dazed Barabbas standing alone in the street.

"You, boy!" thundered an enormous soldier, causing eleven-year-old Barabbas to jump. He shouted in broken Aramaic, "Fetch me some water!"

Unsure of the soldier's strange words, the wide-eyed boy froze.

The hulking behemoth lumbered over to the shaking child, towering over him. "Didn't you hear me, boy?" he seethed. A ferocious backhand sent him tumbling backward. Searing pain rushed through the barely conscious boy, his face and clothing bloody from a broken nose and split lip. Barely conscious he wiped the blood from his nose, unaware of the monster's approach. With brutish indifference, the boor struck him again, this time even harder, sending him spinning away to land facedown, unconscious in the dirt.

The massive legionary stood over the boy. "Get up and get me that water!" When the child didn't move, he continued the mugging, kicking him in the ribs. "Get up, you little turd, I know you're faking!" Receiving no response, he brought his size-sixteen ironclad foot down on the head of the lifeless boy, grinding his face into the sand.

Barabbas's father, held captive at the point of a sword, could take no more. The savagery of the attack had distracted the soldiers enough to release their hold on him. Running to rescue his son, he screamed, jumping on the thug's back, wrapping both hands around the monster's neck.

Adrenaline and the element of surprise provided a momentary advantage until the soldiers' hand slid down to his pugio. The would-be attacker collapsed as the blade plunged deep into his side. With a frightening mix of rage and delight, he turned, driving his knife into the father again and again, refusing to let him fall. The manic-driven assassin then turned, preparing to do the same to the child at his feet when a voice of authority shouted for him to stop.

"That's enough!" shouted the Centurion.

On the edge of insanity, the giant was poised to stab the child but was stopped by the point of a sword against his throat.

"I said that's enough!" barked a raspy voice, his blade breaking the skin above the giant's Adam's apple.

A battered young Barabbas, passing in and out of consciousness, heard the Centurion say the words, "Stand down or I'll kill you myself!"

With every legionnaire watching, the massive brute straightened his frame, looked briefly into Atticus's eyes, then backed away.

Even young and less battle-scarred, Atticus struck fear into all those under his command.

Wiping his blood-stippled face, the hulking legionnaire sauntered away. Barabbas, his face in the dust, turned his head just enough to see his dead father lying beside him.

*****

"Barabb!" Isa cried, shaking him. "Can you hear me? We have to leave now!"

Returning from his lapse into the past, Barabbas's eyes met Issachar's.

"Barabb, if we don't go now, the timing will be ruined and our planning lost."

Barabbas rose to his feet, in full command of himself. "We can't let that happen, can we, Isa?" Leading the way, Barabbas moved swiftly into the street with Issachar right behind him.

CHAPTER 18
Antechamber

Vitus and Orel found themselves trapped in a subterranean grotto, swallowed up in absolute darkness without a torch. Unable to see anything, Orel reached back toward the stairs while trying to maintain his footing.

"I can't feel anything," he said, trying to keep calm.

"Stay where you are. We can easily get separated in this blackness."

Fighting panic, Orel thought of Lamech's words: *An ancient evil has descended on the Romans.* He turned slowly in the darkness, flailing his arms for any point of reference.

"Blind as a bat," muttered Vitus, wishing he could maneuver the way bats did in the dark. "Keep calm," Vitus remarked, sensing Orel's anxiety. "Talk to me so I can track your voice."

"I'm here. Haven't moved a step."

The cavern air was dank and heavy with the smell of decay. "What is that stench?" asked Orel.

Vitus brushed away what he thought were cobwebs from the back of his neck. The tomb-like air served to muffle and distort their voices, making them sound distant from each other.

Orel, who suffered from claustrophobia, talked to calm himself. "This must have been what it was like for Rabbi Toile," he remarked.

"Who's Rabbi Toile?"

"Years after his burial, they discovered he had only swooned."

"They buried him alive?"

He was entombed in a mausoleum, woke up in there, and for the second time died in there."

"How long before they realized it?"

"Two years had passed before they rolled the stone away to deposit another member of the family. They found his mummified remains at the entrance. He had been trying to claw his way out, poor devil. He had wiggled free of his grave bindings but couldn't budge the weight of that stone alone. No one could. He likely died of starvation or insanity."

"That's a great story, Orel, thanks for sharing!"

"That's not going to happen to us! Is it?"

"Not unless you talk us to death. Follow the sound of my voice. I shouldn't be more than a step or two away from you. If you reach up, you can feel the top of whatever it is we're in. If we work together, we should be able to find a fulcrum release to reengage the stairs."

"Okay, I'm heading in the direction of your voice."

Vitus prevented Orel from crashing into him with an outstretched arm. "I think I feel the retracted stairs above me, but I can't budge them," cried Vitus. Standing side by side, the two men exerted considerable energy until Vitus shouted, "Stop! We could dislodge something that might prevent it from functioning completely. For now, let's accept the fact that we're not getting out the way we came in."

His statement sent a mini shockwave through Orel. "What now?"

Vitus, in complete control, kept things calm. "We'll get out the way the assassins came in. But exercise caution. There may be other hidden levers that could trigger things down here." Orel took a moment to digest this information before speaking.

"Let me get this straight. We're blind, can easily lose all sense of direction in this blackness, and oh yes, let's not forget there could be other traps waiting for us? Did I miss anything?"

"Move slowly. Finding a wall will help us navigate our way. Stay close, just not too close. Don't want both of us falling into the same entrapment."

"It feels like we're not alone down here, like someone or something is watching us?"

"What could be watching us? I can't even see the hand in front of my face." Vitus downplayed Orel's remark, but he was sensing the same thing. What he thought were cobwebs brushing his neck were the hairs on the back of his neck standing up.

They stopped when Vitus's fingers come in contact with something solid. Moving his hand along the rough surface of the wall, he straightened his frame. Not realizing Vitus had stopped, Orel bumped into him.

"Geez, man!" yelled Vitus.

"Sorry, did you find something?"

"The wall. Reach to your left, get your hands on it. You should be able stand up without hitting the top."

"That smell is getting stronger. Something died down here."

"Maybe it's Aurelius's corpse."

Orel's eyes strain for any glimpse of light; he was a blind man in unfamiliar surroundings.

"How far do you think this thing goes?"

"You know these grounds better than me. If this is an escape tunnel that empties outside the compound, how much farther do we have to travel?"

"A fair distance from ambassador's quarters to the outer wall, maybe five hundred paces (half a mile). That's assuming we're moving in a straight line, not a winding maze!" Orel decided to share his secret with Vitus. "There's something I need to tell you. Something I haven't shared with anyone."

"Let me guess. You're not really Jewish. No, wait, you were a member of the underground, but they kicked you out for failure to pay dues."

A smile broke across Orel's face, though neither man could see it.

"Come on," said Vitus, "that was funny. Listen, we're not going to die down here, so hold off on the final confessions." Vitus paused for a second. "At least, I'm pretty sure we're not going to."

"Very reassuring. Listen, thanks, but you really stink at this comforting thing. Anyway, it wasn't a death confession, but oddly enough, death is a part of the equation."

"I'm listening. What deep, dark secret have you been keeping to yourself?"

"We haven't known each other long enough to call ourselves friends, but I feel like I've known you my whole life. I wouldn't have come down here if I didn't trust you." Vitus stopped and turned his head, looking directly into what he imagined to be the face of the man behind him.

"I've never made friends easily. Until I joined the special ops unit, I didn't really trust anyone, but I trust you. Only a friend would come into a place like this." They began moving forward again in the blackness.

Orel continued, "I'm not sure why I decided to help the immunes that night. It was like I was compelled or something. But inside that chamber, I noticed something no one else did." Somehow, the inability to see each other in the darkness made it easier to communicate, to understand what made the other man tick.

Vitus's interest, now piqued, encouraged Orel to continue. "So what did everyone else miss that you didn't?"

"A concealed mark hidden on one of the dead."

"What kind of a mark?"

"A small tattoo behind the ear, easy to mistake for a birthmark but definitely Hebrew lettering, a compound word made up of two parts." Both men stopped simultaneously, breaking the rhythm.

"The word, what was it?"

Orel was confident in Vitus's mastery of Aramaic, but how could a soldier of Rome be competent in a language that only highly educated Judeans would understand? But since he'd come this far, why stop now?

"The first part is *Tsal*, meaning shadow, and second, *mavet*—"

Elated, Vitus cut him off in mid-sentence, "Death shadow." He deciphered in the darkness, "It means shadow of death!"

A stunned Orel nodded in the blackness. "Yes," he sputtered, "but how could you know that?" The intensity of the moment had caused him to lose track of their captivity.

Sidestepping the question, Vitus shared his thoughts, "Only a Judean would bear such a mark. Logic dictates that he was an infiltrator."

Orel was impressed by the quickness of Vitus's mind.

"But are the Zealots so well-connected they can infiltrate a Roman peace delegation?" Vitus paused for an instant. "You kept this to yourself because you feared it would lead back to the priest. Lamech was a high-ranking priest who still has considerable connections and clout. It's the perfect cover, a ranking member of the Roman-friendly Sadducees. You were wise to keep this to yourself." Even in this darkness, the light began to dawn. "A military compound that just happens to be the generational home of a wealthy priest with a secret underground tunnel that leads up into the ambassador's quarters? Lamech is in league with the Zealots with who knows how many other wealthy patrons, all financing the nationalistic cause of Zionism. Do you know the identity of the tattooed man?"

Orel, still holding out hope for Lamech, offered an alternate thought, "Something doesn't make sense. If the tattooed man was a Zealot operative, why was he killed?"

"A living but missing staff member might have raised questions. But the assassins could never have imagined a Judean guard getting involved on behalf of Romans."

"If they had the ambassador, what difference would it make if one more staff member was missing?"

"In this kind of operation, the trick isn't just pulling off the assignment. It's doing it so the enemy doesn't realize they've been had. But thanks to you, the tattooed man provides a lead."

"The dead man?"

"Sometimes dead men have more to say than the living, and this guy is going to tell us plenty!"

"What about Lamech?"

"That's not for me to decide. If he is involved, and everything points to that, he's up to his ears in it." Realizing they'd come to a halt, Vitus got them moving again.

"I've been thinking about this tunnel," said Orel. "It could be an old aqueduct. My people have history with this kind of construction. They provide an internal source of fresh water during times of enemy siege."

"I don't doubt it, but—" He interrupted himself. "Phew, that stench is becoming unbearable!" In the same breath, Orel tripped over something, causing Vitus to reach for his dagger.

"What happened? Are you all right?"

"Stumbled on something in the darkness," Orel replied, Vitus keeping his weapon ready while listening intently. "My foot slid off something hard. Almost rolled an ankle." Kneeling down, he felt around in the darkness. "It's a bone—correction, a lot of bones."

"Bones?"

"Feels like…a skull!"

Vitus took a breath. "Human?"

"I think so." Stooping down again, he ran his hand along the basin floor. His voice was quiet. "The place is littered with bones, and some of them haven't been here long."

"There's something down here with us," Vitus cautiously replied.

"Something?" Orel replied. "You mean like an animal? Wait, did you say *was* or *is*?"

"I've been listening to it breathing since you stumbled over that skull."

Orel's throat tightened, reflexively forcing an involuntary swallow. Unexplainably, the temperature in the cavern had suddenly dropped. "Someone or something is watching us," he whispered.

Orel dropped the skull, reaching for his sword, peering into the blackness. "I can't see anything!"

"Quiet! Our sense of hearing is our greatest ally right now, so calm yourself and listen."

"I hear it," Orel spoke in a whisper. "It's breathing heavily. What do you think it—"

"It's moving toward us."

Both men shifted their feet, ready to engage whatever it was that was approaching. Its breathing was queer, but it sounded more human than animal.

"It's close…steps away," whispered Vitus. "Get ready."

Shoulders hunched in the cramped space, adrenaline flooded through each of them.

"Vitus! Orel!" a familiar voice called, piercing the tomb-like silence. It was Scipio. "Call out! Where are you?" Scipio's shadowy torch briefly revealed the stalker's shape. Grunting and shielding its eyes, it retreated back into the darkness. Vitus tried to process what they'd just seen.

"What in the hell was it?" cried Orel.

"Over here, Scipio! Keep following the sound of my voice!"

Scipio and three more ops soon stood next to them with torches and long swords.

"This is quite a situation you're in down here," said a relieved Scipio. "You think it might have been a good idea to bring a torch down here with you? Or do you possess another superpower you haven't told us about?"

"You have no idea—" Vitus paused. "You arrived just in time."

Scipio was puzzled, unsure of Vitus's meaning.

"Lord, what are all these bones? Looks like a lion's den." Scipio's torch revealed skeletal remains littered everywhere. "Some of these are human!" he said with a shudder.

"No time to explain," said Vitus. "Hand me a torch and follow us."

Being unable to stand fully erect in the cramped tunnel, they moved at best possible speed. If they couldn't catch the creature, they could at least find where this underground channel led. They followed until the underground shaft divided into two forks.

"What are we chasing?" asked Scipio.

"No time to explain. Orel and I will take the left channel. Scipio, you and Anthony take the right shaft. Didius and Cyrus, head back to the staircase. Bring the rest of the Ten. Leave one man at the top of the entrance so we don't get trapped down here again."

Without delay, the six separated, moving in three different directions.

"It can't be much farther," said Orel. "We should be outside the compound by now."

Vitus's eyes were continuously moving in the shadowy light, scanning for any movement. He abruptly threw an arm to Orel's chest, halting them both.

"Stop! Do you hear that?"

"Yeah, it's the same sound. It's around that bend." They readied themselves, but this time, it was their turn to bring the attack. Leading the charge, Vitus lunged around the corner to find a dead end. Spinning 180 degrees, he looked up, then down for any clue that would make sense of the disappearing act.

In disbelief, Orel stated the obvious, "It's gone!"

CHAPTER 19
Simon Says

Situational camouflage is intentionally deceptive. It's designed to misdirect us from critical underlying issues, and Barabbas, the leader of the Judean underground, was not what he appeared to be. Roman legionnaires stationed in Judea called this choreographer of death the Phantom. Under his tutelage, the Zealots had methodically chipped away at Roman resolve.

Barabbas was a facade, a veil of deception who played his part well, guarding a secret that might backfire, costing him his life. He clung to the hope that if he succeeded in carrying out his part in this ruse, he'd achieve what mattered most to him: the reunification and independence of Israel. Only then would he be free to divulge who and what he really was. Every Zealot was branded with a mark of unity and identity.

"I'm a patriot, not a criminal," Barabbas argued. "It's the damned Romans who strike fear into the hearts of our countrymen." Tonight, his gestures were demonstrative and his speech impassioned as he addressed a small circle of men in a darkened room. The flame of an oil lamp produced a dancing shadow on the wall behind him. Zealots held to the proposition that they were freedom fighters, not terrorists. But the murder of Ambassador Aurelius may have pushed things too far, putting Judea directly in the crosshairs of a major Roman reprisal.

Barabbas was an inspirational leader. He saw as plausible what others saw as impossible. "If only," speaking his thoughts aloud, "the promised one, the Messiah, would show himself, we could lead our people to freedom." Unfortunately, no one knew when the prophesied messiah would come on the scene.

During a moment of repose, Barabbas allowed himself to daydream. *What if I'm the Messiah?* His eyes sparkled at the thought. *It's not impossible,* he mused. *No one has given more in trying to deliver our people! What if I'm the one the prophets wrote about?* His brief reverie was cut short by an intrusive thought. *Could the ancient prophecies refer to the Nazarene?* With conflicted feelings, he explored this alternate path. *If even half of the things they say about him are true, his influence could work powerfully for our cause. Messiah or not, together, we could break Rome's stranglehold on our land!*

Locals had been buzzing about Jeshua for months. They said he was a craftsman by trade, but his words and the crowds that followed him belied that. His sermon in Capernaum drew such large numbers he had to deliver it from the side of a mountain. Since that day, Herod, Pilate, and the Jewish religious authorities had been on alert.

Taking all these things into consideration, Barabbas had always believed the true Messiah to be a military leader capable of overthrowing foreign occupiers; at least, that was the general view. Until now, the Nazarene had only been a distraction because he drew attention to himself and away from Zionism.

"So tell me, Abiel," Barabbas posed the question to a fellow Zealot and confidant, "what do you think?" Tonight, the secretive group broke bread in the house of a villager in league with the underground movement.

"What do I think of what?" Abiel's response sent a stream of partially chewed meat spraying across the room.

Other members reclining at the two-foot-high table groaned and waved their arms in disgust at his boorish manners.

"What?" Abiel asked in a puzzled tone, spraying a second explosion of predigested particles on his compatriots clearing the table. Abiel and his juice-drenched beard were left sitting alone.

"The potential is staggering," affirmed Barabbas, "if it were to turn out that the Nazarene really is the promised one." The troop of assassins burst into laughter, offering a triple-tongued cry of victory, causing Barabbas's wonderment to fade into a sarcastic smile. "It doesn't matter whether it's true or not, only what the masses believe or are willing to believe. His power to command them would be unparalleled!"

The room was silent as the magnitude of Barabbas's words sank in. Even Abiel stopped shoving bread into already overloaded cheeks and sat motionless. Knowing he had their full attention, Barabbas smiled.

Saul was the first to break the silence. "What should we do? Reason with him or bribe him? What do we even know about him?"

"He comes from Nazareth!" said Hophni. "Whoever heard of anything good coming out of Nazareth?"

"You're right, we don't know much about him," interjected Barabbas. "We don't know what he believes or what his politics are." Pausing, he tore away a morsel of bread from the flattened loaf, dipping it in the *sop*. "That, my friends, is what we must find out!"

Issachar, always at Barabbas's side, entered the conversation. "At least he's not like that locust-eating Baptizer, shouting about repentance and living like a wild man. He pushed that crazy act too far when he called out Herod's indiscretions."

"I like John," Barabbas chirped in. "Any man with the courage to stand up to that blowhard Antipas is okay by me. You're right, Issa, the Nazarene isn't like John or anyone else. That's why we've got to learn as much about him as we can." He shifted his attention to Simon on the far side of the circle. "That's why Simon is going to get friendly with Jeshua."

Simon's body stiffened; the eyes of every man settled on him.

"Why do I deserve such a privilege?" His volume slowly increased as he rose to his feet. "I'm willing to die for the cause as much as any man here! But I'm not willing to waste my time listening to a self-proclaimed prophet!"

Grinning, Barabbas walked to the far end of the circle and rested a hand on Simon's shoulder.

"I don't know if he claims to be a prophet or not." Barabbas's voice was calming. "But thousands think he is." Barabbas exhaled. "We all know your dedication is unquestionable, Simon. That's why you're right for this assignment. You're the only one who can infiltrate his circle without giving away your true intentions."

Feeling a little foolish, Simon looked down at the floor. "No one is more talented at making an enemy believe he's their friend."

When you judge the time to be right, talk to him about us. If he's open to listen, get word to us, and we'll arrange a time and place to meet."

"And if he won't listen?" asked Simon. "Or worse, hates the cause?"

"Then we've lost nothing but time. Finish your meal, all of you. We've work to do."

*****

Walking briskly along a cobbled street, Barabbas repeatedly looked over his shoulder, taking great caution to be sure he was not followed. The covering on his head was for stealth, not piety. Standing at the gate of a rich man's home, he glanced left then right to be certain he was alone. His fist hung suspended in air, reflecting on the path he'd chosen. Again, he visualized the brutal death of his father as seen through the eyes of an eight-year-old, his village consumed by flames. As a young man, he dreamed about a wife and children, but the dream was not to be. He was the pundit of death, a stone-cold killer who could take a life without hesitation if it served the cause. Instead of doting over a family, his waking hours were spent scheming of ways to rid Judea of the disease that was Rome.

The old gate's hinges squeaked open, granting him entrance.

"Come in quickly," urged a voice in the darkness. "You haven't been followed?"

Barabbas nodded that he had not.

"Is it done? Did you convince Simon the Zealot to do it?"

The Phantom nodded affirmatively.

CHAPTER 20

In Search of a Monster

Gathering at the stairs that lead up to Aureliu's quarters, the Ten huddled to collaborate.

"We hit a dead end at the end down there in those tunnels," said Vitus. "Be alert," he paused, "something is down there. It was stalking us in those lightless tunnels. We heard its labored breathing as it readied itself to attack. Scipio's call to us was almost too late. We glimpsed it in the shadows of his torch before it vanished."

Only Didius found his tongue. "What did he look like?"

"Like I said, we only glimpsed it for a second before it retreated into the darkness."

"It? You meant him, yes?"

"I don't know what I mean! It wasn't an animal, but it didn't look human either." Vitus shook his head. "Like nothing I've ever seen." He cautioned the Ten, "Never go down there alone, no fewer than two or three. The floor is littered with bones, some of them human." Other than Vitus's voice. there was no sound but the hissing of flickering torches. "Scipio and I must report back to Atticus. By now, he surely will have reached his boiling point. The rest of you search the tunnels," repeating his words with conviction, "stay in groups, watch each other's back!"

Anthony, the oldest member of the Ten, his hand resting atop his long sword, offered his opinion, "Let's waste no more time discussing it. Let's split up and map out those tunnels."

Vitus approved. "Leonidas is the best tracker. Decima and Caius should stay with him. If the thing is still down there, Leo will find it.

Julius, Virius, Cyrus, and Didius can run down the different tunnels. We need to know which one was used by the attackers."

"We better go," said Scipio. "The Centurion is going to have our heads."

"Orel, you're with me," Vitus ordered then paused. "If that's okay with you?"

Orel nodded, quickly joining him and Scipio. At the top of the stairs, two immunes blocked their way. "Orders from the Centurion. You are to accompany us immediately."

"Of course," Vitus replied.

The immunes led them to the base medical treatment area. There they found an impatient Centurion waiting for them with the base physician. The look on Atticus's face wasn't welcoming.

"What part of 'Bring them back with all haste' didn't you understand, Scipio?"

Scipio tried to explain, "Sir, I—"

But Atticus would have none of it. "Button it! Whatever the hell you've been doing over there, it better be more important than obeying a direct order. We've been here hours waiting for you to see this!" Atticus ferociously pulled back the covering, revealing Aurelius's mangled remains. Vitus and company are taken aback by the condition of the body.

Scipio stepped in for a closer look. "What did they do to him?"

"Oh, so now you want answers," Atticus bellowed. "While you three were over there playing in the water, we've been trying to put the pieces together, and I mean that literally!"

Making no excuses, Vitus quietly asked, "Where was he found?"

"What's left of him was flopping around on a roadside cross some miles outside Sychar."

"They have eyes on our movements!" Vitus was quick to remark.

"You think?" answered an agitated Atticus.

Shaking his head in disbelief, Scipio stared at the disfigured corpse. "The troop found him in this condition?" He studied the remains, trying to make sense out of it. "Could these wounds"—pointing to the neck and chest—"have been caused by scavengers?"

"He wasn't out there long enough," said Atticus. "We passed that area two days earlier. That babbling idiot, Flavius, claims the troop was led to him."

"You're kidding," said Orel.

"The fools chased the Zealots right into an ambush. The rebels must have feigned surprise for Flavius, then took off running. He obliged them chasing right into a crossfire of arrows."

Vitus shook his head in disbelief. "How bad was it?"

"Twenty men wounded, nine mortally after three volleys, and the attackers vanished. Flavius's exact words: '*It was like they were invisible, like fighting ghosts.*'"

"What about Sergeant Oppius?"

"He wasn't with that patrol. His experience would likely have recognized the neat little trap, and those men would still be alive."

"The Zealots are toying with us, steps ahead of us. They planted Aurelius's body in a place they knew our men would find it," said Vitus.

"That's my assessment as well but take another look. What else do you see?"

Clearing his throat, Orel moved closer, waving off the decaying stench. "He bears the wounds of crucifixion, but what are all these other wounds? Did the sadistic dogs have to torture him too?"

The Centurion was caught off guard by Orel's remark, as the Zealots were his people.

"Apparently not," said Scipio. "Check out the gaping hole on his left. He may have bled out before asphyxiation." Standing with arms folded across his chest, the Centurion watched with pride as the trio slowly assemble the puzzle.

"Scipio's right," added Vitus. "He bled out in minutes, but not from the wounds to his torso. The slash across the throat is the fatal wound." Vitus's eyes locked with Atticus, who was staring back at him, waiting to hear him tell the rest of it. "The massive tissue loss to his chest and lower torso were not caused by a weapon," he said softly.

Scipio looked warily at Vitus. "Then what caused them?" he asked, stepping next to Orel for a closer look. "You're right." He grimaced. "The flesh looks like it was torn away by some kind of animal, but we know he wasn't out there long."

"I know of no death more gruesome than crucifixion," said a solemn Atticus. "An official Roman crucifixion includes three legionnaires and a Centurion. The execution teams keep sour wine on hand because it helps them get through what can be a several-day ordeal. I was ordered to oversee one, and I'll never forget it. Crucifixion isn't as much about inflicting pain on the victim as it is about scaring the crap out of the people who see it. That's why the order isn't given to take the body down after death is pronounced. They want it rotting out in the sun for weeks, encouraging the birds and beasts to take it apart. The spectacle makes an indelible memory on anyone who sees it. That's not the case here. Aurelius wasn't out there long enough for this to happen."

Vitus glanced at Orel before laying out his thought, "What if these marks were made by something else?"

Orel's throat tightened at this remark. "Like the thing we saw in that grotto?"

"What's that you say? What happened over there?" demanded Atticus.

"We know how the attackers got in and out sight unseen," said Vitus. He had the Centurion's full attention. "We discovered an entrance in the floor of the chamber leading down to an underground passageway. That's why the chamber doors were bolted from the inside."

Atticus nodded, knowing where Vitus was going with this. "The water you sent Scipio for…you hoped it would detect what the naked eye couldn't see." He exhaled with a sigh of relief. "Very clever, but what was that comment Orel made about the thing in the grotto?"

"The bad news is we didn't find the passage that leads outside of the compound. Anthony and the rest are still down there searching for it." Vitus paused, fumbling over his next words.

"What is it?" asked Atticus. He turned to look again on what was left of Aurelius's corpse. "You think these bites came from something you encountered down there?"

Vitus nodded. "We were trapped down there without torches. We both sensed it in the darkness."

"It?"

"Yes, *it* had the ability to see us, even though we were totally blind. It was coming in for the kill. Scipio's shout and torch saved us."

"What was it?"

"It shielded its eyes from the light of Scipio's torch as if in pain."

The Centurion was frustrated. "Confound it, man, what did it look like? Was it an animal?"

Neither man answered his question.

"Are you saying there's some kind of monster living beneath this compound?"

"Whatever it is, we didn't get a good look at it."

"Do you back this account, Orel?"

"Yes, but there's more. Vitus didn't mention the bones. I think we stumbled into its lair. Just before the attack, the air became very cold. My breath turned to steam."

Atticus rubbed the top of his close-cropped scalp, not knowing what to make of this.

"Whatever it is," Orel continued, "it's been down there a long time. There were a lot of bones. I picked up what I'm certain was a human skull."

Atticus, a battle-hardened warrior, had seen things that caused other men to lose control of their bowels, but this had him mystified. He turned to Scipio, who nodded in the affirmative.

"Well, this puts a new twist on things, doesn't it?"

Vitus hesitated. "I've never felt fear in combat, but this thing made my flesh crawl."

Orel concurred, "It was like the darkness came alive, a feeling of pure evil."

The Centurion massaged his deformed eyelid. "So you believe these wounds were from fangs tearing away flesh?" Atticus took one more look. "Do you know the kind of power it would take to inflict these kinds of wounds from an animal's jaw? I can't imagine a man... it's impossible!"

The three men offered no reply.

"So tell me, how does your monster fit into all this? This well-planned attack was thought of and carried out by a cannibalistic beast?" He looked again at the body. None of this makes any sense? If this…creature was under the rebel's control, something went very wrong that night!"

"I think that's it," said Vitus. "Something went very wrong. I think the insurgents are trying to disguise the truth by using misdirection. The different kinds of wounds are meant to distract us from what actually happened that night. Why crucify him then slash his carotid? You don't cut a man's throat if your intention is to prolong his agony by crucifixion."

"But why kill everyone else in that room and kidnap the ambassador? That doesn't make sense either," Scipio chimed in.

Atticus squared his shoulders then offered a conclusion, "The kidnapping and the crucifixion are a cover-up, neither one part of the original plan. They lost control of the situation."

Vitus pointed to the slash across Aurelius's throat. "It's the same wound we found on the rest of the butchered staffers. The Zealots never intended to kidnap Aurelius. He was killed in that chamber with the rest of them. They took his body with them because the creature surprised them as well. Later, the insurgents crucified his already dead body, leaving a trail of bread crumbs for Flavius to find."

"It makes sense now," said Orel. "The tattoo I found on the staffer's body—he wasn't a staffer, he was a Zealot. It must have been his scream, not the ambassador's, I heard that night!"

Vitus was surprised by Orel's disclosure but thankful it was no longer a secret from the Centurion.

"What's this about a tattoo?" Atticus turned to Scipio and Vitus. "You both knew about this?"

"Not me, sir, this is the first I'm hearing about it," said Scipio, looking quizzically at Vitus.

His muscled arms hanging at his sides, Atticus shook his head. "I thought we had an understanding about this." Giving Vitus a portentous look, he then turned to Orel. "Tell me about the tattoo. There be must be a good reason you kept this to yourself."

"Commander, it didn't occur to me until this moment that the man bearing the tattoo was the same man who shrieked. I think he was killed to be silenced. When Mercurius invited me to look closer, I discovered Hebrew lettering, צלמות, behind his ear. It translates as 'shadow of death.'"

The Centurion couldn't help being impressed with Orel. "What is so important about that tattoo that you would keep it a secret?"

Vitus interjects, "The creature might have attacked him first."

"Yes," Orel affirmed, "before it jumped on the ambassador."

Atticus's eyes darted between the two men, trying to keep up. "What about that mark?"

Orel cautiously continued, "Judeans, even extremists, have a compartmentalized culture. Secret societies are plentiful here. 'Shadow of death' has to be a code for the Zealot secret society. The massacre happened inside the post compound. The tattoo clearly ties at least one person in that room to the insurgents. I didn't want to—"

"You didn't want to implicate the priest," said Atticus. "These are Lamech's ancestral grounds. You figured you'd give him the benefit of the doubt, hoping that conversation with him would prove your worst fears unfounded."

This time, it was Orel's turn to be stunned!

"I already knew about the mark. I checked the bodies myself before assigning them to the burial detail." Turning to Vitus, he added, "Did you really think I'd miss a thing like that? I asked a scribe to translate the letters, which I haven't yet shared with Post Commander Mercurius. Need-to-know basis only." He chuckled in his gravelly voice. "It wasn't much of a stretch to come up with Lamech as a conspirator." Atticus turned to face Orel, "I didn't know as yet if I could trust you."

Vitus grinned from ear to ear, having even greater appreciation for his commander.

Atticus winked at Vitus with his good eye. "Never underestimate me, kid!"

"I won't make that mistake again, sir."

"Orel, only a valiant warrior would put himself in harm's way for a soldier he barely knows. Your knowledge and intelligence have proved invaluable, and it's clear you don't hold with the tactics of the Zealots or you wouldn't be standing here. We need you. The agreement between the Jewish Sanhedrin and Rome is tenuous. Emperor Tiberius has put the brakes on what we can and can't do. If there is a connection between Lamech and the Zealots, we'll find it eventually, and your continued help might make things go easier on him. If you're willing, tell me about the conversation you had with Lamech."

*****

Later that evening, members of the Shadow of Death met in the house of Shimron. There was great concern over the Romans' encounter with the *beast*.

"It's only a matter of time," insisted Iri, a Levitical priest, "until the Romans, no matter how boorish they appear to be, put things together!" Greatly agitated, he stood to his feet. "I told you Barabbas's plan to raid the compound was too great a risk! Now here we are!"

"We don't need to be reminded of your great wisdom, Iri," snorted Shimron. What we need is damage control, a consensus on how to proceed from here. We knew the creature was becoming increasingly vicious and extremely difficult to control. We must take action now while we are still able to do so!"

"Lamech will never agree to this. Ichabod is still his son, and Lamech, whether we like it or not, is still crucial to our plans," said Tola, another Shadow member.

Korah, a Pharisee, stately in appearance and speech, held the greatest influence over the group. He stood up, slowly drawing the attention of all. His words were measured, offering logic and foresight. "Lamech is not the man he once was. We all know this. He becomes more forgetful, more removed from reality daily." Korah continued, "This *chevah* must be removed, its connection to Lamech notwithstanding. Up to this point, the chevah has served a purpose, but the Phantom's botched massacre demonstrates that time has passed. We are in a perilous position. The longer we ignore this, the greater the chance for failure or discovery by the Romans."

"Lamech will not agree, I tell you," interrupted Tola, "and we dare not push him out of the picture. The compound is still his ancestral home."

Standing perfectly still, Korah waited for the explosive Tola to finish, maintaining eye contact with him until Tola looked away. Finally, Korah resumed his address, "Lamech is failing, weak in body and mind, lacking the stamina to even sit with us in counsel tonight. He won't object to our plan to relocate the *chevah* because we aren't going to tell him."

"There are holes in this plan," said Shimron. "First, how do we restrain him? He's grown so powerful that rope no longer holds him. So tell us, how do we transport him if we can't bind him?"

"With double or triple shackles if necessary!"

"Second, where do you suggest we put him? Until now, he has gone undiscovered, hiding here in the grotto, coming out only at night. Lamech's servants are afraid to get close enough to feed it. In the last full moon cycle, it killed one of them down there. How can we, release it into the countryside? It would have to fend for itself, and after what happened to the ambassador, cannibalism is a frightening reality!"

"I don't see that as our concern." A moment of silence incurred as the circle considered the consequences of divorcing themselves from the man turned monster, but none dared pretend they wouldn't be happy to rid themselves of him.

"Yes, Korah, Lamech is not the man he once was, but he is a man who earned our respect in the past. Even in his diminished state, you think he won't notice that Ichabod is gone? It is, after all, his son!"

"His bastard son! And no, I don't think he will. Lamech's mind has become wistful. He believes El Shaddai's plagues are the blight that troubles our Roman enemies. So allow him to live in his world of fantasy."

Isa spoke up, "The question then is where to put him."

Korah recognized the debate to be over. "I know of a suitable place. Its people are cursed, raising herds of pigs and practicing dark arts. He will fit perfectly into such surroundings."

"Where is this place?"

"They call it the Gadarenes."

CHAPTER 21
Infiltration

Rays of sunlight warmed the back of Simon's neck as he scaled the grassy hillside. "How did I let him talk me into this?" he muttered, shaking his head. "'No one can do this but you, Simon,'" he mimicked Barabbas's words in a higher pitch. "'No one is as clever!'" Somehow, saying the words aloud made them even more infuriating.

Simon's life was secretive; he had few friends, never letting his guard down. Above all else, insurgents valued their privacy.

Still hot about his assignment, he continued to fume, "Get close to him, Simon. You'll know when the time is right to speak! Right, because I'm a *seer* like the ancient prophets!" Two men just ahead of him turned and stared. "What's your problem?" he snipped. "Here's a thought, try *minding your own business!*" His brashness produced the desired effect as the men turned away.

The fishing village of Capernaum was Jeshua's base of operations. Wanting no further attention, Simon quieted down. *I'll move slowly,* he thought, *follow him around for a few days, maybe weeks, blend in with the rest of these sheep.* The incline of the hill had become a little more challenging, forcing him to be more deliberate with his footing. "I'll study him, figure out what makes him tick, and convince him I want to dedicate my life to his cause. Once I learn his weaknesses, I'll know how to manipulate him. He'll either work with the Zealots or face public scandal. The beauty of a rumor is it doesn't require any basis of truth. Perception is everyone's reality. All it takes is one insider willing to reveal the truth. His religious enemies will eat him alive!"

As his climb leveled out, Simon found the place teeming with people, thousands of them. He had intentions of getting close to the front, but there was little room to maneuver in this overcrowded landscape. He scrunched down between people, expecting an angry reaction to his forceful intrusion but received none. Thousands arrived before him, and streams of people continued filtering in. He'd never witnessed anything like this. The atmosphere was strange to him, a different kind of feeling.

Jeshua watched more than ten thousand people file in. He bowed his head, offering a silent prayer.

A well-dressed group of men sat on Simon's left. Regular folk took extra care to give these elitists space. Their phylacteries identified them as Pharisees. Beyond this group sat another equally snobbish religious order, the Sadducees. Behind them, a few Roman legionnaires were there as insurance against riots.

Simon jumped when the man next to him started up a conversation, "It's amazing, isn't it? All these people!"

Simon nodded weakly, wondering who else might be hiding in this crowd.

"I hear they're coming from as far as Syria now. Word of him spreads like wildfire."

Simon feigned innocence. "It would seem so. Have you heard him speak before?"

"Oh, yes, that's why I got here so early to get as close as possible. Don't want to miss anything!"

Simon scratched his bearded chin. "You mean his sermon?"

The man laughed without making a sound, then laid a hand on Simon's shoulder. "I'm Joseph," he chuckled.

Not sure what to make of this guy, he replied, "I'm Simon."

"Well, Simon, there's a lot more to this man than sermons! Oh, don't misunderstand me, he has the wisdom of Solomon, and his words are spellbinding, but there's much more."

"Such as?"

Another silent laugh followed, Joseph wagging his head in disbelief. "Where have you been, Simon?

Simon just shrugged.

Joseph paused to study Simon's face.

"This man turned water into wine at a wedding in Cana, and you heard nothing about that?"

Another shrug followed.

"When he prays, the earth seems to stop and listen. He's opened blind eyes and brought life to dead crippled legs with a single touch! I've seen it!"

"I meant no disrespect. I had no idea that he—"

"Young man, keep watching. See for yourself."

Simon could only imagine what this guy would say if he knew who he was talking to—a Zealot commissioned by the Phantom to check Jeshua out. Still, there was an irony in this conversation that he couldn't ignore. "I'm looking forward to it," he told his talkative neighbor.

Turning away from the still chattering Joseph, he focused on the young rabbi. Eleven—he counted five men on his right, six on his left—regular townspeople and not a single dignitary among them. A hush cascaded through the crowd. As the Nazarene stood, the masses leaned forward with anticipation.

His persona was amazing, humble yet electrifying. Simon studied him intently, the way he so effortlessly commanded the crowd, captivating them without uttering a word. There was something about him that even the charismatic Barabbas couldn't compare to. Simon was certain the Nazarene would make an earth-shaking ally. Jeshua's greeting to the masses was both general and specific, causing each person to feel like he was speaking expressly to them.

"You're blessed when you're at the end of your rope," his voice easily projected to the multitude. "With less of you, there is more of God and his rule. You're blessed when you feel you've lost what is most dear to you. Only then can you be embraced by the one dearest to you."

Joseph was right. Jeshua's words were magnetic but also uncomfortable.

"You're blessed when you're content with just who you are—no more, no less. That's the moment you find yourselves proud owners of everything that can't be bought." (Matt. 5:3–5 MSG)

Simon shifted his weight uncomfortably. *He couldn't possibly know who I am or why I'm here,* he thought, trying to calm himself. When Joseph laid a hand on his back, he jumped forward.

"It's all right, Simon. It was same for me the first time I sat where you are. Don't be afraid. It will be all right, I promise."

"You have heard the law that says the punishment must match the injury: 'An eye for an eye and a tooth for a tooth,'" Jeshua continued.

Simon's eyes grew wide with concern, wondering if someone told Jeshua about him. "Impossible," he muttered, attempting to get hold of himself. In the same instant, Jeshua looked right at Simon, culling him out of the crowd.

"But I say, do not resist an evil person! If someone slaps you on the right cheek, offer the other cheek also. If you are sued in court and your shirt is taken from you, give your coat, too. If a soldier demands that you carry his gear for a mile, carry it two miles. Give to those who ask, and don't turn away from those who want to borrow" (Matt. 5:38–41 NLT).

Simon was stunned and sure the Nazarene knew everything. He turned his face from Jeshua's gaze, his legs feeling like they were paralyzed. He could only remain seated as the words bore into his soul.

"You have heard the law that says, 'Love your neighbor and hate your enemy. But I say, love your enemies! Pray for those who persecute you! In that way, you will be acting as true children of your Father in heaven, for he gives his sunlight to both the evil and the good, and he sends rain on the just and the unjust alike'" (Matt. 5:43–45 NLT).

Hours passed—or were they only minutes? Simon was fighting the battle of his life. He hated this teaching of love and humility, but he also detested the religious know-it-all pontificators who acted and treated others like El Shaddai created the earth solely for them.

The bright morning sky had dissolved into the subdued afternoon rays when Jeshua made his concluding remarks. "These words I speak to you are not incidental additions to your life, homeowner improvements to your standard of living. They are foundational words, words to build a life on. If you work these words into your life, you are like a smart carpenter who built his house on solid rock. Rain poured down, the river flooded, a tornado hit—but nothing moved that house. It was fixed to the rock. But if you…don't work them into your life, you are like a stupid carpenter who built his house on the sandy beach. When a storm rolled in the waves came up, it collapsed like a house of cards" (Matt. 7:24–29 MSG),

The crowd burst into applause. Never had they heard this kind of teaching. As the crowd slowly dispersed, Simon was motionless, his head in his hands, struggling to make sense of what he'd heard and felt. He suddenly jumped from an unexpected tap on the shoulder.

"Who are you? What do you want?" Simon asked.

"I'm Peter, and this is John." Simon recognized them as two of the eleven disciples that sat at the table with Jeshua.

"Are you his bodyguards?"

Peter smiled. "No, nothing like that. He's calling for you, Simon." Simon's name and circumstance suddenly transported Peter, who had also been called Simon, back in time.

*****

Crouching at the edge of the shoreline, his hands and knees coated in sand, Peter mended fishing nets in the early morning light. "Simon!" called a familiar voice. Shading his eyes from the sun, Peter followed the sound of his brother Andrew's voice. Winded from running, Andrew yelled, "Simon, I found him!"

Peter brushed the sand from his hands, "Who did you find?"

"The Messiah! I've found him!"

Pursing his lips, he gave Andrew a look.

"Wow, Messiah?" he said sarcastically. "Where has he been keeping himself?"

Andrew grabbed Simon's arm. "Come and see!"

Now Simon was annoyed; he was losing daylight and still had extra work on the nets before he could begin fishing but was taken in by Andrew's enthusiasm.

"Help me roll up these nets, and we'll go together."

Together, Andrew and Peter walked up to the Nazarene. Jeshua looked intently into Simon's eyes and said, "You are Simon, son of John, but you will be called Cephas, which means Peter." From that moment forward, Peter never left his side.

*****

"How do you know my name?" Simon the Zealot said, feeling for his concealed dagger.

"You won't need that," Peter calmly replied. "No one here is going to harm you."

"What does he want with me?"

"Only to speak with you. He's calling you, Simon, in the same way he once called John and me."

In a state of emotional confusion, Simon reminded himself that this was what he came for. His brain in a fog, he gazed blankly at each man. Peter laughed at his languid expression, helping to release some of Simon's tension. "Come and see for yourself."

CHAPTER 22

The Mysterious Gadarenes

Though he hadn't seen *it*, he had heard enough to make his next decision a no-brainer. The Centurion dispatched twenty regulars to assist the eight special operatives still searching the underground matrix of tunnels. His instructions were clear: "Have them report back in three hours or less with or without the monster." The discovery of this mysterious creature had introduced an x factor into the mission's equation.

Joining Scipio and Orel, Vitus followed the Centurion outdoors for a breath of fresh air, leaving the nightmarish remains of the ambassador behind.

"A different course of action is needed if we expect to get out from under this mess," said Atticus. "It's time we catch these insurgents by surprise instead of the other way around."

The trio nodded in agreement.

"Using the Ten to pursue the creature seems a poor investment of resources to me. If they come back empty-handed, I'm going to dispatch them elsewhere."

"What about us?" asked Scipio.

"You two will be heading in a different direction." Atticus turned to address the Judean guardsman. "Orel, isn't your time for reporting back long overdue?"

Slapping his forehead, Orel responded, "I totally lost track of time in this melee. Yes, it's past time I checked in." He paused to consider Atticus's question. "But I'm part of this now and intend to see it through. I will return as soon as I've checked on the priest."

"Considering the current state of things, I'd say it's Lamech, not you, that's in hot water," interjected Vitus.

"Unfortunately for him, you're probably right, but I'm still concerned for his welfare. He's well advanced in age, and I've neglected my duty. I hope the other two guardians have kept a close watch on him. Lamech has always been feared by his enemies and revered by his allies, but this past year he exhibited disturbing signs."

In a hurry to take make his departure, Orel turned to the Centurion. "I'll be back after I've checked in on Lamech's welfare." Watching Orel depart, Vitus turned to the Centurion. "Is there anything we can do to help?"

"Maybe," he answered in his gravelly voice, "just a little downtime with some food and some R&R." Blinking several times, he rubbed his always irritated eye. A smile broke over his face. "Why not visit that well in Bethany? Maybe you'll get lucky and run into that young Judean woman again."

The remark caught Vitus off guard.

"I guess you thought that little episode at the well was your little secret, didn't you?" he chuckled.

"Flavius's big mouth," sighed Vitus.

"That's the second time today you've underestimated me."

Vitus nodded. "I didn't think that was information I needed to report."

"You put three legionnaires in the infirmary, blew your cover in the process, and you think it's not important enough to report?"

"Sir, the way you handled troop assembly the next morning, I thought—"

"Don't sweat it, kid, that silver-spooned blowhard and his three little rat tails had it coming. They chose the wrong door to kick in, and it cost them. I just wish I could have seen their faces when it went down. My concern is you blowing your cover."

Head down, Vitus tried to explain, "Sir, I—"

Atticus waved him off. "Tough guys can't afford soft spots. You can't lose yourself like that, no matter the situation! Special training or not, matters of the heart make us lose our edge. Don't let them be your Achilles!"

"Yes, sir."

Looking off into space for a moment, the Centurion's thoughts became spoken words. "Wishing I had the time to get back to Sychar. There's a well there and a woman"—he paused—"but I'm not the one who has to worry about blowing my cover." Shrugging his shoulders, he started walking. "I expect you and Scipio back for morning inspection."

While Scipio headed for a Jerusalem tavern, Vitus was hopeful of a second meeting with Rebecca at the well.

*****

On the eastern side of the city, members of the Shadow of Death held an emergency session. Korah, the acting spokesman, addressed the furtive group.

"New developments demand action. The Romans have discovered Ichabod and are actively hunting him. If there is even a shred of sanity left in that demented mind, his capture could unravel the tapestry of secrecy we labored to preserve."

"This will be no easy task," responded Iri, the scribe. "First, we need to find him and then trap him like the animal he has become without injuring ourselves—all of this under the nose of the Romans down in the tunnels where they are searching for him." His remark was immediately followed by numerous heated discussions.

Korah stood, signaling for quiet. "What Iri says is true, but we have an advantage over our enemies. Ichabod has been cared for these past years as you would a pet. As his condition deteriorated, his level of care increased. Lamech's servants supply him with food. When news of Ichabod's unfortunate interference reached us, I took it upon myself to investigate further. Ichabod is fed on a schedule, the same hours every day, which means he's been conditioned and responds to routine. According to one servant, he appears daily for provisions in the same hour and place. We know what the Romans don't: the time and place we can snare him."

"He's a wild beast!" shouted Shimron. "You're not the only one who investigated. Lamech's servants fear for their lives. Their torches keep it at bay long enough to drop provisions and run. They claim it won't come into the light, staying only in the shadows. One servant reported that its visage had become terrifying, barely human in appearance. Ezra, Lamech's eldest servant, says it is beyond frightening."

Sitting cross-legged on the floor, Shimron was disgusted. "How will we catch it if it won't come into the light? Barabbas claims it's vicious and strong enough to overpower several men. Whatever Ichabod has become, it isn't normal or natural!"

All conversation ceased as an eerie silence settled over the room. After an uncomfortable period of silence, Korah spoke, "No matter how beast-like Ichabod has become, he is still human, still a man. He may be totally insane but still eats and defecates like a man and therefore can be trapped like a man. We have soldiers at our disposal who are skilled at laying traps. Out of respect for Lamech, we'll take him alive, if possible, or drag his dead carcass out, if necessary."

Korah squared his shoulders, waiting for debate, but none was offered.

"If we capture it—excuse me, him alive, we'll transport him under the cover of night. Our men will cross the Jordan just south of the Sea of Galilee. From there, they will deposit him in the Gadarenes."

*****

Dressed in Judean attire, Vitus waited by the well in Bethany, but there was no sign of Rebecca. *Where is she?* he wondered. Most of the local villagers who came to the well were women. It was just another day of the week for them, a place to spend a few minutes to gossip and gather local news. These ladies knew the faces of all who frequented this place, and few, if any, were male, especially at this hour of the day. Several of the younger women, taken by Vitus's handsome features, made him aware they were interested. He smiled but didn't encourage them.

His heart jumped when he saw her in the distance. Her movements were graceful, even while balancing water pots atop her shoulders. She looked downward, preoccupied by something other than the task of drawing water. Her face and form were seared into his memory from their first meeting. As she drew closer, he swiftly stood to his feet; he felt like something was caught in his throat. Casually looking up, she spotted Vitus at the well. A shy smile lightened her face; her eyes moved down, then quickly back up to meet his. Gently, she lowered her urns, resting them on the parched ground. They stood motionless, aching to go to each other but unsure of the next move.

CHAPTER 23
Vitus and Rebecca

Rebecca's stare drew the attention of women nearby; some responded with a smile, others feigned indifference, but all were taken in by the emotion of the moment. Her facial expressions ran from elation to uncertainty. *Is it really him?* She had hoped, even prayed to see him again. She impulsively raised her hand to her mouth, then looked down, away, and finally into those green eyes.

Vitus felt like a thirteen-year-old, his arms dangling awkwardly at his sides. Taking a breath, he advanced, stopped, started again, and stopped again, laughing at himself.

Feeling both relieved and ecstatic, she covered her mouth with both hands, laughing at his unassuming behavior. *Is this the same man who dismantled four Roman soldiers?*

With newfound confidence, he started again, but another woman stepped in front of him, close enough for him to feel the heat of her body.

Her voice had a raspy purr to it. "Hello, I'm Tezra. You're not from this village, are you?"

Tezra was striking and in her early twenties. She, like Rebecca, was a daily visitor to the well. They knew each other by sight but had little in common. Tezra was accustomed to the stares and comments from men who appreciate what they saw. An exotic beauty who unapologetically used flirtation to exert power over the opposite sex. Twisting her neck from side to side, her auburn hair faithfully followed sway.

"No," answered a momentarily distracted Vitus, "not from here." He was flattered but annoyed by her intrusion. Tilting his head, he tried to peek around her to check on Rebecca's reaction to all this.

Tezra countered his every attempt to sidestep her; his indifference only seemed to further intoxicate her. Her large eyes offered the same invitation she'd used on dozens of unwitting males, but Vitus was quickly tiring of this game.

He spoke softly but affirmatively, "Excuse me, I—"

"Shhh," she whispered, revealing a dazzling smile, playfully placing a finger against his lips. "What brings you to my town, mister?"

Another Judean maiden rolled her eyes, having seen this act before. Tezra used the same tactic on her prospective fiancé.

Vitus tried once more to sidestep her, but she placed both hands against his chest, gently restraining him, but Vitus had enough. Putting his hands under her elbows, he lifted and spun her out of the way. "Stay," he stated.

Tezra was stunned at this turn of events. She'd never been rebuffed by a man. Her playfulness turned to anger. Those alluring eyes become flaming orbs. "Who do you think you—"

"Shush," he whispered, placing his finger against her lips, then turning away, he left her stunned and embarrassed. His eyes found Rebecca at the well, hauling up water; she ignored his approach, focused only on her task. He quickly joined her, but what would he say? Rebecca had no such problem.

"What are you doing here?" she snipped. "Don't you have pressing business with Tezra?"

Vitus left no room for uncertainty. "I have no interest in Tezra."

But Rebecca continued her work as if he were invisible.

"I'm not here for anyone but you."

Rebecca stopped her labor, looked away, then into Vitus's eyes. "I know." She sighed. "I'm glad you came. I'm pleased to see you again."

Her change in tone refreshed his heart. All the other women at the well, excluding Tezra, went about their business, pretending not to hear their wonderful exchange. Vitus relieved her from drawing water, continuing until both vessels were full. "I'll carry them for you later if you'll allow me, but for now, can we just talk?"

Rebecca smiled and nodded, and the two walked toward the market area. Dressed like a Judean, he inquired about a particular bracelet one merchant was displaying. Then without haggling, he paid the asking price, despite her objections.

"Did you say anything about our last meeting to your family?" he asked.

"You mean, did I tell them how I was rescued by a man who fought four soldiers, risking his life to protect me? Of course! How could any person keep from speaking of such things?" She smiled, looking into his eyes. "You're the bravest man I've ever met. I still can't believe what you did!"

Vitus dropped his gaze, a little embarrassed.

"But I didn't mention the part about you being Roman. That will remain our secret for as long as you wish it."

Vitus wasn't exactly sure how he felt about the last part of her statement.

"What I am can stay between the two of us for now, but as for what I did that day, I would do it again without a second's hesitation."

"We don't know each other very well. All I really know is your name and that you are a soldier." She reached for Vitus's hand, and he was quick to respond.

They spent the next few hours talking, asking and answering questions, learning more about each other. He told her how he had been forced to leave Judah and about his life in Tuscany. She listened intently as he described his mother's beauty and untimely death by the Zealots. Her voice was laced with sadness and empathy. "How terrible for you," she whispered.

"It was a long time ago, but in here," tapping his heart, "it's still fresh. I dreamed of my father every night until this past week."

She looked at him with curiosity. "What happened this past week?"

Vitus smiled. "Since I met you, I'm not the same, not so angry all the time. You've cast a net over my obsession."

"No," she countered, "it was you who came to my rescue that day. What would have happened to me if you hadn't been there?" Her large expressive eyes held him spellbound. "Our meeting that day was more than my good fortune. I'm convinced that Yahweh had you there that day to save me, and you have done so in more ways than you know."

The hours had flown by, and Vitus was thinking of her family's concern due to her delayed absence, especially after her recent episode.

"Let's get you and the water back home to your family. I'm sure they are concerned for your safety by now."

She placed a hand to his cheek, which he quickly caressed. The water sloshed as he hoisted the pole atop his shoulders.

He laughed aloud. "How does a little thing like you balance these heavy containers so much better than me?" When she didn't reply, he quickly changed the direction of the conversation. "Tell me about Jeshua. Have you been to any of his meetings?" She stopped at his question.

"Are you interested in the Nazarene?"

"More than you can imagine."

CHAPTER 24
The Call

Simon the Zealot lengthened his stride, trying to get in sync with the taller Peter's gait. Making some mental notes, Simon studied the former fisherman who couldn't seem to stop talking. Peter was more outgoing than the quiet, more serious John.

Simon should have been ecstatic. He was on his way to achieving the goal of infiltrating Jeshua's inner sanctum, but he couldn't shake the nagging feeling that something was amiss. He would proceed slowly, cautiously, feigning undying admiration for Jeshua, doing what he did best, talking his way in. *It'll work*, he assured himself, but the unsettled feeling in his gut persisted.

While Simon plotted, Peter continued yammering about his mentor. "He's absolutely amazing! Never known anyone like him. None of us have, right, John?"

John offered a silent nod in agreement.

"He has a way of cutting through the nonsense you've heard all your life, but his eyes—that man can look right through you with those eyes." Peter tried in vain to imitate Jeshua's look, coaxing a chuckle out of John.

"Not even close," John stated.

"You can't hide anything from him." Peter's words induced an involuntarily swallow from Simon. There was no doubt in Simon's mind that Peter believed Jeshua to be the Messiah. "When you look into his eyes, it's all there—kindness, authority, and love." Peter smiled broadly, "When he smiles, you realize you've been given a fresh start."

Unlike Peter, John listened and observed. Something about Simon's demeanor was disconcerting to him. John's voice was deep and rich, like the sound of distant thunder. "Are you all right, Simon?" he asked.

Peter broke from his stream of words, surprised by John's question.

"I'm fine," Simon responded, trying to remain confident.

One hundred feet away, they spied Jeshua, surrounded by listeners from the crowd. Trying to settle himself, Simon stated the obvious. "Looks like he's trying to make his way to us through the crowd."

A small shiver ran through Simon, remembering Peter's words: *You can't hide anything from him.* "Doesn't look like he's going to make it with all those people hanging on him."

"It's always like this," said Peter. "They can never get enough."

"Nor can we," added John. "These people are getting answers to questions they've wondered about all their lives. He's not just approachable. He cares and they know it."

The crowd was suddenly unnerved when a man dressed in rags emerged out of a cluster of trees. There was a collective gasp when their fears were realized. "Leper!" one cried with dozens of others joining the chorus.

"Unclean!" They pointed and shouted.

The man with leprosy fell to his knees. The crowd demanded his immediate departure.

"Rabbi," the leper spoke with the tone of a man whose spirit had been crushed. "If you're willing"—he paused—"you can make me clean!" (Matt. 8:1–4 NLT)

Leprosy was not just a terrible illness, it was a death sentence, stripping away personal dignity, depriving its victims of contact with family and friends. It began with the extremities; the loss of sensation in a finger soon became paralysis, followed by disfigurement and deformity. It was slow-acting acid, eating away its prey with ulcerated sores that penetrated to the bone. Once diagnosed, a leper was quarantined from villages, towns, husbands, wives, and children. A leper was the ultimate outcast, forced to announce, "*Unclean!*" to anyone passing by, but rarely was such a proclamation needed because they were avoided like the plague that infected them. The Pharisees insisted that leprosy was the visible evidence of inward sin, the result of something either they or their parents had committed.

"Unclean!" The cry had the same impact as yelling, "Shark!" The horrified crowd tripped over each other, trying to get away from him, leaving Jeshua standing alone with a clear path to this walking dead.

Simon's heart raced, but Jeshua didn't retreat. He advanced, walking to the man whose face was on the ground. A collective gasp broke the open-air silence when he placed his hand on the leper's shoulder. Simon witnessed the smile Peter spoke of earlier.

"I am willing." His words displayed compassion wrapped in authority. "Be whole."

Simon, like the rest, couldn't believe his own eyes as the transformation began: deformed knuckles popped, his spinal column straightened, his swollen misshapen hands and missing fingertips rejuvenated, and oozing bloody scabs gave way to healthy, glowing skin. Simon rubbed his eyes, trying to digest the impossible. The man, who moments ago looked and smelled like death, was now the picture of health. Everything he had lost to this disease was suddenly all back. The only evidence it was the same man were the blood-stained rags he was still wearing.

Hot tears ran down the man's cheeks as he looked at his hands and felt his face. He put a bear hug on a smiling Jeshua, who was enjoying the moment with him. Then suddenly he fell to his knees in worship. Taking him by the hand, Jeshua lifted him to his feet and whispered in his ear. The man's eyes filled up as he thanked Jeshua again and again before leaving. The astonished crowd was beside themselves. Finally, a few found their tongue offering praise to God.

Simon leaned over to Peter. "What just happened here?"

Peter took in a shallow breath. "No matter how many times we see him do things like this, it's just as unbelievable."

"Are you saying this is a regular thing with him?"

The lively Peter was pensive. "He's a great prophet, a messenger from El Shaddai whose words and deeds are nothing short of incredible, as you just observed. No one can deny he is unique."

Wearing a bewildered look, Simon glanced over at John, who smiled back. "None of us," said John, "can predict what he might do next." His eyes rested on Jeshua. "One thing I know, before he's done, he's going to change everything!"

The crowd again closed in on the Nazarene, creating an impassable barrier between the disciples and their leader. During that moment, Simon accepted an invitation to join them for dinner.

"I must first attend to certain responsibilities," he explained to Peter, knowing he needed time to process all that had happened. He briefly considered getting a message to Barabbas, but how could he explain the miracle of the leper? He couldn't deny Jeshua's actions and words, couldn't rationalize any of it away. *I can imagine what would happen if I told Barab what I saw today. Heck, I saw it and I don't believe it!* Leaning back against the courtyard wall, he tapped his head against it several times.

*****

Following the directions Peter had given him, Simon knocked on the door of Matthew's impressive home. A house servant holding a basin of water and a towel opened the door, gesturing him to enter and have his feet washed. Simon sat, removing his sandals, but he was stopped by a servant who did it for him. Sounds of talk and laughter drifted in from an adjoining room. Simon estimated the servant to be no more than twenty. "What is your name?"

Surprised by the question, he looked up. "My name, sir?"

"Yes, what's your name, boy?"

Remembering his status, the younger man lowered his head to finish the task of drying this guest's feet.

"I'm called Samuel."

"Tell me, what does your master do to own a dwelling like this?"

Surprised at such a bold question, Samuel blinked. "He travels and studies with the Rabbi."

"Yes, of course, but what did he do before traveling with the rabbi?"

"He was a tax collector."

Simon's eyes grew wide at this revelation. "A Roman tax collector?" he asked defiantly. "Your master worked for Rome, stealing our people's hard-earned money to give it our enemy?

Keeping his head down, Samuel didn't reply.

"What's his given name?"

"Levi."

"It doesn't make sense," he said aloud, not caring someone might be listening. "Why choose a former tax collector for a close associate? How could this be anything but harmful with the people? A Jew will remember forever the face of the man who collects a poll tax. After he skims from the top, the rest goes directly into Roman coffers."

"If you'll follow me, sir, there is a place for you inside."

At a Judean dinner, guests were seated on the floor around the table which stood about two feet off the ground; chairs were never included. Simon squatted down, joining the already seated guests around the table. Peter stood, intending to announce Simon but ended up feeling a little foolish when Jeshua handled the introductions.

"Welcome, Simon. We've all been looking forward to spending this time with you."

Simon nodded politely, deciding to go with a humble approach.

"Thank you, Rabbi, I'm grateful and honored to meet you."

Servants scurried about, readying the dinner table while Jeshua spoke, "The people seated at this table are my friends and dedicated disciples. Each one has responded to *the call.*"

Simon's eyebrows furrowed. "The call?" he repeated.

"On your left is Andrew and Peter, his brother, sons of Jonas from Bethsaida, fishermen who are now fishers of men. On your right is Bartholomew from Cana, the son of Talmai, an Israelite without guile. The man smiling next to him is James, John's older brother, the sons of Thunder"—Jeshua smiled—"children of Zebedee and Salome, another fishing family from Bethsaida and Capernaum." Making his way down the table, Jeshua motioned again, "This is

James the Younger, son of Alpheus and Mary, who live in Galilee. Next to him is Jude and his brother, Thaddeus."

Servants lay out the first course of sop served with green herbs and loaves of unleavened bread. Jeshua signaled to the far side of the table, "This is Matthew, son of Alpheus, from here in Capernaum. Matthew—"

"Is a publican," Simon blurted out, his hatred for Rome trumping his control, which he immediately regretted. "Forgive me. Old habits."

The awkwardness of the moment dissipated from the smile on Jeshua's face. "It's all right, Simon." Jeshua showed no sign of anger as if he expected the outburst. "Yes, Matthew was a tax collector, also our host for this wonderful dinner." In no hurry to continue, Jeshua's eyes traveled to Matthew, who was doing his best to keep his cool. "The name Matthew means 'gift of God,' and that's what he is to us, but we call him Levi. He's the brother of James, both sons of Alpheus and Mary."

Simon breathed a breath of relief as Jeshua continued, "Next, we have Philip"—putting a hand on the shoulder of the man next to him—"a fisherman from Bethsaida. He has a warm heart but a pessimistic head. He enjoys doing things for others. Now if we can just get him to finish what he starts."

Philip and the others burst into laughter at their master's accuracy.

"This is Thomas, a Galilean, a man with childlike faith and great courage." Pausing for a moment, Jeshua looked deeply into the eyes of Judas Iscariot but without condemnation. "This is Judas, son of Simon who lives in Kerioth and the only Judean of our group."

Shifting his position, Jeshua faced the masquerading Zealot.

"Judas holds the flame of nationalism close to his heart, much like you, Simon."

Feeling the eyes of every man upon him, Simon shifted his position.

"You're a Canaanite, Simon, a former fisherman and a man with true heroic zeal. You and your compatriots regard your cause as a means to Israel's purification. My friends"—Jeshua pauses—"meet Simon the Zealot."

Simon's stomach dropped; his plans had backfired. Instead of setting a trap, he had been caught in one. Soaked with perspiration, his mind raced. *I've been set up but by who?* he thought, quickly settling on Barabbas as the culprit. *So this is what betrayal feels like.*

Feeling the release that comes when you realize you've been completely screwed, Simon slumped back, staring at Jeshua. "So what happens now? Is it the Romans or the Herodians waiting to arrest me?"

Jeshua smiled. "That's not why you're here, Simon. You haven't been betrayed by your compatriot as you imagine."

Flabbergasted, Simon jumped to his feet, searching the eyes of the men seated around the table. "How does he know these things?" His gaze returned to Jeshua. "How can you know what I'm thinking? Are you also a mind reader?"

"I knew what was in your heart when you sat next to the talkative Joseph on the hillside this morning."

Simon slowly settled back down to the floor, never taking his eyes off the Nazarene.

"I know who you are deep inside"—he tapped his finger to his own chest—"just as I know each man in this room."

His penetrating words calmed Simon's racing mind; no wonder Peter couldn't stop talking about him. He began to wonder if Peter was right—if Jeshua was the One. For the first time in his life, Simon made no excuses; it was clear he didn't have to.

"You came here hoping to find out who *I am*. I'm offering you the opportunity to realize your dream in a way you never imagined. Lay down your sword, Simon. Follow me."

CHAPTER 25
Metamorphosis

The Centurion was livid, trying to contain his temper after hearing her explanation. "What do you mean you can't?" he snarled. "I've spent a full day's journey just to see you!" He stormed about her hovel in a fit of anger, tossing several of her meager possessions to the floor. "You have no idea of the risks I've taken for you, wench!"

The woman allowed the brute to throw his tantrum. When she finally spoke, her voice was barely audible. "Things have changed, and I've changed."

His massive fist pummeled a small table, sending parts of it flying. "We had a deal," he ranted, fumbling for words, "an...understanding! Whatever you want to call it. My support in exchange for your services!"

With eyes downward, her only reply was silence.

He towered over her, still seething. "Do you understand what I could do to you, woman?" Atticus had passed the many hours on the road imagining the lustful romp in her bedroom. "What happened to you?"

She began to explain, "Earlier today, I met a man who changed my life."

Atticus lost track of the number of men he'd killed with his hands. Enraged by her frankness, he raised his hand ready to knock her unconscious.

With eyes closed tightly, she grimaced, anticipating a surge of pain. It wouldn't be the first beating she'd taken, but none of the other men were as intimidating as Atticus. Surprised when the blow didn't come, her squinted eye spied the Centurion heading for the door.

"I'll find another whore!" he shouted. "One who appreciates the offer!" He regretted this statement the moment it escaped his lips, her saddened image burned into his conscience. It made no sense, yet he knew it was true. This was not the same woman he struck a bargain with less than a week ago.

After Atticus departed, the woman of Sychar stepped out of her house and took in a deep breath; everything felt different. A smile came to her face; in fact, she couldn't seem to stop smiling. She thought of the beating he almost gave her and wondered, *Did he see it?* A pool of water just outside her door reflected the visible difference in her face. The corners of her mouth no longer turned downward, and her eyes looked alive for the first time in years. Then she remembered the water jug; she must have left it by the well. A person who did the same chore six days of the week didn't make such a mistake, but this had been no ordinary day.

Villagers had referred to her as "*that woman.*" She was the brunt of jokes, the fodder for rumors. For years, she'd been shunned and isolated, but not today. Today, she felt like a lady.

The locals of Sychar gathered around her. "Tell us again what he said," asked one of the men, baffled by the obvious change in her.

"Why would a Jew have a conversation with a Samaritan, especially a woman?" asked another, trying to make sense of it.

As word of this development rushed through the small town, she was quickly surrounded by curious villagers.

Her excitement was refreshing and contagious as she tried to explain what even she didn't completely understand. In one day, she'd gone from outcast to a person of interest. How quickly it all turned around, but there she was, boldly speaking to the people of the village.

A feeling of giddiness welled up from within her. "I don't know why," she said, responding to the question.

"We all know the problems between our people and his. A Jew will travel miles out of their way to avoid this place, yet you say you found him sitting by the well?" so said one village elder.

"I know you will think this strange, but it was like he was waiting there just to talk with me! I don't know how I know this. I just feel it!"

Excitement among the people grew despite an inclination by certain leaders to dismiss her as ridiculous. But none could dismiss how undeniably different she was. The crowd pressed in closer, anxious to hear more about this amazing stranger.

The whispers began. "Could this man possibly be who she thinks he is?"

"There's something about him: his eyes, his voice, not like any other man I've known."

"Yeah, and we all know she's known a lot of them!"

An eruption of laughter followed, but the woman didn't try to defend herself, causing a stillness to blanket the place.

"He told me everything about myself," she said soberly. "He knew things I'd never told anyone, things only a prophet could know! When he asked me for a drink, I released all my years of hatred and disappointment on him. 'How dare you,' I snapped! Are you ignorant or just dull?' I steamed. 'Where does a man like you get the nerve? Are you really willing to defile yourself by drinking from my cup?' Oh, it was terrible the way I spoke to him." She now had the complete attention of the crowd; even the elders were hanging on her next word. "He didn't repay my anger with more anger. Instead, his gentleness melted my bitterness.

"'If you only knew the gift that God has waiting for you,' he said, 'or who it is that asks you for a drink, you'd be the one asking me for a drink. I have a kind of water that you've never tasted, a kind that quenches a person's thirst forever'" (John 4:10 NLT). She sighed, reliving the moment in her mind.

"I'm no fool." She stiffened. "I've heard plenty of come-on lines in my day."

"You can say that again," snickered the same tormentor, but this time, his remark drew the ire of the crowd.

"Hold your tongue!" yelled one woman.

"Yeah, leave her alone, you clod!"

The crowd became single-minded in reviling her tormentor, leaving the woman amazed.

"His passionate words swept me off my feet, but not in a dreamy kind of way. My heart was pounding. 'Please, sir,' I practically begged him, 'give me some of this water.'"

"And…what did he say?"

"To get my husband." She paused a moment to gather herself. "At first, I couldn't bring myself to look at him. 'I have no husband,' I finally answered.

"'Woman, he said, 'you've spoken truthfully…for you've had five husbands, and you're not married to the man you're currently living with.'"

The people were awestruck, first by the way a total stranger could have intimate knowledge of a woman they considered worthless but also by the courage of this woman's frankness. How could an outsider, no less a Jew, know such things? Most people knew about the woman's indiscretions. A few even knew about the Centurion. There were precious few secrets in a town the size of Sychar, but she hadn't lived in Sychar her entire life.

"He's got to be a prophet!" one man insisted, causing yet another buzz.

"Is there more?" a feminine voice asks.

The woman continued, "After I regained my composure, I asked him a question that had always puzzled me. Why do Jews insist that Jerusalem is the only acceptable place of worship while we Samaritans worship at Mount Gerizim?"

The listening crowd was spellbound, for this was the question all of them wanted an answer to but none had ever received.

"Believe me, dear woman'"—she scrunches her face again, trying to emulate the Nazarene— "the time is coming when it will no longer matter whether you worship the Father on this mountain or in Jerusalem. But the time is coming—indeed it's here now—when true worshipers will worship the Father in spirit and in truth. The Father is looking for those who will worship him that way." (John 4:21, 23 NLT)

"I know when the Messiah comes," she continued, "he will explain everything." Her face was glowing, reliving the peace of that moment with Jeshua.

"So," asked one impatient villager, "what did he say about the Messiah?" Frustration grew as they tried to extract the words from her. "What did the man say?"

"It's hard to explain. It was like his words were inside of me."

"What about the Messiah? What did he say about the Messiah?"

Smiling, she repeated his exact words verbatim, "'*I am the Messiah.*'"

The encircling crowd seemed to hold its collective breath.

Keeping his distance, Atticus squatted, trying, if it were possible, to hide his hulking body. He listened with interest, still angry but also curious. The woman had spoken truthfully, but it still made no sense to him. How could her kind of woman make this kind of change? He continued to listen.

"The meddling fool," he mumbled, referring to the Nazarene. "I'll teach him to involve himself in my personal business."

To his left, a villager stood, staring at his disfigured eye. In no mood, he returned a vicious glance, causing the startled man to nearly fall over himself, trying to back away. He resumed his muttering, "No Jew travels to Samaria. Why did this one have to?" His temper flaring, he continued, "You just had to mess things up for me!" Atticus, getting hotter by the minute, was spoiling for a fight and didn't care who heard him.

"Another Jewish Messiah…that makes him a dangerous insurrectionist. If he has this kind of impact on Samaritans, imagine what he'll do in Judea. Yes"—he nodded decisively—"it's time we paid more attention to the Nazarene."

CHAPTER 26
Redeploy

A trumpeter finch's song did little to lighten the Centurion's dark mood. The unexpected turn of events during his last visit to the village of Sychar was still fresh in his mind. In his fury, he came dangerously close to injuring the woman, yet only days later, his resentment toward her had faded, and this apparent change of heart was surprising even to him. He revisited the woman's considerable courage in his mind.

"No!" she rebuffed him.

He chuckled at the thought of that little-framed woman standing up to a brute like him until a secondary thought turned his mood foul again. "The damned Nazarene!" he said aloud.

"Sir?" said Mercurius's chief aide, Numa scanned the room. "Who are you talking to, Commander?"

Numa's voice had an irritating quality, making Atticus wince from its pitch. "Where am I going to find another arrangement like that?" he fumed, still intoxicated with the curve of her bare olive skin.

Numa's inquisitiveness wasn't out of concern. It was self-seeking and derisive. "Commander, are you all right?"

The Centurion's steely eyes bore into Numa, briefly considering the pleasure he'd garner from pummeling this self-serving pest. But reason trumped momentary gratification. Barabbas and the Zealots were his prime targets, not Numa or Jeshua. These he would reserve for another day.

Numa was a *Tesserarius*, an ambitious young administrative officer. His aristocratic silver-spoon attitude irritated Atticus like a burr in his sandal. Atticus equated Numa's value to a pile of excrement. In the old days, Atticus would have broken his nose without a second thought. However, Numa's family held gravitas in the senate, making him virtually immune to regular military discipline. So for now, at least, Atticus would resist his natural tendencies, sure that the little piss pot's day would come soon enough.

"Commander, these matters require your immediate attention! The senate is demanding a progress report on the Judean insurgents. Also, the post commander has voiced his concern over the missing patrol you sent to Samaria, and finally, Governor Pilate has stated, and I quote, 'I want Aurelius's assassins crucified or impaled before the month is up!'"

In field combat, Atticus was cunning and ferocious, but in diplomacy, his skills lagged. This new assignment has several areas that had forced him out of his comfort zone. He turned his attention to Gaius, his personal staffer.

"What news from Oppius?"

"We have received no report, sir."

"Damn! What about Anthony? Do I have his report on the grotto?"

"Sir, Anthony returned last night before you arrived. He said he would report his information to only you."

"Good soldier, that Anthony. Unlike the rest of you, he follows direct orders." He looked with disgust at the growing stack of communiqués on his desk, exhaling emphatically. He turned to Cato, another officer of low rank called a *principalis*. "Isn't that right, Cato?" Before Cato could finish his nod of agreement, Atticus promoted him to the rank of *optio*. "You can begin with morning inspection of the rest of the troops. I want those men ready to move out by midday or there will be hell to pay."

"Haven't you forgotten something, Commander?" Numa spoke in his habitual condescending tone. "Post Commander Mercurius and chain of command?"

Atticus's eyes flash with contempt, slowly pivoting in the direction of this tall two-legged toad. His always raspy voice was pronounced. "You can instruct Commander Mercurius that I'll meet with him this afternoon—after the troop has departed!"

Undeterred, Numa didn't let it go. "I remind you, sir, that the post commander outranks you and that you answer to him, not the other way around."

Seated staff members tenuously shifted their weight.

"Yes, and now that you've reminded me, you can scurry back to your cushy little post and continue to pretend you're a real soldier."

Numa leered back at him, his teeth on edge. As Atticus rose to his feet, Numa was the only man foolish enough to make eye contact with him.

"I suggest you get moving before I assign you a task more closely aligned to your talents, like cleaning the company latrines."

Numa appeared pathetic as he stormed out of the room. "You won't get away with this!" he retorted.

Atticus looked like a man who just finished a satisfying meal. "I just did! Pompous little—" he mumbled. "Gaius! Get me some breakfast, man, I've worked up an appetite. And while you're at it, have Anthony and Vitus round up the Ten. Get them here posthaste. Anyone else here got something to say?"

There was only the sound of crickets. "Good. The rest of you, get out."

They wasted no time clearing the room.

Moments later, Anthony presented his report in an almost regal manner. "Commander, as per your orders, we discovered several more connecting tubes in the subterranean cavern." Anthony was flanked by the rest of the Ten.

Intent on finishing his breakfast, Atticus waved his spoon, motioning Anthony to take a seat. "You can give your report just as well sitting down as standing, so please"—he again gestured to the empty chair—"sit. Improve my line of sight and digestion."

Anthony respectfully complied.

"That's better. Now please finish what you started. What else have you learned?"

"Sir, our investigation was hindered by cramped overhead space and the absence of natural light. Coping with both of these factors slowed our movement and our ability to report sooner. Using extra caution, we explored each tube, always anticipating the possible attack from the creature. We divided our numbers into small groups. It was nearly impossible to detect the direction from which sound traveled. This also slowed our communication."

Atticus leaned back in his chair. "I take it the creature remains at large?"

Anthony nodded. "That's correct, sir, and our frustrations grew as tunnel after tunnel dead ended, but Decimus's discovery explains the creature's disappearance."

Atticus leaned forward, his interest piquing.

"He noticed marks on the floor and wall that looked out of place to him. After methodically examining stone after stone, he uncovered a camouflaged fulcrum at the base of the wall. When manipulated correctly, it opens the way to a cleverly concealed portal."

Anthony's belabored way of speaking was trying Atticus's patience. "Can you pick up the pace, soldier? You've got me dangling here!"

Anthony's cheeks flushed, and his attempt to prevent an involuntary swallow caused further delay. "These are our conclusions."

"Thank the gods!"

"Judging from the number of debris and bones covering the cavern floor, the creature had spent considerable time down there, perhaps years."

"Are you saying it lives down there?" asks Vitus.

"We know that it's moving freely through those tunnels, and we concur with your conclusion. Its vision exceeds the limits of a normal man, possessing an animal-like ability to see in the dark. We were using torches. It didn't. Whatever it is, it can see in total blackness."

Unhappy with the direction of this discussion, Atticus redirected to Vitus. "You said it was human."

"We were only able to catch a glimpse of it, but its shape looked more like a man than an animal, but...something about it wasn't human. In the shadow of Scipio's approaching torch, it was crouched, ready to attack the way an animal stalking its prey would. I've gone over it in my mind, trying to construct the details, but it happened too quickly in little to no light." Vitus took in a shallow breath. "If Scipio hadn't shown up at that precise moment, I might not be here telling this. It fears light. Shielding its eyes, it retreated into the darkness."

Atticus turned to Scipio. "What did you see?"

"Not much," he replied. "We followed the sound of their voices through the darkness, which wasn't easy, but we had no idea what was happening. I saw something move but thought I might have imagined it."

Atticus turned back to Vitus. "How can you be sure it was going to attack if Scipio hadn't arrived."

"It was feral, beast-like. We listened to its breathing in that darkness, definitely abnormal. I knew it was watching us, measuring us. We were virtually defenseless, and it knew it."

"Maybe it has the sense a bat does in the darkness," said Scipio.

"Whatever it is, it's enormously powerful," interjected Anthony. "It possesses unworldly strength. It took three of us to pry open the release fulcrum decimus discovered. That thing had to do it alone!"

"You can't be sure it was alone," said Atticus.

Anthony was quick to respond, "There was only one set of foot-prints at the exit to the chamber."

Atticus hesitantly asked his next question, "Were they human?"

This time, the quiet Decimus answered for himself, "It was unclear, sir, but all the tracks were the same. Most of the floor is stone with a light covering of dirt."

"You said you found the tracks on the inside," Vitus remarked.

"That's correct," said Anthony. "Beyond the chamber was another underground corridor that ran a thousand yards and emptied into a cave-like formation and finally into a dense pine forest. A significant amount of blood had recently been spilled in that cave. Whether it was the creature's or someone else's, we don't know."

"It could have been from Barabbas or one of his men as they exited," Scipio suggested, "or maybe the ambassador's."

"I don't think so," said Anthony. "The blood was fresh—my guess, not more than two days old. We think someone set a trap for the beast, someone it would have recognized by sight, scent, or sound. Even if they did manage to catch it off guard, it would have taken several men to overpower it, which could explain the blood we found there." The operatives and their commander silently considered the possibilities.

"If you're right," Atticus theorized, "someone went through a lot of trouble to get rid of whatever it is that's been hiding down there. But why do it now? It can't be a coincidence."

Atticus paced, then suddenly stopped, looking straight ahead. "What if Barabbas didn't know the creature was down there or that it even existed? Its sudden appearance in Aurelius's chamber would be disastrous." He glanced over at Vitus, inviting him to join his inductive line of reasoning. "Think about that gnawed-looking corpse. It's the only thing that makes sense and everything that followed after the attack. The crucifixion, even the kidnapping, was a cover-up for what really happened."

"The man with the mark that Orel uncovered in Aurelius's chamber," added Vitus, "must have been one of Barabbas's men that was killed by the beast." His eyes were bright with revelation. "The throat-cutting was another part of the cover-up."

"Then it wasn't the Zealots who came back for the creature. They weren't privy to its habits or even its existence. The second group, unlike the first, was careful about cleaning up their mess. There were no bodies at the site of the struggle," Anthony confirmed.

"The creature is probably still alive," said Vitus. "Anthony's idea about the beast being caged is probably correct. It was taken alive for the same reason it had been kept alive: someone cares about it. But who? And where is it now?"

"For our purposes, the creature's whereabouts is inconsequential," Atticus concluded.

"What do we tell Pilate?" asked Vitus. "He keeps pressuring Mercurius for answers and results?"

"It's time we get to the bottom of this. You're right, Vitus, the beast will not lead us to Barabbas, but it does point us to a second party involvement."

"Sir?"

"It's not hard to imagine why this second party wants the creature out of the way. Its trail will eventually lead us back to its caretaker."

"Caretaker?" remarked Scipio. "What caretaker? It's feral, hunting to survive."

"I don't think so," said Atticus. "Make no mistake. Whatever it is, it's only survived this long because it's been sheltered and fed. We need to find the person who's been keeping this dark little secret, and I know where we begin." Atticus's eyes shifted to Anthony. "You will take the lead on this. You will not demand but cautiously question the priest. Always keep the emperor's protective attitude toward Judea in mind."

Vitus, a bit set off, immediately challenged the order, "Sir, shouldn't Orel be the one to interrogate Lamech? After all, he—"

"Absolutely not! He's too close to the old man."

"It won't go well when he learns we've boxed him out."

Atticus's expression turned icy. "Kid, I like Orel, but that's where it ends. Lamech has to be held responsible. Don't let your friendship with this Jew cloud your judgment."

Atticus's remark struck a chord deep inside Vitus, who had kept his own unique heritage hidden from the Centurion.

"Anthony is the right man for this."

"I respectfully disagree. Orel is the only man with an inside track on this. His relationship with the priest is an asset, not a liability. I trust him as much as I do any of the Ten. He proved his value the day of the assassination."

Atticus could only smile. "I'll consider your argument, but for now, you and Scipio are going to Capernaum, and you're taking Orel, our greatest asset, with you."

"Capernaum? Why Capernaum?"

Rubbing his disfigured eye, the Centurion explained, "I want eyes on the Nazarene and his band of twelve."

Vitus's expression asked the question for him. *Do we really want to do this now?*

"I don't like loose ends. The Nazarene's impact on Judea is too great to simply ignore. The stir he's created among the populace has thousands coming to listen to him. I've seen firsthand his ability to control minds. If he sympathizes with the Zealots, things could quickly escalate to a full-scale revolution, and if they haven't already approached him, they certainly will. You will operate in a strictly covert manner for now."

Once Vitus and Scipio had left, Atticus addressed the rest of the Ten.

"Leonidas, Julius, Caius, Didius, Virius, and Cyrus—you six will head for Samaria. I want to know why we haven't heard from Sergeant Oppius. I want a status report on him and the patrol. Let's put those amazing skills of yours to work."

Leonidas, a puzzled look on his face, probed for an explanation. "Sir, didn't you send Gaius with instructions for Cato and the regulars to move out this afternoon?"

Atticus rested his muscular arms on his desk. "Cato and the regulars are going to Gaza. They shouldn't get in too much trouble out there in the desert. If Oppius is in trouble, I need the swift and powerful ops to get him out of it."

A smiling Leonidas nodded.

"All right, gentlemen, off with you, and send reports back to me as soon as possible. Anthony, you and Decimus will carry out my earlier orders regarding the priest, but remember to tread lightly with Lamech. See what you can find that will help us. Orel, when he returns, may still hold the key to penetrating the old man's secret."

*****

A solitary figure hiding in the morning shadows had been doing his best to eavesdrop. Not everything was clear to the surreptitious Numa. But one thing was certain: the Ten were not part of Atticus's regulars. The Centurion had given them elite status, treatment, and responsibility. Having gathered all he could for now, he snuck away before being discovered. To find out exactly what was going on, he'd need a confederate, someone within the ranks that could help him bring Atticus down, and he had a pretty good idea who that someone might be.

CHAPTER 27
Lamech

Vitus was steamed as he headed for the courtyard palladium. The Centurion's decision to bypass Orel in favor of Anthony in dealing with Lamech, he thought, was a huge mistake, and now he further compounded it by shuffling them off to Capernaum. Orel would see this scheme as a betrayal, the priest having acted as his mentor. Vitus had little to no experience dealing with moral dilemmas. How could he be less than honest with his friend? Vitus had to figure out how to balance his friendship with Orel against the Centurion's effort to get the truth out of Lamech.

A voice called to him across the courtyard. "Vitus, over here!"

It was Orel. Both were pleased to see each other.

"Have you checked in on your priest?"

"On him and my two associates. He will likely accuse me of dereliction of duty once we sit down together."

"Oh, then you haven't spoken with him yet?"

Orel gave Vitus a curious glance. "No, not yet. Why do you ask?"

Annoyed with himself for prompting this line of questioning, Vitus didn't answer.

"What is it? What's up with you?"

Vitus looked down, trying to hide his facial expression.

"Come on man, spill it! What's eating you?"

"The Centurion is sending us to Capernaum to check in on the rabbi from Nazareth. We're leaving tomorrow, and he was hoping we could talk you into joining us."

Orel smiled. "I'm spending more time in service to Rome than Judea. Is the Centurion worried about the large following that the Nazarene has gathered to himself?" Orel shrugged again. "Sounds like an interesting assignment. This Jeshua sounds pretty amazing. I welcome the chance to see him up close. Guess the commander is going by his gut."

"Atticus hoped you'd willingly accompany us."

Orel was confused. "As I said, glad to go with you, but after I've spoken to the priest, there are questions needing to be asked."

Vitus took a second to speak. "Yes, Atticus is anxious for those questions to be asked, but he wants someone else to ask them."

"Let me get this straight. After all I've done to help you Romans, I'm excluded from this critical investigation of the priest?" Orel's anger ramped up as he continued, "So the Centurion wants my help and service but only when it's convenient?"

Vitus places a hand on his friend's shoulder. "He thinks your relationship with Lamech will affect your judgment. Is he right?"

Annoyed, he brushed Vitus's hand from his shoulder. "Guess you had to ask that question."

"I don't question your integrity, and I've experienced your loyalty, but that's why I need to ask. The old man is family to you. It would be close to impossible for a man like you to put loyalty aside and be completely objective. Can you stack your feelings in a corner while you interrogate him? Can you ask the kinds of questions that could incriminate him?"

Orel considered Vitus's reasoning. "Still be better if I ask them then some legionnaire!" He looked into his friend's eyes. "It's already set in motion, isn't it? Who?"

"Anthony."

"It's not going to work. He's a renowned Sadducee of considerable influence. Lamech has made extensive concessions to the Romans, including his personal estate. But that doesn't make him a confederate! He's the son of a Levite, a devoted follower of Elohim. Besides all that, his health has been disintegrating these past few months. If he's even well enough to entertain their questions—and that's a big if—he'll see this as betrayal of trust. On the other hand, if he is involved in a secret society, he'll die before divulging anything of value." Orel halted abruptly. "There's something else."

"Not another tattoo?"

Orel smiled. "He was trying to warn me just days before our encounter with the chevah."

"The chevah?"

"It's a Judean term for the thing that nearly ended both our lives in that grotto. He strictly warned me to keep my distance from Roman military, rambling on about the pestilence that was about to fall on them, relating it to the historical carnage our God leveled on the Egyptians."

"He was referring to the very first Passover."

Orel looked surprised.

"I'm half Judean, remember?"

"There's more. I don't know how, but Lamech knew I'd discovered the secret mark in the ambassador's chamber. He kept asking me if there was something I wasn't telling him."

Vitus rubbed the back of his neck. "That's crazy. How could he possibly know? The news of you helping Mercurius could easily get back to him, but the mark? How? Unless you told someone else. Did you?"

"Not until I confided in you."

Vitus smiled and nodded. "Then there's no way he could have known. You're building this up in your mind."

"I'm telling you, he knew. He was pushing me to come out with it. I'd been thinking about the meaning of the mark. Do you remember the two words?"

"*Tsal* and *mavet.*"

"Good, now turn the phrase around, shadow of death becomes 'death casts a shadow.'" Orel's mood changed. "Do you believe in things you can't see? Ever felt a shiver run through your body but didn't know why?"

"I'm not sure I know what you mean."

"You know what I mean! There are things we can't see or touch, but they're just as real."

"Are you talking about demons and spirits?"

"Lamech, the tattooed corpse, and the chevah are all linked. One or two things could be coincidental, but all three converging together? No way. I sensed something in the priest's chamber the next day as he ranted about a pandemic plague. It was just the two of us, but there was something strange—a chill, a presence. Maybe the old priest hasn't been singularly faithful to El Shaddai. Maybe he's gathered some invisible allies?"

Vitus would admit there were occasions when things happened that couldn't be explained. "The only allies that matter to me are my sword and comrades."

"I'll go with you to Capernaum after I get what I need from Lamech."

*****

Orel was less than satisfied with Judah and Seth's report regarding Lamech's well-being.

"We covered our designated areas and stood our posts, just as you instructed," Judah answered, responding to Orel's look of displeasure.

"How often did you check in on him during my absence?"

The two men glanced at each other. "We didn't," said Seth in a defensive tone. "When he's in his house, he has servants that attend to his needs. We did our job, and they did theirs."

Orel deliberately slowed his speech, pushing his words through his teeth, "Our job is to protect the priest whether he's inside his house or walking the grounds! Didn't it occur to you that there might be a reason he hasn't left his house in three days? That he might be ill? The man is aged and frail, exposed to horrific violence in his own backyard!"

Completely caught off guard, Seth stuttered out a reply, "Sur-surely his servants would have—"

He froze at Orel's extended palm. "Take a walk with me."

The three men crossed the courtyard, passing through the garden portal that led to Lamech's house. Orel respectfully touched the miniature Torah on the door lentil. He pounded three times on the massive door, waiting several seconds before pounding again. Ezra opened the door to them.

"Greetings, Ezra, we've come to check on your master's welfare. May we come in?"

Squinting, Ezra's eyes shifted from man to man, his expressionless face never changing. His words and tone were an indictment to their negligence of the priest. "He is not well today." He focused solely on Orel. "You alone may come in." He gave a reprehensible glare to Judah and Seth. "The two of you may wait in the garden."

Ezra led Orel to the aged priest's study where he found Lamech seated, waiting. It had been less than a week since their last conversation, but Lamech looked like he'd aged several years. The old man slowly lifted his head that was resting on his chest, acknowledging his chief bodyguard. "You have news for me?" His speech was slow and labored, upsetting Orel, who did his best to hide his concern. "Speak up, man, what is the nature of this visit? Have your Roman friends begun to understand the danger they face from El Shaddai's wrath?" His voice and body were frail.

"Sir, I—"

"I have always held you in high regard, my friend." The old man made no attempt to stand up. "You're more than a guardian. You have always treated me as a father, and I regard you as a son. For that reason, I warn you again: distance yourself from the Romans."

Lamech's boldness was not unusual, but his degraded condition and slurred speech were concerning to Orel, who wondered if he was coherent. "Sir, I share the same feelings for you. I remain your faithful protector and I haven't compromised my loyalty to our people or the Lord. I assist the Romans in their search for Zealot cowards whose mindless and brutal attacks will eventually force the legion to retaliate against us with full force. These insurgents have no regard for the safety or welfare of our people!"

Lamech slowly turned his head until Orel's face was fully visible. The old man's pupils appeared to be glazed from advanced cataracts.

"When his vengeance finally falls, it will be our enemies, not our people, who suffer the consequences. That's why you must separate yourself or be consumed with them."

"My *kohen* [priest], please understand that I've come to help and protect you if I can."

The old priest cupped a hand behind his ear. "Speak up, Orel, protect me from what?

"The military is coming to question you about the hidden tunnels under this dwelling, the tunnels the assassins used to enter and exit the ambassador's quarters."

"Let them come!" The defiant priest punctuated the point with his index finger. "The governor shall hear of these accusations as will Emperor—" His outburst was interrupted by a look of confusion.

Orel rushed to catch the slumping priest, keeping his head from hitting the floor. His labored breathing completely stopped.

"Sir!" Orel shook him, trying to rouse him, and then he listened for a heartbeat.

Seth and Judah sat patiently in the beautifully tended court, waiting for their captain to emerge. When he finally did, there was no need to question him. His countenance told them that Lamech had died.

*****

Numa was furious. "He thinks he can talk to me like that?" Halting his pacing, he threw an explosive uppercut at an invisible enemy. "No one treats me like that and gets away with it! Pompous, hard-ass, crazy, dim-witted fool!" Numa was reliving the moment he was sliced up like a garden salad in public and was hell-bent on revenge. "He thinks he can humiliate me and that's the end of it?" The formation of a plan blistered in his brain as he headed for the field barracks. Who better to be his confederate than the son of a wealthy patron like himself?

Bursting into the enlisted men's barracks, he squinted, trying to see in the darkened hall. He moved about the rows of bunks as though they belonged to him. Resting legionnaires jumped to attention, respecting his rank.

His tone was demeaning. "Where is Flavius?"

The barrack soldiers wisely remained silent, except for one foolish legionnaire who offered an answer, "He's not here, sir." The young soldier had inadvertently provided Numa an excuse to unload his pent-up anger.

Now in full bully mode, he let it fly. "Do you think I'm blind, soldier? That I don't have the eyes to see that?"

The wide-eyed young legionnaire now realized what he had done. "No, sir, I—"

"Let's try it again, shall we? This time, try to come up with an intelligent answer instead of sounding like the idiot you are." Spittle sprayed on the young soldier's face. "Think you can manage that?"

The cowering legionary nodded yes.

"Speak up! Or do you need help moving your lips as well?"

"No, sir. I mean yes, sir."

Numa scoured the room for a response. "Where is Flavius?"

*****

Later that evening, two men met in a tavern called Delayed Justice, a favorite haunt of legionnaires. Mixing business with wine, they took precautions, needing to be sure they were alone. The place was loud enough to cover their guarded conversation. Numa was intoxicated and even more obnoxious than usual, splashing his drink on the man across from him. Flavius was also smashed and having trouble forming a coherent sentence.

"He's been spe-specially tra-trained, I tell you!" he said, letting go a deep-throated belch. "Th-thinks he's betterrr than the rest of us, but he's nothing! A nobody!" Flavius gripped the table, attempting to stop the room from spinning.

"That nobody singlehandedly put the ten of you in the base infirmary."

"Four," Flavius replied, holding up four fingers.

"For? For what?"

"Four, not ten! He put four of us into the infirmary."

"Right, thanks for straightening me out on that 'very' important detail. The story I heard was that your friends had to drag your carcass back to the base after the pounding he laid on you!"

"Wh…what's it to you anyway?"

Numa's grin was evil. "How'd you like to return the favor?"

Flavius blinked repeatedly, liking the sound of Numa's offer. He tried to stand up but thought the better of it. "What makes a g-guy like you care about a guy like me?" Sliding back, he raised an eyebrow, the light beginning to dawn even in his inebriated brain. He pointed at Numa across the splintered table. "You want me to help you get him. Why do you care what happens to him?"

"I don't care, pinhead, I'm after a bigger fish, and Vitus is the one who can help me catch him."

At the far side of the room sat Issachar the Zealot, listening intently to the duo's inebriated conversation.

"Now listen," Numa continued, "the Centurion is sending Vitus and Scipio to spy on the Nazarene."

"You mean Jeshua?" Flavius loudly blurted.

"Shush! Quiet, you idiot!"

Flavius raised a finger to his lips, gesturing he'd tone it down. "You mean Jeshua?" he whispered, still too loud for a secretive discussion.

Numa wagged his head, annoyed at having to deal with this moron who was beneath him. "Atticus thinks the Nazarene has a connection to the Phantom. I want you to assist me in messing up their little cloak and dagger game."

"Wha-what I gotta do?"

The dark-skinned man from the opposite side of the room was standing next to their table. His Latin, though fragmented, was clear enough for them to understand. "Gentleman, may I join you?"

Both Numa and Flavius stared at him, wary of this unexpected intrusion.

"What do you want?" inquired Flavius.

"I am Issachar, forgive me. I overheard your conversation, and I have a proposition to offer you that could be profitable for all of us."

Everything about this man was distasteful to the elitist Numa. Still, he motioned for him to sit.

Issachar's eyes shifted from man to man. "It seems we have something in common: the ruin of certain Roman soldiers."

CHAPTER 28
Flashback

Thousands of shimmering diamonds danced on the Jordan River as the sun triumphantly rose. The shore was stippled with thousands of Judeans waiting for the arrival of Jeshua. He'd earned the reputation of being a man of the people, not like the Pharisees who regarded most commoners as unworthy of their time. On the contrary, Jeshua's persona was magnetic, virtually irresistible.

The open sandy shore was quickly turning into a standing room only situation. People were coming in numbers to hear his teaching, many hoping to see a miracle. Others wanted to hear more about their God that Jeshua was calling their heavenly Father. He was not standoffish, not afraid to touch them when he prayed for them, so they waited patiently, no matter how long it took. Wherever Jeshua was, seashore or hillside—they come by the thousands. The never-ending stream of people was emotionally draining, yet he never turned his back to anyone needing help. However, even on the busiest of days, Jeshua made time to be alone and pray.

An exceptionally large number of people followed him here from Capernaum. Vitus, Scipio, and Orel had joined them, blending in, dressed as locals. Their arrival was delayed because of Lamech's untimely demise, and Vitus refused to leave without Orel. The three men reached Capernaum late that evening, long after the Nazarene had concluded his day. After making camp for the night, Vitus waited for a moment when they were alone to talk to Orel, offering sincere condolences for the loss of a friend and mentor.

"I'm sorry about the way this all went down. Had to be hard to take."

"He was an old man whose health was failing." Orel exhaled long and slowly. "But there's no doubt I'm the one responsible for pushing him over the edge."

"No, that's not true. It was going to happen no matter who approached him. Look at it this way: he didn't die alone because you were there with him."

Orel nodded. "Maybe. At least he didn't have to endure Anthony's accusations."

Scipio returned with fresh water, unaware of the nature of conversation he just missed. "Maybe I missed something because I still don't understand why he wants us to waste our time on this preacher instead of chasing down Barabbas," smirked Scipio.

"It's called direct orders. You were standing next to me when the Centurion issued them. At least your body was." Shielding his eyes from the sun's morning rays, Vitus scanned the horizon for Jeshua. He spotted him sitting quietly with his back to the river and his eyes closed. Elbowing Orel, he motioned in the direction of the Nazarene. "What's that all about?"

"He's praying."

"Praying?" Vitus repeated suspiciously.

"What's he praying for?" Scipio's inquiry had a kind of childlike innocence to it.

"How would I know that?" snapped Orel.

"Ahh, just thought you might know," muttered Scipio, but Orel wouldn't let it go.

"Because I'm a Judean, right? We're all the same—seen one, seen 'em all!"

Scipio raised his hands in surrender. "Didn't mean anything by it and just thought you would have a better idea about him than me."

"Everything he does involves prayer. At least that's the news—" Pausing, Orel suddenly had an epiphany. "It's funny it never occurred to me how agitated he got when I mentioned his name."

"What? Who got agitated?" asked Scipio.

"Lamech."

"Lamech? I thought we were talking about Jeshua."

"We are—I mean I was—I mentioned Jeshua to him in passing several weeks back. His reaction was surprising, way over the top!"

Vitus picked up a stone, juggling it in his hand. "Because you mentioned his name, I wonder if Lamech's associates feel the same way about the Nazarene?"

"It's possible, I suppose."

"More like plausible. Did he say anything else about the rabbi?"

Orel slumped back, thinking over the question, "'Sabbath healer' is a term he used in reference to Jeshua and not in a complimentary way."

"Sabbath healer?" remarked Scipio.

"He practically spit the words back in my face. I just chalked it up as an overreaction and put it out of my mind until today. Sabbath healer," he repeated the phrase again with a faraway look in his eyes.

"Sabbath healer. What does it mean?" asked Scipio.

"I think you understand how sacred the Sabbath is to my people," he addressed his thoughts to Vitus.

"*Our* people," Vitus insisted, staking claim to his own Judean heritage. "It's revered, but what's that got to do with—"

"It could mean that the stories are true. At least Lamech believed they were."

"What stories?" Scipio asks.

"About the Nazarene. He doesn't restrict doing amazing things to the other six days of the week. He continued doing miracles on the Sabbath. That's why Lamech was so adamant! The fourth commandment: revere the Sabbath and keep it holy!" Orel was on a roll. "The Pharisees and Sadducees are both emphatic about it. Absolutely no work is to be done on the Sabbath. Noncompliance is a serious offense."

Scipio couldn't believe it. "All this fuss is about a holy day? The whole thing is religious nonsense."

"For a Judean, Sabbath begins at sunset, and there are dozens of rules governing the preparation of food, the care of animals—anything that requires work. Even laying out clothing for the next day is forbidden. If Jeshua has been *working* on the Sabbath, it would be a serious breach of Mosaic code. The Pharisees and Sadducees would be all over him."

"Wait." Scipio couldn't believe what he was hearing. "So you're saying that if the Nazarene does something amazing on the Sabbath—a miracle, whatever—these religious power brokers will try to bring him down, even though he's helping your people?"

Vitus chimed in, "It's what Romans call *disgregarsi*—unspeakable disgrace."

"Right," says Orel, "they would consider it their duty to publicly harass and discredit him."

"No wonder he's praying." The three burst into laughter until a group of parents steering their children through the crowd snatched their attention.

Orel resumed discussion with Scipio, "We're not talking about the general populace. Just look around. Jeshua's popularity is stunning. It's the pious demigods who can't stomach him. They see themselves as Elohim's exclusive keepers of truth."

Vitus validated, "That would explain Lamech's angry reaction."

Scipio motioned toward the determined parents. "What is that group up to?'

"They're hoping Jeshua will bless their children, place his hand on them, say a few words over them."

While Orel was speaking, the parents were intercepted by a couple of Jeshua's disciples. Thomas and Judas, probably due to the short night, were less than cordial to these resolute pilgrims.

"I'm sorry, but you can't bring your children to him for a blessing. We would have to allow everyone to do that," explained a somewhat irate Judas. Thomas joined him in shooing away both parents and children until Jeshua put an end to it.

"Don't push these children away! Don't ever get between them and me. These children are at the very center of life in the kingdom. Mark this: unless you accept God's kingdom in the simplicity of a child, you'll never get in" (Mark 10:14–15 MSG).

With a shrill whistle, he regained the attention of the parents. Squatting down, he extended both arms in a welcoming fashion. At first, the children froze, looking to their parents for approval.

"It's all right," Jeshua laughed, his white teeth gleaming in contrast to his tanned skin. He widened his extended arms, inviting them to return. "Don't be afraid," he assured them.

The youngest girl was the first to run to him. She was quickly followed by a flock of charging kids whose collective weight pushed him backward, sprawling on the ground. For an instant, the people were silent, even a little frightened. But laughing, Jeshua regained his balance, gathering the giggling children into his arms. Thomas and Judas, who were quieted by his rebuke, couldn't help but laugh as well. Fathers openly chuckled; mothers, trying to be proper, covered their mouths, giggling with delight, and thousands in the crowd shared in an unforgettable moment of pure joy.

Giving the children his full attention, Jeshua talked and listened to them to the delight of their parents. Laying a hand on each child's head, he was caught up in a childhood memory of his own.

*****

The carpenter shop was active. Joseph was teaching eight-year-old Jeshua how to plane down a cedar chest. Curly chips of wood fell to the floor as Joseph guided the plane against the rough-hewn planks. James, Jeshua's younger brother, walked into the shop to announce that supper was ready.

"Put your hands here and here," instructed Joseph, pointing to the wooden tool. "Be careful, my son, its sharp edges can cut you as easily as it does the wood." Additional shavings littered the floor, filling the workshop with an aromatic smell of fresh cedar. Completely forgetting his mother's instructions about dinner, James was focused on his big brother.

Mary popped her head into the workshop where James stood motionless with his mouth open. "There you are," she said, placing both hands on her hips. "Did you tell them?"

James bowed and shook his head.

Mary, placing her hands on both sides of James's head, moving it up and down like you would a puppet, spoke in her deepest voice, "Abba, Jeshua, supper is getting cold!"

Joseph leaned against his worktable and chuckled. "Yes, Emma," he replied, bringing a tiny smile to his wife's eyes while Joseph's hands rested on the head of a smiling adopted son.

*****

Meanwhile, twenty-two-year-old Scipio had enough of these children. Leaning forward, he whispered to Vitus, "Oh yeah, this guy, Jeshua, is a serious threat to the empire right up there with the Phantom! A born killer I tell you! C'mon, you kidding me or what? Holy...the man is hugging children!" he exclaimed. "We're wasting our time out here, Vitus!"

Exercising patience with his high-spirited comrade, Vitus's tone was calm and slow. "You're probably right, Scip. But on the other hand, what if this was very convincing window dressing? Either way, we have orders. So until we see the rest of his act, we're not going anywhere."

Vitus scanned the colossal crowd. "These people haven't come here because he's good with kids. There's something unique about him. And that, my friend, demands we take a closer look." His eyes rested on Scipio. "The Centurion is a master at dealing with mayhem." Turning back to Orel, he continued, "He wants us to find the link—if it exists—between the Nazarene and the Zealots. He won't tolerate excuses or failure, so we will deliver neither." Stretching his neck to relieve tension. "You're right, Scip, this display by Jeshua doesn't exactly fit the profile of an insurrectionist, but—"

"Damn right!" snapped Scipio.

"But we've seen only a small sample," Orel interjected. "All these people are confirmation of that."

Vitus nodded in agreement.

"I've been curious about him for a while," said Orel. "Stories circulating about him are nothing short of incredible. I welcome the chance to see for myself. I'm all for carrying out the Centurion's orders."

By the time Jeshua began his public address by the seashore, the crowd had swelled to eight thousand people. Putting his back to the

Jordan worked to amplify his voice, carrying easily to the throng of thousands.

"Be careful not to practice your righteousness in front of others to be seen by them. If you do, you will have no reward from your Father in heaven. … But when you give to the needy, do not let your left hand know what your right hand is doing, so that your giving may be in secret. Then your Father, who sees what is done in secret, will reward you" (Matt 6:1–4 NLT),

The people listen in stunned silence, pondering the term: *Heavenly Father*. With straight backs and ears tuned, they strained to take in every syllable. Many were stunned. Did they hear him correctly? Did he just connect God to their family tree? A collective gasp cascaded over the crowd when Jeshua referred to the great *I Am* as *Yahweh*, meaning Abba or Daddy.

They blinked in astonishment, having always been taught that the transcendent Elohim was fearsome and removed. Judeans could only call on his name in moments of desperation when there was no other avenue to turn to. But Jeshua was telling them that God was not only awesome but took a personal interest in them, the way a loving father would. The people were so quiet that a woman weeping in the crowd was heard. For the first time in their entire lives, they'd been given hope, not condemnation. Time seemed to stop as Jeshua delivered an irresistible message.

Serving as temple guardian, Orel spent years in the company of religious leaders, but he had never listened to anything like this. His natural instincts signaled caution, but he was finding himself drawn in by the authority of Jeshua's words. *How could he reconcile Lamech's anger against the majesty of this rabbi?* he wondered.

"You have to admit he is special," said Orel, offering his opinion to his companions. "Is there any wonder why people are fascinated with him?"

As the Nazarene continued, Orel listened intently for contradictions relating to Mosaic codes, but even if there was something, it wouldn't explain the priest's extreme hatred for the Nazarene.

Jeshua's speech was articulate and authoritative. "Your Heavenly Father knows what you need before you even ask" (Matt. 6 NLT).

There was no common ground between the Nazarene and the bloodthirsty Zealots. Orel's mind reeled. He wondered how deep the old man's involvement was with them. Because of Lamech's sudden passing, he never got the chance to question him about the part man, part animal subterranean beast.

The passing of Lamech expedited the decision of the enigmatic Shadow of Death. For years, the priest had cautiously guarded the secret of his son who, at a tender age, fell victim to his father's occultist rituals. A dark spiritual force steadily disturbed the boy as he grew, slowly disfiguring his appearance, mind, and spirit until at last he was no longer man but chevah. The entity within gave him freakish strength but also reduced him to a beastlike mentality. Its control over him continued to increase until the possibility of breaking free seemed impossible. How did the son of a prominent priest like Lamech end up this way?

More than a decade earlier, a much younger Lamech was enticed to join a secret organization. The clandestine circle included high-ranking religious dignitaries who regularly took part in its hedonistic rituals. Men like Isa, Korah, and Lamech knew of the warnings of the Prophet Isaiah.

"These people…honor me with their lips, but their hearts are far from me. And their worship of me is nothing but man-made rules learned by rote. What sorrow awaits those who try to hide their plans from the LORD, who do their evil deeds in the dark!" (Isaiah 29:13, 15 NLT)

Instead, they did the very things that guardians of the faith were supposed to protect Judah's citizenry against. Lamech, engulfed in fertility ceremonies, forsook the Mosaic Law he'd sworn to uphold. A Syrian priestess became pregnant with his son during one such ritual. As the child grew, he was repeatedly exposed to the incantations of his mother. He became violent, difficult to control. Eventually, the thing his mother had helped turn him into turned on her, crushing her windpipe with effortless strength. Lamech took to hiding him in the underground confines of his mansion.

Far too dangerous to be free, he was chained and cared for by the priest's most trusted servant, Ezra. But his condition continued to deteriorate until he was reduced to the status of a wild beast. The evil power that controlled him increased as did his physical strength until at last, no chains could securely bind him. By that time, Lamech had lost much of his faculties from worry and advanced age.

CHAPTER 29
A Nonnegotiable Deal

Issachar would never have imagined legionnaires and Zealots working together toward a common goal. Not only was it about to happen, but he was the one who arranged it. Issachar was a pragmatist. He didn't believe in fate or even luck. It wasn't destiny that allowed him to overhear the inebriated conversation of Numa and Flavius. A tavern might be the only place where a Roman and Judean could share the same space without fear of reprisal.

Issachar understood the transformative nature of wine. A normally tight-lipped man could easily lose his inhibitions after a few healthy drinks. Issachar's rebel compatriots had called his struggle to learn Latin a waste of time. But this knowledge had allowed him to eavesdrop on the enemy's conversation without drawing suspicion to himself. Fate had nothing to do with it; diligence and dedication had everything to do with it.

Barabbas sat with fellow Zealot leaders waiting for the meeting to begin. Saul, Hophni, Abiel—all key figures in this circle of secrecy—were seated at their usual places. They were joined by a late-arriving Issachar.

Hophni opened the meeting with a somber tone, "To my knowledge, we've received no report of any kind from Simon."

All eyes in the room shifted to Barabbas, but he offered no verbal response, just a nod of agreement.

Hophni turned to Barabbas. "What do you have to say about this? Where is Simon? And why haven't we heard from him?"

Issachar, who had barely had time to sit down, sprang up with an announcement.

"My brothers, I have news that I think you will want to hear!"

Barabbas's expression was evidence that he was not pleased with this interruption.

"I'm sorry, Barabb, but this is critical information."

Barabbas was deliberate in replying, "It better be, Issa!"

Just as Issachar had predicted, the circle of men were enthralled as he offered details of his encounter with the two Romans. Those who had regarded him to be a buffoon now gave him their full attention.

"These Romans are cautiously anxious for our help. One of the men I spoke with has an inside track on the plans being charted against us and is willing to work with us."

"It sounds too good to be true," a sarcastic Saul retorted. "You know what they say when something is too easy. How do you explain your good luck? I suppose it was fate that brought you to the right place at the precise moment?"

Issachar chuckled. "No, it wasn't luck or fate."

"What if this is a trap to get you to lead them to our doorstep? Have you even considered that?"

Issachar grinned. "These men didn't approach me. They had no idea I could speak their language. This, friends, is the opportunity we have been waiting for, and it didn't just jump into my lap. I made it my business to regularly visit a certain tavern, hoping to gather information from drunken legionnaires. Yesterday it paid off. This is not a Roman trap. It's a gift! Now shall I tell you the rest?"

"We will hear it," said Barabbas.

Issachar's gray eyes sparkled as he related the tale. "The man I spoke to, Numa, is blinded by his hate for his superior officer. He has agreed to share information if it will help bring a swift end to the Centurion and his special mission." Issachar leaned back, taking the liberty of a slow deep breath.

The Zealot leaders, sensing the gravity of this, were restless to hear more.

"I will insist our future meetings include just the two of us. The other soldier, Flavius, was in a drunken stupor but still complained about the arrangement." Issachar looked around the unusually silent room. "So what do you think?"

Barabbas was the first. "Exceptional work, Issa. Think of what we could do with this information. How will you get word back to the Roman?"

"It's already set for tomorrow evening in the same place."

This decision raised several concerns from the group, but Barabbas interjected before anyone else could comment.

"Let this be the last time you meet in a tavern. Even drunken men have eyes and ears."

"A private setting offers more protection," Hophni interjected. "You must be the one to set the time and place, and make sure you're not followed. Romans cannot be trusted."

Issa smiled inwardly as he listened to Hophni broadcast his hypocrisy. This was a man that helped plan Aurelius's kidnapping and who belonged to a clandestine society, and Romans were the ones who couldn't be trusted?

"It's nearly impossible to be followed if the meeting is set in a remote area outside the city," added Barabbas. "First light is good when it's still difficult to see. But the place must also be identifiable so Numa won't get lost. You know these Romans," chuckled Barabbas. His levity helped break the tension of the moment. "You tell him the Zealots will be happy to kill as many of his people as he is willing to inform on."

Issachar would implement the Phantom's wise counsel. The ancient olive press, outside the city limits, was accepted as their next meeting place.

*****

At their next rendezvous, neither Issachar nor Numa enjoyed a level of comfort. Issachar was the first to speak, "The Zealots are ready to work with you."

Numa looked left, right, and behind him, then said, "We're alone."

Issachar wasn't sure if that was a statement or a question. "Yes, as we agreed," he responded with caution.

"I'm sure of it. I arrived early and watched you approach from a distance."

"A good start to our friendship, yes?"

Numa's eyes flashed fire. "This is not a friendship. It's a business arrangement, nothing more. I don't like you. I'm here because we have common interests. You kill the men that threaten both of our welfares, I provide you with the information needed to get the job done."

A wry smile pursed Issachar's lips. "Then we understand each other."

Numa's face was cold, expressionless. "I have the critical information about soldiers who have been tasked to deliver a serious blow to the cause of the Zealots. The risk is greater on my end, the reward on yours."

Issachar's distaste for Numa could be heard in his voice. "We Zealots risk our lives daily for our nation, so don't lecture me about risk! Tell me about those names you mentioned earlier."

"First, let's be clear. The termination of Centurion Atticus is the desired result, but I'll settle for publicly disgraced, demoted, and being labeled as a failure."

"I know of this Centurion." Issa paused. "He's not a man easily killed. It will take careful planning and, of course, your assistance if we're to accomplish this. What's the second demand? Do you plan to take his job?"

"No, I don't want what he has!"

"You hate him more than we do! Tell me why I should trust a man who betrays his own people."

Numa squared his shoulders. "Because we're both after the same thing, and this is the only way to achieve it."

Issachar nodded in agreement. "What is your second *request?*"

"The field leader of the Ten is called Vitus. His death is not negotiable. Kill as many of the others as you're able to, but he must die. Is that understood?"

Issa responded with a wry smile, "Perfectly. You provide me with the details of their plans and movements, and we'll take care of the rest. Are we in accord?"

Numa extended and shook Issa's hand, but he wanted to bathe as soon as possible. Interestingly, Issachar felt the same way.

"Give me something to get started?"

Without delay, Numa relayed Oppius's location and current orders as well as Vitus's assignment.

"Beware that you don't underestimate the power of the ten soldiers. They're formidable and none more dangerous than Vitus. It will take many men"—he repeated emphasizing the point—"many men and the element of surprise."

Issa didn't look alarmed.

"Do you have a plan?"

"That's not your concern. I'll be in touch."

"How will I know when the deed is done?"

"You'll do what you always do. Keep your nose in the wind for the smell of death."

As the two men parted company, Issachar was extra careful to make sure he wasn't being followed.

*****

Barabbas and other key members awaited Issachar's arrival in the house of Hophni. "How did the meeting go?" asked Hophni. "Was it worth it?"

Issachar, looking his usual disheveled self, ignored him and asked a question of his own. "I thought Simon would be here by now. Has he sent word?"

This time, it was a sullen Barabbas who ignored Issachar. "What have you got for us, Issa?"

Issachar's broad smile revealed remnants of the previous day's meal still lodged in his teeth.

Barabbas leered at his slovenly appearance. "I think you've been spending too much time around Abiel. You've picked up his boorish manners."

"I have news about the Centurion's men. The bulk of his legionnaires are hunting our men in Samaria." He paused to temper his excitement. "It seems that Imperial Rome has taken steps to wipe us out using a small but specialized group of soldiers. The Ten, as he called them, will be using precision strikes to take us down."

Saul challenged Issachar, "Ten? Ten Roman soldiers?" he asked in disbelief. "How can ten legionnaires accomplish what whole companies couldn't? He's playing with you. It makes no sense!"

"The Ten are not regular legionnaires. They're deadly warriors with fighting skills that enable them to take on and defeat much larger forces. Numa called them killing machines, pledged to capture or kill the Phantom and his troop."

The room was bathed in silence.

"How can we identify them? Are they working independent of the regular army?"

"They will do both but at times will become invisible, working much like the Zealots. But now because of this alliance, we know the assignment and location of a key field leader."

"Excellent!" shouted Abiel. "Cut off the head of the snake, and the whole snake dies. Where do we find him?"

"His name is Vitus, and according to Numa, he is the most dangerous of these warriors, without equal. He warned to underestimate him would be a fatal mistake."

"Is that so?" Barabbas sneered. "We'll see about that."

"Numa insisted on several conditions before he gave up this information."

"What does the traitor request?"

"Not requests. Two demands: first, the death and or public disgrace of the Centurion."

Barabbas grew impatient with Issachar's slow pace. "Speed it up, Issa, what else did the traitor demand?"

"The assurance that Vitus would draw his last breath. This is an absolute."

"If I have my way, this Numa will join the list of Romans who take their last breath!" Barabbas voiced a demand of his own. "Where is this Vitus? And how many of the ten are with him?"

"He travels with two men. One is a Judean, the other is one of the Ten."

"One of our people travels with him?" he snarled. "Is he a Samaritan?"

"No." Issachar's eyes met Barabbas. "He's a former temple guardian, the bodyguard of the dead priest, Lamech."

Arms dropping to his sides, Barabbas wagged his head in disbelief. "The bodyguard of the priest…that's just great! He will have spent hours with Lamech. This could prove very bad for us!"

"I know this man," Saul interjected. "His name is Orel."

Barabbas sighed. "Orel could be more dangerous than the Roman. Who knows what that crazy old man may have shared with his bodyguard?"

"Lamech was a major player in the Shadow of Death, but he took the same oath we did to take our secret to the grave," said a concerned Hophni.

"He had lost most of his faculties toward the end. We can't be sure what may have slipped out of the mouth of that once brilliant mind."

Silence reigned until Issachar spoke, "The three men are currently in Capernaum."

Barabbas turned to stare at him. "Why in the name of the El Shaddai would they go there?"

"To see the Nazarene, of course. That is also his current location. You said it yourself. The Nazarene is a persuasive, powerful personality," said Hophni. "You so much as suggested he could be *the One*. Or have you changed your mind on that?"

A sly smile molded on Barabbas's face. "It appears the Centurion has noticed him as well. He's clever, this Roman. We send Simon to sway Jeshua to our side, the Centurion sends Vitus, with a Judean, anticipating such a move on our part. The SOB is clever."

"So what's our next move?" asked Issachar.

"It's time we check in on Simon."

"Simon?" said Saul. "What about Vitus?"

"Yes, we're going to get Vitus, and Simon is going to help us."

The Zealot leadership was tuned in, awaiting Barabbas's next remark.

"It will take considerable planning and stealth, but this special soldier is going to have a sudden death experience. Saul, you will gather six of our best soldiers. Be sure at least two of them are Sicarii. Have them wait for us in Capernaum."

"What's the plan?" asked Issachar.

"Vitus will think he's about to accomplish his mission, namely capturing the Phantom. If we do this right, the three of them will think they're tracking us back to our lair, but we will be leading them to their deaths!"

"An ambush!"

"A trap. Why risk our soldiers' lives against such a formidable warrior?"

Issachar wasn't sure if Barabbas was being serious or sarcastic.

"Numa warned us not to underestimate him, so we won't. After the savage attack on Aurelius, a key leader in the Shadow of Death told me they had moved the chevah out of the underground grotto because it had become too dangerous. I saw the look of fear in Korah's eyes. He said they had to act immediately or it would be too late."

The Shadow of Death had pledged to do whatever it took to achieve national independence, including a tryst, but were stunned by the beast's horrific savagery that day.

Issachar shrugged. "Why tell us all this now, Barab?"

"The creature now roams the region of the Gadarenes. After my conversation with Korah, I sent Judah and Ezekiel to locate him."

There was an uneasy stirring when Issachar asked, "Why send Judah and Ezekiel to spy on the creature?"

Again, Barabbas sidestepped Issa's question. "They returned unharmed because they kept their distance as I instructed them to. It dwells in a cave near a cemetery, a place where the Gentiles bury their dead. It roams the countryside because they can't restrain it. Local authorities have tried to bind it with chains, but it breaks free of them. Apparently, its strength increases daily. The nearby towns-people live in mortal fear of it."

The evil grin on Barabbas's face was disturbing. "We will not engage Vitus. We will entice him and his companions to follow us into the waiting arms of the chevah, where it will tear them to pieces!"

CHAPTER 30
Who Is Pushing Whom?

Having deployed the last of his special operatives, Atticus kicked back in his officer's chair to take a breather and review the events of a very long day. His hands clasped behind his head, he was envisioning the Samaritan woman and what might have been when a soft tapping at his door interrupted those thoughts.

"Commander." His Staff Sergeant's muffled voice called through the outer wooden door.

Frustrated by the interruption of his fantasy, Atticus cursed under his breath. "Can't I get a damned moment to myself? Come in, Gaius!"

Gaius entered and stood at attention, offering a salute.

"Commander Mercurius requests your presence posthaste, sir."

"Post what? Holy…can't that man do anything around here without me? I have to do my job and his too? Hell, I should have gone with the Ten!" Gaius ducked an object whizzing past his head. "Posthaste my—"

A wary Gaius remained at attention, even though the Centurion's scowl warned him to stay down. Still bemoaning the woman, Atticus exhaled an exasperated breath, "There was a lot more to that woman than just looks!"

Gaius didn't know how to get back to the post commanders' urgent request. Atticus, reading the dilemma on his sergeant's face, let out one last rant, "I swear I'll even the score with the Nazarene if it's the last thing I do!"

Gaius tried again, "Sir, Mercurius has requested that you come without delay"—pausing for a second—"but I suppose it's a little late for that now."

Atticus glared at Gaius and asked, "Any other gems from the PC?"

Gaius swallowed. "He said the Phantom would probably arrive before you did."

"Come again, soldier?"

"Sir, I'm only delivering a message."

Making his exit with intent, Atticus nearly walked over Gaius. Upon arrival, he was immediately ushered to the PC by two sentries.

"Commander." Atticus's raspy voice echoed in the empty room. "You sent for me…posthaste," he added, emphasizing the latter.

Mercurius walked from the far end of the long rectangular chamber, grasping a communiqué in his fist. "This missive," he stated, extending the scrolled note, "is from Tribune Lucius, bearing the seal of Governor Pilate."

Atticus grimaced at the name—unforgotten bad blood. Unrolling the scroll, Mercurius read: "Centurion ordered to meet Prefect of Judea tomorrow morning at the Praetorium."

Atticus wasn't pleased. "Why summon me? You're the post commander!"

"Lucius is senior military advisor to Pontius Pilate, and for your information, he's been after me since the assassination. As you know, Caesarea is the center for Roman military personnel here in Judea, and Lucius oversees most of these legionnaires."

"And I care about this because?"

"Because this time, my dear Centurion, he asks to see you, not me, and you'd better be wary of him. He has an unparalleled aptitude for recognizing and playing angles to his advantage. He's made himself an invaluable resource to Pilate by relieving him of the daily nuisances of military procedure."

Atticus stood tall. "I wasn't sent here to powder the backsides of pseudo-military blowhards. With all due respect, that's your job."

The even-tempered Mercurius was not swayed by Atticus's brashness. He was a man that appreciated the truth when he heard it.

"Lucius is only an annoyance. It's Pilate's repressive treatment of the Jewish population. Last week, the governor, not Lucius, sent legionnaires to Jerusalem to parade through the city, displaying Tiberius's image on the clasps of their uniforms. The Judeans revere the *Torah,* and it forbids graven images. So you tell me, is the prefect ignorant, defiant, or just stupid?" The usually calm Mercurius became loud and animated. "He mints coins bearing the emperor's image, something Antipas was careful to avoid. He tops this off by draping imperial banners throughout the city, further shoving the insult down their throats!"

Mercurius's uncharacteristic brashness surprised Atticus. "I've heard Jewish religious leaders have taken to demonstrating in the streets of Caesarea," Atticus remarked.

"Who could blame them? But does the governor take a step back? Of course not. He threatens executions if demonstrations continue."

"The man is a tactless imbecile!"

"I agree, but Lucius is forced to deal with the fallout, making our dealings with him all the more difficult. Pilate's despotism bolsters the cause of the insurgents. If it continues unchecked, it could drive Judea into open rebellion, exactly what the Zealots want."

"What's this got to do with me?" snorted Atticus.

"That's the question, isn't it? My sources tell me that Lucius has been alerted to a rumor." Mercurius turned his back to Atticus, trying to keep from staring at his disfigured eye. "The rumor goes something like this: a former Centurion's rank and commission were suddenly and uncharacteristically restored and sent on an undisclosed mission to Judea." Mercurius turned to face Atticus. "Lucius is a man that will entertain rumor but demand verifiable data."

"So he thinks he can extract the truth from me?" Atticus chuckled.

"As I said, the man is skilled at leveraging angles. He'll do whatever it takes to get what he wants from you, especially if it helps him douse the flames of insurrection."

"I'm familiar with the tribune's methods. I've dealt with him in the past."

Lucius sent no military escort for Atticus; a possible oversight but more likely a signal of disrespect. Atticus could care less; his present concerns were the welfare of Oppius and his young phenom, Vitus. He did regret Vitus's absence; it was a lost opportunity to tutor his protégé on his unique brand of political diplomacy.

*****

Upon his arrival to Caesarea, Atticus received no welcome. As he and Anthony, the only member of the Ten not on assignment, moved through the courtyard, he spoke openly, "You're wondering if this visit concerns our failure to produce the culprits in Aurelius's assassination." The two men walked in lockstep cadence as they climbed the stairs to the *Magister Militum's* office. "It doesn't. This is about past history between me and Lucius. There's a bug up his butt about a rumor that he'll use to extract his pound of flesh from me. Prefect Pilate will probably be absent from this meeting. You, my young friend, are here to remind me to hold my temper and conduct myself with the proper military decorum. Think you can handle that, soldier?"

Anthony, the most proper of the Ten, was uncomfortable with the notion of correcting a senior officer.

"I'll do my best, sir." They were stopped at the top of the stairs, checked, and escorted inside.

One of the sentries announced them, "Tribune, the Centurion has arrived!"

Lucius was younger and taller than the compact, more powerfully built Centurion. He motioned from his seated position for them to advance. The tribune's skin was pale and untethered by the Judean sun. He openly displayed his many medals of honor to impress and intimidate competitors.

In sharp contrast, Atticus brandished only the scars that crisscrossed his body; these were his medals of valor. The tribune was well-aware of Atticus's distinguished heroics but treated him with little respect. The Centurion held Lucius responsible for the injury to his eye and his military demotion. The tribune liked to quote a proverb of his own making: "Study a person's past, and you'll uncover the weapon to best use against them in the future." He advanced his career by leveraging opponent's secrets against them. The threat of exposure was enough to convince a rival to cooperate or suffer the consequences.

Lucius disliked Atticus from the very start because he achieved his advancements through results not posturing. He would enjoy venting his frustrations on the legend of the Varus Wars, or so he thought, but had grossly underestimated the man behind the legend.

"Welcome, Centurion." Lucius's greeting was self-serving, refusing to even rise from his chair. His tone was cold and removed. "You've been summoned here at the pleasure of His Excellency, Pontius Pilate." Making no pretense, he stared directly at Atticus's damaged eye. Squaring his shoulders, he cleared his throat. "The governor is presently occupied with other more important matters of state. Today, you will speak only with me." Motioning with an outstretched hand, he added, "You may dismiss your subordinate and sit."

Atticus had no intention of giving Lucius the psychological advantage of looking down on him by sitting down. His response was "Thank you, Tribune, but my guardian and I prefer to stand."

This sent a flush of adrenaline through Lucius. "The governor has ordered you to disclose your mission here in Judea."

"Tribune, two days ago, I was summoned by Post Commander Mercurius. He held a missive marked 'Urgent' bearing the prefect's crest. I was ordered to drop everything and report to Caesarea with all speed. So here I stand at the governor's pleasure, as you stated earlier, yet now you tell me he has other more important matters to attend to."

Lucius's nostrils flared. "Insolent...you dare to lecture me?" His folded arms fell menacingly to his sides. "Let me be direct, dimwitted bumpkin. As far as it concerns you, I am the governor! Your recent promotion carries no weight here in Caesarea." Close to losing control, he stood, thinking his height would give him an advantage over the shorter Centurion. "Now, Commander, you will inform me of the details and progress of your secretive little operation. Then I will decide whether to pass it on to the prefect or have you demoted for wasting our time. Do I make myself clear? Or am I speaking too fast for you?"

Atticus displayed the slightest little smile. "Absolutely clear, sir," he calmly replied.

Lucius grinned pretentiously, pleased that he had put the great military champion in his place. His tone, once again, sounded official. "Now as I stated earlier, I require a full—"

Once again, he was cut off in midstream, "Tribune, it might interest you to learn that I anticipated such a meeting with the prefect before you summoned me."

Lucius's smile faded to a frown, concerned with this change of direction.

Using instincts and guile, Atticus rendered a report devoid of any real information. "It's true that I was sent to Judea on special assignment, and I expected, at the appropriate time, to be summoned by the prefect. But it was you, not the governor, who summoned me because you obviously have no idea as to why I'm here in Judea. The men who commissioned me answer directly to Tiberius. I have sworn an oath to divulge no measure of this mission unless instructed by them to do so. I proceed on a need-to-know basis only. If Governor Pilate had been contacted by these men, he would surely be present for this meeting because there are no matters more important. It's clear—a term you've used several times today—that you have not been contacted by them. Therefore, Tribune, since my superiors have not seen fit to divulge any details relating the nature of this mission"—Atticus grinned fearlessly, knowing he was burning the petty bureaucrat to the soles of his feet—"it would be a direct violation of my orders to do so now."

"In the name of Pontius Pilate, Prefect of Judea, I demand you divulge the nature of this mission!"

Atticus was sarcastically deliberate. "Sir, perhaps it is I who have spoken too fast for you. Let me start again. As I have stated, my mission is strictly classified, a need-to-know basis only. These are the orders of the *Magister Utriusque Militum* in Rome!" Motioning to Anthony to join him, the Centurion did an about-face, showing his back to Lucius. Before walking away, he turned around to face his old enemy for one last jab. "I will remain in Caesarea the rest of the day should the governor have any questions for me. At such a time, I will gladly share with the prefect how willing you were to potentially endanger a clandestine mission by going over his head. Otherwise"— Atticus held the tribune suspended in midair—"I see no reason for us to meet again. Unless, of course, some part of my mission requires additional soldiers. Then I will submit a request for you to dispense as many legionnaires to my command as I deem necessary."

Turning for the last time, he was joined by a silent Anthony. The two men exited, walking stride for stride. Anthony, eyes straight ahead, fought back a smile of admiration, absolutely astounded by the *chutzpah* of his commanding officer.

CHAPTER 31
Miracle Worker

The past three days had rushed by faster than Vitus would have dared to imagine. Special ops were known for precision and speed, not sitting around in fields, observing clouds, or listening to homilies. Initially, his assignment to Capernaum felt like punishment, but the hours had flown by. Jeshua's voice was authoritative but not repressive, capturing Vitus's imagination along with the rest of the masses. The way Jeshua interacted with so large a crowd was astonishing. It was as if he spoke to each person individually.

Yesterday, they watched him cup his hands around a blind man's face. The man let out a gasp. "I can see!" he shouted, laughing and crying at the same time. People in the crowd who were close enough watched as glazed pupils turned crystal clear.

"Unbelievable!" Orel muttered, thinking about that scene. At the end of each day, Scipio, Vitus, and Orel discussed what they'd seen and tried to imagine the Centurion's reaction to their report.

Sitting crossed-legged, Scipio shrugged. "How do we explain any of this? I watched the Nazarene do it, and I still don't believe it. If we report this stuff, he'll toss the lot of us into the infirmary and have our heads examined!"

Orel put words to his thoughts. "Seeing is believing, yes? So why does my brain keep searching for a rational explanation? I think I know the answer, but it's Rome's worst nightmare."

Vitus gave him a curious glance. "What is it?"

"Jeshua is the Messiah."

"The Jewish prophetic deliverer?"

"If it occurred to me, you can bet the multitudes are considering it. There's something else gnawing at me."

"Does it have something to do with Lamech's crazy notion?" asked a scowling Vitus.

Orel nodded. "Lamech hated Jeshua with a passion, but after watching him up close these past three days, I keep asking myself, why? He ranted about him, warned me to never mention his name. Lamech painted him as an infidel, a destroyer of Judaism."

"Sounds like he was afraid," said Vitus.

"Afraid of what?" asked Scipio.

"The legend. The ancient prophecy," said Vitus.

Scipio shook his head. "You lost me, Vite."

Vitus turned to Orel. "Lamech was disturbed, you said so yourself. Add his mental state to his fear of religious change, and you get hysteria. He may have also feared that people would see Jeshua as the Christ."

"I thought we were talking about the Messiah?" said Scipio.

"*Messiah* is the Hebrew word for Christ. Both refer to a deliverer."

Scipio forced out a laugh. "To rescue these poor Judeans from the terrible Romans, right? No offense, Orel."

"None taken, Scip." Turning to Vitus, he spoke in Latin, "How can anyone not be impressed with this man?"

"The religious leaders don't look impressed," countered Scipio.

"Maybe they're frightened too," said Vitus. "The Centurion sent us to sniff out insurgent connections with Jeshua, but how do we ignore the stench of jealousy of these, so called, religious leaders emit. They attack relentlessly with pretentious questions. They remind me of circling buzzards, waiting for the right moment to devour their prey. I can picture them privately spinning their webs, hoping to publicly discredit him." Stretching out his arms, Vitus took in a quick breath. "And you think they're not afraid of him?"

"But the man skillfully handles everything they throw at him. They keep falling on their own swords," said Orel happily. "Yesterday, it was the Pharisees and Herodians with that suicidal tax question, remember?"

Vitus laughed sarcastically. "Who could forget? Jeshua wields his words the way we wield our swords."

Parrying the air, Scipio playfully enacted the encounter. "Teacher," he said, making himself out to be a Pharisee with a nasal problem, "we know you have integrity and that you teach God's ways with accuracy!"

Laughing, Orel and Vitus ate up Scipio's performance. "More, more!" they clamored.

"Teacher, you care not about popular opinion or playing to the crowd."

"Boo!" cried Orel, razzing the bad guys.

"So tell us honestly," asked a hammy Scipio, "is it right to pay taxes to Caesar or not?" Shaking his head in disgust, he added, "Damn hypocrites, sham artists!"

Orel was still chuckling. "But Jeshua would have none of it!" Taking his turn to impersonate the Nazarene, he continued, "Why do you play games with me? Show me a coin!"

"Yeah, that was great!" said Scipio, jumping in again. "And the genius hands him a silver piece. 'Whose image and name is on it?'"

Vitus got in on the fun. "Caesar's!" he shouted in a voice of authority. "They never even saw it coming."

Orel took the last act. "Give back to Caesar what is Caesar's and to God what is God's (Matt. 22:17; 18–22 NIV). The fool slinked away, tail between his legs, wondering how Jeshua did it to them again!"

The three broke into laughter until Orel quieted down. "Maybe they've got good reason for being afraid," he mused. "I mean, think of all the outrageous things we've seen in such a short time."

Vitus swallowed involuntarily at the thought.

"I'm starved," said Scipio, his short attention span shifting to his stomach. "It looks like Jeshua has finished for today. What say we head for the nearest town and find something to eat?"

As the three took their leave of the Nazarene, Vitus got the unsettled feeling the underground might approach Jeshua tonight.

CHAPTER 32
Setting the Trap

A solitary figure moved stealthily through the seated crowd, stopping at a patch of grass large enough for one person to sit. This was as close to the Nazarene as he dared to go. No one in this mesmerized crowd of listeners had noticed him, and that was good for the moment. This darkly clad figure wasn't alone; his confederates were hiding nearby in plain sight. Just two weeks ago, Barabbas gushed about Jeshua's unlimited potential, but opinions and perspective were subject to change. Jeshua's teachings weren't militant nor political; the kingdom he talked about was different, otherworldly.

Barabbas sent Simon, a trusted soldier, to convince Jeshua that the *righteous* cause of the Zealots could easily align with his own. However, after two weeks and no word from Simon, Barabbas would wait no longer.

"Should have done the job myself," he fumed, "but today, I'll remedy that mistake."

The people were so actively engaged with Jeshua's teaching that Barabbas felt no need to sit down, forcing those nearest him to stretch and strain, trying to see around him.

This is too easy, he thought. *These people are nothing more than sheep.* But his confidence took a hit when his eyes met Jeshua's. The penetration of his gaze was unsettling. *Does he know who I am?* His mind raced. *Has Simon betrayed me?* he wondered, fighting to hold his emotional ground.

Jeshua commanded the multitude the way a captain commanded a troop. "Your Father knows what you need before you ask him" (Mark 6:8 ESV).

Barabbas was staggered by the thought—Almighty God a heavenly Father? Never had he heard this kind of teaching, nor had any of the listening thousands. The word *father* triggered a childhood memory of Barabbas's own father.

"Barabbas"—his father kissed the top of his head—"*Abba* loves you."

The young boy delighted in his father's affection, but the pleasant memory took a sudden excruciating turn. The recurring nightmare of his father's horrific death had begun to invade his waking moments. Losing himself in this daytime nightmare, he covered his ears to drown out his father's screams. Engulfed by fury, he swore aloud, "Nothing but spilled Roman blood will be enough!"

Aware that he'd had another episode, Barabbas shook himself. How long had it lasted this time? He was still standing, which was a good sign that the spell was short and that it may have gone unnoticed by the people around him. Jeshua was still speaking, and Simon was sitting to his left. Barabbas continued to stand, resolutely waiting for Simon to notice him.

A man, tired of trying to see around Barabbas, voiced his complaint, "Hey, do you mind? You're blocking my view!"

Barabbas ignored him.

"Hey," the man turned up the volume, "did you hear me or what?"

Barabbas was no longer concerned about drawing attention to himself; in fact, a small disturbance might actually help. The Phantom's disregard for others started a swell of frustration.

Additional people joined in the grievance. "Why can't you sit down like the rest of us!"

But Barabbas wasn't about to give up his vertical advantage. He wanted to be noticed and not just by Simon.

*****

Leaders of the Shadow of Death were agitated by the attempt to skirt their questions.

"I ask you again," said an irritated Korah, "what happened to the leader of the ops and his companions? Did they follow you to the Gadarenes?"

"Enough of your endless droning," added Shimron. "None of us care about Simon's mission or his loyalty!"

"*Were you successful?*" Korah hammered out each word. "Did they follow you to the Gadarenes? And are they dead? The demise of these men not only keeps our bargain with Numa alive. It also removes the trail that could lead them back to us."

Barabbas was quick to respond, "So now it's your bargain. That's funny since none of you had a hand in this arrangement!" Barabbas refused to be rushed or bullied by these religious blow-hards. "Patience, gentlemen, each thing connects to another, and it's essential that you hear all of it."

Reluctantly, a red-faced Korah, returned to his seat.

*****

Simon turned an ashen gray color when he spotted Barabbas staring at him. The day he'd been dreading had arrived. Barabbas didn't tolerate excuses. The Zealots would not only consider Simon's mission a failure; they would see him as a traitor. There was only one outcome for that kind of behavior. Ironically, Barabbas's plan for Simon to talk his way into the Nazarene's confidence couldn't have gone smoother, but Jeshua wasn't the one caught off guard. Simon was.

Simon was a changed man, as zealous as ever but for a different cause. He feared his explanation would be met by a knife in his throat before he could finish his sentence.

Peter was concerned by the obvious change in Simon's face and body language.

With a sideways jerk of his head, Barabbas motioned to Simon the Zealot to meet him a distance away from the crowd. A visibly shaken Simon stumbled getting up, then quietly slipped away. He was approached by two Sicarii who escorted him to the meeting site.

Barabbas's mood was indifferent. "Where have you been, Simon?"

Simon tried to maintain his old courage. "Here with the Nazarene where you requested."

Barabbas stood head and shoulders above his old compatriot. "Why did you fail to report?"

"I infiltrated their ranks as you—"

Barabbas refuses to hear the rest, having already made up his mind. "What could have prevented you from reporting back to us, I wonder?"

The Sicarii stood directly behind Simon, waiting for the Phantom's order.

"You've become one of them, haven't you, Simon?"

The Sicariis' unsheathed blades rested on both sides of his rib cage.

"Of all of my soldiers, I considered you the most capable and cunning. We were more than compatriots. We were brothers." His voice rose slightly in volume. "Weak-minded fool, you know the price of betrayal!"

Simon was but a heartbeat away from death when a voice stopped the Sicarii, "Take our lives also!" It was Peter. He approached with John at his side.

Bartholomew, Andrew, and James joined in, "That goes for us too!"

As he did so often, Peter assumed the role of spokesman. "It's true, Simon failed his mission, but that doesn't make him a failure and certainly not a traitor. Everyone who encounters the teacher is changed, most for the better, and Simon, the former Zealot, is no exception. If he's guilty, so are we. Will you kill all of us?"

Barabbas was stunned by the courage and devotion shown to a man they barely knew. Maintaining his poker face, he shook his head in disbelief. He knew there was something different about these men. He signaled to the Sicarii to sheathe their weapons.

"What a waste." These were the last words he would ever speak to Simon. "Imagine what we might have accomplished."

*****

Korah's teeth were clenched in frustration. "Will this wearisome monologue about Simon never end? Yes, the Nazarene has become troublesome, but your directive was to locate the special operatives, not the rabbi!"

"I was about to tie all these things together when you interrupted me yet again," Barabbas continued. "Please sit down. Let me give you the news you've been waiting for. I was set to take my leave of Jeshua and his party when one of my men pointed out the Romans in the crowd, disguised as locals. They looked no more menacing than a ripple breaking on the shore.

"The day was far spent when we broke camp. I didn't leave until I was sure they had noticed me. We chose a heavily traveled road leading away from Capernaum, hoping our three pursuers could follow without being detected. The heavily traveled road also served to camouflage a second party of our men trailing them." Barabbas smiled in appreciation of his own devious ability. "I'm not the gambler that some suppose. Insurance, gentlemen, in case the three moved against us before reaching our intended destination. They split up, trying to remain inconspicuous." Barabbas enjoyed Korah's fidgeting from this little game of delay he was playing

"Well?" said an animated Korah. "Are you waiting for Passover? Get on with it, man!"

"The trick was getting them to follow us across the lake without giving the ruse away, no hesitation at the shore, nothing to cause them pause."

"How did they get a boat?" asked Shimron. "Galileans are ready to fight anyone who dare touch their boats or nets."

"With the help of local fisherman sympathetic to our cause, we arranged for an unattended boat to be waiting for them. We slowed our pace to be sure they wouldn't lose sight of us and to give our men following behind them time as well."

Korah smiled for the first time, "You are a clever—"

"I didn't account for the sudden change in weather. A violent squall with ten-foot swells came crashing down on us about halfway across. My men barely kept us afloat. We couldn't see anything, lost sight of the other boats. Survival was our only priority." The sunbaked lines on Barabbas's face relaxed, replaced by a look of wonderment.

"Mysteriously, the waterspout just ended, going from crashing gale to flat sea. Damndest thing I've ever seen. We bailed water and searched for signs of the others. I'd hoped the storm had finished the Romans for us, but they were still afloat, bailing just like us." Now Barabbas got serious. "I can't swear to it"—his voice barely above a whisper—"but I think I saw the Nazarene out there."

"Jeshua?" said a surprised Shimron. "You were hallucinating."

"My eyes were stinging from all that water spray, but it was right after the storm died. I spied another small craft, not ours or theirs, and there was a man standing at the bow with outstretched arms as if he had just ordered the maelstrom to stop. I know how crazy it sounds, but I witnessed him do fantastic unexplainable things that same day!"

"Have you lost your mind?" Shimron cried divisively.

Korah mocked him as well, "Ridiculous! Your brain was as waterlogged as your boat! Only El Shaddai has authority over nature!"

"As I said, I wouldn't swear to it, but if you could have seen the things Jeshua did that day in the crowd—"

"Enough!" shouted Shimron. "Not another word of this blasphemy!"

Barabbas, recognizing the impasse, moved on. "My men were exhausted when we finally reached the other side of the lake. Our second boat and men were lost in the storm, leaving us without backup. Against these odds, we knew our best chance, maybe our only chance, was the chevah. We waited for the Romans luring them to the Gadarenes."

"Get to the point," demanded Korah. "Did the *special* soldiers perish at the hands of the beast?"

Barabbas paid no regard to Korah's rants. "In our depleted condition, it took the rest of the night to reach the location you'd described. The predawn light was barely enough to identify the Gentile—"

"Cemeteries," said Korah, impatiently finishing his sentence for him.

"Yes, cemeteries, freestanding tombs. These Gentiles have strange customs."

"Get on with it!"

"Not wanting a repeat of the Aurelius fiasco, I kept the chevah in front of us and the closing operatives behind us."

"It was there. You saw it?"

"There was no mistaking the sounds coming from a nearby cave."

Several Shadow leaders swallowed.

"It sounded human for a moment, but then it didn't, weird sounds coming out of the darkness, painful guttural cries. I don't frighten easily and fear no man, but a chill ran through me. I knew the Romans would soon be on us, so I signaled for the men to flank both sides of the cave opening. Its cries turned to terrifying screams and multiple voices, then all sound suddenly stopped as it emerged." Barabbas took a long breath, while his listeners anxiously awaited the next word.

"It was worse than the attack on Aurelius's chamber—far worse. Its eyes were lifeless, and it reeked of death. For the second time in less than a day, I thought I was going to die, but I couldn't have scripted it any better. The chevah ignored us and charged the approaching Romans. The dusky morning rays outlined the shape of the galloping beast. It was on the leader before he could draw his weapon. He tucked and rolled, reaching for his short sword, but the next man wasn't as fortunate. Shredding both armor and flesh with its claws, it went for his throat. The leader tried to stab it from behind, but with frightening speed, it spun around, latching onto him."

Barabbas paused, virtually reliving the story.

"I tell you it's no longer human. The thing flung the leader with incredible force into the side of the mausoleum. Incredibly, he got to his feet, but the chevah battered him with his compatriot's body. Coming from behind the Judean struck a glancing blow, but it grasped and crushed him as if he were a small child. That's when I realized I had to escape, but its black eyes caught sight of me."

"How did you get away?" asked a solemn Korah.

"It was set to charge me when it saw the leader had regained consciousness. That distraction gave me enough time to get to the boat."

"Then it's done," stated an ecstatic Shimron, an evil glint in his eye.

"It nearly cost you your life, but your daring scheme worked," remarked Korah. "It did work, didn't it? The chevah did finish them?"

"No one could survive that onslaught, not even an ancient Assyrian. The beast was preparing to devour them as we pushed away from the shore."

CHAPTER 33
On the Heels of the Phantom

Bruised and bloodied, Vitus rose from his infirmary cot using sheer willpower. Scipio tried to do the same but staggered sideways before being steadied by the Centurion.

"Sir," both saluted, which Atticus waved off, shaking his head at the sight of them.

"The two of you look like hell. Sit down before you fall down."

Both willingly obliged.

Atticus had brought the base *medicus,* with him to check up on them. Vitus's left eye was swollen shut, his scalp was seeping blood, he had several cracked ribs, and his right arm was lacerated from shoulder to elbow. Both men were a bloodied, contused mess. Scipio's movements were slow and deliberate, symptoms of a concussion. The creature had launched both of them into the crypt with such force that bits of stone were still embedded in their skin. Scipio's legs were shredded, his torso a mass of purple, and his face was gashed from forehead to chin. Atticus's eyeballed the pair in disbelief.

"It wouldn't have surprised me to find regulars in this kind of condition but—" Maintaining his tough-guy aura, Atticus turned to the infirmary physician. "How long before they're back on their feet?"

The doctor gave Atticus a look of disbelief. "Commander, these men are fortunate to be alive. Soldiers who undergo this kind of trauma are generally prepared for burial. They may never—"

The Centurion cut him off, "Doc, you have no idea what kind of men these are or what they're capable of!" He turned his back to the doctor. "Did Orel survive?" he asked with concern.

Vitus nodded, wincing with pain. "He's pretty banged up, sir, they're attending his wounds in the home of Lamech."

"I hold him in high regard. He's a good man and soldier for a Judean."

The qualifier caught in Vitus's throat.

Atticus had already moved on. "How many men did they throw at you?" He was still trying to figure out how this happened to his elite soldiers.

"Sir?"

"The Zealots, how many? Fifty? One hundred? They took you from behind, didn't they?" A robust stream of obscenities bounced off the infirmary walls. "Backstabbing cowards!"

"Four, sir."

The Centurion paused. "Come again?"

"Four...there were four of them."

"Four? Four Zealots did this to you?" Atticus ran his hand along the back of his neck, wearing a look of disbelief. "The ten of you took on an entire company during your training mission! Hell, you took on half of them all by yourself!" His focus centered on Vitus. "Something is amiss."

"Maybe I should start from the beginning," said Vitus.

The attending physician broke in, "Commander, these men should be resting, not exhausting themselves with explanations."

Atticus dismissed him with a wave and rested his large body on the edge of Vitus's cot.

Vitus's story was similar to the one Barabbas shared with the Shadow of Death but from a totally different perspective. He began at the hillside at Capernaum, the unofficial headquarters of the Nazarene.

"As you ordered, the three of us made our way to Capernaum, blending in with a stream of pilgrims. The rabbi was holding an open air meeting a mile or so from the Sea of Galilee. We were stunned by the number of people that gathered that first day—Galileans,

Judeans, people from Jerusalem and Idumea, some coming from as far as Tyre and Sidon. After watching him for a day, it wasn't hard to see why. News of him spreads like wildfire, and the people come by the thousands."

"That alone makes him extremely dangerous. What about the insurgents?"

The physician continued to work on Scipio.

"The Zealots were there."

"I knew it!"

"They were conversing with one of his disciples."

"It was a prelude to a bloodbath," Scipio interjected, holding his throbbing head.

"We were too far away to make out what they were saying, but two of the Sicarii looked like they were ready to carve up the one called Simon."

"I've had dealings with the Sicarii—deadly accurate with the blade. But you said you couldn't hear what they were saying. How did you know the disciple's name was Simon?"

"Another one of his disciples, a tall one with a big mouth, called out his name."

Atticus leaned back and crossed his arms.

"Tell me you got something more than that name."

"The Zealot leader is a big man," said Vitus. "Whatever the tall one said to the Sicarii, it worked because they put away their weapons and withdrew. It was obvious to us that something had soured between Jeshua's men and the insurgents, but as to its nature, we have no clue."

"But then our luck changed," added Scipio, who winced from the pain. "We decided to watch, not attack, hoping they would lead us to a bigger catch, maybe even the Phantom."

"We didn't realize they were baiting us," said Vitus.

"They must have done a good job selling it."

"They did, like they planned it all out ahead of time. I think they were expecting us." Vitus paused for a moment and took a breath, trying to manage the searing pain. "They took a heavily traveled road. We followed from a safe distance, keeping alert to the possibility of an ambush."

"Tell him about the lake, Vite!"

"What about the lake?" Atticus asked. "They cornered you at the shoreline with your backs to the sea, right? Additional men were hiding under fishing boats." He shook his head, pushing away the notion. "Still wouldn't have been enough to defeat you or leave you in this kind of condition."

"Nothing like that, sir, we followed them across the sea, keeping them in our sights."

"The storm! Tell him about the storm!"

Vitus cocked his head, a little annoyed with Scipio, unsure how much of the story he wanted to share with the Centurion. "We got caught in a ferocious storm halfway across, and none of us are competent sailors. Couldn't hear anything over the howling wind. Our small boat was bobbing like a cork! The wind, waves, and rain filled the boat. We were sinking." Vitus flashed Scipio a look.

The Centurion unfolded his huge arms. "And yet here you both sit," he added with a touch of sarcasm. "You boys had quite an adventure, didn't you? Sicarii, scary storms. Tell me." He grinned. "Was the storm part of the Zealots' plot too?"

Twenty-one-year-old Vitus took his commander's ribbing in stride.

Atticus smiled. "It would have been all the same to them if the three of you had drowned in that maelstrom. And don't kid yourself. That storm was a lot harder on the three of you. Those guys know their way around sailing vessels."

Scipio could no longer contain himself. "It was crazy, sir, everything just stopped. I mean, the storm did, sir, completely and suddenly, and then there they were on the horizon like they'd been waiting for us. We should have seen it coming. Why didn't we?"

Atticus looked directly at Vitus. "You wanted those Zealots so badly you could taste it. When you let the past rule the present, it clouds your judgment."

"But our training—"

"Training only takes you so far, kid, you learn to trust what's in here"—pointing to his head—"and here." He pointed to his gut. "You were up against their best. How do I know that? You were expertly targeted. Someone went through a lot of trouble to set you up for the kill. The question we better find an answer to is how they got that kind of intel. We'll talk more about that after I hear the rest. What was waiting for you on the other side of that lake?"

Vitus took a moment to answer as he considered Atticus's conclusion. "It was first light when we reached shore, all of us dog-tired. We found their boat, but there was no sign of them. The storm, however, provided a muddy trail that was easy to follow." Vitus shook his head, realizing the Zealots had parlayed that situation too. "Convenient," he whispered. "We kept going, climbing a pretty steep cliff. At the top was a mesa that was a burial site with hundreds of graves."

"We had a bad feeling about that place," said Scipio.

"It was the same feeling we had in the darkness of that grotto. We started making our way through the tombs when a fearsome moan stopped us dead in our tracks. It sounded otherworldly. Before we could locate the source, this thing was on us, shrieking."

As he listened to their tale, the Centurion looked stoic, unflappable. Having served as both soldier and troop commander, he'd seen things that might cause lesser men to collapse.

"So now we know what happened to the creature," sighed Atticus.

"It was on me in a flash, forcing me to move instinctively, shifting to survival skills. I dodged and rolled, trying to gain time, but I cleared a path right to Scipio. Sorry, Scip." He stopped to apologize, but Scipio waved it off. "The thing flew into Scip, and I stabbed at it, but it kept moving at a speed that was ridiculous. Nothing about it was normal. Not even an animal can move that fast, tearing through Scip's armor as if it were made of wax."

Vitus's account even caused the physician to stop stitching up Scipio, prompting Atticus to chuckle at the stunned look on the doctor's face.

"As I stabbed at it a second time, it spun around, using Scipio as a shield and weapon against me. I stopped my forward motion, avoiding a head-to-head collision but couldn't stop its advance. Things started getting fuzzy. It grasped and launched both of us, one in each arm, with great force against the stone tomb. I lost consciousness after that."

Atticus rubbed his misshapen eyelid, trying to put the pieces of this bizarre story together. "It hurled the two of you simultaneously?"

Vitus nodded.

"Do you realize the kind of strength it would need to do that?"

"I do now," said Vitus.

"How is it you're alive? Did Orel save your hides?"

"No, the thing must have turned on him after discarding us. That's what he later told us. We never saw the insurgents, but I heard one yelling to the other seconds before being flung into a stone wall. The voice shouted, '*You did it, Barab!*' as the thing ripped into us."

"By the gods, it was Barabbas you were following! But that changes nothing. How did any of you survive?"

At that instant, a messenger rushed into the infirmary. "Sir, the post commander urgently requests your presence in the officer's hall."

Getting up, Atticus told them, "We'll finish this as soon as I return. Heal quickly. I need the both of you." Atticus exited, following the young messenger out the door.

The doctor finally finished his work. "You're lucky to be alive," he remarked with grave bedside manner. "You need time to heal. If you go back too soon, you'll reopen these wounds. Don't push your luck."

Staring up at the ceiling, Scipio asked, "What are you going to tell him?"

"I don't know," said Vitus, his feet hanging over the side of his cot. "The truth, I guess. What else?"

"I can picture his face when you tell him the Nazarene's part in all this. Maybe you should omit that." Vitus leaned back, putting his good arm behind his head, thinking over Scipio's suggestion.

"We were slammed so hard against that wall it should have killed us," said Vitus. "Maybe we were hallucinating."

"Yeah, my vision was blurred, and my head felt like it had been split in two, but I'm certain I saw the creature kneeling at Jeshua's feet just before I passed out," said Scipio.

Just to be clear; there were four boats caught in the maelstrom that evening. The lead boat contained Barabbas, followed by Vitus, Scipio, and Orel, then a second Zealot boat, and finally, a fourth boat containing Jeshua and several disciples. Barabbas was correct. It was indeed Jeshua he saw standing up in the boat with his arms outstretched against the wind. It was impossible to hear because of the droning gale winds, but Jeshua had just issued a command to the storm, telling it to put a muzzle on it.

Vitus, going in and out of consciousness, caught a glimpse of Jeshua. So what really happened that morning in the Gadarenes? This indeed was the place members of the Shadow of Death had transported Lamech's beast-like son. Several of the townspeople tried to bind it with iron chains, but it broke them as easily as if they were made of straw. After frightening away a stonecutter, it took up residence in the unfinished mausoleum of a rich man.

Area pig farmers were still bringing their herds to graze, but none got within a mile of the beast. Barabbas believed his plan had worked out perfectly. Vitus and company had suffered certain demise at the hand of the raging Chevah. However, in the midst of all the violence and confusion, he had missed the debarkation of a fourth boat. Jeshua had arrived.

CHAPTER 34
Oppius

Striding step for step, the courier and the Centurion made their way to Mercurius's quarters. By design, Atticus was always tardy when responding to a summons, but the word *urgent* coupled with his concern for Oppius made this different. Following military protocol, the courier started to announce their arrival, but Atticus hurriedly shoved him aside.

"You sent for me, Post Commander?" he said, stating a fact more than asking a question. "*Urgent* is the word I was given."

"Yes, perhaps you'd better take a seat."

Atticus refused this courteously. "I don't need to sit down, let's have it!" he demanded, causing the courier to wonder which of these men was the ranking officer.

A man with less patience than Mercurius would have taken offense, but instead he looked with concern at the powerfully built Centurion. He knew Atticus's explosive temper and personal history, wondering if he would maintain appropriate military decorum. Mercurius held the notion that words could take on a life of their own. Thoughts could be distracting, even troubling, but they took on greater impact once spoken. The hulking Centurion's body language was explicit. He was expecting the worst.

Mercurius's speech was solemn, apologetic. "I'm sorry to tell you that Sergeant Oppius has been killed. I realize he was a good—"

Atticus wouldn't let him finish. "And the rest of the men?"

The PC was taken aback. This was not the response he was expecting. "You surprise me, Commander."

Standing tall, Atticus eyed the PC. "When I catch the SOB responsible for this—and make no mistake, I will catch him—he'll be lashed with a *flagrum* till his flesh hangs in strips from his body. I'll be there to listen when he begs for death, and if by some miracle he survives that beating, I'll impale what's left of him on a pole so the birds can peck out his eyes, the rats devour his organs, and the Judean sun rots his corpse! Now, sir, I ask again. What happened to the rest of my men?"

Atticus's savagery sent a shiver through Mercurius. "Only one of Oppius's regulars lived to tell us the tale. Our enemy used an old but time-proven plan: take out the leader, leave the regulars in confusion without direction. The news gets worse. Your special operatives were ambushed responding to the agonizing cry of a surviving legionnaire."

"How many casualties?"

"Julius and Caius are dead. Virius is severely but not mortally wounded. A dozen legionnaires were stripped naked and had been nailed to crosses." Mercurius paused. "One of them was Oppius. The rocky terrain afforded the Zealots invisibility. Oppius's patrol was the first to be caught flatfooted in a crossfire of arrows. They were sitting ducks, half of them slaughtered before they could employ the defensive shield tactic."

"So once again," snarled Atticus, "we were outflanked and outmaneuvered with no avenue for retreat, nowhere to go but into the Sicariis' waiting arms of death."

"Leonidas gathered information from the first attack from its sole survivor, saying they arrived just short of too late."

"Better if they had been too late."

"The rest of the ops split up, four pursuing the retreating insurgents, two attending to the wounded. They cut Oppius down but too late."

Atticus slammed his helmet down hard against Mercurius's desk. "Damned butchers! They knew we were coming!"

Mercurius nodded. "There's no question they have us on our heels, always a step ahead. But how?"

"Isn't it obvious? Someone on the inside is feeding them information? We have a mole."

Unconsciously, Mercurius sat down, his mind evaluating Atticus's theory.

Atticus gave voice to his frustration. "Two more of the Ten are in the infirmary, fortunate to be alive. They barely survived a sophisticated ambush that required coordinated effort." "These attacks leave little room for doubt that the insurgents are getting help. I sent Vitus and Scipio to Capernaum dressed like Judeans to find the connection between the Nazarene and the Zealots."

"Wait, you think Jeshua is in league with the Zealots? You have intel to suggest this?"

"My gut is my best intel. Barabbas was there, having a side session with some of the Nazarene's disciples."

Mercurius straightened up. "Great Jupiter! The Phantom was in their grasp, and they let him walk away?"

"Don't call him that. There's nothing otherworldly about him. He's a bloody hatchet man! They didn't know it was him. They were listening from a distance, maintaining their cover. Vitus made the call to follow, not confront them, hoping for a bigger catch. They followed them, never realizing that they were being lured to their death."

*****

Orel had a noticeable limp, but if Jeshua hadn't intervened, he wouldn't be walking at all. The three men were separated upon their return to the military base. Orel was refused treatment at the infirmary by medical technicians claiming he was not Roman military, but the real reason was his Jewish heritage. Without the Centurion on hand to counter those decisions, Orel was forced to leave the base and his friends to seek help from a Judean physician. It didn't seem to matter that he risked his life to save Roman soldiers. Scipio and Vitus were seriously wounded and in no condition to counter the attending officials. Now one week later, Orel had returned to the infirmary.

"What are you doing here, Jew?" a sentry sneered. "You don't suppose I'm letting you in here, do you?"

"Let him pass," shouted a still recuperating but alert Vitus from across the room.

Keeping his eyes trained on Orel, the sentry called back to Vitus, "But, sir, he's a—"

"A Judean? Good to see you're right on top of things, soldier," Vitus answered sarcastically. "This *Judean* saved my life more than once. Now step aside before someone gets hurt!"

"I wasn't going to hurt him, sir."

"He's not the one I'm worried about. Stand down, soldier!"

A smiling Orel stepped around the bewildered legionnaire to join his convalescing friends.

"Vitus, Scip—you're both looking well."

"Compared to what?" asked Scipio. "How is it you look so good?"

"The truth is you both look terrible. It's a miracle you're alive." Orel's words hung heavily in the air.

"Scip and I have been trying to piece things together. But neither of us can remember much of anything after we collided with that tomb. How did the insurgents manage to relocate the monster without being killed? We can't figure out how any of us survived. How did you?"

Orel was not quick to answer. "Are you sure you're ready to hear this?"

Vitus nodded. "Absolutely, I've got to know!"

"Let's start with you telling me what you remember," said Orel.

"I remember Scipio flying headfirst into a stone wall and, despite my best efforts, being slammed into the same wall."

Orel waited for him to finish. "That's not exactly the way it happened. The thing hoisted the two of you above its head with terrifying strength, like you were weightless."

"Before I blanked out, I think I remember it going after you." Vitus wrestled with bits of recall. "I was being loaded into a boat, voices all around me."

Scipio smirked. "Vitus thinks he saw the beast on his knees in front of the Nazarene!"

His smile faded when Orel remarked, "He did."

For a moment there was silence, no one speaking.

"What happened out there, Orel?" asked Vitus. "How did you manage to defeat it and save us?"

Orel looked at each of them, wondering how he could tell them the truth. He was almost certain they wouldn't believe him.

Scipio pulled himself to an upright position, tearing away strips of bandages that covered his left eye. "So how did you do it?"

"I didn't. When both of you went down, it came after me. I wasn't going to die without putting up a good fight! I reached for my dagger, but compared to the chevah, I was moving in slow motion. It ripped into me."

The dimly lit infirmary was quiet; everyone in earshot was listening intently.

"We were dead men, all of us, if he hadn't shown up at that exact moment."

Scipio was so distracted he forgot about his pain. "What are you talking about?" he demanded. "Barabbas wouldn't have helped—"

"Not Barabbas, Scip, he's talking about Jeshua."

Orel was done holding back. "Yes, Jeshua. I was finished, hemorrhaging blood, when it suddenly backed away, cowering. I was face down, breathing in dirt, when I caught sight of him. I thought I was hallucinating. He must have crossed the lake right behind us in that maelstrom. I blinked several times, trying to clear my vision. Jeshua was walking toward me. With each step, the beast became more unraveled, finally falling to the ground, screaming and contorting."

Orel's story was too fantastic to be true; yet, somehow, they knew it was.

"'What do you want from me, Jeshua, Son of God?' it screamed."

Vitus and Scipio glanced at each other but said nothing.

Orel shook his head. "He commanded it to reveal its name."

"Was he armed?" asked Scipio.

"Not with any weapons I could see, but the cowering chevah obeyed. *'My name,'* it said, *'is Legion,* for *there are many of us inside this man.'* Then like a general, Jeshua ordered them to come out. Can you imagine?"

"So it could speak but a legion of devils? A Roman legion contains more than a thousand soldiers!" Vitus shivered, thinking of the fear he felt in the darkness of that grotto. It was pure evil.

"Its voice was terrifying. Even in my nearness to death, it went right through me. It—I mean, they begged Jeshua to send them into a herd of swine feeding on a nearby hillside. Seconds later, a thousand pigs rushed down the hill to a watery death. The panic-stricken pig herder couldn't get away fast enough!" Orel paused to take a breath. "Do you believe me?"

Vitus answered cautiously, "If we hadn't seen the things Jeshua did in Capernaum... But what about the mortal wounds you described earlier? There are no visible marks on you."

Orel smiled. "You and I were down there in that grotto. Have you ever asked yourself how we survived that experience?" Orel looked into the eyes of his friends. "You question my story because my body doesn't bear it out. My life spark was nearly gone when he knelt next to me, lifting me up to a sitting position. My fear disappeared when he spoke to me, and the searing pain stopped when he placed his hand on my gut." Orel opened his tunic to show them. "See, no damage or scars. I felt power surge through me, healing everything except for my right leg. I think he left it that way so I wouldn't think it had been a dream or something I imagined. This is what I was wearing that day." He pulls out a bloodstained garment from his bundle, putting his fingers through a hole where the fatal blow had been struck. "He instructed one of his disciples to give me water, then he attended to the both of you."

"To us?" cried Scipio.

"That's right."

"I guess his power worked better on you. We're not exactly in the best of health here. Maybe he's partial to Judeans," Scipio chuckled then winced from the pain.

"I can't explain it, but the inside of me was healed too. I started to thank him, to pledge my life to him. He smiled and helped me to my feet, then he attended to the both of you."

Vitus shrugged. "I don't remember any of that." There was no other feasible explanation for how they escaped the monster that had knocked the stuffing out of them.

"What became of the creature—err, man?" asked Scipio.

"That, my friend, is the most amazing part of the story! His transformation was as radical as the storm that went from turbulent waves to calm sea. His voice and appearance became normal. He stood, talked, and acted like a man. He begged Jeshua to let him go with him, but he told him to remain there and show the townspeople the wonderful things God had done for him." Orel shook his head. "I tell you the whole thing was incredible!"

"More like inconceivable," said Scipio. "The monster turned man is now an ally of the Nazarene? The Centurion isn't going to buy a word of this."

CHAPTER 35

Reversal

Some people thrive on hate; they harbor memories so odious that it takes only a scent in the air or the sensation of a cool evening to rekindle the smoldering embers. They're obsessed with the demise of an old enemy. Like a ravenous wolf stalking its prey, they wait for the opportune moment to strike. They subsist on vengeance; nothing else, they believe, will liberate them from their cancerous existence. Hatred is unbiased, infecting rich, poor, wise, foolish, strong, and weak alike. Hatred tells its victims they control the fire burning within, that a controlled fire provides warmth and comfort, even survival. But a blazing fire is always one step away from disaster.

Atticus had reason to hate Barabbas even before Oppius's death, but now he was overcome with revulsion. "Clear the room," he bellowed. "Everyone out—now!"

The room quickly emptied, leaving Atticus alone with the massacred corpse. Romans believe a soldier's soul lives on after death, but if the body isn't buried, the soul will never find rest. Atticus gave no credence to such a mystical idea, yet he refused to allow fallen soldiers under his command to be buried in mass graves. The bloody, often mud-encrusted bodies, were to be identified, if possible, and respectfully buried on the battlefield where they fell. But not Oppius; his body had been returned to Atticus for special burial preparation and honors. This was the accepted practice for Roman generals.

As enemy armies engaged in hand-to-hand combat, fighting became so intense that fallen comrades were either stumbled over or maneuvered around. If the battle ended in retreat, bodies would later be dragged away using makeshift bayonet hooks, then gathered into piles for cremation. For Atticus, it wasn't about moral or religious beliefs; it was about loyalty. He rose in rank the hard way, demonstrating courage, instinct, and intelligence in the heat of battle. More than anything else, Atticus saw himself as a soldier. He was one of them.

Clasping Oppius's blood-stained hand, he forced back a tear and whispered a solemn oath, "I swear to you, the devil will pay for this. I swear it on my life and our friendship. Rest now, my friend, you've more than proven your mettle."

Intending to fetch an orderly for burial preparation, Atticus was caught off guard at the sight of Vitus in the entryway. "I said I wanted everyone out!" he barked.

"Yes, sir, but this is where I remain."

Atticus offered a nod of appreciation, acknowledging a shared mutual respect. "Shouldn't you be in the infirmary?"

"My place is here, Sir." Still in pain, Vitus gingerly walked over to the Centurion. "What are your orders?"

Placing a huge mitt on Vitus's shoulder, he relented, "Let me first attend to Oppius, rest in my quarters for the remainder of the afternoon, and we'll talk later." Atticus would never mention to his young protégé how much his support meant. Though they were nearly a generation apart, they were very much the same man. For all but eight years of his life, Vitus has been fixated on avenging his parents. Only recently had this singular focus altered because of Rebecca.

*****

That evening, the two men met in a tavern. Several flagons had taken the edge off Atticus. "Tomorrow, I'll assemble the remainder of your unit," he said in a moderate tone. "The Ten are now only seven, including you and Scipio, if you're up to the task."

"We will be."

"Good. How is Scipio coming along?"

"You know Scip, hard to kill, fast to mend."

Atticus nodded and then began to relay the grisly details of the attack on the rest of the Ten.

"Julius and Caius were killed by arrows to the throat and chest. The doctor"—Atticus snorted—"doubts that Virius will ever use of his left arm again. The arrow that punctured his shoulder blade severed muscle and tendon." The Centurion took another swallow of wine but maintained his focus.

Vitus was hot. "It wasn't supposed to go like this," he protested. "Not for an elite fighting force!" He took a drink of Atticus's wine. "Our men are better warriors, and we had the element of surprise!"

"*Had*—that's the key word. When you walk into a waiting barrage of arrows, everything is equalized. They baited us on two fronts with a plan to divide and conquer."

Vitus stared in disbelief at the Centurion.

"Ah, the light dawns as at last you see the panoramic view! We were duped, not twice but three times. It was a miracle that the three of you escaped from the Gadarenes alive."

"But how did they pull this off? It doesn't make sense. They would have to know times and places of our—"

"That's right, kid, they would need advanced knowledge of our movements. And clearly, they had it!"

Vitus blankly stared at the Centurion.

"Do I have to spell it out? Your covert mission is in the wind. Now it's time to use that knowledge to our advantage and catch them in their own trap. For weeks now, Pilate has been demanding a progress report on the Aurelius massacre. Let's give him one! Since the presence of the Ten is no longer a secret, let's get Pilate off Mercurius's back and sucker punch Barabbas at the same time—two birds with one stone. How does that sound to you?"

"It sounds great, especially the part where Barabbas takes a punch."

"Anthony and Didius will travel with me to Pilate. I'll lay out the mission as it was outlined by the senate subcommittee. Bringing the governor up to speed no longer matters because our enemy already knows our plans before we execute them, but that's about to change. I may have to oversell a few points to Pilate, might even arrange a little demonstration for him. Pilate will rail on me for not making him aware of the mission sooner. I will humbly agree but press him for replacements. He will spurn my request like the pompous ass he is saying, something like, 'Why do you need additional troops if those soldiers of yours are so extraordinary?'"

The Centurion's guttural belch reverberated across the room, causing a dozen men to raise their cups to him. After a quick cursory scan of the tavern, he continued his impersonation of the governor of Judea. "'If these special ops are half of what you say they are, they should be sufficient to complete the mission!'" Atticus snickered. "He'll finish up with, 'Any senator foolish enough to put a man like you in command should have his head examined!'" Sitting back. Atticus smiled broadly. "Of course, refusing to give me the additional troops is exactly what I want—fewer regulars and fewer distractions. When he's done shooting off his big mouth, I'll drop the news that we know who killed Aurelius and will capture him by the end of the week."

This last statement drew a look of concern on Vitus's face.

"Spit it out, kid, what's troubling you?"

"Sir, should you tell the governor you are ready to abduct the ambassador's killer at this point?"

Atticus chuckled in his raspy voice. "Let me worry about that."

"What about me and Scip? Why are we on the sidelines during this visit?"

"Well, let's see. For starters, you both need a little more downtime to recover. Look at you." He tossed his hand toward Vitus. "Also, I want the two of you to act as bait again once you've sufficiently healed and get me an update on Orel's condition. That man is a good soldier."

A smile lightened Vitus's face. The tough guy cared. "I will, sir."

"Before you go, finish telling me how the three of you managed to cheat certain death."

"Sir, you have a lot of things to attend to. I shouldn't take any more of your time on that tale."

Atticus stared back at him, gingerly rubbing the always irritated eye. He was not buying what Vitus was selling. "How did the creature end up in the Gadarenes? Is it still under the control of the insurgents?

Vitus was slow to respond, "I can say with certainty that he's been neutralized."

"He? You mean *it*, don't you?"

"It turns out that it's a man."

The Centurion was more than a little surprised. "That's a very different story from the first time you encountered it. Look, I don't care if it's man, animal, or—"

Vitus broke in, "It poses no future threat to anyone."

Atticus's massive hand scratched his midday stubble. The look on his face begged the question, *What is it that you're not telling me?* "So the thing is dead? You managed to kill it?" He tried to make sense of the veiled approach.

What Vitus remembered wasn't totally reliable, and if he shared what Orel told them, Atticus would likely judge Orel as no longer reliable. He decided to share a shortened version of what he could recall of the ordeal.

"Sir, in the truest sense, the beast is dead and out of the picture."

Atticus stood to his feet, shoving his chair out of his way. He trusted this young underling as much as he had ever trusted anyone. "So your skills were up to the task after all! I wish I'd been there to see the thing go down."

"You wouldn't have believed it."

"Kid, from what I've already seen you do, I'd have no trouble at all!" Atticus knew that Vitus was guarding something, but he wouldn't push it. "I'll make an adjustment in my report to the governor, tell him that the wild man responsible for the assassination has been eliminated. Is that accurate enough for you?"

Vitus nodded.

"For all we know, the creature may have been Barabbas's trained attack dog." Atticus chose his next words as carefully as a man making his way through a field of cattle droppings. "We'll give Pilate what he's asked for, news that Aurelius's killer is dead. Of course, there's always the possibility he might ask us to produce the body."

Vitus thought for a moment. "There was a large herd of pigs grazing out there. You know pigs, once they get a whiff of a corpse, there wouldn't be much left to find."

Atticus nodded. "After a few more days of rest, I want you, Scipio, and hopefully Orel to revisit the Nazarene. At my next staff meeting, I'll be sure that Numa hears about the impending arrest of Simon the Zealot, from Jeshua's inner circle, playing up the idea that Simon is the key to Barabbas."

"Commander, you should know that the masses flock by the thousands to the Nazarene. They practically worship him."

"From what I hear, the people are ready to coronate him!"

"Simon is a member of Jeshua's inner circle now. Arresting him will likely create a riot."

A muscle in the big man's temple flinched. "Even if I thought he was dangerous, I wouldn't be so foolish to openly arrest him. I have no concern for his welfare or his crowd-pleasing rabbi. I'm after bigger fish. I'm about to drop a story in Numa's lap that will start the kind of fire we need."

*****

Rebecca had only seen the Mediterranean Sea once in her life, but she imagined starting a new life there with Vitus, far away from the scorn and ridicule of family. Aware of the kind of problems a marriage with him, would create, she had a heart-to-heart conversation with herself, but it was no use. Each trip to the village well was filled with hopeful anticipation of seeing him.

Today, she was having a conversation with a woman who recently returned to Emmaus after a twelve-year hiatus. This woman, twenty years her senior, had already formed a bond with her. Her warmth and kindness were calming, but Rebecca was in for a shock.

"You're a woman now, but your face hasn't changed. I knew your mother, father, and sisters. Are they well?"

Rebecca was taken aback.

"When I last saw you, you were no more than five, bouncing on your father's knee." Her gentle voice stirred childhood memories.

Rebecca smiled. "You voice is familiar. I remember you talking with my Emma. You had a son a little older than me."

The woman's face displayed surprise. "I'm amazed you remember that. You were very young."

"I can almost see his face. There was a man too. He was tall, and I was frightened of him."

"My husband. I suppose he was scary to some of the people in Emmaus. He was a soldier," she said pensively.

"A Roman soldier?"

"Yes." The woman paused. "An officer."

Rebecca chose her next words carefully. "If I may I ask, where have you been these many years?"

Sadness settled over the woman who stared at the ground.

"It's a long story, my daughter." She paused. "Some things are beyond our control."

Rebecca was silent.

"Twelve years ago, I was forced to leave home and family."

"Why? Who would do such a terrible thing to you?"

A smile lit the older woman's eyes. She remembered being just as innocent and naive as Rebecca. "The illness that threatened my health also struck fear into the hearts of Emmaus's people. Fear can do terrible things. Good people forced me to leave my home." Her eyes well up. "The disease took everything I cared about—my home, my son, and my husband."

Rebecca, feeling at a loss, stated the obvious, "But you look so well now!" Somehow, this woman's past seemed eerily similar to her present situation. Could this be an omen? She wondered. "What happened to your husband and son?" she asked softly.

The woman offered a halfhearted smile. "Decimus sent our son to his ancestral home in Tuscany for his safety."

"Decimus was your husband?"

"Yes, and Decimus fell victim to the man he had been after." Hot tears again streamed down her cheeks as if these tragic events had only recently happened. "He suffered a terrible death at the hand of the Zealots."

Rebecca began to process the tragic details. A child of mixed heritage that would be about the same age as Vitus, her husband, the Roman officer, killed by the Zealots, just like Vitus's father—there were too many matching pieces for it to be coincidence.

"I'm so sorry"—Rebecca wrapped her arms around the woman, trying to console her—"for all the pain you've suffered." Inwardly, she wrestled with these disturbing details. One piece didn't fit—Vitus's mother was a casualty of the Zealots, so this couldn't be the same person.

"It's all right," the woman sighed, "it was long ago. It's foolish for me to carry on so."

"Emma, there's something I'd like to ask you, but I fear it might cause you more pain."

"Judging from the aggrieved look on your face, you'll have no peace unless you do. It's all right, little one, ask me."

Rebecca blurted out, "Is your son's name Vitus?"

CHAPTER 36
A Twist

Members of his staff fidgeted uneasily in their seats, waiting for the meeting to begin. They'd heard the Centurion, who would soon arrive, was on the warpath. They stood in unison as he entered the room, carefully avoiding eye contact. Numa seemed especially anxious to get this over with.

Atticus was curt. "Take your seats." The silence was broken by the sound of chair legs sliding over stone floor. His icy stare traveled from soldier to soldier. "Let me speak plainly. In my estimation, the lot of you are about as valuable as what exits the south end of a swine!" His real target was the traitorous Numa, but attacking the whole assembly served his purpose. "Sergeant Oppius was a superior soldier. He deserved better." Atticus paused. "After desecrating his body, they hoisted it on a pole, intending to send a message, and what was that message?" Again, he paused, waiting for one of these fools to offer an answer, but none dared to. "That scum bucket you've dubbed Phantom is telling us that he is in control. He violates one of our finest soldiers, mocking us, daring us to do something about it!" Atticus's white-knuckled rage had the entire staff quaking. "The lot of you make me vomit!"

There was no comment or excuse offered, all eyes looking down.

"What? No snappy comeback from our distinguished Tesserarius?" His remarks were directed to Numa. "Two of my best soldiers were served up on a platter for the damned Zealots!" He gave them a look that might melt steel. "Incredibly, they survived."

No comments, no eye contact.

"*Gentlemen*, we're going to get to the bottom of this, or I swear, by the gods, one of you will be the Phantom's next trophy!"

No comments, no eye contact.

"Well, what do you to say for yourselves?"

"Sir, we—"

"Shut up, Gaius, you wouldn't recognize a good plan if it crawled up your crack. Anyone else?"

No comments, no eye contact.

"I'm done playing the fool for Barabbas and his butchers. It ends today!"

Numa saw his opportunity. "Sir, it sounds like you already have a plan worked out."

"Sir?" Atticus's sarcastic tone was biting. "That's a twist coming from you, Tesserarius. You're correct, I do indeed have a plan that not even you geniuses can screw up! Until now, we've been reacting, following false leads, lured into their tidy little ambushes. Give the devil his due. He's kept us off balance, kept us on the defensive. We have nothing to show for our efforts but death and injury because we never knew where he will strike next—until now." Atticus's dangling comment promoted a rumble of discussion.

"Sir?" asked Gaius cautiously. "How can you possibly know this?"

The Centurion straightened his frame. "The Nazarene is going to help us."

"The Nazarene?" Numa blurted out. "Why would a man who has no interest in politics help Romans?"

"And just how would you know that? Have you been attending his meetings?"

Caught off guard and embarrassed, Numa attempted a recovery. "Common knowledge and local tavern talk," he snapped.

"Let me tell you what isn't common knowledge. One of his disciples is a Zealot. Simon the Zealot," he continued, "is a member of Jeshua's inner circle. Perhaps Jeshua isn't as far removed from nationalistic politics as you imagined."

In the next few minutes, Atticus relayed the details of a plan that he had no intention of implementing, feeding false information that he knew Numa would channel back to Barabbas. "Governor Pilate has ordered me to send what's left of the Ten to a meeting in Caesarea, all except Vitus and Scipio. I'm sending them to arrest Simon. Before I'm through interrogating him, he'll tell us everything: patterns of operation, strongholds, and hideouts, including the location of the Zealots' next attack. Gentlemen, we will catch him in his own trap and nail that insurgent to the same cross that held Oppius."

Smiles and nods of affirmation transformed the mood of the room from solemn to jubilant.

"Questions?"

Numa smiled. "It's a good plan, sir, I'm impressed."

"You're impressed? How magnificent! Maybe you can impress the rest of us by performing competently."

A red-faced Numa held his emotions in check; he needed more information, so he chose his words carefully. "Even if Simon has gained the confidence of the Nazarene, how can you be sure his information will be current or reliable?"

"Two men I would trust with my life paid dearly to obtain that information for us. I'm sure because they watched Simon conversing with Barabbas while the Nazarene droned on about a kingdom that's *not of this world.*"

Numa nodded, acknowledging that the Centurion had indeed covered the angles. But how, he wondered, could he get the details he needed?

"When will you initiate the plan?"

"Timing is critical and execution tricky, which is where you come in. I need assistance in working out the particulars, getting everyone in the right place at the right time. I'm not worried about the Nazarene getting word to Barabbas. He recruited Simon for non-revolutionary reasons. It's Simon who has other plans.

"There is little time to waste. The intel we get out of Simon will have shelf life. Jeshua will be holding meetings outside of Bethany within the week. In the morning, Anthony and the operatives depart for their meeting with Pilate. Vitus and Scipio will be in Bethany by midweek. The beginning of the end is about to commence."

*****

At the conclusion of the meeting, Numa slunk away to a prearranged meeting with Flavius; it seemed the timing for defectors was equally critical.

"One more meeting," he snickered, "will be sufficient to take care of Vitus and company forever." Even more important to Numa was that the Centurion suffered public humiliation and military disgrace. He was so preoccupied that he failed to notice he'd been followed.

Lurking in the shadows was a man he didn't know but who was perfect for this kind of assignment. He waited for Numa to enter the tavern, giving him time to get comfortable, then he casually followed, sitting at a table suitable for listening to another man's conversation. He portrayed himself as the kind of man who'd come to drink, but he listened intently to every spoken word.

*****

On the other side of the city, three men met privately behind closed doors. Atticus began the conversation, "The pieces are in motion now. If all goes well, Orel will bring me information from our traitorous friend, Numa, that should include the name of his coconspirator." Atticus took a breath in. "I want to gut him and be done with it."

Vitus leaned in closer. "Glad we're on the same side."

Atticus smiled.

"So it's set. Scip and I will bait the trap by arresting Simon the Zealot, when the crowd isn't engaged with Jeshua."

"Let's be clear about this. You're going to *ask* him to accompany you under the pretense of answering a few questions. Arrest him only if it becomes absolutely necessary."

"Got it, and upon leaving the camp, expect the Zealots to be waiting for us."

"Are you sure you're up for this? I'm not going to gamble your lives over this. I need you to be straight with me!"

Vitus grinned; no one would ever believe this side of the Centurion existed. Vitus's relationship with Atticus was far more than soldier to officer.

There was no hesitation from Vitus. "I'm more than ready. What about you, Scip?"

Scipio nodded and winked. "Absolutely."

"All my life, I've been waiting for this. Barabbas murdered my parents. I won't fail."

Waiting for Vitus to finish, Scipio repeated the plan aloud, "We're going to lead the Zealots to the waiting arms of thirty regulars. Will thirty regulars and the two of us be enough to handle Barabbas and his Sicarii? Are we certain that none of these legionnaires have thrown in with this conspiracy?"

"Numa isn't a field soldier, he's an administrator with no connection to infantry regulars. But after tonight, I'll have a clearer picture. The Judean guardsman is an amazing soldier and ally. Orel has forced me to reconsider this whole Judean situation, something I didn't think was possible."

Vitus broke into a silent chuckle.

"What's so funny soldier?"

"Yesterday, Orel was saying the same thing about you, sir."

Atticus raised an eyebrow.

"What if Barabbas doesn't show up when we spring the trap?" asked Scipio.

"He'll be there. No man with a head as big as his will miss the chance to take out the operative sent to kill him. Just before he plunges the knife into your heart, he'll want to look into your eyes, savor the sense of hopeless that comes when you realize you've been played."

"Twist and double twist—I can't wait!" said Scipio.

"Neither can I, kid, neither can I."

*****

Just as planned, Orel shared the information he learned with the Centurion that evening.

Atticus rubbed his hands together with delight. "Excellent. Just as I expected." He shook the guardsman's hand so hard it jarred his whole body. "I'm in your debt, Orel. I know you see Vitus and Scipio as family. If you're still willing to help, I'd like you to travel with them to Bethany. The three of you make quite a team."

Orel nodded. "I'm in."

"Answer me one question before you go."

Orel figured this would be about the trio's miraculous escape from the Gadarenes, but it wasn't.

"That night of Aurelius's assassination, Mercurius told me your assistance was invaluable. You not only surprised him, you have me perplexed, and that's not easy to do. Why does the bodyguard of a priest jump in and help his enemy?"

Orel stood motionless as if searching for the answer. "I've asked myself that question several times. My answer will probably surprise you again. I believe God's invisible hand directed me that night. I have no logical explanation for many of the things I've witnessed these past weeks. I'm convinced that Elohim is at work here and that his purposes are higher than any Jew's or Roman's."

CHAPTER 37
Reunion at the Well

She studied every line of his face, searching for a recognizable feature. She promised she would be discreet, but she couldn't look away. She had to find out if it was him. The woman didn't have the look of a person whose illness had nearly killed them. After twelve years and numerous doctors, her prognosis was no better and her pockets empty. Sadly, every visit had ended with the same phrase: "I'm sorry, there's nothing I can do."

Dejected and penniless, she resigned herself to wait for death to overtake her, but all that changed after her encounter with the young rabbi from Nazareth.

Her chestnut hair had streaks of gray, but her face had the look of a woman in her late thirties. The village well at Emmaus was bustling with activity today, and thanks to Rebecca, she had come at the right time of day to see him. She hoped to stay out of his line of sight but get close enough for a good look. She had often tried to picture him as an adult. Could this really be him? Taking a breath, she moved closer, then abruptly stopped "What if it isn't him?" she whispered.

Orel and Scipio visited Emmaus's local pub, affording Vitus the privacy to meet with Rebecca. He has arrived in the midmorning hour, the usual time of Rebecca's arrival at the well. His keen peripheral vision alerted him to a would-be stalker. Turning casually, he scanned the landscape; his eyes came to rest on a woman who was doing her best to look inconspicuous.

The last thing an undercover soldier wants is attention, but this inquisitive woman was definitely interested in him. Deciding the direct approach was the best way to end this guessing game, he walked toward her, smiling, hoping to keep her calm.

Her knees went wobbly as he approached, wondering if she would be able to speak.

"Woman," he said, speaking in Aramaic, "is there something I can help you with?" His body language and tone held no threat. "Are you looking for someone?"

Her eyes filled up at the sound of his voice. Embarrassed, she bowed her head toward the ground. Marshaling her courage, she took a step toward him. Her gentle voice was almost apologetic. "May I ask your name?"

Caught off guard by this question, he replied, "Who are you?"

Hot tears stream down her cheeks. This was her son! She was sure of it! For years, she had prayed to see him, to speak to him. She resisted the urge to run to him and kiss him, and for the first time in his military life, Vitus was unsure of what to do next.

She could stand it no longer. "Your name is Vitus. It means new life! I'm"—she paused—"I'm your Emma!" She covered her mouth, shocked at the sound of her own words.

Vitus was stunned at this declaration, wagged his head in protest. "My mother is dead!"

"I was dead!" She brushed away tears. "Dead to my husband, to my people, and you!"

Vitus shook his head again, trying to weigh this woman's sincerity against his rising anger. "You cannot be my mother! My father buried her!"

The woman's interwoven fingers were pressed against her chin. She couldn't lose him again.

"Dear woman, I know you think I'm your son, but—"

She persisted, "Your father, Decimus, was a Roman officer." Her eyes filled again. "You adored him." A smile lightened her countenance. "And you look so much like him." She sighed. "same eyes and mouth." Her cadence hastened. "He sent you away to Tuscany."

She searched for any sign of recognition or acceptance, knowing how contrary all this must sound.

Vitus was perplexed. How could she know these things? But Decimus had given him specific details to the manner of his mother's death, and they were confirmed by Claude. The Zealots murdered her eleven years ago, then also claimed his father's life. But the facts remained—this woman knew specific details about his life; what other plausible explanation could there be?

"Why would Decimus lie to me? He was an honorable man, not a narcissist." His face flushed red.

"To protect you."

Vitus's green eyes widened. "From marauding rebels, right?" He smirked. "I remember his last words to me: 'I'm sending you to a place where you'll be safe where those animals that killed your mother can't get to you.'"

"He thought he could bury the truth with me, it was meant to spare you. Both of us knew the certainty of my death." The woman had taken a risk meeting Vitus like this, and it wasn't going the way she had hoped. Her analytical son reminded her so much of her husband that she lapsed back into her painful past.

*****

The illness had begun with nothing more than an irregular menstrual cycle, but every doctor's diagnosis would be the same: "You have an incurable blood disorder." As the unyielding disease progressed, her large eyes became sunken orbs.

This beautiful Judean girl and handsome Roman officer met at the village well in Emmaus. Decimus was highly intelligent with the commanding presence of a great leader.

The Roman Senate enlisted him to take charge of its military campaign in the always troublesome region of Judea. His charismatic leadership caused him to gain favor over more experienced officers. He was assigned the rank of *Magister Peditum*, with authority nearly equal to a governor. The responsibility for solving the festering insurrection in Judea lay squarely on his shoulders.

When others hesitated, Decimus moved decisively, always in control of situations, people, and his emotions—until he met her. Her soft brown eyes captivated him; she would not be another of his conquests. He tried to deny her power over him, but his heart was undone by her gentle spirit.

Roman military protocol forbade military personnel from marrying foreigners. But neither that nor the heated objections of her family could deter Decimus. They believed their love was deeper than custom, regulation, language, or discrimination. But matters intensified after they were married; her Judean father declared her dead to the family, leaving her isolated and inconsolable. She drowned her sorrows in the care of her newborn son, showering him with the love she'd been denied.

By the time Vitus reached eight, she was very ill. A Jewish woman with a hemorrhaging menstrual problem was ceremonially unclean and prohibited from attending synagogue. Because the bleeding never stopped, she couldn't complete purification rites. Local religious elders pronounced her cursed by God. Her sadistic illness was slowly killing her.

Decimus faced a difficult decision in what to do with their son. There would be no help from her disenfranchised family. With the child already having night terrors, he feared he would be scarred by the long-protracted death of his mother. Exhausted in mind and body, he sent Vitus to his ancestral home in Tuscany where he would be spared the rejection and ethnic bigotry his mother had endured.

With Vitus out of danger, Decimus devoted himself to caring for his ailing wife, but it took its toll on his ability to command. He missed critical signs of danger, eventually following bogus intelligence leading him to believe he had trapped the insurgents in a canyon hideout. He realized too late that he'd been baited into an ambush that would cost the life of every man in his troop. Arrows rained down like hail stones until the massacre was complete. This was the coming out party for Barabbas, the beginning of a legacy.

Barabbas's legend continued to grow until one Roman legionary dubbed him the Phantom.

*****

Vitus was speechless, thoughtfully considering this alternate reality.

"You were barely eight," she reasoned. "We didn't know what was best for you. Your father wanted to protect you from the physical and emotional pain tearing us apart. I was gravely ill with no hope of recovery."

Vitus slumped back against a nearby stone wall.

"Claude never approved of your father's decision to marry a Judean, so he told him I was dead and that he needed his help to raise you."

Vitus was quiet. "How can I know what to believe now?" he asked.

"The truth, my son, is that you're only half Roman. You know this to be true, but whether you accept it or not, you are my son. I'm the daughter of Zaccur, your Judean grandfather. You grew up speaking the language of two nations. The customs of our people live deep within you. You must know these things I'm telling you are true!"

Her words struck a chord inside him, a kind of calm acceptance. "What happened to you, Emma?"

She looked deeply into the eyes of her son. "After twelve years of fighting a losing battle with my disease, I was alone, penniless, and destitute—death was my only companion."

Vitus squeezed her hand, wishing he could have been there to help.

He studied her carefully. "There was no visible evidence that suggested such a struggle."

He was so engrossed in her story he didn't notice the person standing behind him.

"Listen to her, Vitus." Rebecca's voice caught him off guard—not an easy thing to do.

"Rebecca!"

Smiling, she stepped between mother and son. "I see you two have met," she said softly. Sliding an arm around the woman's waist, Rebecca pulled her close, hugging and kissing her on the cheek.

"Isn't she wonderful?" the woman remarked, causing Rebecca to display her dimples. "She's the reason I found you," she stated but paused to correct herself. "No, it was Yahweh that has done this, but Rebecca has been his partner." She patted Rebecca's shoulder, then resumed her amazing story. "I was very thin and weak, skin stretched over bones. In those final moments, I prayed to Yahweh to see my son one last time." Rebecca held her close. "When I opened my eyes, there was a young man kneeling beside me. The disease had taken most of my vision. 'Are you Vitus?' I asked.

"'My name is Luke,' he said, 'I'm a physician, and I've been sent to get you.'

"His gentle touch was comforting. He saw my face in a dream," he said, "and a voice told him where to find me and to take me to Jeshua. The man isn't even Jewish!"

"This doctor took you to Jeshua?" Vitus asked, anxious to hear more.

"He carried me most of the way. I was too weak to walk. He was so positive that I was going to be healed that I started believing it too. Jeshua was already attending to the needs of the crowd, walking among the people when we arrived. The people pressed in against him, so many of them calling him, vying for his attention. Even if I had all my strength, I knew I couldn't push through that crowd. My heart sank, and my body went limp.

"'Don't give up,' Luke cried. But I collapsed, despondent and exhausted. The crowd pressure became so intense it separated me from the doctor. I could see Jeshua walking toward me. Unable to stand, I stretched out my arm as far as I could, hoping to touch the hem of his tunic. People stepped on and tripped over me, but I felt his garment brush my fingers as he passed by. My vision instantly cleared. I could see perfectly, and strength returned to my body.

"Jeshua stopped, 'Who touched me?' he cried.

"Everyone withdrew, afraid to be labeled as the guilty offender.

"'Someone here touched me,' he insisted, 'I felt power flow from me.'

"I stepped toward him, head bowed to beg his forgiveness, but he smiled and took my hand, caressing it. I can't tell you how wonderful it was. He told me I had amazing faith and that my days of suffering were over."

Rebecca, welling up with tears, hugged her tightly.

"When I later examined myself, the hemorrhaging had completely stopped, just as he had said."

Vitus felt like he'd fallen out of a tree. His mother was alive, and her story was miraculous. The driving force of his life had always been centered on avenging his parents, but now that goal was altered. His mother didn't need to be avenged; she received something far better, and from Jeshua, the man Vitus had been spying on. Time stood still as Vitus tried to digest the life-altering revelations of the past hour. Suddenly the three of them were joined by Scipio and Orel. It seemed only fitting that these four people should be the first to meet each other. He wondered, if the Nazarene somehow had played a part in this reunion as well? The two people he most trusted were about to meet the two people he would lay down his life for. Vitus began the introductions, "Orel and Scipio, my two greatest friends, meet Rebecca and my mother." At this pronouncement, both men displayed the same jaw-dropping look of surprise. After a detailed explanation, the five of them bonded the way a family did when overcoming a common struggle. Vitus was elated at the realization that his mother was alive but also conflicted. If his father lied about his mother's death, what else did he lie about?

CHAPTER 38
Crosscurrents

It was a forty-mile hike from Sebaste to Jericho, where Jeshua was holding open-air meetings. A three-day walk for a civilian, two days for a legionnaire, and one for special ops. Since Vitus and company were still mending physically, Atticus had allowed for additional time, including a short stopover in Bethany. There was also the question of their battle readiness, but even physically compromised, they were far more capable and dangerous than regulars.

Atticus's plan was for the regulars and operatives to rendezvous at Jericho in three days. This would give Vitus time to rejoin Orel and Scipio before they reached the city. After the two groups met, the regulars would take the longer route passing through eastern Judea into Perea. This was the route most Galileans used because it circumvented Samaria. Judeans held such contempt for Samaritans that they'd willingly add an extra day of travel to avoid incidental contact. Vitus, Scipio, and Orel would rest an extra day, then take the shorter less-traveled route to preserve energy. If all went as planned, both groups would arrive the same time in slightly different locations.

As they entered Samaria, Vitus's thoughts were on Rebecca, his mother, and Jeshua to whom he owed a debt of gratitude. Orel interrupted his friend's solitude of thought.

"You're miles away. What's going on in that head of yours?"

Vitus smiled but made no response.

"You're not the same intensely focused guy I've come to know these past months. Who are you? And what've you done with my friend?"

Vitus smiled but kept his gaze straight ahead.

Orel wouldn't let it go. "It's Rebecca, isn't it?"

Vitus gave him a quick look.

"Yup, that's what I thought."

"It's Rebecca, my mother, the Nazarene...but mostly Rebecca, I guess. It's crazy the way he's become so entwined in my life, all our lives."

"It's remarkable," said Orel.

"You boneheads may see it that way, but I don't!" added Scipio. "To me, he's just an assignment, and that's what he's supposed to be for all of us."

"Come on, Scip, we wouldn't have survived that attack in the Gadarenes if it wasn't for him."

Walking briskly, they looked straight ahead, not at one another.

"According to Orel, but we don't really know what happened out there. Neither of us remembers anything!"

"We were unconscious," Vitus insisted. "The thing would certainly have finished us off!"

Scipio continued to look straight ahead.

"The three of us have gotten pretty close these past weeks. You've had the same chance to judge his character as I have," remarked Vitus. "Why would Orel make up a tale like that?"

"I'm saying the rabbi isn't even a soldier. How could he do what we couldn't do? The thing tossed us around like helpless children. How could an untrained civilian handle that kind of raw power? Maybe Orel was delirious and imagined it. Maybe the creature lost interest and moved on. I know one thing for sure." Scipio snorted. "Before this guy"—he gestured toward Orel—"we were brothers, even closer than brothers."

Vitus stopped abruptly, staring at Scipio. Orel was silent as Vitus and Scipio faced off.

"Is that what this is about? You think Orel is more important to me than you?"

Scipio looked down at the ground. "A lot of things have changed, Vite, you said it yourself. Rebecca, your mother, and now the Nazarene. Things are not the same. You're not the same."

It took a moment for Vitus to respond. "You're right, Scip, a lot has changed, but not everything." He placed a hand on Scipio's shoulder. "I value your sword, strength, and friendship as much as ever. There's no one I trust to guard my back more than you! We're still brothers. The only thing that's changed is our family has expanded." He shot a look over to Orel. "I have another brother now, and so do you. We're blood, Scip."

Scipio nodded in agreement. "Sorry, Orel."

"No problem, Scip, I'm glad to be here with both of you."

*****

In the city of Phasaelis, a pit stop for Roman legionnaires, Barabbas was meeting with several key leaders of the Shadow of Death. As always, Issachar was at his side. Issa was concerned about the increased frequency of Barabbas's spells, which were now occurring in the day. Only Issachar was close enough to notice what was happening to him.

Barabbas was attending this meeting to discuss an urgent matter but had been unable to speak because Shimron and Korah were engaged in a vehement argument.

"You're not facing the facts," Korah stated emphatically, "the man has become a greater danger than the damned Special Forces. It's time we call the Nazarene's activities what they are—a clear and present danger. We've been so concerned about a few soldiers that we've turned a blind eye to the bigger issue."

"Which is?" asked Shimron.

Korah gave Shimron a look of disbelief. "If the Nazarene is allowed to continue on his present course, he will completely win over the uneducated masses if he hasn't already. There are undercurrents, rumors about him being the *Messiah*. Can any of you deny this?"

No one commented.

Barabbas believed Korah was right, having previously entertained the notion himself. This was the reason that he had sent, Simon, to join Jeshua's ranks.

Korah continued, "He's bewitched the masses with tricks and sorcery. Tobiah, the scribe, was an eye witness. Five thousand fed from nothing but two fishes and five barley loaves!" Korah grew increasingly agitated. "The rabble are comparing him to Moses who gave us manna from heaven! How much longer before they hail him king?"

Barabbas, exasperated with the arrogance of these men, broke into Korah's tirade, "Where would that leave all of you?" His innuendo caught them off guard. "Is it his words or the authority behind them that most concerns you? With each passing day, he usurps more of your power over the masses." Barabbas had no intention of making such statements. He was ecstatic to share his news that the Zealots now had a Roman conspirator who had already turned over the Centurion's plans to them.

But his remarks had Korah on the verge of losing his self-control. "You think because they call you Phantom you can speak to me this way? That the likes of you can now tell us what is correct? Your job is to keep the Romans off balance and out of our affairs. But it seems that assignment is too difficult for you and your men!"

Barabbas, usually a master at deflecting personal jabs, was having trouble maintaining his cool. "Perhaps, my fine gentlemen, you should ask yourselves what you're really after since you can't seem to agree on a course of action," he retorted. "When I told you about the Nazarene's potential to be a great help or threat, you rebuked me, told me to concentrate on the Romans. I came here today to tell you that I'm poised to deliver what you requested: an end of the special ops threat, but I couldn't even get the words out. All you can talk about is bringing down the Nazarene. Yes, he is popular with the masses, but a clear and present danger? He's a soft soap Messiah, who speaks only of love and peace."

"You're a fool or blind or both if you can't see the danger he presents!" said Korah.

"Oh, I see the danger, sir!" Barabbas was dangerously close to alienating his greatest benefactors. "It is you who are incapable of seeing it!"

"How dare you lecture us!" Shimron's eyes flashed with fury. "Your instructions were to take out the ringleader along with the rest of this insignificant force of special soldiers!"

Barabbas tried to speak, but Shimron talked over him, "Only weeks ago, you boasted about the ambush at the Gadarenes—*slaughtered* was the word you used. They had been slaughtered beyond recognition by the chevah. Now days later, we hear that this Vitus is still alive, but we shouldn't worry because once again, you've come up with the perfect solution if we move quickly. So tell me, Phantom, which is it? Are you incompetent or a liar? As for myself, I think you're both. What else, I wonder, have you lied to us about?"

A bead of perspiration trickled down Barabbas's temple, struggling to control the fire raging inside him "I'm not a liar or a fraud! We Zealots fight for love of country to liberate our people. My men have sacrificed everything, even their lives!"

Issachar watched his friend's nostrils flare, a sign that he was about to lose it. Pushing his shoulder-length hair back, Barabbas revealed the tattoo, צלמות, behind his left ear, the emblem of the Shadow of Death. "Every one of my men bears this mark as a sign of commitment to the cause. Tell me, Shimron, what have you sacrificed?"

Appealing to reason, Barabbas switched gears. "These special ops are like no other threat we've ever faced. They're capable of bringing down the entire Judean underground, which is why we must beat them to the punch!"

Ira, a priest who regularly made inflammatory statements, pushed back the sleeve of his tunic, revealing the same identifying mark worn by the Zealots.

"I also bear the mark of the SOD," added Ira in an accusatory tone. "We brand ourselves in spite of the Torah's warnings." His expression was almost emotionless as he stared at Barabbas and Issachar. "It's not your passion that's in question, it's your judgment. You worry about falling pebbles, we worry about boulders. Perhaps your concerns are correct. The operatives might shut down the rebellion. They may even catch and crucify you and your lieutenants before it's all over." He flashed a wicked smile. "Wouldn't that be a shame?"

Ira's comments invoked a flurry of undercurrent from the seated company.

Barabbas pictured the point of his short sword exiting the back of Ira's throat. He pushed him too far this time. Barabbas rose to his feet, his hand on the handle of his weapon.

"Barabb!" Issachar shouted, his eyes large as saucers.

Barabbas's eyes looked lifeless, his killer instinct overcoming his reason. Issachar jumped to his side, ready to defend him.

The armed contingency of priestly bodyguards immediately moved to intercept the threat, their gleaming swords all trained on the two men.

CHAPTER 39

To Catch a Ghost

The atmosphere was so emotionally charged that one wrong word might trigger an eruption of violence. Tola, one of the three scribes, stood to his feet, signaling for calm. "Brothers, let's calm down. Our enemies are outside these doors, not inside." His voice was steady and calm. "My brothers, let us think about what we are doing here. Please put away your weapons. Let's sit down and resume our business"—he glanced at Ira—"and keep a civil tongue."

Tola's influence was evident; everyone except Barabbas and Issachar returned to their places around the knee-high tables. Tola tried to clarify the situation, addressing his remarks to Barabbas who was still on his feet. "These men"—gesturing to those seated—"are worried that the Nazarene will bring the full power of the empire crashing down on us." Tola was composed, unruffled; his interlocked fingers rested on the table before him.

Barabbas and Issachar returned to their seats.

"I'm sure you're familiar with the phrase 'There is no king but Caesar.' This is the only truth that concerns Emperor Tiberius as it relates to Judea and its surrounding regions. It is, therefore, incumbent upon us to strike a balance that will maintain the status quo. Survival first, freedom second—these are our priorities, where our bests interests lie. I will agree there are moments when it's hard to determine where our best interests lie." He looked directly at Barabbas. "I hope that you are able to see the bigger picture in all this. If you cannot, our passions and pathways have already separated."

Barabbas took in a breath and squared his shoulders. "Our interests lie with securing freedom for our people."

"Whose people?" said Shimron sharply, causing the tension level to climb again.

Barabbas made his position clear, "With or without your help, we will take down the Special Operatives. I can say with absolute certainty that the Nazarene has no political aspirations. I could present clear evidence to support this, but your ears and hearts are already closed."

A disappointed Tola was silent. Realizing there was nothing else to say, Barabbas and Issachar began to make their exit as the eyes of their former allies burned into them.

"Can we afford to let him go?" asked Shimron in a quiet voice. "We may yet have need of him."

"No," remarked Korah, "let him go. Our business with the Zealots is finished. If they do manage to take out what's left of the Ten, it will still serve our purpose. Any repercussions resulting from their actions from this point on will be viewed as acts of desperation, but we will have plausible deniability. Rome will see us as the men who worked toward a peaceful coexistence with Caesar."

"We don't need assassins to bring down the Nazarene," quipped the ill-tempered Ira. "We need brilliant debaters and scholars who can publicly discredit him. Catch him with his own words and build a case of blasphemy against him. It is time I call in a favor from Annas, our former high priest. He has the ear of Caiaphas, his son-in-law, the current high priest. They already lean in that direction, so let's nudge them to issue a warning. Anyone who calls the Nazarene the Messiah will be immediately excommunicated from synagogues and the temple."

*****

On schedule, Vitus, Scipio, and Orel approached Jericho around midday. The pilgrims who swelled the roads with their numbers would lead them to Jeshua. Wherever the Nazarene traveled, thousands followed.

Even from a mile away, the hillside teeming with people was visible. Scipio scanned the landscape, bringing a reaction from Vitus. "You're not going to do that when we get there, are you?" Vitus remarked to Scipio.

"Stop looking around so much, you're making me nervous," said Orel.

They'd rehearsed the plan a dozen times during the long walk—wait for the opportune moment, peacefully approach Simon, and don't arouse suspicion. Barabbas should already be there waiting for them. This would be his second attempt to kill them. If things went according to plan, they would lead the insurgents into the waiting arms of thirty legionnaires. But Vitus didn't know that Numa had arranged a double bluff with Issachar's help. Two naive legionnaires, thinking they were following the Centurion's orders, would soon approach them with last-minute changes. The two soldiers would intercept Vitus less than a quarter of a mile from Jeshua's meeting place, carrying a missive that bore Atticus's seal.

From a distance, Vitus and Scipio saw two legionnaires in full gear standing along the side of the road, actively checking the parade of passing pilgrims.

"Something is amiss," said Orel.

"What are those fools doing here?" asked Scipio.

The soldiers' eyes light up, having spotted Vitus and company walking toward them. They stepped through the flow of traffic to meet them, offering military salutes and drawing curious stares from the passing travelers.

"Put your hand down!" Vitus tried to muffle his stern response.

The soldiers quickly aborted their salutes. "Sorry, sir—," one replied.

"Don't 'sir' me," said Vitus, "you're destroying our cover!"

The legionnaire on Vitus's left spoke first. "We have an urgent message from Commander Atticus."

Vitus wondered how these two geniuses ever picked them out of the crowd, figuring it had to be from a detailed description from the Centurion.

"Let's get out of this flow of people," said Orel. Vitus nodded, and the five made their way to the side of the road, an easy task considering how Judeans wanted to avoid contact with Romans.

Vitus read the orders: "Do not proceed to Nazarene's meeting place or approach Simon the Zealot. Rendezvous with large troop first."

Vitus was puzzled by the unusual change in orders. The missive wasn't in Atticus's own hand, but that was not unusual. He had dictated messages to scribes before, and the wax seal impression was spot on. "I don't get this," he mumbled to Scipio and Orel.

"Neither do I," remarked Sipco, "but orders are orders."

Vitus turned to the messengers. "You two will accompany us."

The five men turned and waded into the incoming tide of pilgrims. After two miles of backtracking, Scipio began to bellyache, "Guess this trip wasn't long enough. What's a few more miles. No big deal, right? I mean, we're only the walking wounded here!"

The words were barely out of his mouth when the Zealots emerged from the travelers moving toward them. Blades gleaming, the insurgents rushed the five head-on while a second group attacked from behind. The attack was so swift that the young legionnaires were stabbed in the throat and ribs before they could deliver a blow.

There was no time to shout instructions. Vitus and company relied on training and instinct moving faster than their assassins. Scipio and Vitus were at half strength; Orel was whole but lacked specialized combat skills.

The Sicarii were deadly with the short blade but still no match for the speed and athleticism of these special ops. Barabbas had hoped the stream of travelers would limit the trio's ability to defend themselves.

As the fighting intensified, additional insurgents rushed in to fill the circle vacated by pilgrims running for their lives. Orel went down, stabbed in the shoulder blade. Fifteen Zealot warriors also went down, but there were still too many of them. Vitus and Scipio stood back-to-back, surrounded and exhausted, unsure if the blood on them was their own or their enemy's. The rebels moved in for the kill but were stopped by the command of the Phantom.

"Hold!" barked Barabbas to his men. "Lower your weapons!" he shouted to Vitus. "Let's talk."

Vitus and Scipio stood resolutely.

"You have my word my men will not harm you while under my protection."

"Why should we trust a murderer and terrorist?" shouted Vitus.

Barabbas stood tall at six feet, wearing a smirk of triumph. "What choice do you have? Now lower your weapons so we may attend to our wounded and you to yours."

Scipio and Vitus, crouching with weapons extended, looked at each other for a brief moment; the decision belonged to Vitus. When he lowered his sword, Scipio followed. The Sicarii pounced on them, binding their hands behind them.

Vitus protested, "You said we could attend to our wounded friend."

"Later," he smirked. "Take this one," having pointed at Orel, "along with the rest of our wounded."

At the hillside clearing where Jeshua was teaching, a commotion stirred the placid throng. Travelers who just witnessed the attack were filtering into the seated masses, sharing their disturbing news.

"We barely escaped with our lives! It was horrible!" a woman told the person nearest to her. The news rippled through the crowd.

Always aware of his surroundings, Jeshua responded to the troubled crowd.

"Come to me, all of you who are weary and carry heavy burdens, and I will give you rest. Take my yoke upon you. Let me teach you, because I am humble and gentle at heart, and you will find rest for your souls" (Matt. 11:28–29 NLT).

The crowd calmed down as Jeshua continued, but six men spread throughout the multitude simultaneously moved to the outer edges of the crowd. Leonidas, Julius, Caius, Didius, Anthony, and Cyrus came together to confer.

"They should have been here by now," said Leonidas with a sense of alarm. "The attack has to be the reason."

"Let's go," cried Anthony.

"Yes, but to where?" asked Caius.

Anthony assumes leadership. "In the direction those frightened Judeans just came from."

"What are we looking for?" asked Leonidas.

"This is Vitus and Scipio we're talking about," said Anthony. "They'll have left a trail of death behind them for us to follow. Let's move!"

Moving wounded men was a difficult and time-consuming task; moving a lifeless corpse was even worse. Fifteen Zealots went down; only four of them were still alive. The insurgents dragged the dead bodies into the untamed undergrowth. Then, by Barabbas's order, the remainder of his forty men split up. Twelve would stay behind to tend to the dead; the others would carry the wounded along with Orel, Vitus, and Scipio to a prearranged dwelling outside Jericho's city limits.

When they arrived at their destination, Vitus and Scipio were tossed to a corner of the room. They protested the lack of care for Orel, reminding Barabbas of his promise.

"He's not dead yet," Barabbas quipped, "but that won't be the case if he doesn't receive attention soon. You'd be wise to not waste precious time that would be better used assisting him. Cooperate with us, and we'll save your comrade. Oppose us, and it won't go well for any of you."

Vitus struggled to contain the hate coursing through him.

"Issa," Barabbas called to his friend, "we've killed what? Five hundred Romans?"

"More like a thousand," Issachar replied.

"Have you ever seen one with eyes like this?" He nodded toward Vitus.

"Nope, this one hates you with a vengeance from hell. He stinks of it!"

Barabbas sat down about three feet from a trussed and bloody Vitus, shaking his head in disbelief.

"Tell me, Roman, how did you and these others escape the beast? I watched him pitch you like a bale of hay. You were helpless in its grasp! The three of you were set to be his next meal."

Vitus's blazing eyes were locked on Barabbas, but he didn't answer.

"Yet here you are. still alive. but for how long? That's the question."

Vitus didn't reply.

"For as long as I wish it and not one second longer, Roman!" The Phantom leaned back, studying the sheer revulsion Vitus held for him. "What is it that causes you to hate me this much, Roman?"

Vitus, convinced they were all going to die anyway, decided to speak. "You think yourself a hero, a freedom fighter," he seethed. "You're a terrorist, a murderer, a common thug who enjoys what he does."

Scipio's eyes flashed in disbelief. "Vite, don't!"

"You murdered my father, a great soldier of Rome."

Barabbas nodded. "I knew it, the officer with special training much like your own."

"You know nothing about it!"

"I know everything about it, Roman dog! I was just a boy when Roman legionnaires slaughtered the people of my village. The memory of it is still fresh, still haunts my dreams and waking hours. They descended on us like locusts, forced me to watch as they savagely beat my father, so don't tell me I don't understand!"

Vitus was taken aback by Barabbas's story, his own hatred momentarily stemmed. He felt an unexplainable affinity for the man he had spent most of his life planning to kill.

"How did you escape?" Vitus asked with a sincerity that surprised the Zealot leader.

Barabbas paused, considering whether or not to answer him. "That's the amusing part," he said sarcastically, "it was a young Roman officer that saved me. He told the soldier pummeling me that he'd kill him if he didn't stop."

Vitus was silent.

"What was your father's name?"

Vitus stared at his captor; the situation had moved from strange to bizarre. After a short delay, he replied, "His name was Decimus."

Barabbas's face showed recognition. "I remember him, he hounded me, forced me to kill him. He was a fool, and you followed in his footsteps, but unlike him, you're going to die a slow and painful death. But before you do, you're going to tell me everything. If necessary, I'll torture and kill your friends, one at a time, while you watch. If your resolve still holds, I've been told there's a young woman you care about."

Vitus's calm turned to rage. "Your intel is faulty. There is no woman."

At that moment, a Roman legionnaire stepped forward. It was Flavius.

"Rebecca." Flavius smiled wickedly. "Her name is Rebecca." He was delighted to finally get his revenge for the beating Vitus gave him. "You thought you were so special—"

Vitus cut him off, "I'm going to kill you!"

Flavius laughed. "You're not going to be around enough to kill anyone! And after you're dead, I'll go back to that little tramp's village and pay her a visit." Flavius was suddenly struck by a ferocious backhand, knocking him to the floor. Barabbas was there, standing over him.

"Traitorous dog, who gave you leave to talk? Utter another word, and I'll kill you myself! Stay down there on the floor and crawl away, out of my sight, like the dog you are." He turned back to a distraught Vitus. "I hold all the cards, Roman, but if you tell me what I want to know, I'll spare the girl, maybe even kill this traitor for you. What do you say?"

Head down, Vitus didn't respond. Barabbas's promises were worthless.

"No comment?" He turned to Issachar. "Kill his friends. Start with the wounded one, and take your time. We're in no rush!"

One of the Sicarii flipped Orel over with his foot. "This one has lost a lot of blood. We only have to—"

The enraged Phantom grabbed Vitus's head, propping him up to ensure he watched.

"*Are you deaf?*" he shouted to the Sicarii. "Open him up so this one can watch his intestines slide out."

243

The Sicarii, knife in hand, was poised to pierce Orel's abdomen but suddenly dropped to the floor. Chaos enveloped the room. Leonidas and Didius attacked with furious speed on the right while Anthony and Cyrus advanced from the left. The close-quarter battle magnified their remarkable abilities, the larger enemy force falling fast and silently.

"Don't kill the leader!" shouted Vitus. "The Centurion needs him alive!"

CHAPTER 40
Prisoner

Leonidas stood less than a foot from Barabbas's face. "So this is the terrifying Phantom," he chided, then delivered a blow to his sternum that sent him stumbling backward. With his hands bound behind him, he looked like a sheep trussed for slaughter. Leonidas wasn't yet finished; crouching down, he mocked him in Aramaic, "Not so scary now, are you, Phantom?"

A dejected, hurting Barabbas wondered how it had come to this.

"Leonidas," called Anthony, "your time would be better spent helping me untie these two."

Leonidas grudgingly nodded and rose.

Vitus could think of nothing but getting help for Orel, whom he believed had been seriously wounded. "Cyrus," he called, "Orel needs immediate attention!"

Cyrus was the Ten's acting medic, having two years of medical training. He had defended his village from rogue marauders, driving them off, surprising himself in the process. When the opportunity came to train under Dmitri, he believed it to be a higher calling and left his medical dream behind.

"We arrived just short of too late," said a beaming Anthony, working with Leonidas to free Vitus and Scipio. Scipio massaged the rope burns on his wrists while surveying the remains of the mostly deceased Zealot troop.

Rising slowly, Vitus stood over Flavius's mangled corpse. Scipio stood next to him. Neither could look away. Scipio nudged the head with his foot, then checked for a pulse.

"One less enemy of Rome," Scipio stated in Latin.

Vitus followed in Aramaic, "One less sadist to threaten Judeans." Rubbing the bump on the back of his head, Scipio nodded in agreement.

Still gazing at Flavius, Scipio asked Vitus, "What's the word Judeans use when they strongly agree?"

"Amen!"

As he stared at Flavius's lifeless body, he was both pleased and disappointed. Finally turning away, he joined Cyrus still at work on Orel's gashed back.

"How is he?"

"He's lost a lot of blood. The Sicarii use circular blades."

"Does that cause a more serious wound?" asked Vitus.

"No, it probably saved his life. The wound is wide but not as deep. He's lucky. It missed the artery by a thread or he'd already be dead. There's some muscle damage, all repairable once I get the bleeding stopped."

"So he's going to be okay?"

Orel, lying on his stomach and in considerable pain, grunted, "Can't get rid of me that easy."

A smiling Cyrus tapped the back of Orel's head. "Stop moving around or I'll let you bleed to death."

Ignoring both Cyrus and pain, Orel tried to sit up. "Scipio, check behind the ears!"

"Of these Zealots? Tell me why."

"Just do it," he winced.

Scipio and the rest of the Ops examined the fallen insurgents.

"Each man has a tattoo," said Anthony, "some kind of identifying mark. It might be Hebrew, but I have no idea what it means."

Taking a breath, Orel pushed out his words, "Tell them, Vitus."

Surprised, the operatives turned toward Vitus who began to explain, "You're right, Anthony, the letters are Hebrew. The word translates 'Shadow of Death.'"

"Hold still, Orel," yelled Cyrus, "before I stitch the wrong parts back together!"

Grabbing a fistful of hair, Scipio ferociously yanked Barabbas's head sideways, to reveal the same mark.

"What's this all about, Phantom?" demanded Scipio.

His silence resulted in Scipio kicking him in the ribs, and Barabbas writhed in pain. "I asked you a question!" said a seething Scipio. "What's the matter, *beast* got your tongue?" He was about to lay into him again when Vitus stopped him.

"Take it easy, Scip, remember, the Centurion wants him breathing,"

Scipio bristled. "Broken ribs and breathing is not the same thing."

"It symbolizes our loyalty and dedication to the cause," remarked Issachar, breaking the silence. "Now leave him alone!"

"Issa, shut up," urged Barabbas.

Issachar obeyed the instruction, turning away with contempt.

Satisfied that he'd done all he could do for now, Cyrus got Orel into an upright position, which made talking less painful. Orel tried to explain, "It's their philosophy. It connects the Zealots to David, Israel's greatest king. In his most famous psalm, David wrote about a place that is both figurative and literal. 'Though I walk through the valley of the *shadow of death* (*tsal-mavet*), I will fear no evil.'"

After listening intently, Issachar offered a passionate response, "We put away our fears and vowed to fight Roman oppression and cruelty! You accuse us of murder, but who are the real killers here?" Vitus, unmoved by Issachar's babblings, glanced at Flavius's lifeless corpse, then back at Issachar.

"You made the deal with this one, didn't you?"

Barabbas pleaded, "Issa, please, don't say anything else."

"No, Roman, I did not! He was nothing, only a messenger following—"

Barabbas kicked Issachar over. "Shut up, you fool!"

"Numa," remarks Vitus. "It was Numa who sent those two soldiers with bogus orders, knowing it would cost their lives."

Scipio was steaming. "Time we give Numa what he's been ask-ing for."

Vitus smiled. "I'd be very surprised if the Centurion hasn't taken care of that already." Turning to Anthony, he asked, "Speaking of Atticus, you guys were supposed to be in Sebaste, putting on a show for Pilate, while we led the rebels into the waiting arms of a company of regulars."

"Barabbas is sly," Anthony allowed, "but so is the Centurion." "He pulled a double bluff of his own, sending us ahead of you to hide among Jeshua's listeners. Atticus kept it from you, hoping to blind-side the Zealots into taking the bait, which they did. The troop of legionnaires was just a decoy, but when Numa sent those false orders, things got a little dicey."

"The wax-sealed orders," said Vitus. "I'm guessing Numa lifted Atticus's signet, hoping its absence wouldn't be noticed until it was too late."

Anthony interrupted with a sense of urgency, "We should clear out of this place as soon as possible. Too dangerous to stay any longer."

Vitus turned to Cyrus, "Can Orel travel?"

"If you don't want those stitches to open, we'll need to build a litter."

"I can walk, forget the litter."

"I'll see to it," said Anthony. "What about you and Scipio?"

"I'll make it. What about you, Scip?"

A hurting Scipio gave Vitus a thumb's up.

"Okay, then, as soon as that stretcher is ready, we move out."

"Someone has to get word to the Centurion," said Antony.

"I'll do it," said Leonidas. "I'll take one of the horses the regulars used."

While Leonidas rode furiously to Sebaste, his companions worked quickly. While one group scouted for a new campsite, a sec-ond attended to the dead. Anthony and Didius took the assignment of guarding Barabbas.

Orel was not regressing, which gave Vitus one less thing to worry about. His thoughts rushed back to the Nazarene, thinking of the way their paths had intersected. Could destiny have taken a hand here? His encounters with Jeshua had saved the lives of his friends and family. Dmitri's platitude echoed in his mind, *Our life's pathways are already laid out before we take a single breath.*

*****

Two days later, Leonidas returned to the now deserted Zealot hiding place, carrying new orders from the Centurion. From there he followed clues that only a member of the Ten would recognize. Vitus is the first to greet him. "That was faster than I expected!"

"A small company of reinforcements are a half a day behind me. They should arrive by morning."

"How did the Centurion react to the news about the Phantom's capture?"

"The way you imagined he would: no visible emotional display, but inside, the man was dancing. He couldn't hide his delight when I described the way it went down."

Vitus broke into a smile. "I wish I could have been there when you told him."

"The first thing he asked about was his wounded prodigy. He was more concerned about you than the capture of the damn Phantom. He was also concerned about Orel. Has that old buzzard changed his mind about Judeans?"

Again Vitus smiled, knowing the other side of the Centurion.

Leonidas surveyed the camp. "Any sign of rebel activity?"

"No, it's as silent as Barabbas. Has me worried."

"I told Atticus about Numa's order switch, the death of the young legionnaires, and your team being captured."

"Oh, man, that must have blown the top of his head off!"

"The stream of obscenities blistered my ears."

The two friends burst into laughter.

"I almost feel sorry for Numa. Can you imagine his fate when Atticus gets his hands on him?"

"It's already done. When I mentioned Numa forging his signet...holy, things really got ugly!"

"What happened?"

"An official report will be sent back to Numa's family, telling how their son died bravely in battle. The Centurion wouldn't tell me what he really did to him."

"Numa was a staffer. He never even sniffed a battlefield!"

"That's not what the report will state. It seems the poor guy was the victim of, are you ready for this? A Zealot ambush."

"I suppose none of us will shed any tears over that parasite," said Vitus. "What about Atticus's orders?"

Leonidas slapped his forehead, "Right, the orders that I nearly killed my horse for racing back here." Leonides read from the missive:

> Do not transport prisoner back to Sebaste.
> Enlist aid of regulars to transport Barabbas to
> military compound in Jerusalem. Post round the
> clock guard. Pilate heading to Jerusalem. Will
> join you there.

"The Centurion," Leonidas continued, "wants first crack at the Phantom, before Pilate arrives. He seemed certain that there would be a rebel attempt to free Barabbas during transit to Jerusalem. He said, and I quote, 'Expect it.'"

CHAPTER 41
Jerusalem

The Centurion had delivered on his promise to Pontius Pilate to capture or kill the Phantom. Ready to conclude his business with the governor, he offered his closing remarks.

"Prefect, with Passover holiday nearly upon us, I've ordered my men to transport the war criminal, Barabbas, to the Tower of Antoni, Jerusalem's most secure prison."

Tribune Lucius jumped to his feet in protest. "You had no right to make that decision! The arrangement was for him to be imprisoned here in Herod's Caesarean Praetorium."

Ignoring Lucius's outburst, Atticus defended his decision to Pilate. "The distance from Jericho to Jerusalem is shorter and safer, a half-day journey compared to the two-day trek to Caesarea. Additionally, the Jewish Festival of Unleavened Bread compounds the danger of transit because of pilgrim-congested roads. To transport Barabbas to Caesarea under these conditions is tempting fate. Even in a weakened state, the Zealots will attempt to free their leader. We reduce the enemy's strategic advantage by taking the shorter, direct route to Jerusalem. Finally, Prefect, since you intend to make your annual trek to Jerusalem for Passover celebration, it seemed prudent to have the war criminal there waiting for you." Atticus rested his hand on the handle of his sheathed sword, waiting for permission to leave, but Pilate was deliberate, forcing the Centurion to wait on his pleasure.

Pilate began, "I've made no secret of the fact that I don't like you, Centurion, and I'm not inclined to change my opinion."

Atticus should have been put off by this remark, but he wasn't. He knew Lucius had poisoned the prefect against him. Atticus had never been a man to play the game of political expediency for the sake of advancement.

Pilate continued, "I'm less than satisfied with your explanation regarding the ambassador's assassin. I want evidence, not assurances that the job is done." Pilate tilted his head toward Lucius, who'd been silent since his initial outburst. A barely perceptible smile lightened Pilate's eyes as he turned back to face the Centurion. "That being said, I am impressed with the rest of your work in this matter. Your leadership over this diminutive fighting unit is impressive. Their actions were decisive and swift, lopping off the head of the insurgent snake. And unlike my tribune, I am in complete agreement with moving Barabbas to Antoni prison. My officials estimate two million pilgrims will be traveling for Passover. It will be challenging even for my official transport to get through such congestion. I look forward with anticipation to my visit to Jerusalem. I will personally oversee the Phantom's examination."

Atticus's damaged eye twitched when Pilate attached the ghost-like status to Barabbas, a term he detested.

"We will take full advantage of Jerusalem's bulging populace! More eyes to witness the denigration of their national hero! It couldn't have worked out better! He'll be crucified on their holiest holiday and on the highest hill overseeing Jerusalem. The residents call that place Golgotha, but our executioners refer to it as the place of the skull." This prompted a chuckle from the indifferent prefect. "My report to Tiberius will reflect favorably on you and your men, and you will extend my compliments to them."

The Centurion nodded in recognition of the prefect's unusually high praise.

"Once Barabbas has been imprisoned in Jerusalem, I will see to it you and your men are rewarded."

Atticus's eyes acknowledged only Pilate as he offered the compulsory salute before making his exit. Getting to Jerusalem quickly was his next priority.

*****

Amon and Jothan, Hebrew scholars who had attended Jeshua's forum at Jericho, stood ready to present their report. Both men were indignant as they presented their news to Korah.

Jothan was emotionally charged as he recounted Jeshua's words. "Truly I tell you," Jothan recited, "whoever obeys my word will never see death."

Korah gasped. "Those were his exact words? Are you certain?"

"Positively," asserted Amnon. "I heard them too, and I immediately challenged him. 'Do you think you're greater than our father, Abraham, who died?' I asked. 'Just who do you think you are?'"

Korah's eyes continued to shift between the men, following their discourse. The degree of their emotional investment was disconcerting. "Shimron selected you for this assignment because of your textural scholarship. We sent the two of you for the sake of corroboration as Moses had suggested in using two witnesses. At this stage of our investigation, accuracy is critical. Do you understand?"

Both men nodded.

"All right, then, continue with your report."

Jothan proceeded to quote Jeshua, "You don't know my Father." Jothan paused, taking an exasperated breath. "But I know him. If I said I didn't know Him I would be a liar like you but I do know him and obey His word. Your father Abraham rejoiced at the thought of seeing my day; he saw it and was glad." (John 8:19–20 NLT)

Amnon broke in, "'You're not yet fifty years old, but you've seen Abraham?' I said, but that deceiver just kept going. 'I tell you the truth,' he said, "before Abraham was, I Am." (John 8:58 NLT)

Korah's jaw dropped, momentarily stunned. "Unbelievable! He's claiming to be God! This is the ultimate blasphemy!" he raged. "I can appreciate your outrage. Is there more?"

"We were enraged and quickly searched for rocks to stone him, but when we looked up, he was gone."

"What do you mean gone? He slipped away through the crowd?"

"No, there wasn't time. He was gone, like he vanished."

"I will share all of this with my colleagues, except that part about his disappearance. I don't want that mentioned again, is that clear?"

Both men, glancing at each other, nodded.

"My thanks to you both."

In an ill mood, Korah presented Amnon and Jothan's report to members of the SOD (Shadow of Death), repeating verbatim the Nazarene's words as they were relayed to him. The place broke into an uproar. Shouting and cursing, they demanded immediate action against the Nazarene. The boisterous Ira was the most vocal of all.

Ira's high-pitched voice rose above the crowd. "What more do we need to hear?" he asked, ripping his tunic. "He is worthy of death!"

The charged atmosphere morphed into mob mentality. Korah, seizing the opportunity, raised his voice above the tumult. "We have, at last, the element we've needed to take down the Nazarene." The room quieted. "Let me be clear, these events have already been set in motion."

The ever-caustic Ira broke in, "What events?"

"You all know we have sought the means to penetrate the Nazarene's circle of twelve *disciples*." He uttered the word *disciple* as though it left a bad taste in his mouth. "Barabbas failed to do this with Simon the Zealot, but we have succeeded!" With all eyes riveted on him, Korah savored his moment of power. "One of Jeshua's twelve has agreed to our terms."

"How reliable is this information you're selling?" demanded a jealous Ira. "It sounds a little too good to be true!"

Tola, the most respected member of the group, stood to add credibility to Korah's words. "So reliable," he added, "that price and payment have already been struck—thirty silver coins."

"Why would this person turn on his mentor for such a paltry sum? It barely pays the price of a burial!"

"What makes a man do anything?" snapped Korah. "Jealousy, delusion, power struggle, or just plain greed? I don't care about his motives as long as they serve the greater good. The sum of money we offered is inconsequential to him. He was all about getting the deed done."

"What, specifically, have we agreed to?" asked Shimron.

"On the night of the Passover, our insider will excuse himself at the conclusion of the meal, feigning a matter that simply can't wait. He will meet us at a prearranged spot, and from there, he will lead our men to the place they will be staying for the night."

"And he has agreed to do all this, knowing we intend to turn his teacher over to Pilate for crucifixion?" asked Ira.

"Do you take me for a fool? Pilate was never mentioned. He will assume the Nazarene will be brought before the Sanhedrin," said Korah, "and we let him think that."

"So you lied?" said Ira.

"Withholding information isn't lying," Korah replied.

Ira nodded and smiled in agreement.

"What about Barabbas?" asked Shimron.

"What about him?" said Korah.

Shimron continued, "The operatives who captured him did what no other Romans could do, delivering a crushing blow to the Zealots. Interestingly, it happened much the way Barabbas warned it might, making his words sound prophetic."

"His misfortune, not ours," added Ira. "We were right to cut him loose when we did."

Tola's temper flared. "You really are a coldhearted bastard, aren't you?" For Tola, such language was out of place. "Misguided or not, the man was dedicated to our cause and served us faithfully for years. His arrest is not just his misfortune. It's ours as well. If he talks, our heads are in the noose along with his."

Ira was first to respond. "Unfortunately, you're right," he bellowed. "Why couldn't the man have the decency to die with the rest of his soldiers?"

"Pontius Pilate is about to make his annual trek to Jerusalem for Passover," said Korah. "When he arrives, he will celebrate, interrogate, and execute his long-awaited prize, the Phantom."

"Barabbas will be imprisoned here in Jerusalem?" asked Ira. "Shouldn't they take him back to Pilate's palace in Caesarea?" Ira's eyes grew large as he considered the situation. "If he implicates us, we will deny everything!"

An annoyed Tola rebuffed him, "Can you deny the tattoo you so blatantly displayed to Barabbas? If he wasn't sure before, he is certain now that we all have them. If he talks, our situation becomes unpredictable. We must come up with a plan of our own concerning Barabbas."

CHAPTER 42
Reunion

Leonidas and Anthony finally settled on the safest route for reaching Jerusalem. After weighing the risks of overcrowded highways versus off-road trails, they decided it was better to face what they could see on the open road than be blindsided by what they couldn't in the outback. Orel continued to protest from his makeshift stretcher, insisting he could walk, but Vitus wouldn't relent.

"Stay in that litter or those wounds will be the least of your problems!"

Orel begrudgingly settled back.

Barabbas and Issachar, fettered hand and foot, were poked and prodded by several of the regular reinforcements sent by Atticus. After tripping over their own feet for the first hundred yards, the two men worked out a complementary rhythm. Being clasped in leg irons was a new experience for both.

Anxious to impress their counterparts, the regulars stayed on high alert, continually checking for signs of trouble on the swollen highways. Employing Vitus's directions, the troop maintained a twenty-foot perimeter of defense. They traveled in a formation of legionnaires three deep on every side. The regulars were on the outer walls of this moving rectangle and the ops the center core. The logjam should keep pilgrims intent on passing them in single file. Vitus had noticed several suspicious faces in the crowd searching for an opening, then disappearing after finding none. If archers should attack, they would employ the shield defense posture. The regulars were startled when Anthony yanked a young man inside the moving wall of defense. It happened so fast that only Vitus's shout kept Anthony from plunging his short sword into the young man.

"Wait, check for the mark!"

Maintaining a steel grip on the young man's wrist, Anthony forcefully manhandled him, checking behind the ear.

"He's clean," he scowled. "You came this close"—displaying the space between thumb and index finger—"to the end of your life!" He shoved the visibly shaken youth outside of the moving convoy.

"I think the kid soiled himself," said Anthony, the most soft-spoken of the Ten. "That was not my intent."

"Don't worry about it," Scipio yelled from the far end of the perimeter. "He shouldn't have been in such a hurry to push past us!"

"We're five miles outside the city limits," Leonidas estimated. "One of us should run ahead to alert the prison guards to be ready to receive our 'special' prisoner."

"Send two of the regulars," said Scipio.

Vitus shot him a smile. "I think Leonidas might have something else in mind." Leonidas's wide grin accentuated his rugged features. "The fastest man should be the one to go."

"Look at him," said Anthony. "He can't wait to burn off some energy."

As soon as Vitus nodded, Leonidas cleared the front buffer of soldiers and broke into a measured gallop.

"If he keeps that pace up, he'll reach the city in fifteen minutes," said Scipio.

Several hours after Leonidas's departure, the troop marched into Jerusalem, having suffered no further incidents. Roman sentries, alerted by the fleet-footed Leonidas, stood ready at attention. Behind the sentries was a company of twenty soldiers ready to escort the prisoners to the tower prison. The Fortress of Antonia, as it was formerly known, was built by Herod the Great, Antipas's father. Its impressive walls were 115 feet high and surrounded by a 165-foot-wide ravine—it was an impregnable prison. The former palace was now a military headquarters where six hundred Roman soldiers were garrisoned.

As he crossed the penitentiary threshold, Barabbas exhaled. He'd heard how badly the prisoners of Antonia were treated. The only escape was death either by torture or suicide. Roman guards kept a careful watch, intent on foiling a prisoner's attempts to prematurely end his suffering. A man who refused to eat would be force-fed by prison guards. Every interrogation began with a flogging or examination. The intent was to break the will; questions may or may not be asked later. Each strike of the *flagrum* ripped away small chunks of meat and muscle from the victim, reducing their backs to hanging strips of flesh. Administrating forty stripes will almost certainly kill a man, so an examination was limited to thirty-nine or less lashes, followed by several days of a ghastly crucifixion. Barabbas knew this is what awaited him.

The cross had become Rome's *pièce de résistance* for prolonging agony. A victim of crucifixion might finally die for any number of reasons: cardiac rupture, heart failure, asphyxia, arrhythmia, pulmonary embolism, or any combination of these. Even sepsis caused by infection from flogging was a possibility. A naked prisoner, nailed to a cross, might last three days. Still fettered, Barabbas dropped to the floor of his cell, unafraid to die, but never expecting it to end like this.

"I should have gone out like a warrior," he choked, wondering if he'd have the courage to endure it like the man he'd been purported to be. Slumping down to the cell floor, he relived yet again the ordeal of his father's death.

*****

The sun's early morning rays were just beginning to break Jerusalem's eastern horizon. The Centurion had ridden relentlessly through the night, his exhausted horse staggering through the city gate. The city stable master was appalled by the animal's condition but lodged no complaint with Atticus.

His always raspy voice barked at the stable master, "The men who brought in the criminal, Barabbas, where are they?"

The stable master motioned in the direction of a nearby barrack.

"In there." He pointed, being careful to avoid eye contact with this physically imposing soldier. "Some were taken to the infirmary."

Leonidas, who had kept a lookout for him, was the next man he saw.

The Centurion's fatigue caused his damaged eye to look even more pronounced. He was hell-bent on getting to the Phantom before Pilate, wanting to make him answer for Oppius's death. But in his present state of exhaustion, he might forget where his best interests lie. This made him thankful for Leonidas's company.

First stop was the infirmary to check on the health and well-being of his young protégé and his friend Orel. He found Orel in good spirits and Vitus never having to be admitted. It hadn't taken Vitus long to see through his commanding officer's guarded façade. If anyone could cool down his murderous intentions, it was Vitus.

After assembling both regulars and operatives, Atticus's mood moved from morose to upbeat.

"Some of you care about the praise of politicians, some could care less. Let me state that I'm pleased." He paused to redirect. "No, proud of the way you handled yourselves, averting what could easily have turned into a crisis. You kept your wits, stopped an enemy that had previously been unstoppable."

Standing at attention, the soldiers kept their eyes forward but beamed inwardly.

"You combined brains and brawn, leaving the Zealots with no recourse." Straightening his posture, he saluted, and his salute was quickly and enthusiastically returned. "See to it you get treatment for any and all wounds at the infirmary. Dismissed!"

As the company disassembled, Vitus and Scipio continued standing at attention with broad smiles.

"Glad you stayed behind," said Atticus. "We need to talk."

After several minutes of pointed questions, Atticus reached over to tap Scipio's shoulder. Scip got the message, leaving the two men alone to talk. Neither was much of a conversationalist, but Vitus became what Atticus needed: a voice of reason. Vitus could read the grizzled warrior better than anyone; only Oppius had known him better.

"I'm heading over to the prison."

Vitus nodded silently.

"I took a vow to avenge Oppius's death." He paused, taking in a breath. "But now that I have him, I—"

"You think you have no choice," said Vitus softly, "that you will dishonor Oppius if you don't kill him. Sir, no one wants that devil to suffer more than me. You know the role he played in my father's death."

Atticus squinted, correcting him. "You mean the death of both your parents."

Vitus lowered his chin. "That's what I was told and believed, but my mother is alive."

Atticus was taken aback but didn't interrupt.

"It's a long story, sir, I won't take up your time with that now. What's important now is not letting Barabbas regain control. He's the one with no options, not you. Sir, you know what the governor will do when he arrives. Why not let things take their logical course? Barabbas will be publicly disgraced and brutally executed. In the end, that death will be worse than anything you could inflict on him." Vitus paused, looking directly in the Centurion's eyes. "Sir, if Sergeant Oppius were here, I know he'd be satisfied with that."

The Centurion could feel his temples pulsating as he climbed the stairs of this once great fortress. Though he issued strict orders to the ops to preserve Barabbas's life, his own resolve to follow these same orders was in question. He visualized himself entering the Phantom's cell and closing the door behind him. His massive fists furiously pummeled him until his face was unrecognizable. Ignoring his plea for mercy, he plunged a dagger into his throat.

Beads of perspiration seeped from Atticus's forehead as followed the guard to the cell. Vitus's words echoed in his head. "Let things take their logical course. If Oppius were here, he'd be satisfied with that."

As the guard unlocked and pulled back the heavily rusted door, a stench, thick and ripe, assaulted his nostrils. The sentinel pulled the door closed, leaving him in a room that had no source of natural light. As his eyes gradually adjusted, he could see why the place stank. The floor was covered with filthy straw and human feces.

Barabbas sat at the far side of the cell, the picture of dejection. His face was severely swollen, no doubt a beating from the guards. The buffeted prisoner looked up at him, expecting more of the same.

"Get to your feet!" Atticus sneered in broken Aramaic.

The battered prisoner, wincing from cracked ribs, pulled himself up.

"It appears I'm not the only one lacking the patience to wait for your formal examination."

Barabbas was wobbly, barely able to stay upright. He hadn't been given food or water since he'd arrived. The Centurion recognized dehydration when he saw it. Pounding on the cell door, he called out, "Bring this man some water immediately!" When no response was forthcoming, he issued a threat. "If he dies of thirst, the prefect will execute you in his place."

Without delay, the guard scurried off to fetch water.

Barabbas squinted at the Centurion through swollen eyes, his words punctuated by pain. "It's you," he whispered, having a better command of Latin than Atticus did Aramaic. "You saved my life more than twenty years ago in Gazara when I was a child."

"Whatever you're up to," quipped Atticus, "you can save your breath. It won't help you!"

"It was during the Varus wars. My village had just been burned by legionnaires, my people were rounded up like cattle. You were a young officer but with the same defiant spirit. A monstrous legionnaire beat my father to death in front of me. He would have killed me…but you stopped him. I can still hear your words. 'Stand down or I'll kill you myself!' A moment ago, when you ordered the prison guard to bring me water, I recognized that unmistakable raspy voice. It hasn't changed in all these years."

Atticus was silent; he remembered the occasion happening just as Barabbas said it did. He was stunned by the irony of the situation but maintained a stony countenance. "Do you think that little story impresses me?"

"Then you do remember?"

"I'll admit that I've made mistakes in my life, but I make it a point not to repeat them. The governor is on his way from Caesarea. He is looking forward to his time with you. That is the only reason I haven't already killed you." Atticus would never admit that it was his young protégé, not the governor, that had given him reason for pause. "There's a cross out there waiting to receive your naked body, spikes waiting to be driven through your hands and feet, and a crew of executioners that will take extra care to ensure you have time to consider all the throats you've slashed as you hang there, praying for death to come. I want you to be haunted by the faces of Aurelius, Oppius, and others that you ordered crucified until your muscles give way or your heart finally gives out."

Though in great pain, Barabbas spoke in a clear, unfazed voice. "You do realize that you're just as responsible for those deaths as I am because it was you who saved me all those years ago."

"As I said, I try to learn from my mistakes, not repeat them, and I'll be there to watch when you take your last gasping breath."

Silently, Barabbas looked away.

CHAPTER 43

The Dream

There are some who believe that dreams are nothing more than the wanderings of the subconscious mind. But all of us have experienced dreams that stay with us, the kind we can't shake. Somehow, we know the dream is different, supernatural. It was this kind of dream Claudia, the wife of Pontius Pilate, experienced.

Tossing and turning, Claudia's sleep was contentious, restless. She finally drifted off in the early hours of the morning, only to endure an ominous nightmare.

"Let go of me!" she shrieked, trying to break free of the dream's dark specter. Its evil laugh coursed through her like a bolt of lightning. "Pontius!" she cried, propping up on her bed but still in the grip of the dark dream.

Her husband, Pontius Pilate, trying to rouse himself from a dead sleep, called to her, "Claudia, wake up!"

She stuttered, "Must warn you…before it's—"

An eerie sensation sent a shiver through Pilate.

"*Claudia!*" His voice was loud as he shook her. "*Wake up!*"

"No!" she cried, catapulting herself forward, sending them both sprawling to the stone floor.

Pilate had never believed in spirits, but this episode challenged that notion. After getting her back in bed, he peered into the silhouetted darkness. Thankfully, the apprehensive feeling had lifted, but he still wasn't at peace as they climbed climbed back in bed.

"Are you all right?" he asked softly.

"I don't know," she replied. "That dream was important, a warning from the gods, but the memory of it escapes me!"

"After such an experience, not remembering might be a good thing."

"No!" she insisted. "The specter in my dream didn't want me to warn you, Pontius. There is grave danger ahead. I feel it inside." Her eyes filled up. "It was horrible, dark, and monstrous!"

Pilate swallowed involuntarily. "It was only a dream," he assured her. "Try to get some rest. Everything will look different in the morning."

*****

The early morning rays brought no relief to Claudia. Sitting with her legs tucked under her, she struggled, trying to recall the dream. Pilate was reviewing the plans he had formulated back in Caesarea, their new residence. The city of Caesarea was an urban delight that boasted a cutting edge seaport. The newly built city replicated the Roman forum, with a temple dedicated to Caesar Augustus. Its governor's palace was magnificent, but Claudia had been reluctant to accept the city as home.

Pilate had divided the trip from Caesarea to Jerusalem into two parts. They had traveled to the plantation city of Jericho, stopping there for a two-day rest. The second leg of the journey and his entrance into Jerusalem would be all about making an impression. Fully rested and robust, he would enter the city with a full escort of soldiers one week prior to Passover.

Claudia stood barefoot on the cool stone floor of her bedchamber, still haunted by the previous night's dream. "What if the dream was a warning from the gods, and I can't remember it," she ruminated. Her somber mood was interrupted by Dena, her maid servant.

Dena had an effervescent personality. "Good morning, Mistress, ready to go out and see the sights? What's wrong? What's troubling you?" Dena was more than Claudia's servant. She was a trusted friend. Claudia's eyes told her all she needed to know. Though they were miles apart in social status, they were two sides of the same coin.

Dena had been a part of Pilate's household staff since their days in Pompeii. "Did someone die?" Dena asked.

"No," Claudia said and paused. "I had a terrible dream from the gods."

Dena sat beside her. "Do you want to talk about it?"

"I can't."

Dena's smile was contagious. "You know how I am with dreams. Tell me about it. Perhaps I can tell you what it means."

"It was awful and horrible, but it's gone from me."

"Let's get some light in here." She pushed back the tapestry-like window coverings, flooding the chamber with light.

"It is a beautiful morning," Claudia states, "even if it is Judea."

Escorted by a larger than usual contingency of guards, the women set out for Jericho's open-air market. Claudia was usually an enthusiastic shopper, but today, she was distracted and careless with the merchant's wares.

"Why did we have come here?" she huffed, turning a hammered copper kettle into a projectile. "Of all the places they could have assigned him, why did it have to be Judea?" Another item went airborne, but her personal guards disheartened the merchant's complaints. Distracted and angry, her thoughts continued to rush back to her husband who had claimed to have no choice in the matter.

"To refuse the offer of governorship in Judea," Pilate told her, "is the equivalent of political suicide." He left no room for discussion. He knew she wanted to stay in Pompeii, but his decision was final—it had to be.

Pilate was sent to the most rebellious outlying region of the empire, but it was never a question of if he should go, only how soon he would be ready.

Claudia loved the status of being a dignitary's wife in Pompeii, which indulged her with luxuries of the elite, like indoor plumbing, heated baths, even ingenious open-air skylights.

Dena examined a colorful pottery vase. "This one has promise, don't you think?" She presented it to Claudia. "Or is it too decorative to be practical?"

"I don't care for it," she answered curtly.

"Mistress, do you wish to leave?"

"Yes…no…I don't know! It's too early to eat, but even if it wasn't, what would they offer us here? Unleavened bread and water? Everything is distasteful! We can't even shop without being harassed by these brutish guardians." Concerned about Zealot reprisals, Pilate had doubled Claudia's personal escort, which further suffocated her. "Yes, Dena, let's leave. I need something to drink that isn't water."

They were about to leave when she noticed him on the opposite side of the marketplace. She'd never seen this man before, yet his face was very familiar. He stood tall and walked with a commanding presence, but there was gentleness about him. She wouldn't say he was handsome, yet there was something about him. It was improper for a governor's wife to stare at a Judean, but she couldn't take her eyes off of him.

She nudged Dena to look in his direction. "Do you know who that is?" she whispered.

Dena shrugged. "Should I?"

"It's the young rabbi from Nazareth, I'm certain of it."

Capitalizing on Claudia's fascination with the man, Dena smiled. "So much for your sour mood." She chuckled. "What makes you think it's him?"

"It's obvious."

"You've seen him before then?"

"He was in the dream that I couldn't remember until this moment."

The superstitious Dena was both frightened and intrigued. "You're positive this is the man you dreamed of?"

"I've never been more certain of anything!"

Dena displayed a troubled look.

"What's the matter? What is it?" prodded Claudia, but before Dena could answer, the guards encircled them. On the opposite side of the square, a keyed-up beggar was crying out for help?

"Jeshua, son of David!" he shouted.

People who had begun to gather around the rabbi were trying to quiet him. "Shush, quiet down," they told him, but the blind beggar refuses to be silent.

"Jeshua, son of David!" he shouted again, even louder.

Jeshua stopped and turned toward the man. "Call him over," he instructed, and several very willing people happily obliged.

"It's okay," one man said. "He's calling for you." Several men directed the blind man to the Nazarene.

"What is it you're so determined to get from me?" asked Jeshua. Falling to his knees, he raised both hands.

On the opposite side of the street, the two women were spellbound. "He's blind," Claudia whispered to Dena.

"My sight, son of David, if only you would have pity on me." Jeshua broke into a full grin. "Bartimaeus, son of Timaeus."

Claudia was mystified. "How does he know the name and lineage of a wretched beggar?"

The crowd was quickly growing, making it harder for the women to see. Claudia, wanting a closer look, tried to cross over, but her guardians wouldn't allow it.

"Take your hands off me!" she fumed, but she was silenced when Jeshua looked directly at her. With his hands still on Bartimaeus, he spoke aloud but to her, not Bartimaeus.

"I know who you are," he said, softly looking directly at Claudia. With eyes wide open, she drew in a breath.

"It's all right." There was no hint of rejection in his tone. For a frozen moment, there was no sound, no other people, just the two of them.

*****

Suddenly, the dream with all its terror came rushing back to her. She was standing in the court of judgment, struggling to push through the crowd of people blocking her way to the young rabbi. Its dark but flaming torches highlighted Pilate, who was standing in front of the Nazarene. He was trying to quiet the angry mob. Claudia called to him, trying to gain his attention, but to no avail. He couldn't hear or see her. As she pushed into the thickened crowd, a soldier grabbed her arm, jerking her toward him.

"Where do you think you're going?" he scoffed.

"Pontius!" she screamed.

"Shut up!" the brute roared, dropping her to her knees with a backhanded assault. Blood gushed from her nose, turning her white tunic red. Still not satisfied, the soldier pushed her to the ground with overwhelming force. Pulling one arm up behind her, he shoved his foot against the back of her neck, grinding her face into the dirt. He sneered, "Who do you think you are? The governor's wife?" His evil laugh paralyzed her. Her mouth was filled with clots of dirt, making it difficult to breathe.

"How can this be happening to me?" she cried. She had a searing headache from the blow to her face and the foot pressed against the base of her skull. Yet, her view of the Nazarene was somehow unobscured. Standing beside her husband, his tunic was filthy, completely bloodstained. From his puckered temples came rivulets of blood caused by a makeshift crown of thorns pushed deep into his scalp. His battered face was turned downward. He didn't say a word.

"What should I do with your king?" Pilate asked the mob.

"No!" she screamed convulsively, her lips caressing the earth. Just then, Jeshua looked up at her. It wasn't fear, anger, or hate; she saw in his eyes only concern for her. He didn't speak, but she heard his voice inside of her.

"It's all right," he whispered.

"Take him away!" the mob retorted. "Crucify him!"

In a last-ditch effort, Claudia screamed with all her might, "Pontius, no!"

*****

Suddenly, Claudia was back on the village street with Dena beside her. Jeshua was still smiling, his hand still on the blind man's shoulder as if none of what she just experienced happened.

Jeshua turned and spoke to Bartimaeus. "Go your way now," he said. "Your faith has healed you."

There was a collective gasp from the crowd as the blind man's eyes quickly transitioned from milky white to crystal clear.

Bartimaeus leaped and shouted, "I can see! I can see!"

Jeshua broke into a laugh as Bartimaeus put an inescapable bear hug on him. "Thank you, thank you, son of David, thank you!" Saying it a thousand times still wasn't enough for Bartimaeus. "Thank you!" he said again and again.

Claudia's bodyguards were stunned like everyone else but remembered to pull her back from the press of the crowd.

As Jeshua walked away, he glanced one last time at Claudia without breaking stride. She fought her impulse to run to him. "This isn't Pompeii," she reminded herself. "It's him," she declared to Dena, watching the crowd moving away from them. "The man in my dream."

"I know," said Dena. "He was in my dream last night as well."

CHAPTER 44
Political Combustion

Pilate's arrival in Jerusalem had created just the kind of spectacle he'd envisioned. He knew this circus-like display was contrary to Rome's current policy, but he didn't care. The Imperial Senate had been seeking a calmer, less confrontational occupation with Judea's general population by reducing its military presence there. In case of an emergency, the acting governor could mobilize a three-thousand-soldier auxiliary unit, most of them conscripted from Samaria and Caesarea.

Tiberius appointed Pontius Pilate Prefect of Judea in AD 26. His seven-year administration hadn't quieted Judean hostility toward Rome. Pilate employed demonstrations of force at regular intervals. His credo was to meet violence with violence whenever warranted and even when it wasn't. His punitive policies inflamed nationalists like Barabbas and frustrated Tiberius.

Pilate was euphoric, visualizing Barabbas being crucified on Jerusalem's highest hill.

"It couldn't have been planned any better." He chuckled. The thought of Barabbas's demise combined with the Jewish weeklong Festival of Unleavened Bread had him feeling downright giddy. He was so anxious to get started that he decided to leave Claudia in Jericho for an additional forty-eight hours.

*****

As the governor approached Herod's palace on the west side of the city, the Nazarene was entering Bethany, a suburb of Jerusalem. Jeshua had delayed a visit to Bethany, despite an urgent plea from the sister of a best friend who was deathly ill. He waited another four days before responding to Martha's pleas, causing his disciples to be totally confused.

"Lazarus is dead," he told them, "and for your sakes, I'm glad I wasn't there to save him." When Jeshua finally arrived at the house of Lazarus, he had already been entombed.

"The teacher is calling for you," one of the mourners whispered to Martha who was sitting shiva. An emotional Martha left the mourners behind to meet with Jeshua. Waffling between disappointment and confusion, she stopped several feet from where Jeshua stood. Her fingers opened, then closed into tight fists; she was torn between telling him what she really thought and falling at his feet. Martha's stoic nature won; she stood her ground.

"Lord," she spoke, breaking the awkward silence, "if you had only been here, my brother would not have died!" Pausing for a moment, she continued, "But I know even now, God will give you whatever you ask for."

Jeshua, feeling the pain in Martha's heart, responded, "Your brother will rise again."

"I know he'll rise again on the last day," she responded, but her words sounded hollow even to her.

"I am the resurrection and the life," he declared. "Everyone who believes in me will live, even though they die, and whoever lives and believes in me will never die." He looked deeply into her eyes. "Do you believe this?"

Lazarus's burial site was a crypt hewn from a rock wall formation. As they stood together in front of the entrance, they were joined by the younger sister, Mary, and the mourners.

"Isn't this the person who opened the eyes of a blind man?" one mourner whispered under her breath. "Couldn't this man have prevented the death of his friend?"

At the entrance to the sealed tomb, Jeshua wept, triggering another wave of emotion from the mourners. "Have them roll the stone away," he told Martha, who was horrified at the request.

"Oh no, Rabbi, it's been too long. The smell will be insufferable!"

His heart was broken for both Martha and Mary, but this was the very reason he delayed his arrival.

"Didn't I say that your brother will rise again?" he asked.

With a stunned look in her eyes, Martha nodded yes. Forcing down a swallow, she turned to relay the command to her servants.

"Do as he says," said a solemn Martha. "Roll the stone out of its furrow."

Six stunned servants exchanged bewildered glances, but it was their job to obey, not question. Positioning themselves, they strained to overcome the inertia of the large round stone. After several moments of straining and grunting, they cleared the entrance to the mausoleum.

Jeshua's face became flint-like as he ordered death to relinquish its grip on his friend.

"Lazarus!" he called with authority. "Come out!"

(Quotations in the above passage, taken from John 11:15–45, are author's own paraphrase.)

A stench wafted out of the open tomb, dropping servants to their knees, gasping and gagging for air. Lazarus wasn't just dead. He was ripe. And then suddenly, he wasn't! News of this magnitude could not be contained; it spread like a raging wildfire.

If Jerusalem would have had a local periodical, the news article would have read something like this: "Trussed up like a mummy, the dead man hopped out of his tomb, like a child in a sack race. The Nazarene told the family to untie him and feed him."

Each time the account was repeated, a rhetorical question followed: "Is there any doubt that this man is the Messiah?"

*****

Like Pilate, Herod Antipas had departed his primary residence in Galilee for his palace in Jerusalem. Though Antipas was sometimes referred to as King of the Jews, he was not Jewish. He was, however, a polished diplomat, and for the past six Passovers, he had done his best to ease tensions between Pilate and Jerusalem's citizenry. Arriving ahead of the governor, he had taken special pains to enlist the help of the pro-Roman Herodians who always cheered Pilate like a conquering hero.

"Prepare the way for the prefect!" they shouted to the praetorian guardsmen hauling Pilate's carriage litter. Diplomatic relations between Pilate, Antipas, and Caiaphas would accurately have been described as tenuous. Caiaphas's regard for Antipas was slightly above the grime between his toes.

"The man is a buffoon!" he said, a term Pilate had often used when discussing Herod with his tribune, Lucius. Pilate was more respectful of Caiaphas but only as a means to a political end.

The Roman prefect could never have imagined that Barabbas would become a major player in a trade that would force his hand. Pilate would have to make that deal or face political suicide. Instead of condemning Barabbas as a murderer, he would be forced to execute the Nazarene.

*****

Members of the Shadow of Death met in Iri's Jerusalem residence.

"Did you arrange the meeting with Caiaphas?" Tola asked anxiously.

Korah seemed impatient with Tola's question. "I've been speaking with his father-in-law, Annas, one of our greatest allies. Annas has promised to take our request to Caiaphas."

"Did you impress upon him the seriousness of our situation?" asked Shimron.

Looking annoyed, Korah continued, "I explained the danger that all of us face if Barabbas's tongue is loosened by the examiner's whip."

Tola interrupted, "We must know if Annas is serious about helping us. We can't wait with fingers crossed. If he isn't, we will be forced to take other actions!"

Korah's exhale demonstrated his frustration. "This is a former high priest we're talking about, not a common temple Levite! What would you have me do, twist his arm behind his back? We're in no position to make demands!"

The circle of members was silent, none asking for or offering suggestions.

Korah broke the silence, "There is too much at stake here for him to do nothing. He has as much to lose as we do. If the SOD's link to the Zealots is discovered, it will lead back to the Sanhedrin and Caiaphas."

A grim kind of silence pervaded the room.

"Annas will persuade his son-in-law to dust off an old Passover custom."

"What custom?" asked Shimron.

"Every Roman governor wants to ingratiate himself to Judean citizens during Passover. A former governor had set a precedent—one prisoner pardoned—upon the citizenry's request."

"I can think of no reason for Pilate to honor such a request," said Tola. "What would possess him to release a man he's been after for years? A man he hates with every fiber of his being?"

"For once, I must agree with Tola, it's impossible," said Shimron, but Korah wore the look of a man who knew something no one else in the room did.

"Annas and Caiaphas want the Nazarene and his antics out of the way as much as we do. When I told Annas a deal had been struck with one of the Nazarene's confederates, light rushed into his tired old eyes. We have an accord. You arrange the betrayal the night of Passover and deliver him to Caiaphas. He will do the rest, bringing capital charges before Pilate, demanding execution."

There was a sudden scurry of voices. "What assurance do we have for any of this?" asked Tola.

Shimron jumped in, "Even if he would agree, what would possess Pilate to release Barabbas?"

"Just one hour ago, we received news from one of our men who followed the Nazarene to Bethany. Caiaphas received the same update."

"Which was?" asked Shimron.

An evil smile cracks the corners of Korah's mouth. "The rabbi has outdone himself this time. Under the watchful eyes of more than a hundred people, it is reported that he brought a man named Lazarus back from the dead."

"Impossible!" roared Tola. "Another one of his tricks!"

"This Lazarus was reported to have been dead four days when the Nazarene arrived. The mourners and family have sworn to it," said Korah. "Upon hearing this news, Caiaphas tore his clothing."

"Everyone will soon be following him!" yelped Tola.

"The Sanhedrin is ready to do whatever it takes to stop him, even if it means killing Lazarus. Caiaphas plans to bring charges of blasphemy and treason before Pilate's judgment seat. He will state that the Nazarene claims to be God. We will select the crowd that will influence that trial and provide corroborating witnesses. The crowd will turn mob-like if necessary, shouting to Pilate that he is no friend of Caesar if he releases the Nazarene. Pilate will have no choice but to cave to public pressure and execute Jeshua while correspondingly releasing the people's choice, Barabbas."

CHAPTER 45

Eastern Gate

It was almost midday when Jeshua neared Jerusalem's eastern gate, properly called *Sha'ar HaRachamim*, or Gate of Mercy. An unmistakable buzz of anticipation filled the air. The avenue that would provide Jeshua passageway into the city was teeming with people, ten thousand of them. It had even been rumored that Lazarus, the man brought back from the dead, would accompany him. Youthful admirers who had been faithfully surveying the horizon sent back the message, "He's coming!"

People who had been standing for hours started to chant, "*Hosanna!*" meaning "Save now." Jeshua was riding on a donkey, stepping over palm branches and articles of clothing that the crowds had adoringly strewn in his path, the proverbial red-carpet treatment. This was the kind of welcome that only the anticipated Messiah could receive.

From his balcony, Pilate watched with concern as Jeshua continued his ride toward the temple.

"Send out a detail of legionnaires," he ordered. "I want order maintained. Instruct them to make arrests if there is even a hint of a rebellion." The display had caused him to temporarily lose focus on Barabbas.

Hours after Jeshua's majestic entrance, pilgrims continued to stream into Jerusalem. Among them were two women from Emmaus: Rebecca and Vitus's mother.

They talked continuously along the way, making the long trip seem shorter. Rebecca took the opportunity to learn as much as she could about Vitus. "Tell me, Emma, what kind of a child was your son?" A smile lightened the lines in her face as she conjured up memories she thought she'd never revisit.

"He was seven when I wrapped my arms around my little boy for the last time. He was a loving child, fiercely protective of me. Our married life was considered taboo on both sides of the cultural divide." She sighed. "It was hard for him to grow up under those kinds of conditions. Even at that age, he could read the sadness in my eyes. He would sit next to me and put his arms around my neck, kissing my face. 'Don't cry, Emma,' he'd say in that little voice. I tried to hide my feelings from him, but he was too smart." She paused abruptly. "Too many times, he would come home with bruises and blackened eyes. He was defending me from the hurtful words of other children." She wiped away a tear from her cheek.

Rebecca hugged her neck and kissed her. "That's all in the past now," she lovingly consoled her.

"In some ways, my son reminds me of Jeshua. He's powerful, yet compassionate, caring, but never one to be pushed around."

"Your son is all of those things and more, which is why I love him so much. I suppose it's also why I love Jeshua."

"Rebecca," a distant but familiar voice called to her. She tried to trace its direction. "Rebecca," the call came again, a little louder this time. "Over here!" Orel was waving and walking toward her, smiling. Taking care not to frighten her, he stopped several feet away.

"Orel!" A smile lit up her face.

Moving a step closer, he bowed to the older woman. "Good morning. Good to see you again, Emma."

She bowed in response, a slight smile pursing her lips. "Thank you, sir."

"You both look well. I assume you're here for Jeshua?" Then he quickly added, "And, of course, Passover."

Rebecca nodded. "Yes, we're both anxious to see him again but didn't expect the city to be this crowded, but Jeshua is not the only reason we're here." She sighed. "But also—"

"To see Vitus, of course."

"When news of Barabbas's capture reached Emmaus, we knew Vitus had to be involved. We were told he had been taken to Jerusalem to stand trial for his crimes."

"Is my son well?" the woman broke in. "Has he been injured? Is he here in the city?"

Orel smiled and nodded. "Yes, he is here." He took her hand. "He is recovering from some wounds, but I assure you, he's fine and will be irate if he learns I delayed in bringing you to him. Please come with me." As they walked together, Orel continued conversing, "The multitudes of people that have invaded this city seem to believe something special is about to happen." He paused. "So do I. This rabbi is not like anyone I've ever known. I'm convinced he is the One."

Rebecca nodded in agreement. "I, too, believe he is the Messiah. What about Vitus?"

"Vitus," said Orel, slowly shaking his head. "That's another story."

*****

Claudia entered Jerusalem under heavy military escort. Once inside the prefect's palace, she demanded an immediate audience with her husband.

"It's urgent that I see the governor!" she insisted. Within minutes, she was standing outside Pilate's door. "Pontius, I need to speak with you!" Pilate signaled for the room to be emptied.

"My dear," Pilate began, "I didn't expect you so—"

"Pontius!" she cried, looking more like a child than the governor's wife.

"What is it, Claudia? Have you been harmed?"

"No, no, I'm fine. I mean, no, I haven't been harmed, but I have to warn you of the grave danger you're about to face."

Pilate stared into the eyes of this unnerved woman and shrugged. "Grave danger?" he quipped.

"You must not take part in the death of the Nazarene!" she cried then anxiously relayed her dream.

"Stop this, Claudia!" he demanded, concerned for her mental state.

Biting her lower lip, she wondered how he could be so obtuse and tried again. "You must not be part of the execution of this righteous man," she stated with large and foreboding eyes. "The gods have warned me about him."

Pilate paused at this remark. "Claudia, I have nothing to do with—"

"Don't let them push you into this!" she repeated.

He shook his head. "Who is trying to push me into doing what?"

Claudia obviously believed what she was saying; this was not just an emotional outburst. "Members of the religious elect," she exhaled. "They're planning to trap you, force you into ordering his execution." Tears streamed down her cheeks.

Pilate was at a loss, not because he believed her story but for her state of mind. He tried to calm her. "I'm the governor. This religious rabble may think they run things here, but I'm the one in charge." Thinking of his mutual alliance with Caiaphas, he dismissed the notion of an open confrontation between them. He stood up preparing to leave, but Claudia pulled him to herself, throwing her arms around him.

"Please, Pontius, listen to me. Everything I had dreamed came rushing back to me when I saw the Nazarene in Jericho. Dena was with me, but this time, I wasn't dreaming. I was awake and saw a vision of the events about to happen. You must prevent them from hurting him!" She staggered backward, putting her hand to her forehead. "He's no ordinary man, Pontius. If they manipulate you into taking part in this, you'll regret it for the rest of your life. We both will. You must not provide them a scapegoat!"

Pilate had never seen this kind of passion from Claudia. He stared at her in silence then spoke, "I'm the governor!" he asserted. But inwardly, he wondered who it was he had tried to convince.

CHAPTER 46
A Few Silver Coins

Judas Iscariot was emotionally despondent. Fewer than twenty-four hours ago, he led a company of three-hundred Judean temple guards to a garden called Gethsemane, a favorite evening spot of Jeshua's. While Atticus, Vitus, and Pilate slept, Judas pointed Jeshua out to the torch-bearing mob. Judas identified him in that dimly lit garden by planting a kiss on his cheek. The Nazarene didn't put up a fight; his only request was the release of the others with him.

While the rest of the disciples scattered, Judas stayed, studying his former mentor. Jeshua's eyes remained on Judas as they arrested him, but incredibly, his expression was empathy for his betrayer. Judas was haunted by that look, unable to get it out of his head. The inner voice that whispered to him, pushing him to betray the Nazarene, now condemned him with an unholy vengeance.

"Why did I do it?" he cried. "He warned me, even identified me as the one who would betray him as we dipped our bread together in the *sop*! He saw me doing it before I did it!" Judas staggered, getting to his feet; the only thing the wine did was dull his senses. Suddenly, a thought, perhaps a ray of hope, presented itself. "Maybe I can still undo this. Maybe it's not too late!" he gasped. A frantic, unsteady Judas tracked Korah down, finding him on the stairs of the Temple. Rushing his words, he tripped over them.

"You...you handed him over to the R-Romans so Pilate would condemn him!" said Judas in an accusatory tone. "That's not the way you said this would play out. Y-you lied!" Wiping drool from a corner of his mouth, he struggled to concentrate. "You said it would be ha-handled by the high priest!"

Korah was disgusted and insulted by the nerve of this turncoat. How dare this fool approach him and on the steps of the temple no less! Only because he was openly confronted did he reply, "I said the charges of blasphemy would be brought to the high priest, and they were. The charges made against him were worthy of capital punishment. According to Roman law, only the governor may issue a verdict of death. Caiaphas did what he had to do."

Falling to his knees with hands clasped in front of him, Judas made a last-ditch plea. "I've made a grave error," he moaned, "betrayed an innocent man!"

Korah had heard enough. "Fool!" His tone was laced with revulsion. "What did you think would happen when you greedily accepted that blood money? Thirty silver coins in exchange for your cooperation! Whatever regrets you have now, they're yours, not mine." Korah turned to walk away but stopped to face a weeping Judas one last time. "We're finished here. Don't let me see your face again, ever! Are we clear?"

The icy cold truth surged through Judas's brain. *No way out!* Pulling a small leather pouch out of his tunic, he threw it at Korah's feet. Thirty silver coins spilled out on impact, bounding and trickling down the temple stairs. Without another word, Judas rose and descended the stairs, leaving Korah with a vacant stare.

Unable to cope with unrelenting guilt, Judas purchased a reasonable length of rope. In his dark emotional state, he walked to the outskirts of the city. There he found a tree that overlooked a precipice. After fastening one end of the rope to a limb, he tugged at it, making certain it would do its job. His eyes glazed over as he looped and tightened the opposite end around his neck. Seconds later, his lifeless body dangled over the precipice. The rhythmic sound of the twisting rope both mourned and mocked him.

*****

Snorting and twisting his bulky body, the sleeping Centurion resisted Scipio's attempt to rouse him.

"What the hell?" he roared in that gravelly voice. "This better be important!" He squinted with his good eye through the darkness, identifying Scipio as the culprit, tilting his head in disbelief. "Didn't I send you away to get rest? What are you doing here, disturbing me?"

"Sir, I would never risk wakening you if it wasn't gravely important, but you'd have killed me if I hadn't come to you."

"I might kill you anyway."

"Please, Commander, you've got to come with me right now if there's to be any hope of stopping this."

A disoriented, Atticus tried to digest Scipio's words. *Any hope of stopping what?* he wondered. "What in blazes are you rambling about? Has the Nazarene created a riot?"

"No, sir, it's not him. I mean, yes, it's the Nazarene, but it's the mob that's creating a riot and threatening the prefect, demanding his release!"

Atticus scowled, "The mob is threatening the governor?"

Flustered, Scipio tried again. "They've arrested the Nazarene, but they're demanding his release."

Taking a lengthy exhale, the Centurion settled back into his cot. "Why should I give a damn if the governor releases the Nazarene? Let them do as they please with him!" he groused.

Scipio's volume increased, forgetting who it was he was addressing. "Not the Nazarene," he shouted! "Barabbas! The mob is screaming for a trade! Barabbas for the Nazarene!"

"They want what?" Atticus was now fully awake. "Holy jumping…why didn't you say so?" he howled, stumbling to get his tunic and outer gear on as quickly as possible. "Where's Vitus?"

"Orel is trying to find him."

"Orel again," remarked the Centurion. "He knows where he is?"

"He knows. We split up. I came to get you, and he went to get Vitus. We're supposed to meet up before it's too late!" As the two men beat a path from Atticus's quarters, they were joined by the Centurion's personal guards.

"Release Barabbas?" Atticus muttered. "Over my cold corpse!"

*****

Korah had exhausted the last of his political favors, but he was confident it was finally going to happen. He'd pulled the rug of public approval from under the Nazarene's feet. Conventional wisdom says one can't stop a tidal wave, but Korah didn't become a key leader in the Shadow of Death by conventional thinking. He marshaled the forces of the high priest, Pharisees, and the SOD to work in concert for one goal—to bring down the Nazarene. He cut ties with the Zealots, gambling that time would work in his favor if he moved quickly. Too many powerful people had too much to lose for this to fail. Pilate would be cornered into making the Nazarene the scapegoat.

"It's come together more beautifully than I had anticipated." He chuckled in Tola's ear but was suddenly haunted by the thought, *Is this too easy? Are there unseen forces at work ensuring the Nazarene's demise?* He quickly dismissed the notion as ridiculous nonsense. "The only thing left is for Pilate to make it official."

Tola's eyes remained fixed on the empty platform of the judgment hall. "I hope you're right."

"Oh, I'm right, it's over! His disciples have scattered like frightened sheep. One of them even sold him out for a price. The Nazarene's moment in the sun is over. Of course, Pilate will do his best to save face, but in the end, he'll succumb to the pressure. Caiaphas controls the tone of this ugly crowd. He won't let the prefect wiggle off his hook, not Caiaphas. He'll squeeze him, force him to play his final card, in keeping with the custom of Passover. But Caiaphas will cast the last and final lot, insisting that Barabbas, the one man who could have indicted our secret order, be released."

"Incredible," said Tola, his face lighting up with admiration. "How did you ever pull this off?"

*****

Vitus and Orel arrived at the place known as the Pavement, Pilate's judgment seat, but there was no governor or prisoner, only a docile-looking crowd mulling around. Vitus looked at Orel, who shrugged. "They were here when I left," he assured him.

Away from the view of the crowd, Jeshua stood waiting inside, back from his excursion to Herod. Since Jeshua was a resident of Galilee, Pilate tried to pass the buck, or in this case, the denarius to Antipas. "Why not let Antipas deal with his own subject?" he reasoned. However, Herod, also known as the Fox, was having none of it. After a brief conversation with Jeshua, he sent him back to Pilate with the message: "This is your problem, not mine."

Initially, Pilate, called from his bedchamber, was only annoyed by the council's predawn intrusion. He tried to dismiss it as a religious and not a civil matter, but it soon became apparent that he was the pawn in the council's clever scheme. Incredibly, the dream had become reality. Pilate stood face-to-face with Jeshua, listening to the restless crowd outside.

"You are accused of high crimes against the state. They claim you call yourself a king."

Jeshua didn't reply.

"You refuse to answer me?" said an exasperated Pilate. "I hold the power to take or preserve your life."

The Nazarene remained silent.

"Why won't you speak to me?"

"I was born into this world to be a witness to the truth," Jeshua finally responded. "Anyone who desires to know the truth recognizes it when they hear my words."

"Really? So tell me, what is truth?" Pilate asked with a sarcastic tone.

"Bring him out!" the mob shouted. "Bring out the Nazarene!"

Orel, standing in the press of the crowd, turned to a man next to him. "Where is he?" he asked.

The man looked at him strangely. "Where have you been? Pilate sent him to Herod hours ago. The prefect thinks we're stupid, but I can assure you the people in this gathering aren't stupid!"

Trying to garner more information, Orel asked him to explain, but the man refused to add anything more.

"How long has he been gone?" asked Vitus, directing his question to the same man.

"Several hours," he hesitantly replied. "When that criminal appears again, it will be for the third time."

"Third time?" asked Orel.

"That's right. The governor is trying to wiggle his way out of passing judgment on him."

"This man is not a criminal!" said Vitus. The noise level around the praetorium reached a crescendo as Pilate walked out with Jeshua. Atticus and Scipio joined Orel and Vitus in time to see a fettered and battered Jeshua led out. Pilate gestured with both hands for silence, knowing what he was up against as he stared down this bloodthirsty crowd.

How did it come to this? he wondered. *How did they manage to usurp my power?* He sat in the governor's seat of judgment, knowing it was just a sham. His voice pierced the cool evening air. "I find nothing wrong with—"

But his words were instantly drowned out. Pilate's guardsmen stepped forward, weapons ready. Pilate stood to his feet; the tumult momentarily resided. "It is your custom that one prisoner may be pardoned in honor of Passover." Pilate was resolute; he would not show weakness to this lynch mob. "Shall I pardon your king?"

Korah, arms crossed on his chest, wore a Cheshire grin, glancing back at Tola.

"Watch this," he mouthed.

A singular voice shouted, "We have no king but Caesar!" This sent a chill through Pilate. His power to spare the Nazarene's life was gone. The singular voice was joined by the crowd. "Not this man! Give us Barabbas!"

A chant rose from the throng, "Barab-bas, Barab-bas!"

Pilate nodded to the head guardsman who led Jeshua off for flogging. Reaching for a pitcher of water, he rinsed his hands, stating publicly his opposition to this man's death.

Atticus could not believe his eyes, his damaged orb blinking furiously. He was about to get ugly and disorderly. "No, no, no, you can't allow this! Barabbas is a murderer and a terrorist! He can't be granted freedom! Not after all the Roman soldiers he's butchered. Not after all we've gone through to get him!"

Vitus, who had as much reason to see Barabbas executed as the Centurion, was startled by the outburst. Atticus pushed through the mob to where Pilate was still standing. He gestured violently. "You can't do this!" he bellowed. Vitus and Scipio pushed through, trying to intercept him, knowing this behavior could get him killed, but restraining Atticus was like holding back a charging bull.

"You can't do this!" his raspy voice declared. "I won't let you do this!" He began to scale the steps of the platform. Praetorium guardsmen rushed to block his way. "You'll free that bloody assassin over my dead body!" he brazenly shouted to a wide-eyed Pilate.

"That can be arranged," the governor stated, standing behind his bulky guardsmen.

CHAPTER 47
Unthinkable

"Arrest him! Get him out of my sight!" Pilate's demeanor didn't support the image he had striven to portray: the governor who had everything under control. Ten elite guardsmen latched on to the riled Centurion.

"Get your filthy paws off me!" snapped Atticus, whose physical strength was terrifying when aroused. His swinging elbows floored the first wave of guardians. Trying to settle things down, Vitus and Scipio got between charging guards and the raging Centurion, but their intentions were misinterpreted. In the short but intense battle, all but two guardsmen were rendered incapacitated.

"Sound the general alarm!" shouted Pilate. "Get more soldiers in here!" Pilate's judgment hall was about to spiral out of control when Orel averted disaster.

"Centurion!" Atticus paused at the sound of Orel's distinctive calm voice. "Commander, we are willing to die for you if that's your wish."

Atticus halted his juggernaut-like actions. Orel's message has registered; Atticus would not sacrifice any of these valuable men over the likes of Barabbas. He reluctantly raised two massive arms above his head.

"I surrender! Let these others go!"

Scipio and Vitus laid down their weapons.

Caught off guard by this sudden reversal, the lead guardsman barked out directions, "Bind them securely!"

Pilate was relieved, angry, and embarrassed all at the same time. "Take the lot of them to the tower and wait for my orders," he sniped.

Orel was taken as well, but Pilate rebuffed them, "Not that one."

Surprised to be released, Orel made an appeal on behalf of his friends, but the governor refused to listen. For Pilate, this long and humiliating day couldn't end soon enough. Releasing Barabbas while sending the Nazarene to his death seemed incomprehensible, and yet, that's exactly what he did. His hands, still moist from his display of public washing, felt filthy.

With hands bound behind them, Atticus, Vitus, and Scipio marched off to the Antonia prison. One of the guards whose nose had been broken during the scuffle, shoved Vitus from behind, sending him stumbling forward. The convoy of legionnaires burst into laughter.

"What's the problem?" the soldier snorted. "Having a little trouble staying on your feet?"

Scipio's hot temper flared. "Wow, aren't you a brave one now that our hands are tied behind us?" Signaling the troop to halt, the leader positioned himself inches from Scipio's face, then unleashed a 225-pound backhand strike to the face, sending the defenseless warrior down like a sack of potatoes.

Squaring his shoulders, Atticus glared at the guardsman. "Soldier," he grunted, "you'd better hope they kill me in that prison." His hoarse sounding voice was deadly calm but ferocious. "If they don't, I will find you, and when I do, my hands won't be bound."

"If it were up to me, you'd already be dead! Get him up." He nodded toward the fallen Scipio. "Let's finish this." As the trio was lead past an open court, the distressing sound of a whip striking bare flesh caught Vitus's attention. Even though his line of sight was obscured, he could see it was the Nazarene taking the beating.

*****

Inside Antonia's walls, the prison guard was in no hurry to take Orel to his newly interned prisoners. The guard's foul-smelling breath was so rancid, Orel imagined he saw a faintly visible cloud as he spoke.

"You have a visitor." His words possessed neither stamina nor conviction. "Ten minutes," he cautioned Orel, "no more."

Keeping his distance from the odious attendant, Orel was grateful to see Vitus and the others alive and offered a silent prayer of thanks to Yahweh. How things had changed for him. If anyone would have told him four months ago that he'd be visiting Roman soldiers in a Roman prison, he'd have laughed in their face.

The crude iron door moaned as the guard opened it just enough for Orel to slip in sideways. "Ten minutes," he repeated, as he locked Orel inside. His aroma lingered in the air, even after he was gone.

"How did you manage to get in here?" asked Vitus, who stood to greet his smiling friend.

"I'm surprised," said Atticus. "People in Antonia don't get visitors, especially those who have threatened the prefect."

"Mercurius," answered Orel. The Centurion massaged his always irritated orb, trying to figure Mercurius's angle in this.

"Mercurius?" said Atticus. "Does his influence stretch all the way from Caesarea?"

"He's here in Jerusalem. He took leave and traveled here as soon as he heard the news of your successful campaign. He couldn't wait to see the infamous Phantom in the flesh. When I told him what had occurred and of your plight in this place, he went to work, and here I am."

"Good old Mercurius. I misjudged him," chuckled Atticus.

"We don't have much time, so let me explain." Orel spoke quickly as he relayed key details of Mercurius and Pilate's meeting.

*****

"Post Commander Mercurius," said Pilate, "come in. I wasn't expecting you here in Jerusalem."

Always one for decorum, Mercurius snapped off a salute.

"Shouldn't you be minding things back in Sebaste?"

"Thank you for seeing me, Prefect. After years of fighting the Zealots, I wanted to see the so-called ghost for myself. You can imagine my disappointment when I learned of his impending release."

"You know what happened out there?"

"The Judean guardsman, Orel, learned I was in the city and sought me out. He relayed the unfortunate series of events that led up to your decision."

Pilate stared at Mercurius for several seconds before responding, "The damned religious blowhards had me by my short hairs, and they knew it!" he fumed. "But the Centurion's antics undermined whatever semblance of authority I had left. I won't deny his value as a field officer, but his raging insolence left me no choice. He must answer for it."

Mercurius, careful not to interrupt Pilate's speech, waited for the right moment. "Prefect," he began, "you're absolutely correct about the Centurion. The man has no understanding when it comes to politics or diplomacy." Mercurius was careful to maintain eye contact. "He's as delicate as a wild boar in a pastry shop, but as you indicated, a great soldier, the best at what he does. Who else could have so effectively led the special ops team?" He paused. "And without them, we'd never have trapped the Phantom."

Pilate stood to his feet. "Are you suggesting I forget this incident? Do you suppose that I can afford to let these men go unpunished?"

"No, Prefect, I'm not here to second-guess the governor, but allow me to point out other options moving forward."

His interest piqued, Pilate settled back into his chair.

"Because of years of involvement with the Judean underground, I may be aware of certain things you haven't considered. For example, how do you imagine the Roman Senate will react to the news that two Special Operatives are being executed after successfully completing their mission? They'll hear of how the Ten disemboweled the Zealot movement, depositing its elusive leader right on your doorstep. When the committee discovers it was you who ordered their execution along with the Centurion whom they handpicked to lead them...well, you can imagine the backlash." Mercurius looked directly into Pilate's eyes. "Furthermore, the importance of these ops will be even more critical once Barabbas is released! We'll need them to hunt him down again, and they'll need the leadership of the Centurion."

Pilate's fingers tapped his desktop as he listened intently. "I have to make an example of them," he said in frustration. "I can't pretend none of this happened, not on the stage where it happened," he insisted.

"Yes, a statement demonstrating your resolve as governor must be made. But there's a way to do it that doesn't include killing them."

"A public flogging?"

"No, Prefect, these men are far too valuable for that. The whip would only compromise their prowess and resolve. There's a way we can satisfy your wounded pride and publicly expose their error."

"I'm listening."

"You've already sentenced the popular Nazarene to be crucified."

"Regrettably, yes."

"You're aware, I'm sure, that an official crucifixion requires a team of three men, headed by a Centurion, acting as overseer. Have Atticus pay penance by assigning him to that charge. Use the other two operatives to fill out the team."

An evil smile tugged at the corners of Pilate's mouth. "That's quite an idea, Post Commander, I never realized what a devious mind you possess." He chuckled. "I save face with the senate, the local military, and the citizenry of Jerusalem." Pilate's jaw tightened as he considers a possible hitch in the plan. "There is a problem. Atticus and his operatives have no experience with this kind of thing, and this execution is too high a profile for slipups." He shifted his weight forward in his chair. "I'll order Asus, the regular Centurion in charge, to assist them. He and his men are scum, but they know what they're doing."

Mercurius rose and saluted. "Thank you, Prefect, I know you won't regret this decision."

"I damned well better not!"

"Shall I deliver your decision to Centurion Atticus personally?"

Pilate shook his head. "No, let the Judean bring them the news, he's earned it. His quick thinking saved their lives twice: outside the judgment hall and again by sending you here on their behalf. But even the gods won't be able to save them if there is a third time!"

"There won't be, I'm certain."

"Tell the Judean his three friends will be spared but not freed until they carry out the execution of the Nazarene. They'll remain under house guard while Asus trains them. Make it plain to the Judean and all three of them that once this is over, I never want to see their faces again. Is that clear?"

"Perfectly."

*****

"Time's up," said the unkempt prison guard as he unlocked the iron door. "You"—the sentry's deep-set eyes settled on Orel—"out now!"

Orel rose. "It seems you are a little behind on your information. The four of us are leaving this place."

"Like hell!" he quipped, wiping his runny nose on his forearm. "You're the only one leaving this cell," he said, pulling open the rust-laden gate, but while he was speaking, four guardsmen arrived with orders to escort the trio out.

*****

Back at his palace, Pilate pondered the pros and cons of a face-to-face meeting with Barabbas. He reveled in the idea of watching the Zealot leader squirm upon hearing the special tortures planned for him. But now it might be the Phantom who had the last laugh. The more he thought about it, the more determined he was to hold Barabbas as long as possible. The prisoner trade was a Passover loop-hole that the counsel played perfectly. There would be little to no repercussions for holding the Phantom until Passover had passed and things had quieted down. He would certainly keep his promise to release Barabbas, but Pilate had no intention of letting him live.

CHAPTER 48
Backlash

Orel and company were anxious to put their prison cell and its keeper behind them. Just before they were released, the lead guardsman lay down the rules of transit to them.

"Let's get a few things straight," said the guardsman. "We're going to take a quiet, uneventful walk across this compound." He was a big man, towering over everyone except Vitus, and surprisingly articulate, leaving nothing to chance. "Do anything that makes me nervous during this excursion, and I'll take your legs out." He paused to be sure his message was sinking in. "There's no telling what might make me nervous, and when I get nervous, I act first, ask questions later." His speech wasn't intended to intimidate; he knew what kind of men these were, and now they knew what kind of man he was. As he concluded his warning, Atticus offered an apology to Vitus and Scipio for getting them into this mess.

"I'm sorry, boys, I never intended for this to—"

The big man stared back at Atticus in disbelief. "That includes talking, soldier!"

This guard reminded Atticus of himself, and having no desire to make things worse, he made no further comment.

The fettered trio was on the way to Centurion Asus's hall of horrors detention center, escorted by thirty legionnaires. If pain and punishment could be considered a form of worship, Asus would be a deeply religious man. He used many punitive procedures, but his forte was torture, which he carried out with gusto. Most Roman officers avoided all contact with him, which allowed Asus to experiment on his victims with virtually no oversight or resistance. He slept like a baby after a long day of paring flesh, yanking bones out of joint, or performing slow visceral castrations. He had no friends or family; his victims' high-pitched screams provided his purpose and contentment.

"Company, halt!" ordered the guardsman.

The sadistic Asus had been anxiously anticipating the trio's arrival, having heard the news of their judgment hall exploits. But he never expected so large an escort for just three men.

"Welcome to my post, gentlemen." Asus's sinister grin revealed several blackened rotting teeth. When the lead guardsman ordered the chains removed, the disheveled Asus takes took a step backward. He was only accustomed to dealing with helpless victims.

"Do I correctly assume that several of your men will remain here to supervise activities?" the craven Asus asked the officer in charge.

"I think the word you're looking for is protect, not supervise," the officer retorted, making no attempt to hide his disgust for Asus. "No, Centurion, none of these men will be remaining with you. This is your business, not ours." After ordering an about-face, he pauses to address the slovenly Asus, "Do your job well, devil. If these men are ill-prepared to carry out the Nazarene's execution, the prefect will have you displayed on one of your own crosses."

Asus's reputation was hardly a secret, and Atticus was well-aware of his penchant for butchery. With a glaring look of disdain, he measured him up and down. The Centurion had always been a fearless warrior, never asking for or giving quarter, victor or vanquished, kill or be killed. Every soldier accepted this blunt reality. Vitus, a perfect example of this mentality, totally sold out during combat. Nothing distracted or dissuaded him, yet he never lost his sense of morality. He fought like a wild animal, but his heart prevented him from becoming one. Atticus shot Vitus a glance which he acknowledged with a nod. The Centurion had always believed that a man's insides were visible on the outside, and Asus looked like a living corpse rotting from the inside out.

"Let's get on with this," stated Atticus.

Relieved to hear such words, Asus nodded. "We start with the fact that there are three men being crucified, not just the one. Second, there is extra pressure to get this done because of the looming holiday of Passover. Third, the other condemned men have already been fastened to their crosses by my men."

"How do we fit into this thing?" asked Scipio.

Asus smirked. "No need to worry about the governor, if that's your concern. Everything's been arranged. My men will handle the dirty work of nailing and hoisting. You will be responsible to oversee the wonderful long process"—a whimsical faraway look came into his sadistic eyes—"and for taking down their corpses once they expire." Bringing himself back to the present moment, he straightened his slumping frame. "These are the orders of Pontius Pilate." He turned his attention to Atticus. "You will take my place out there as sergeant in arms. Crowd control is a concern here. The possibility of a riot looms because of the third criminal's popularity."

This last remark caused Vitus to flinch. "Where is the Nazarene now?" he asked. "Why isn't he out there with the other two?"

Asus's eyes shifted from man to man. "It's going to take him longer to reach Golgotha." He paused. "He received *special* treatment. In fact, it would be wise for one of you to check on his progress." The sadistic troll became even more pensive as he continued, "It's possible that he might not make it there at all." The three men stood silent as Asus's suggestion sank in.

"Explain special treatment," said Vitus.

Shaken by Vitus's tenor, Asus measured his words carefully. "I had him...examined more severely than the others."

Vitus pressed him. "You nearly beat him to death with a *flagrum*, didn't you?" He stepped closer to the cringing Centurion. "How many lashes?"

Atticus stepped between them. "Easy, kid, calm down."

But Vitus wouldn't let it go. "How many, you two-legged toad?"

"Answer him!" said Atticus.

"Thirty-nine."

This time, it was Atticus who was taken aback. His graveled voice relayed fury. "You struck him thirty-nine times? One short of the maximum allowed by law? You never expected him to survive the beating!" Pulling his helmet off, an angry Atticus rubbed a hand over his close-cropped hair.

"Why?" Scipio cursed softly. "Of all people, why punish this man so badly?"

Asus's eyes flashed with unadulterated contempt. "Because I detest him. I hated him from the moment I laid eyes on him. His nauseating virtue…I had to beat it out of him!"

"Monster!" cried Vitus. "You're fortunate that I have no weapon, or you'd already be dead. I studied that man for weeks. The only thing he's guilty of is kindness!"

Atticus broke in, "If this thing goes south and the Nazarene dies before we get him up there, it's your head as well as ours."

Asus's hunched stance made him look much older than he was. "Watch the roads on the way to Golgotha," he advised, rethinking his folly. "It's likely he will have collapsed." Eyes down, he added, "I made him carry his own cross."

*****

Pushing through the crowded streets, the trio was relieved to find that Jeshua had not died on the way. "Better for us," said Atticus, "but not him. An even more brutal death awaits him." Following the road to Golgotha, they heard a sound ringing in the distance; it was the sound of iron striking iron. They arrived to find Jeshua at the mercy of Asus's team of butchers. A hammer drove a seven-by-five-inch shaft into Jeshua's feet, dorsal to heel, anchoring them to the wooden base of the cross. The pain defied description.

The city, bursting at the seams with people, made Orel's frantic search for Rebecca fruitless. He finally gave up the search and followed the crowd to Golgotha. There he found her.

CHAPTER 49
Tetelestai

News of Jeshua's arrest and subsequent conviction had ripped through Jerusalem like a squall over a tranquil lake. Onlookers were repulsed by the condition of his battered body. Stricken with grief, some turned away while others triumphantly mocked him. But all were unnerved by the sudden and drastic shift in the weather. Jeshua's cross was hoisted up at 9:00 a.m. under a cloudless blue sky. Three hours later, the sky had turned dusky black. No one had ever seen a storm turn midday light into total darkness. A flash of lightning silhouetted the three crosses against the dark horizon. Sudden torrential rain and hail, followed by an earthquake sent most of the spectators running for cover. But the rain and hail could not distract the Centurion whose eyes remain fixed on the Nazarene.

Can all this be because of him? he wondered. He could only shake his head in disbelief when the dying Nazarene pushed out the words, "Father, forgive them, for they don't know what they're doing" (Luke 23:34 KJV).

From somewhere deep inside, the Centurion voiced the conviction that had gripped his heart, "This must be the Son of God!"

A soaked runner, gasping for air, handed Atticus orders that bore Pilate's seal. "Waste no further time. End it now," the communiqué read. Atticus stared at the Nazarene's motionless body.

To short circuit a three-day crucifixion, legs had to be broken. Unable to use his legs to push up for air, asphyxiation and death quickly followed. Atticus gestured to Asus's soldiers to carry out Pilate's instructions. Hammers splintered bone and cartilage of the helpless victims, but their screams were muffled by the howling wind. When one soldier moved to carry out the same treatment for Jeshua, Vitus stepped in front of him.

"No need!" he shouted over the deafening storm. "He's already dead!"

The executioner shook his head in opposition. He tried to amplify his voice above the storm, "Orders are orders, dead or otherwise!" He tried again to get to Jeshua, but Vitus would have none of it.

"Stand down," shouted the Centurion. "If the man is dead, he's dead!"

Vitus was certain that Jeshua was dead, having heard him utter his final word in Greek, "*Tetelestai*," he slumped forward.

The executioner extended his lance to Vitus. "We have to be sure!"

Vitus refused it. "I told you, he's already dead!" he shouted back.

"It's our heads if he isn't!" He motioned again for him to take the spear.

Atticus nodded to Vitus. "We have to be sure!" he shouted. "If he's dead, it won't matter, will it? Let's get it over with."

Vitus begrudgingly accepted the javelin. Holding it in one hand, he calculated the terrible damage it would inflict on the Nazarene's lifeless body. With a look of disgust, he thrust the lance into Jeshua's side. As he expected, there was no reaction.

He turned to face the emotionless assassin. "Satisfied?"

There was no reply.

"Get them down from there!" Atticus ordered.

Asus's men, unnerved by the storm, earthquake, and darkness were quick to comply.

"Keep your bloody paws off the Nazarene!" barked the Centurion. "Only those two!"

Water running off them, Vitus and Scipio peered through the storm at Jeshua's body, still draped on the cross. "Thank Elohim it's over," said Vitus.

"It's not over," stated the Centurion.

"What? What do you mean?" asked Vitus.

"The Nazarene is dead," insisted Scipio. "How can it not be over?"

The wind and rain suddenly abruptly halted. Mopping his brow, the Centurion turned down the volume. "I've lived long enough to know I can trust my gut, and my gut tells me it's not over, not yet." He exhaled. "I hated this man for ruining my arrangement with the woman of Sychar, but I was wrong about him, wrong about everything." His voice trailed off.

Scipio was stunned by this un-centurion-like behavior. "Sir, we were only following orders."

"Keep telling yourself that, Scipio, maybe it'll help you reach absolution."

Scipio solemnly removed his helmet.

"We executed the wrong man!" cried Vitus.

Atticus, his head down, nodded in agreement. "I've fought against and killed all kinds of men, hundreds of them. I watched the life drain from their eyes, listened to their last gasp. Death has a way of settling down on a man. It leaves a blank, disconnected stare." He looked again at Jeshua's sagging form. "Death had no such power on this man."

"Because he was the One," interjected Orel, walking toward them. "The Messiah. The day he rode into the city, the people knew it, sensed it. That's why the city shook with cries of *hosanna*." His gaze shifted to Vitus, who lowered his head.

"If we killed the Chosen One," he said softly, "where does that leave us?" The four men stood, silently digesting the gravity of Vitus's words. Atticus was the one to break the silence.

"Let's start by getting him down from there."

They respectfully complied.

As Jeshua's body was lowered, a singular voice called out, "Centurion, may we have a word?"

Two well-dressed men approached the Centurion. Joseph of Arimathea spoke in Latin, "With your permission, we will take his body for burial preparation."

The request surprised Atticus. Touching a dead body made a Jew ceremonially unclean. This was no little concern for a Judean during Passover.

"I'm afraid you're asking the wrong man." He exhaled. "You'll have to take up the request with the governor."

"We already have. He has granted permission for us to receive his body and prepare it for burial."

After looking the men up and down, Atticus waved them on.

"Where are they taking him?" Rebecca gently asked, her tiny frame looking even smaller in rain-soaked clothing.

"Rebecca!" said Vitus. "How long have you been standing there?"

Tears streaming down her cheeks, she turned away. For a moment, she could not speak or even look at him. "How, Vitus?" she spoke with her back toward him. "After all you witnessed, even your own mother, how could you be involved in this?"

Vitus reply was barely above a whisper, "I don't know."

Joseph of Arimathea and the second man, Nicodemus, wrapped Jeshua's battered body in a clean linen covering.

"Look at what they've done to him," said Rebecca, giving Vitus a sorrowful glance. "What you did to him!" Overcome with the emotion, she left him standing there, despair crushing down on him. Orel walked over to join him, putting a hand on his friend's shoulder.

"Let's leave this place, put death behind us."

"I never wanted this," Vitus protested. "I was after Barabbas, not Jeshua. The murderer walks free, the innocent, killed in his place! It's beyond twisted! I listened in disbelief when he asked God to forgive the people who mocked him." He searched Orel's face for an answer, but there was none. "Now he's gone, taking that spirit of forgiveness with him. There's nothing left, Orel, not for me. I've killed the man who brought my own mother back from the dead! The only thing left for me now is revenge."

CHAPTER 50
Second Chance

Vitus hadn't been himself since that day at Golgotha. Neither had Atticus, and the usually upbeat Scipio had turned introspective. The Centurion's regular sneer of defiance had been strangely absent.

Anthony tried to describe the Centurion's peculiar change in behavior. "It's like he's searching for something but doesn't know what it is."

"No ordinary man," the Centurion often repeated to the three who were with him at Golgotha. "Make no mistake," he said solemnly, "the executioners were never in control that day, and those so-called holy men who mocked him, what did they really accomplish? No ordinary man." He mumbled yet again, "He offered no rebuttal to their poison." Atticus pushed out a breath, shaking his head in disbelief. "How does a man maintain his control under those kind of conditions? They reveled in his pain, but what satisfaction did it bring them? It was the Nazarene, not his mockers or Rome, who was victorious that day." His voice trailed off. "No ordinary man." Getting to his feet, Atticus declared, "Boys, I intend to get very drunk in the next few hours. You're all welcome to join me."

Scipio nodded he was in, but Orel and Vitus remained seated, warming themselves at the outdoor firepit. Vitus waited until they were out of hearing distance.

"I think I'm losing my mind," said Vitus, taking in a shallow breath. "Every time I close my eyes, I'm out there again, reliving his final moments. It's always the same. I'm looking up at him. I can't look away. Somehow, he knows the struggle raging inside me." Vitus shuffled his feet. "I'm beginning to lose control."

"These are dreams?" asked Orel.

"Not anymore. Every time I close my eyes, I see him."

Orel was quiet.

"I'm going back to Jerusalem to wait for his release."

Orel didn't have to ask who Vitus was referring to. He knew.

"Do you think this is wise?"

"Wise, unwise—it doesn't matter anymore. I have no choice. Barabbas will be released tomorrow, and I intend to follow him and end his miserable life. If he fails to join his coconspirators, he'll die alone. On the other hand, if he's foolish enough to join them, I'll end all of them."

"Listen to yourself," said Orel. "You're not thinking straight. Barabbas may have caused the deaths of hundreds, but the Nazarene isn't one of them."

Vitus's eyes flashed with anger. "I disagree! He is complicit, and it's time I finish what I set out to when I first arrived in Judea!"

"Even if you succeed," said an exasperated Orel, "what will it accomplish? Killing Barabbas won't bring back the Nazarene. This is a death wish!"

"I've asked Scipio to go with me."

The pained look on Orel's face coaxed a quick apology from Vitus.

"It isn't like that, Orel, you're more than my friend. You're my brother. I'm up against a wall. You're moving in the right direction. I wouldn't ask you to screw things up for my obsession with Barabbas."

Orel stared back at his friend.

"I wanted to tell you," Vitus paused. "This stays between us, Atticus must not learn of it." Vitus calmed a little after sharing his plans with Orel. "By this time tomorrow, either the Phantom or I will be dead." The two men embraced. "Grant me one more favor. If I don't make it back, look after my mother, and tell her"—he paused—"I'm sorry."

Head down, Orel nodded a short yes. "And Rebecca? What should I tell her?"

Vitus's eyes fell to the ground. "Let's not go there."

*****

Standing eyeball to eyeball with Barabbas, the captain of the guard made his feelings known, "If this were up to me," his voice trailed off.

"How fortunate for me that it wasn't," quipped Barabbas.

A powerful backhand staggered him, but he managed to stay on his feet. His left eye rapidly swelled to a slit.

"Get this animal out of my sight!"

As they departed, the guards taunted the soon-to-be freed prisoner. "So this is the great Phantom."

One guard publicized his thoughts to another, "Knock out a few teeth and close an eye, and he looks like any other criminal."

With his freedom so close, Barabbas refused to take the bait.

The guardsmen took up positions in front and behind as the manacles were removed. The soldier behind Barabbas shoved him forward, sending Barabbas sprawling in the dirt. "You're getting off easy, Zealot! The captain wanted to feed your intestines to the prison dogs."

The thought sent a shiver through Barabbas, who defiantly squared his shoulders. As he exited the prison, he was shoved one last time but managed to keep his feet. Steadying himself for the long walk ahead, he thought of the captured Zealots who had not been released. They would be tortured for information or even amusement. He walked on, pondering their plight.

"Poor Issa. A quick death would have been merciful, but these Romans regard mercy as weakness." A mile outside of Jerusalem, Abiel joined him. The two men embraced.

"Barabb, I did what you—"

Holding a finger to his pursed lips, Barabbas shushed him. "Not yet, Abi, we're not alone!" The two revolutionaries' conversation contained nothing of value until they pitched their tent several miles outside of Jericho.

"How many are out there?" whispered Abiel.

"Not many. They think they've been discreet."

"You were pardoned. Why do they follow you?"

Barabbas smirked at Abiel's naivety. "That means nothing to the soldier who hunts me!"

Abiel paused. "Then you know who's out there."

"I'm certain of it. I think he's alone, but if his compatriots are with him, it's trouble for us."

Abiel stroked his beard. "And if he's alone?"

"That depends. Are you armed?"

"Always," Abi grinned, pulling out a variety of hidden daggers.

"Good. If the soldier is foolish enough to take us on alone, he'll die alone."

Abi stared intently at Barabbas. "You expect him to attack tonight, don't you? That's why we camped here instead of joining the others in Jericho."

Barabbas nodded and smiled.

"Who is he?"

"Let's get a fire started, and we'll talk about it."

The thought of hunting up the necessary resources for a fire made Abiel uneasy. "You don't think he'll attack while I gather wood, do you?

"You'll be safe enough. He could have attacked several times today, but didn't. He's waiting for just the right moment."

"And how do we know this isn't that moment?"

"I'm confident it isn't, but if you prefer, I'll do it." With the sun about to set, Abiel wasted no time gathering up enough wood for the night. This game Barabbas had decided to play seemed odd to Abiel. Zealots were always stalkers, never prey.

As the fire gained in strength, Barabbas settled his friend's uneasiness. "The man out there is a young soldier with exceptional skills, but he's a prisoner of his past."

"How do you know so much about him?"

"I understand him. We have a lot in common. Our fathers were murdered by enemy soldiers." Staring into the dancing flames, Barabbas exhaled. "I'm the one who killed his father."

Abiel's back straightened. "That explains a lot, but special skills or not, if he's only one man out there, let's take the fight to him! Why let him make the first move?"

Barabbas's eyes flashed with anger. "This is no ordinary man! He's a killing machine, but I know his weakness."

"What is it?" Abiel's question was mixed with curiosity and concern.

"His hatred for me has eaten away his good sense, compromised his judgment. He is weakened by his raging desire for revenge, and that we will use against him. Besides, I have a little surprise prepared for him."

Abiel wasn't sure what Barabbas meant, but then he notices a look of detachment in his eyes that was all too familiar. Had the Phantom slipped into another one of his flashbacks.

"Barabb! Barabb!" Abiel tried to call him back to the present.

"There was a time," sighed Barabbas, "that I thought—even hoped—that he was the One."

Abiel was relieved but confused. "You've lost me, Barabb. You hoped this Roman was the One for what?"

Barabbas's eyes narrowed. "Not the Roman, the Nazarene! I believed he was the key to saving our nation, but he couldn't even save himself." He exhaled in frustration. "It doesn't matter now." Patting Abiel's shoulder, he added, "That dream died with him."

*****

After two days of constant care by post physicians, Scipio regained consciousness, and Atticus was there when he did.

"Where am I?" he moaned.

"Out of the woods at last," said Atticus. "The doctors were ready to give up on you, claimed you'd lost too much blood. The gray of death was on you, but I told them not this soldier. You don't know him!"

The grizzled veteran didn't hide his thankfulness at the turn of events. He had even prayed when things looked desperate. Scipio tried to sit up. "Easy, soldier, no sudden moves or you'll start hemorrhaging again." That raspy voice sounded like music to Scipio. "Lie still. That's an order, soldier."

Scipio settled back.

"The two of you went after Barabbas, didn't you?"

Scipio nodded, and Atticus asked the question he'd been dreading. "Is Vitus dead?"

Lowering his head, Scipio solemnly answered, "Yes."

The wooden bedpost splintered under the force of Atticus's fist. "Damn!" He jumped up, pacing about the room, trying to stem his frustration. "Damn!" he repeated, rubbing his chronically irritated eye. "Two days ago, I sent what was left of the Ten to find you. They followed a trail of blood to the outskirts of Jericho where they found you, all but dead. So tell me, what happened out there?"

Each word spoken by Scipio was punctuated by pain.

"We trailed Barabbas from the gates of Jerusalem…to open countryside." He paused, trying to push back against the pain. "He was joined by another man, a fellow Zealot, we assumed. The two of them…made camp about five miles from Jericho. Vitus wanted to wait till morning, to separate and flank them, but before morning arrived, we were ambushed. There must have been one hundred of them. They rushed us from every side. There was no escape route. Our only option was to fight back-to-back. Just before I was swarmed under, I caught my last glimpse of him…fighting like a man possessed, trying to get to Barabbas."

The Centurion dropped back down on Scipio's cot. "How did you get away?"

"Honestly, I don't know, sir. I think I took a blow to the back of my head. I'm guessing the Sicarii thought I was dead and tossed me in a ditch. I regained consciousness for a couple of seconds. My head was spinning, but I remember seeing Vitus next to me in that trench."

"When you came to for those few seconds, Vitus was next to you? Are you sure?"

Scipio nodded. "Yes, sir."

The Centurion shook his head. "Something is amiss. Anthony reported that he found you alone in the ravine, no sign of Vitus.

Several of them continued to search for him; the rest carried you back here."

"No, sir," Scipio replied sadly. "There wasn't much left of him. Maybe the Zealots took his body."

*****

The following day, Atticus sent for Orel, wanting to relay the news of Vitus's demise.

"Orel, I have bad news. According to Scipio, Vitus died at the hands of the Zealots."

Orel was strangely silent, making no reply. He didn't have the appearance of a man who just received such news. His reaction seemed odd. "Did you hear me?" Atticus repeated. "Your friend is dead! I expected a show of remorse. Apparently, I was wrong."

Orel rose to his feet.

"Thank you for telling me, Commander, it means a lot to me. I'd heard that Scipio had been severely wounded."

Atticus's good eye opened wide. Something wasn't right.

"He's on the mend. Orel, can I ask you to bring this news to Vitus's young woman?"

"I'll see to it, Commander."

His arms crossed, Atticus watched the curiously uneasy guards-man head out the door.

"What the hell was that?" he asked himself, running a hand over his close-cropped scalp, he was sure Orel was covering something up. He knew Orel believed Jeshua to be the *Mashach*, the Promised One. Jeshua had also penetrated Atticus's heart that day at Golgotha, but things didn't seem as clear now as they did then. He struggled to stay focused, his thoughts running in different directions. "It's been more than three days since those wealthy Judeans carted the Nazarene's body away for burial," he said aloud. He'd heard the rumors that Jeshua was alive and had been seen in Jerusalem. "Ridiculous," he snickered, "I saw him take his last breath." He dismissed the idea as religious hysteria.

Another account had Jeshua standing on the seashore, telling his disciples to cast their nets on the right side of the boat. When they did, they couldn't pull in the catch. It was too heavy with fish. "Ridiculous," he repeated, but he could dismiss the pangs within his own heart. *Did Orel encounter the resurrected Jeshua?* he wondered. *Could that be the reason for his strange reaction to news of Vitus's death?*

He bolted out the door, calling out to the Judean guardsman, who was already a good distance away. "Orel!"

That raspy voice was unmistakable. Orel stopped and walked back.

Atticus placed his huge paw on Orel's shoulder. "My battlefield decisions often determine whether my men live or die." Pausing, he chose his next words carefully. "It isn't my accomplishments or bravado that prompts their obedience. They trust me, believe that I understand them. I recognize fear in a man's eyes when I see it. A man's eyes tell the story, even when he tries to hide it, just as yours do now. What is it you're not telling me, Orel?"

How does he do it? wondered Orel, finding himself in the very position Atticus just spoke of. Slowly, he retraced the events of the last three days to Atticus.

*****

"Tell me again how it all happened," asked Orel, directing his question to the man sitting directly across from him. Orel and Rebecca were guests in the house of Annanias, trying to find plausibility in an implausible conversation.

"You're saying he's alive?" said Rebecca. She painstakingly restated each word to clear away any confusion. "Jeshua is alive!"

"Yes, most definitely alive," answered another guest motioning to Annanias. "Go ahead. Ask him. He was there."

A smiling Annanias nodded in affirmation.

Rebecca was excited and frightened at the same time; it was too much to even hope for!

"How did you find him?" she asked the first man.

"I didn't find him," said Vitus in a calm voice. "He found me."

Rebecca was too overcome to speak.

"Jeshua came looking for you?" asked Orel incredulously. "Why? Why would he do such a thing?" he said, thinking of their involvement at Golgotha.

Vitus's response was measured. "I've asked myself that question a hundred times. Why would he care about me after what I did?" He paused. "Somehow, he knew."

Rebecca's voice was barely audible. "Knew what?"

"That I had died at the hand of the Zealots."

Orel swallowed hard. "Are you saying you were dead when Jeshua found you?"

"I was a corpse in a trench. Ask him." He motioned to Annanias, who smiled and nodded. Rebecca wrapped her arms around Vitus's neck, kissing him again and again.

"It's too fantastic," said Orel. "I need time to—"

"He has the scars on his body as do I." Pulling up his tunic, Vitus revealed a series of crisscrossed wounds, including what had been the fatal blow through his rib cage.

*****

"So you've decided to tell me the truth," said the Centurion in his grating voice.

Orel's facial expression reflected his decision.

"Good, now let's have it! All of it!"

The furrowed lines on Orel's face disappeared; a heavy weight had fallen from his shoulders. Orel relayed the incredible story of two resurrections: Jeshua's and Vitus's.

Amazingly, the Centurion wasn't surprised or unwilling to believe it. It was almost as if he already knew.

EPILOGUE

Vitus was free of the hatred and vengeance that had almost destroyed him. Scipio's sworn testimony, to Vitus's death, marked another failure to tame rebellious Judea. Vitus's given name—*new life*—would prove to be prophetic. Officially listed as killed in battle, all military ties were severed. Except for his uncle Claude's inquiry into his death, his old life had been erased.

Vitus's new life no longer revolved around killing but living. In the years ahead, Rebecca, Vitus, and Orel were to become integral cogs in a movement known as *The Way*. Though it pained him, he would not speak to Scipio or the Ten for the rest of his life. Remaining dead was the only way to guarantee the safety of his wife and child.

The Centurion, however, was the one page of his old life he couldn't leave unturned. In the months and years ahead, Orel would arrange meetings for them in the village of Sychar. The men who once shared culpability in the Nazarene's death now shared faith in a risen Messiah. In the strangest of twists, Sychar, the place where Atticus first declared war on the Nazarene, became the place he would forge a lifelong relationship, asking the woman at the well to be his wife.

As for Pontius Pilate, reports such as this continued to frustrate him: "Attack carried out against Barabbas unsuccessful—Phantom survives." Never letting go of his Antonia prison vow, Pilate leaned on Anthony and his operatives. Anthony hunted the Zealot chieftain relentlessly, almost trapping him on two separate occasions. But as he did in the past, the Phantom managed to stay one step ahead of Rome. However, there was one enemy he could not stay ahead of. Four months after his encounter with Vitus, Barabbas went missing. Eventually, Abiel found him at the bottom of a ravine with a broken neck. What actually occurred remains a mystery, but in Abiel's mind, Barabbas's ever-increasing blackouts were the cause.

As for the secretive Shadow of Death, their celebratory exultation was cut short by the discovery of an empty tomb. They could not effectively quell the next forty days and five hundred eyewitness sightings of a living, breathing Jeshua.

Leaders of the SOD worked diligently to normalize relations with Rome, hoping to regain their former status of co-regency. But their shortsighted intentions could not combat the revolutionary spirit of Judea. In AD 70, forty years after the Nazarene's tearful Jerusalem prophecy, Emperor Vespasian sent his son, Titus, to level Palestine. Titus's presence cast a shadow of death over the city. After breaching its walls, he destroyed and burned everything to the ground, including their sacred temple. Thousands were massacred, including many leaders of the SOD.

There once was a majestic tree which had a mind of its own. It was the straightest, most beautiful tree in Lebanon. It was pleased and proud when it learned the Creator had a special plan for it. But it soon discovered the plan was to cut it down and use it as a pole on which the Creator's chosen one, the Messiah, would be executed. The tree objected to the idea of being used in such a way. The tree wanted no part in the death of an innocent, yet it was chosen for that very purpose. The Creator's plan called for the death of one who was innocent. Only the Messiah, the Chosen One, could accomplish it. The wood of the tree was the resource needed to complete the plan. Though at first, the tree seemed to cast a shadow of death across the land, it was actually an opportunity for life.

GLOSSARY

Abba—Jewish term for father; endearing.

alea iactaest—Latin term meaning *the die is cast.*

Centurion—Military commander of a hundred soldiers.

chevah—Hebrew word for a wild beast.

chutzpah—The quality of audacity, for good or for bad; derives from the Hebrew word *ḥuspāh*, meaning "insolence."

Corona Civica—Highest military honor for a legionnaire.

Decanus—Roman sergeant at arms.

denarius—The standard Roman silver *coin.*

disciple—One who accepts and assists in spreading the doctrines of another, such as Christianity.

disgregarsi—Publicly disgraced.

Elohim—A plural noun for one of the Hebrew names for God; indicates a singular yet plural entity (the Trinity).

El Shaddai—One of the names for the God of Israel, conventionally translated into English as Almighty God.

Emma—Judean term for mother; endearing.

Festival of Unleavened Bread—Yearly Jewish celebration which lasts for seven days; the last twenty-four hours of the celebration is Passover.

flagrum—A whip that has several leather cords, each one knotted with bits of bone or metal.

gradus deiectio—Latin term for a reduction in military rank; a demotion.

Herodians—A political party that agreed with the Sadducees in holding the duty of submission to Rome and of supporting Herod.

Kohen—Hebrew for priest; suggests a personal affinity.

Hosanna—An expression of adoration, praise, or joy.

Magister Peditum—Officer in charge of foot soldiers (ground forces).

Magister Utriusque Militum—A top-level military command in the later Roman Empire, the term referred to the senior military officer of the empire.

Mashach—Hebrew, referring to the promised deliverer "anointed."

medicus—Field doctor.

Messiah—The promised deliverer of the Jewish nation, prophesied in scripture by Old Testament (covenant) prophets.

optio—Second-in-command to the ranking commanding officer.

Pax Romana—The peace which existed between nationalities within the Roman Empire.

pièce de résistance—With reference to creative work, the most important or remarkable feature.

Pharisees—The Pharisees were a major cultural movement and school of thought in Israel. Pharisaic beliefs became the foundational ritualistic basis for Rabbinic Judaism.

Prefect—A chief officer, magistrate, or regional governor.

principalis—A lower ranking officer; operational assistant.

righteous—Morally right or justifiable; virtuous; *holy.*

Sabbath—A day of religious observance and abstinence from work, kept from Friday evening to Saturday evening.

Sadducees—A Jewish sect or party at the time of Jesus Christ that denied the resurrection of the dead, the existence of spirits, stressed the obligation of oral tradition, emphasizing acceptance of the written Law alone.

Sala de mesa—Roman soldiers' mess hall; cafeteria.

Seer—A prophet—one who is able to predict the future.

Sicarii—Experts with daggers; *dagger men.*

Sha'ar HaRachamim—Israel's only eastern gate of the Temple Mount and one of only two used to offer access into the city from that side.

sop—A sop is a piece of bread or toast that is drenched in liquid and then eaten.

stripe—A single lash of the whip.

Tesserarius—Administrative guard assigned to keep watch over the fort when in garrison, responsible for getting the watchwords from the commander and seeing that they were kept safe.

Tetelestai—Comes from the Greek word τετέλεσται, meaning "It is finished" which, according to St. John, were the last words of Jesus on the cross.

Torah—The law of God as revealed to Moses and recorded in the first five books of the Hebrew scriptures (called the Pentateuch).

The Way—The name that followers of Jeshua called themselves before they were called Christians.

tsal and *mavet*—צלמות Hebrew compound word which translates "shadow of death" or "death casts a shadow."

Yahweh—Another name for the God of Israel revealed to Moses, suggests personal and up close.

Zealot—A person who is fanatical and uncompromising in pursuit of their religious and political ideals.

Zionism—A national movement for the protection and preservation of the Jewish nation of Israel.

ABOUT THE AUTHOR

John V Mercurio grew up during the 1960s in Eastern Long Island, New York. Age-appropriate playmates were hard to find in his small rural town, but that fueled an active imagination. He believes it takes a good storyteller to make a good writer. Creativity and a love of history are the ingredients that power his thoughts and writing.

As a college freshman, John had an editorial published in his college campus newsletter. He surprised himself with a raw ability to maneuver words on paper. He met his lifelong partner and wife, Jennifer, at that Midwestern campus but returned to New York where they raised a family of three daughters.

John became what he was destined to be: a teacher with a career that spanned more than thirty years. He has written everything from out-of-the-box lesson plans to op-ed essays. Finding ways to bring history to life has been a lifelong passion. His first book, *A View from the Fish Bowl*, was written for novice educators, offering them a humorous but realistic taste of teaching in the public sector while affording parents a clear sense of what their children experience on a daily basis.

John credits eight years of pastoral experience, while still teaching, as the key to developing his writing style. Asking God's help to inspire and encourage, he combined history, theology, and imagination. *Death Casts a Shadow*, a work of historical fiction, offers readers a way to view life's landscape from a different perspective, a grander scale. John's style of writing is entertaining and educational and offers the astute reader a chance for a spiritual experience.

CPSIA information can be obtained
at www.ICGtesting.com
Printed in the USA
JSHW032114210322
24097JS00001B/13